I0806433

Fastest Brain in the West

Fastest Brain in the West

The Odd Stranger Who Tamed Dodge City

A Novel

Gregory J. Lalire

THORNDIKE PRESS
A part of Gale, a Cengage Company

GALE
A Cengage Company

Copyright © 2026 by Gregory J. Lalire.
Thorndike Press, a part of Gale, a Cengage Company.

ALL RIGHTS RESERVED

This novel is a work of fiction. Names, characters, places, and incidents are either the product of the author's imagination, or, if real, used fictitiously.

The publisher bears no responsibility for the quality of information provided through author or third-party websites and does not have any control over, nor assume any responsibility for, information contained in these sites. Providing these sites should not be construed as an endorsement or approval by the publisher of these organizations or of the positions they may take on various issues.

Thorndike Press® Large Print Hardcover Western.

The text of this Large Print edition is unabridged.

Set in 16 pt. Plantin.

ISBN-13: 978-1-4205-3837-3 (hardcover alk. paper)

Published in 2026 by arrangement with Gregory J. Lalire.

Print Number: 1 Print Year: 2026
Printed in Mexico

Dedication

For my sister Véga Lalire,
with whom I first saw Dodge City

INTRODUCTION

As a matter of practice on the frontier — out of courtesy or a sense of one's own safety — a fellow never asked another fellow where he came from. After all, men all had pasts, most men were armed openly or otherwise, and few men were forever saints. Anyone who met up with Wyatt Matters in Dodge City, Kansas, in the 1870s for even a minute would be tempted to violate that practice. For one thing he was armed with nothing more than a sharp tongue. For another he looked strange with his pudgy arms, stout legs, and colossal nose (standing erect with head raised he resembled a black-tailed prairie dog) and acted equally strange (preferring lecturing over small talk, prodding over harmonizing, mind over matter). For a third, he had no visible means of supporting himself, either respectably or not. And so, during those early days in Dodge, he was subjected to such questions as these: *Where you from, stranger? Where'd you learn that highfalutin jawing? Where you been hanging your top hat, old man? You schooled in Boston, pilgrim? What hole you crawl out of?* He never gave a straight answer if he answered at all. He was from nowhere and everywhere. "All that matters," he would then say, "is that I am here now!"

He had once been, according to rumor, an adventurer or a wanderer or a searcher for something lost with the ability to amaze, amuse, annoy, and anger strangers and acquaintances alike, sometimes all in one sitting, before moving on. He certainly did all that in Dodge City, Kansas, except the *moving on* part. He was a mystery man to me, too, in the beginning. But that would change because he took me under his wing, tried to teach me everything he knew (rattling off historical facts with the rapidity of a Gatling gun), and made sure I never flew away.

By the time I arrived in Dodge City on the shiny steel rails of the new Atchison, Topeka & Santa Fe line in September 1872, some folks were already ready to run Wyatt Matters out of town. Not that he was a hard case or anything like that. He was strange (as I've already mentioned but can't emphasize enough), opiniated, overly critical, and just plain no fun.

Two months earlier, before the town was born, he turned up at Fort Dodge and started to get under the skin of certain prominent men. He was good at that whether the skin belonged to a buffalo hunter, a railroad worker, a government contractor, a soldier, a gambler, a businessman, or a common store clerk, of which I was one. Unlike so many others, though, I for the most part listened to him and stuck with him. I guess in part it was because I was a listener, and he was a talker — boy was he ever! He was old and smart as a whip, and I was a young man who had taken one too many whippings from my uneducated father back in my native Maryland. Although school had mostly been a pain in the buttocks and the knuckles (one teacher specialized in rapping my knuckles with a ruler), I did have an inner drive to know more than my old man and all his nearly forgotten Hannum ancestors combined. All things considered, I might even suggest I had a pretty good head on my shoulders to begin with, and it surely improved under Mr. Matters' guidance. It's all relative. Wyatt Matters had a head that I began to describe as *fathomless* as soon as he told me the meaning of that word.

Oh, and there was the matter of our looks. It is no source of pride for me to say that

Wyatt Matters and I had four physical traits in common, which caused many people who saw us standing together to think we could be father and son or at least uncle and nephew. It has been said that there exists a thin line between a face that has character and one that is deemed ugly. I'll admit that Wyatt had considerably more character than me, but at the same time, he was far uglier to boot. But back to that quartet of likenesses: eyes as blue as the Big Blue River, the largest tributary of the Kansas River (a Wyatt Matters fact); faces as pallid as that of Queen Victoria (whose original name, according to Wyatt, was Alexandrina Victoria); attached earlobes like those of our tenth president, John Tyler (the ear thing was a little-known Wyatt Matters fact; I didn't even know Tyler was No. 10); and enormous noses (called "proboscises" by Wyatt Matters, though he explained that the term usually referred to the noses of mammals, such as the trunks of elephants, but when referring to our noses meant *we've got mighty big 'uns*).

Let me point out that there were just as many differences in how we looked. I was taller and thinner, much younger, and I didn't have long, coarse hairs growing out of my nose or hair sticking out of my ears in tufts. It wasn't clear to me at the start of our relationship why Mr. Matters chose to make Dodge City his home or me his disciple. I did gain that knowledge, however, and I'll get to all that soon enough, and to other important matters such as how law and order slowly developed in Dodge and how I met the love of my life there. You'll also see how I witnessed firsthand how he would become presumptuous if not overbearing yet manage — well, at least until the evening he faced a drunk, armed cowboy in the Long Branch saloon — to talk his way out of any predicament, in part because of his golden tongue and eloquent hand gestures but mostly because my old mentor Wyatt Matters was, as my recently deceased newspaper colleague Bat Masterson stated more than once, "the Fastest Brain in the West."

—Harry Hannum
Lower East Side, New York City
January 30, 1922

Chapter One

Only a week after getting off the train in Dodge City I landed a job clerking at Robert Wright's two-story general store at the northwest corner of Front Street and Second Avenue. Wright was in partnership with buffalo entrepreneur Charles Rath, whose name was attached to the store, but "Plainsman Charlie" spent more time in his beloved hide yard out back while Mr. Wright, with assistance from his twelve-year-old son Bobby, ran the store itself. Mr. Wright hired me because we were both born in Bladensburg, Maryland, and had both taken a notion at age sixteen to seek our fortunes in the West, albeit ten years apart. He was thirty-two, having just celebrated his birthday, and was by any measure a great success: married since 1859 to the former Alice J. Armstrong, father of five children, settled at Fort Dodge in 1868, appointed post trader there, organized and promoted Dodge City, and now just about the wealthiest merchant in the region. I was an impressionable twenty-two-year-old. Although I had worked briefly in the eastern Kansas towns of Lawrence, Elgin, and Atchison as a saloon swamper, cook's assistant, and grain mill worker and had courted a lively gal in Atchison until she ran off with a strapping, bull-necked railroad man, I was still looking to settle down and become somebody.

Before I first set eyes on Wyatt Matters, I had heard much about him from Mr. Wright, who was much more a doer than a talker but couldn't stop himself from palavering about that "wee wiseacre with a big nose for trouble."

On July 8, 1872, Robert Wright and a dozen other men had met at Fort Dodge to form the Dodge City Town Company. Everyone knew each other from their military connections except for one man who looked out of place in his top hat, three-piece blue suit, purple bowtie, and big buckled belt. He was easily the shortest in the group and most likely the homeliest, with the head of a Megalosaurus, the snout of a grizzly bear, and the flapping tongue of a goat (Robert Wright's description). The company decided to offer six hundred shares of stock at ten dollars each, but the short, ugly, well-dressed stranger threw his hands in the air and gave two dramatic thumbs down.

"Objection," he shouted, and all eyes were upon him as if a woman had invaded this male sanctuary. "If you please." He snorted like a bear rudely awakened from hibernation and began to twiddle his oversized thumbs above his silver belt buckle, on which the single word *Original* was engraved in elegant script. There was some rumbling in the room, but before any of the organizers could object to his objection, he continued. "You don't really want to build a town out of the blood of the bison, gentlemen. Such a foul, wretched foundation can only lead to a lawless community and more bloodshed. And I must tell you, gentlemen, this time the blood spilled will weigh heavy on your consciences."

"Who asked you?" said Mr. Wright, speaking for the group. "What's your business here at Fort Dodge?"

"Could be I know somebody here at the fort but no need to get into that long, rather involved story. Let's just say my business right now is your business — town business. I very much want to see the birth of a nearby civilized civilian community, for this neck of the prairie needs more than an Army post, but the birth must be under the right conditions."

"Conditions? There's nothing conditional about what we're doing. Nobody invited you. You're dressed to kill — certainly not a military man or a buffalo runner or a trader or an Indian agent or a squaw man. You must be out of place — an Eastern dandy, I'm guessing. Where you from, mister?"

"It doesn't matter and is certainly of no matter to you. All that matters is my name is Wyatt Matters and I am here to help you gentlemen do the right thing."

"We have never seen you at Fort Dodge before."

"I haven't previously been dressing this conspicuously. I've been tenting on the outskirts, laying low, observing, assessing. I thought I'd dress in my finest on this grand occasion."

"What do you know about any of our business?"

"I know the bison hunters, or buffalo runners as you refer to them, have invaded the Indian hunting grounds along the Salt Fork of the Arkansas River. To obtain hides, they do no running after them. They creep up to a high vantage point and shoot as many bison as they can with their long-range, .50-caliber Sharps rifles. One man, Tom Nixon, kills as many as 120 bison a day, shooting from as far away as 800 yards. At the current alarming rate, 250,000 bison will die before year's end."

"What of it? Tom Nixon is a good shot, a good man."

"Sure, by your standards. And he has a good wife, the former Cornelia Caroline Houston, who is expecting. But that doesn't do the bison any good, let alone the Indians who hunt them for their very survival! Bison hunting by white men is a pitiless, exhausting industry, dripping with blood, gore, and greed. You can't hide the facts."

"Nobody is hiding a thing, stranger. Killing buffalo for their hides happens to be profitable business. How is it you know Tom Nixon?"

"I know more than you can imagine. Last spring, I met a couple of lowly young skinners name of Masterson. The brothers were already so sickened by the whole business, they up and quit and came north to grade the rails."

"The Masterson brothers? Never heard of them. And we don't know you, mister."

"You should know that at least one third of the hides won't be salable because of improper skinning technique. The waste, gentleman, the waste! And what does the military at Fort Dodge do? Nothing. You all look the other way, without a single sign of remorse, while the slaughter continues unabated until the last bison herd has been wiped off the Plains."

"Slaughter? Remorse? What the hell are you talking about, whoever you are?"

"I told you. The name is Matters, Wyatt Matters."

"That's an unusual name."

"It's an original all right." He pointed to his belt buckle. "But I say to you, as Shakespeare said, or rather he has Juliet saying in his *Romeo and Juliet: What's in a name? That which we call a rose/By any other name would smell as sweet.*"

"First he talks of buffalo hides and now he talks of sweet-smelling roses," said another of the organizers. "Those clothes are as outlandish as his words. He may very well be insane."

"I don't know about that, but I know we have no roses at Fort Dodge and that Mr. Matters is not a member of the Dodge City Town Council," said one of the men dressed in military uniform. He then spoke directly to Mr. Matters. "I, for one, have noticed you twiddling your thumbs here and there like a hang-around-the-fort Indian. I am post commandant Richard Dodge, no relation to Civil War General Grenville M. Dodge, for whom Fort Dodge is named."

"That which we call a Dodge by any other name would smell as manly. Pleased to formally meet you, sir. I assure you I try to be noble these days, but I am no red man. My favorite color happens to be purple." He gave his purple bowtie a proud twist. "A man should take pride in his appearance, even here on the wild frontier, don't you agree?"

Several of the organizers looked at each other and rolled their eyes as if Mr. Matters was indeed out of his mind. Richard Dodge, though, merely arched an eyebrow and then chuckled softly. He said only three more words: "Shall we proceed?"

"Certainly, Colonel Dodge," said Robert Wright. "Now about the stock we'll be selling at $10 a share. I believe we are all agreed that . . ."

"I beg your pardon, Trader Bob, but I did have something more to add," interrupted Mr. Matters. "It is something you must all hear."

"Must we?" said Mr. Wright, loud enough to be heard outside on the parade ground. "Listen, stranger, I am the post trader with an official government license, but nobody disrespects me by calling me *Trader Bob.* Understand?"

"I see you carry a lot of weight in this particular circle."

"That's right. I have been put in charge of this important meeting by the men who were invited to attend. You were not *invited.* In fact, I *must* say you are obstructing our business here, Wyatt Matters."

"I only want you to know the facts about rampant buffalo hunting by thoughtless white men."

"We're all white men here. And we all have given this much thought. We are sitting on the edge of the buffalo hunting grounds, and to not take advantage of that fact would be supremely foolish. Commercial buffalo hunting is good, healthy business for *our* upcoming town. Plus, the railroad will be getting here before you can say Jack Robinson. The stretch-dried bison skins are already piling up for transportation to the Eastern markets. You're a white man yourself. What's your game, stranger? You want in on this? You have money to invest? You want to be one of the original shareholders?"

"Not under these circumstances, Trader Bob. And no, no, no, no to your questions. I know all about the railroad and what it means to myself and to everyone else in Kansas, but making money is of no importance to me. Greed isn't one of *my* deadly sins. As Seneca has stated, 'For greed, all nature is too little.'"

"Christ! What hogwash! Who is this Seneca, one of those so-called civilized redskins down in Indian Territory?"

"No. Perhaps you are mixing him up with the great Cherokee Sequoyah, who created a syllabary that made reading and writing in the Cherokee language possible."

"No Cherokees around here, mostly Kiowas and Cheyennes. What's Seneca's tribe?"

"Roman. Lucius Annaeus Seneca, known to history as Seneca the Younger, lived and died before Jesus Christ was born. He was a philosopher, statesman, and orator — the leading intellectual in the time of Emperor Nero, who, by the way, couldn't take Seneca's calm stoicism and ordered him to kill himself.

"Maybe this Mr. Nero had good reason. I believe all of us in the Dodge City Town Company would agree, sir, you have made an ass of yourself and have become an undue hindrance to progress. But this ain't ancient Rome, it's Kansas! So, I won't ask you to blow your brains out. I do, however, believe I speak for Colonel Dodge and the rest of us gathered here today when I ask you to exit this room voluntarily and to leave with a little friendly advice: *You best get the hell out of Dodge.*"

No doubt Mr. Wright meant both Fort

Dodge and the soon to be born Dodge City. Wyatt Matters bowed to him and saluted Colonel Dodge before leisurely strolling for the exit. He did get in some parting words after slowly opening the door: "In summary, I am all for a Dodge town, but not a bison town. Now, I am by no means a religious man, gentlemen, but to count on the ungovernable hunters of those divine but dwindling beasts to create a community of lasting substance and moral value *is* supremely foolish. A high price shall be paid for that foolishness. Those hunters, foul smelling and stained in gore, will come to the new town wanting whiskey, women, and more whiskey. What decent woman would want to come to such a place to live and work and possibly raise a family? Think, gentlemen, think before you act rashly. Good day."

The organizers of the future Dodge City of course did not allow Wyatt Matters to become a shareholder. Perhaps they would have had they realized what kind of bankroll he possessed. But maybe not. Robert Wright was an influential man and his dislike for Mr. Matters was instant and lasting. Mr. Matters lingered at the fort for another two weeks, certainly long enough to show that he hadn't been forced to leave. He spent most of his time telling officers and enlisted men about brutal armed attacks that must never be repeated, including Confederate guerrilla William Quantrill's 1863 raid on Lawrence, Kansas; Colonel John Chivington's 1864 massacre of a peaceful Cheyenne and Arapaho village at Sand Creek, Colorado Territory; Lieutenant Colonel George Custer's 1868 assault on a Southern Cheyenne camp in Indian Territory; and most recently Major Eugene Baker's 1870 slaughter of peaceful Blackfeet at camp along the Marias River in Montana Territory. For some reason he also spent some time at the post laundry talking to the women, mostly the wives of soldiers, who worked there and were permitted to live at the fort. When the day came that the usually considerate Colonel Dodge was ready to order the knowledgeable but maddening civilian to strike his tent, he found that Wyatt had already slipped away during the night.

As Robert Wright and the other original shareholders and founding entrepreneurs soon found out, Wyatt "Original" Matters was not out of their hair. Wyatt later told me he had relocated to Dodge City because in theory a town, even a bad one, was preferable to a fort full of soldiers who didn't want to be there, who took orders from martinets, who didn't necessarily treat women right, and who had no use for a cerebral civilian who could provide them neither drink nor entertainment, only keen insight, which was not in demand.

Wyatt set up his large tent on leafless Locust Street. On the north side of the new railroad tracks, the Rath-Wright general store and a dozen other buildings made up a downtown said to be "in a flourishing condition." Not being one to lay low, Wyatt made his presence felt by going business to business freely offering negative opinions. He complained about the quantity and quality of the red-eye sold at George Hoover's liquor store/saloon (Wyatt was no whiskey drinker himself), questioned the exorbitant prices Robert Wright charged for flour and sugar at the general store (though Wyatt could afford them at any price), rejected the promised "round balls and straight cues" at Alfred Peacock's billiard saloon (Wyatt didn't play the game himself), and dismissed the "cure-all" medicine at Herman Fringer's drugstore (Wyatt often boasted he never had a sick day in his life).

At some point in August 1872 Wyatt aggravated the Dodge City businessmen further by easily sliding into his "I told you so" mold. The town that relied on the buffalo hide business was looking like anything but a peaceful place. It all started because of a street shooting outside of Hoover's establishment that resulted in the burial on Boot Hill of a dark-skinned fellow called either "Tex" or "Black Jack." Nobody seemed to know what caused shots to be fired or whose shot put the fatal slug in Tex — that is nobody but Wyatt Matters, who had done a little detective work on his own and needed to tell Mr. Hoover about his findings.

"What's the shooting to you?" Mr. Hoover asked. "You keep coming in here, yet you never buy a drink for anybody, not even yourself."

"Need I point out the obvious to you, friend? Whiskey and guns are a bad mix. Eighty-one percent of the violence in the West is caused by young, armed men who have been drinking too much. I neither take whiskey nor bear arms."

"Fine. And you obviously aren't young. So, keep out of my saloon. In short, Mr. Matters, stop pestering me."

"Tex was killed right outside your door by a gambler named Denver," said Wyatt, which caused the saloon owner to nearly choke on his cigar.

"What are you talking about, Matters? I don't know anybody by that name. This is Dodge City, Kansas. Denver is in Colorado Territory."

"Likely, Denver the man is on his way to Denver, Colorado Territory, as we speak. That is of small importance. Three nights ago, Denver was in here at his usual table drinking your house specialty, pure Kentucky bourbon, and losing badly at stud poker to another sharp who could mark a deck better than him."

"Black Jack was no sharp. If he was a drinking man, it wasn't in my place. Not that I have anything against his kind, but . . ."

"But Denver must have."

"Why you sticking your nose in a matter that doesn't concern you? You must be crazy, Matters."

"Not by a long shot, Mr. Hoover. Here's what happened right under *your* nose. Denver, his bankroll squandered in your establishment, quit the game with the sharp who couldn't be beat and who carried a derringer in his boot. Denver then borrowed a Colt Peacemaker from an acquaintance at your bar and went out the back door to let off steam. He fired one shot at his empty bottle of your pure Kentucky bourbon in the alley and two shots at the American flag hanging from Wright's general store before he found a better target, firing twice more at the freedman from Texas with skin as black as a new moon. One shot merely grazed the top of tall Tex's scalp, but the second one sliced through Tex's' sizable Adam's apple. Not bad shooting for a Confederate deserter who left Georgia after Sherman's march and reinvented himself in Denver, where he renamed himself after his new hometown."

"How do you know all this? It's impossible!"

"With a little know-how one can know a lot. Could be I know about how Negroes are treated in this country. Could be I once was a Pinkerton man. Could be I got more going on up here than your average detective." Wyatt tapped his forehead and waited, but Mr. Hoover didn't argue the point. "I happened to see Tex's stone-cold-dead body," continued Wyatt. "Saw the broken bottle. Saw the two holes in the flag. Talked to the man who lent Denver the gun. Talked to the sharp who had cleaned him out. Denver had mentioned his wartime escape from Atlanta — it was the pure Kentucky bourbon talking, I reckon. Last thing I saw was Denver spurring a pale horse across the Arkansas River bridge. He was skedaddling as not to face justice — getting the hell out of Dodge."

"All right. Maybe so. But why tell me? Denver means nothing to me, and he's long gone. Nobody's about to go riding after him, unless you have a mind to, which I'd welcome . . . to be rid of you. Too bad about

Black Jack; he never caused any trouble in town that I know of, and I never objected to him walking our streets. We didn't have a single slave up in Ontario, Canada, where I was born and raised."

"It's a crying shame for the man to be shot that way on the streets of *your* town. Tex came here all the way from Galveston, Texas, because he had heard Kansas was supposed to be a good place for former slaves to settle. It's a matter of fact that since the Civil War the number of Negroes in Kansas has risen from 6,237 to 17,108. Well, now it's down to 17,107. So be it. But Tex wasn't just a number. Yes, he was of dusky complexion, but he was a decent man full of hopes and dreams. Yet not you nor anybody else in Dodge gives a damn that he was gunned down by a disreputable Southern shootist."

"Look, like I already told you Matters, Black Jack or Tex or whatever you want to call him, wasn't even one of my customers. Anyway, he's beyond anyone's help now. Dead is dead, whether you be black, white, red, yellow, or a pale-faced son of a bitch from God knows where. So, leave off, Matters." Mr. Hoover tossed his bent cigar onto the floor, ground it into the floorboard with his shoe, and dismissed Wyatt with a wave of the back of his hand.

Much later, word got out — at least to Wyatt, who then shared it with the populace of Dodge — that the killer Denver had bragged about his dirty deed, telling his drinking companions in some low-end saloon that he "shot the big baboon in the top of the head just to see him kick." It hadn't been much of a gunfight — Dodge City's first shooting fatality had been unarmed. But as Wyatt Matters had predicted, more human blood was about to spill, and all because of the wanton slaying of area buffalo, which, according to Wyatt, should really be called bison. (He reminded me maybe two dozen times that the scientific name is *Bison bison* and that the misnomer can be blamed on French fur trappers who in the early 1600s saw these big furry beasts and called them *boeufs* because they were similar to the water buffalo of Asia and the Cape buffalo of sub-Saharan Africa.) Nevertheless, I sometimes slipped up and called these wild bovines *buffalo.* And, though I rarely disputed Wyatt to his face, I never truly believed that all the spilled bison/buffalo blood on the Kansas plains somehow triggered the bloodshed that first year in Dodge. I mean it wasn't buffalo runners who did all the shooting of their fellow man. What the spilling of bison/buffalo in those years did do was accelerate the near extinction of the species by century's end. As I write this, *Bison bison* are making a comeback, but in 1920 only ninety of these bullish but vulnerable herbivores roamed wild in the United States. That, of course, is a fact I dug up myself since Wyatt "the Walking Encyclopedia" Matters has long been gone from this Earth.

Dodge City's first actual gunfight — not counting the one-sided shooting affray that took the life of poor Tex from Galveston — occurred on September 3, 1872. And though Wyatt Matters did not participate in the gunplay, he was involved. I later heard the story from both Wyatt himself and my boss, Mr. Wright. Their stories didn't always jibe, and the papers offered only fragmentary news reports at best, but as far as I can determine, it happened like this:

In George Brown's tatterdemalion (Wyatt's adjective) saloon, a double-dealing (Mr. Wright's adjective) gambler Charley Morehouse squabbled with one Johnnie Langford, possibly over cards, more likely over a woman. Both men were armed, but before any guns were drawn (if that was indeed anyone's intent) Wyatt Matters, who knew neither man, stepped in, seemingly as a peacemaker. "Boys," he told them, "this is typical unavailing behavior by rootless young men.

You should know that three-quarters of the gunfights west of the Mississippi are fueled by excessive whiskey consumption by young men in saloons much like this one."

"What's it to you, mister?" said Morehouse.

"In America, even Dodge, everyone has the right to free speech," replied Wyatt.

"This ain't your scrape," said Langford.

"I know that, friend, but a man's got to say what a man's got to say."

Morehouse now had the false belief that Wyatt was Langford's pal. "If we're going to lock horns, Johnnie, let it be just you and me. Let's play it fair."

"When did you ever play it fair, Charley?"

"Look. I'm willing to pull in my horns if you are."

"I ain't looking for nothing knock-down, drag-out."

"'Course not. Shall we call it a Mexican standoff?"

"I ain't Mex. You best get yourself heeled, Charley."

"Ah, Johnnie. We're all roostered up. I allot upon going to bed and advise you to do the same."

"You always been yellow, Charley."

"Now, why'd you have to pass that remark? You're startin' to get my dander up, Johnnie."

At that point, Wyatt Matters saw fit to intervene once more. "If you fellows are hell-bent on fighting, I'm sure George Brown would appreciate it if you took it outside so no innocent bystanders get hurt."

"That what you're calling yourself, mister, an innocent bystander?" said Charley Morehouse. "I don't believe it!"

"Never mind me. This is about you two. And if you really want to fight fair you ought to go face-to-face like Bill Hickok and Davis Tutt did in the Springfield, Missouri, town square on July 21, 1865. Maybe you heard about it. The two gamblers had a one-on-one quick-draw duel. Deadeye Wild Bill won, fair and square with a helluva long shot, and went on to have quite a career as a Kansas lawman down the road in Hays City, Abilene, and such."

"Dodge don't have no town square," said Langford.

"True. And I doubt it ever will. But Front Street should do."

"I heard Wild Bill shot a friend by mistake in Abilene and gave up marshaling last year to go on the stage back East," said Morehouse.

"You heard right. But don't worry, Mr. Morehouse. You and Mr. Langford are *not* friends."

That was true enough, but the two men didn't step out of George Brown's saloon and go face-to-face on Front Street. Charley Morehouse went to bed. Thing is, he didn't go alone. Sometime in the wee hours, Johnnie Langford and two of his friends (neither of whom was Wyatt Matters, by the way) yanked Morehouse out of bed, interrupting his pirooting with a dance-hall gal. The trio didn't manhandle Charley much, just poured more whiskey down his throat, before returning to the saloon, where Wyatt was telling owner Brown that to advance public manners and health, he should bring in brass spittoons and ban spitting on the floor.

Charley Morehouse's inamorata (another Wyatt word) had fled the bedroom during the invasion by Johnnie Langford and friends. That made Charley so mad he could bite himself. Instead, he went out on the street looking for a fight, and not necessarily a fair one. He brought some of his own friends along with him. It happened that Langford and company had just staggered out of Brown's saloon, and, by chance, Wyatt was right behind them, finally ready to call it a night and head for his tent on Locust Street even though he was completely sober. Forty-rod whiskey didn't give Wyatt pleasure; hearing himself talk for forty minutes straight did.

Morehouse's party didn't give Wyatt the chance to say anything, such as how he was disinclined to take sides in the whiskey-fueled uproar. They opened fire first, but the Langford party quickly returned fire. Bullets were flying around thick as a swarm of locusts, but Wyatt Matters, who always seemed to have all the luck, ducked behind a horse watering trough and escaped unscathed. Others weren't so lucky, although nobody was killed ("Remember," Wyatt later told me, "all the participants were deep in their cups and couldn't shoot straight."). Among the handful of men wounded were the principal adversaries. Charley Morehouse caught a slug in his arm, but it wasn't consequential enough to stop him from dealing cards or bending his elbows at Brown's saloon. Johnnie Langford got it far worse. Shot five times but in no vital organ, he dragged his bloody body into the bushes so that Morehouse couldn't finish him off. The next morning, friends (and again that didn't include Wyatt) transported Langford by wagon the five miles to the Fort Dodge military hospital. Later, Wyatt went out to visit the infirmary, not out of compassion for the wounded man but because Wyatt had great interest in the surgical procedures of post physician Dr. William Tremaine and the relatively new concepts of using clean equipment and keeping dirt out of open wounds. It so happened that Langford, thanks to the good doctor, was well enough to be released. But whether it was wise for him to return to Dodge City was another matter because Charley Morehouse was still there, a free man showing absolutely no remorse for the shootout.

"Johnnie, you better get the hell out of Dodge," warned one of Langford's actual friends.

Wyatt was listening in and couldn't stay quiet. "Hey, I heard that one before," he said. "Not bad advice but not exactly original."

Chapter Two

While nobody was killed in the Morehouse-Langford altercation, a couple days later Dodge City did see its second fatal shooting. Wyatt Matters wasn't directly involved, but he witnessed it. Wyatt was telling a tracklayer how to do his job and how sluggish he and his crew were compared to a Central Pacific crew that had laid a record ten miles of track one day in April 1869. Increasingly annoyed because Wyatt refused a dozen requests to shut his bone box, the railroad man disdainfully prodded Wyatt's purple bowtie. That didn't stop the flow of words, so the tracklayer pulled out his six-shooter and threatened to blow Wyatt's big fat head off. Wyatt arched his eyebrows, adjusted his bowtie, and tugged on an attached earlobe but then decided silence wasn't his best option. Instead, he would talk his way out of the threat by siding with the worker.

"Land's sake, friend, your weekly hours

should be decreased by ten and your weekly wages increased twofold," he shouted, waving a fist in the air. "Do you know how many railroad workers were killed building the transcontinental railroad? Well, I'll tell you, friend — 1,200. Not that the railroad companies kept count; they didn't care enough. Now you don't have to deal with snow and rock avalanches or slipping off cliffs here in Kansas, but the dangers are real — frigid cold, explosions, accidents, disease, wild Indians! You deserve better. Yes, you do — you and all your fellow AT&SF workers."

"How do you know so much about it?"

"Could be I have a railroad connection. Could be I just care about you fellows. You think AT&SF director Cyrus K. Holliday and the other AT&SF bigwigs have your best interests at heart? Ha! You must demand higher pay, less hours, more safety precautions. And if changes aren't made then strike, my friend, for a day, a week, two weeks, whatever, but strike, strike, strike!"

The tracklayer scratched his chin with the barrel of his six-shooter and listened. A half-dozen other members of the railroad crew lay down their tools and moved in closer to hear the big-headed little man with the compelling voice and busy hands that flapped like the wings of songbirds. One of them even let out a hurrah.

"Now, you're talking, mister," shouted the tracklayer, waving his Colt in the air as if trying to flag down a train. "I sure did misjudge you."

"You aren't the first. Let me just add that not everybody in authority with the AT&SF is an uncompassionate, haughty tycoon, but we must never surrender our rights to those authority figures who wield power indiscriminately."

At that point, a brute came running up along the already laid track and tried to drive a railroad spike into the back of the tracklayer's head. The man might have been tipsy, and his aim was off — the sharp point merely nicked an earlobe. The attacker was Jack Reynolds, a hard case who wore an eye patch and called himself One-eyed Jack ever since losing a knife fight in Ellsworth, Kansas, in 1867 (a fact dug up by Wyatt). That morning he had hopped a train and threatened paying passengers with a six-shooter before a conductor disarmed him and booted him off ten miles short of Dodge City. One-eyed wanted revenge against the entire railroad. He had settled for the spike attack on the first railroad man he came to — the tracklayer.

"Land's sake, friend," Wyatt said. "That pirate has run amok. It appears he aims to kill you."

The tracklayer agreed. He spun around, one hand cupping his bloody ear, the other still waving the six-shooter. One-eyed Jack raised the spike again as if preparing for another thrust. The tracklayer opened fire five times in quick succession at close range, each slug penetrating Jack's midsection. Seeing Jack stretched out on the ground, he pulled back his revolver, but accidentally unleashed a sixth shot that tore through the hem of Wyatt's loose-fitting blue coat but didn't touch flesh. Wyatt later said, perhaps jokingly but maybe not, that his blue suit and purple bowtie protected him from bullets the same way that rawhide shields containing spiritual powers protected Sioux warriors from white men's bullets.

The tracklayer apologized for accidentally putting a hole in Wyatt's suit but not for plugging the crazed attacker five times. No charges were made against him, in part because Dodge City had no law yet but also because Jack Reynolds was considered a desperado who had no place in even a lawless town. Nobody bothered to question whether the trigger-happy railroad man had fired those first five shots in self-defense. In fact, the citizens of the fledgling community, glad to be rid of One-eyed, didn't even ask the tracklayer his name and allowed him to finish his work and freely move along out of Dodge at his own pace.

Several weeks after the tracklaying man-killer departed Dodge, I arrived by train, although there was no station yet and nobody to greet me except a three-legged dog who liked the smell of the sowbelly I carried in my bedroll. I had lived and seen employment in three established eastern Kansas towns but had felt like an outsider in each. The last one was Atchison, where I might have fit in eventually had not the first love of my life — yellow-haired, full-figured, half-wild Elizabeth Pepper — bolted like a horse out of a burning stable. After that abandonment, I had trouble showing my face at the grain mill where my coworkers ridiculed me and the owner docked my pay for missed time. Barely going through the motions as a miller and feeling like something less than a man, I up and quit. It didn't take me much longer to quit Atchison, too. I figured I needed to go to a fledging town where a young newcomer could get over a broken heart and had a chance to make something of himself. Since the burly railroad man with a dash of romance took Miss Pepper east, I decided to go west. Not having a horse, I waited for the tracks to reach Dodge before making my move.

The train fare cost me my last penny, so I slept outdoors for three days behind the buffalo hide yard, which smelled none too good, before I was discovered. Several hunters and their skinners wanted to run me off for being a suspicious character, even though they were all more unkempt than me. I didn't take offense. They were just being protective of those hides, which went for $4.25 apiece. I told them I was looking for work. But they could tell right off that I didn't belong in their business, since I didn't own a six-shooter or a derringer, let alone a buffalo rifle, and my pocketknife was something the skinners laughed over.

"Another greenhorn, not worth shucks," said one of the gore-stained hunters as he cleaned the breech block of his four-foot-long Sharps from atop a fifteen-foot-high hide pile. "We sure do get 'em — fellers who don't know dung from wild honey. I'm betting you never did see a buffler, let alone fire a shot at one."

"Last part is sure enough true, but there must be something I can do around here," I said. "My name is Harry Hannum, and I haven't eaten a square meal in three whole days. If I don't get some vittles in me soon, I'm liable to evaporate. I . . . I . . ." I couldn't disguise my desperation, my voice quivering like it used to do back at grammar school in Bladensburg, Maryland, when I had to stand up and recite in front of the whole class.

"This one is a young whiner in mangy duds, last one was an old tongue flapper who dressed funny," said a skinner as he wiped the blade of his long razor-sharp knife on his buckskin pant leg. "You two fish out of water acquainted? The tongue flapper had a funny name, too — Matter, no Matters, that's it, Wyatt Matters." He wiggled the knife as he chortled.

"Never heard of him, sir. I don't know a single soul in Dodge. You see, I only recently arrived by train from Atchison. I need to find work, anything. I need to eat."

"Well, that old tongue flapper sure wasn't looking for no work. He was telling us why we should leave the *bison* for the natives and find new occupations. Crazy bastard! I scared him off by threatening to cut out his tongue. How 'bout it, Pilgrim? You love your tongue enough to stop your whining?"

"Pilgrim tongue ain't as tasty as buffalo tongue," said the one with the Sharps, which he now casually pointed in my direction. "Easier to just shoot him and be done with it."

My laugh was nervous but that was only because my lips were twitching so hard. That brought on mocking laughter from all over the hide yard and revived all the taunting I took at the Atchison grain mill. I eyed the Sharps that was still pointed in my general direction. My knees turned into soggy bread, and my legs trembled. I took a seat in the dirt, which quieted my limp limbs, but that didn't ease my worry or the pain in my empty gut. "I was wondering something, fellas. With all these buffalo hides you've piled up, there surely must be plenty of buffalo meat around."

"Not here, Pilgrim. Out there." The hunter pointed his Sharps toward the open prairie to the southwest. "We take out the tongue and sometimes the hump, but we leave the rest of it on the ground. We deal in hides. No money in buff meat. You're welcome to it. 'Course you'll have to fight the wolves and coyotes for the scraps that ain't yet putrefied in the sun."

"Here, kid, have half a biscuit," said another hunter who had a humped back, gray beard, not many visible teeth, and a scent that even from ten yards away made me gag. "It's too damn hard." He tossed the half-eaten biscuit in my general direction, and I dove into the hide pile to make a one-handed catch. The hunter on top of the pile laid his Sharps down and began to clap. The skinner brought his knife to his mouth and held it with his teeth before joining in the clapping.

"You got good hands, kid," said the gray-bearded biscuit thrower. "You bound and determined to pick up some eating money?"

"You bet," I said with my mouth full.

"Well then, kid, you head out to where the buffler fell, and you scavenge."

"Huh?"

"Be a bone picker."

A few of the skinners laughed, so I figured it was a jest. Not wanting to go on a wild-goose chase on foot, I gathered up my bed-roll (the last of the sowbelly was in my belly along with the better part of the biscuit) and wandered off with no place to go but feeling my chances for finding sustenance were better in town than out in the surrounding emptiness. For another two days my belly and the rest of me continued to suffer before a woman found me sprawled in the weeds behind the Rath and Wright general store. I had fainted from hunger, and some low-life scavenger, perhaps thinking me dead, had stolen my bedroll, my boots, my pocketknife, and worst of all, since I was as heavy hearted as I was hungry, the blue enamel locket that stored the tintype of Elizabeth Pepper, formerly of Atchison, Kansas. Fortunately for me I did not die in Dodge. My savior was kind-hearted, doleful-eyed Alice Wright, who would have helped any stricken man, woman, child, bird, or four-legged beast.

That night in the Wright house after the Wright children were put to bed, I tasted my first buffalo tongue, which apparently was considered a delicacy by diners in New York, Philadelphia, and Boston but immediately made me sick. After a few too many bites and hard swallows, I began picking at my food while apologizing, first to Mrs. Wright and then to Mr. Wright. I told them that back in Bladensburg, Maryland, I had never sampled any part of a buffalo, at which point Robert Wright told me not only had he been born in that very place but also had a father who aided wounded American soldiers during the August 24, 1814, Battle of Bladensburg against the British army. (He did not tell me, but Wyatt Matters later volunteered the information, that it was an embarrassing defeat that opened the door for the invaders from across the Atlantic to march into nearby Washington, D.C., and set fire to the presidential mansion and other public buildings.) Hunger pangs had turned into another kind of stomachache, but I tried to keep my pain to myself. Certainly, I would have welcomed Alice Wright's motherly concern, but I didn't want to chance being put to bed with the children. I admitted to the Wrights, primarily to receive sympathetic looks from Alice, that my own father was a mean drunk who couldn't hold down a job and had never amounted to anything or helped anyone, not even poor little me, in his entire life.

"A man must make it on his own hook," Robert Wright advised me as Alice, her eyes even more doleful now, served her husband another helping of tongue. "You left Bladensburg and your father behind, but perchance one day you shall return home and talk things out man-to-man with him so that you can both make amends and reach a mutual understanding."

"That's impossible, sir," I said, slumping in my chair and holding my belly. "It was in 1867, less than two years after I bolted from Bladensburg to Baltimore for my own sanity, that the old man stumbled onto the Baltimore & Ohio railroad tracks and had a head-on collision with a steaming B&O engine."

"How sad," said Alice Wright.

"Yes, but I have nothing against trains. It was entirely his fault."

"But what about your mother?" she said, leaning close enough to me so that I got a scent of perfume to go along with the pervading smell of recently cooked meat. "Surely, Mr. Hannum, you went back to be with her in Bladensburg?"

"Well, not immediately. Later, I tried, really, I tried. But . . ."

"But what? Tell us, Harry. Talking it out sometimes helps."

She had gone from Mr. Hannum to Harry mighty fast. That pleased me greatly. Speaking in front of her husband about my mother figured to add a little to my pain, but it seemed well worth the telling as it would elicit more of Mrs. Wright's tenderness. "I loved her very much," I said, "and she, well, her mother's love was there but was highly inconsistent."

"A mother's love does not come and go," Mrs. Wright insisted. "The love I have for my children is there constantly, even when they misbehave, and I am certain it will be there no matter what they do or say in future years. It's only natural for a mother to feel this way."

"I suppose that's true, but I'm afraid not all mothers are the same. Some are not so

. . . you know, steadfast. Some, in fact, are — how should I say this — unstable."

"Whatever do you mean, Harry?"

"You see, I was her fourth child. Her first three, my two sisters and brother, who I scarcely remember, died early on during a cholera epidemic. Why I survived always bewildered my mother, and sometimes it felt as if she blamed me for living on and other times she behaved as if I were her fragile flower, the only bright spot in her life of grinding poverty." I paused and remembered how I had used those identical words in describing my childhood to Elizabeth Pepper. Miss Pepper had acted as if my grinding poverty was my own damned fault. I should have taken that as a warning sign, but naturally I had not.

"Do go on, Harry," said Alice. "Unless it is too painful for you to continue."

"I'll manage," I said. My stomach was starting to feel better. "My mother might be described as a prime example of pitiful, unfortunate womanhood. She took a lot from my old man but stuck it out with him even after his cruelty drove me away to Baltimore. Like I said, he was a mean drunk with hardly a shred of decency who built up a ton of hatred for everyone and everything in his life. But he never had enough energy left over to strike her after he got done throwing empty whiskey bottles, cheap dishes, and broken-down chairs. In other words, it was a hellish life for her but could have been worse. And then he died, which in some ways made things better, but now she was alone. Her only son was gone. Her husband was gone. How mother hated to be alone. Better to be miserable with somebody."

"How awful for her and for you," said Alice Wright, as she took hold of my wrist in a moment I found more than touching. I didn't want her to let go. Any contact, however brief, with a living, breathing woman was welcome after Elizabeth Pepper left me in the cold.

"So, what about it?" said Robert Wright as if challenging me to a duel. "Did you or did you not return home to Bladensburg to see your miserable mother after your horrible father had met the train, so to speak?"

I was startled. Robert Wright, like his wife, was really listening to my story. Hearing his harsh male voice, however, sent a bad message to my belly and I started to feel sick all over again. I thought for a moment that vomit would come up before any more words did.

"Maybe, Bob, he doesn't feel up to talking any more tonight," said Alice Wright.

"Nonsense," said Robert Wright, oblivious to the fact I was sinking fast in my chair and holding on to the tabletop with both hands for support. "I take it you failed to see your mother."

"I . . . I tried. At the time I was without a horse and the B&O hadn't yet constructed a branch of its Washington line that ran through Bladensburg. In any case, I couldn't even afford the train fare to Washington. But I was determined, so I left Baltimore on foot. Thanks to several short rides in the wagons of strangers and my own rushing feet, I covered the long journey to the family house in a remarkably short amount of time and . . ." The steady flow of words stopped suddenly as if they had encountered a formidable dam. I had wanted to sound heroic about hurrying to see my mother after my father's death, but I realized I just sounded foolish. It was only thirty-two miles from Baltimore to Bladensburg, and I didn't set out on the trip until three weeks after my father's fatal accident and only then because I hoped his widow, my unbalanced mother, might dig up a few nickels she could spare her only living child.

"And what?" said Mr. Wright.

Mrs. Wright seemed to be holding her breath in anticipation.

"Your mother, I suppose, wasn't home," said the persistent Mr. Wright.

"So true," I said, my head spinning in a different direction from my churning stomach. "I knocked and I knocked on the front door until my knuckles were raw and then went around to the back where I remembered there to be a rusty key under an empty flowerpot. The back door was boarded up and so was one of the windows. The house only had five windows in total."

"Your mother had moved," said Mr. Wright.

"No. It was more than a move. I went to the half-standing back fence where an old neighbor lady who had long feuded with my father and sympathized with my mother stood. I guess she had been there the whole time. She peered at me as if I were a ghost. I walked over to her, unable to remember her name. When I was a boy, I just called her 'the old witch,' and my father used to call her the 'old something that rhymes with witch.' " I don't know why I needed to explain so much to the Wrights, virtual strangers, even though one of them had saved my life. I was running out of breath, if not words. Now I wanted a bed, with children in it or not. "I don't know if the old neighbor remembered I was the surviving Hannum son or not, but she told it to me straight," I said, gasping with every other word.

"Are you all right, Harry?" Alice Wright asked.

"The young man's fine, just a little chocked up," Robert Wright said. "We'll put him to bed in a minute. First things first. We are dying to know what the old witch from my old hometown told you."

I gulped. My eyeballs felt as if they were burrowing into their sockets like a couple prairie dogs into their tunnels. "She . . . she said: *One cloudy day in May, Mrs. Hannum left her empty house for a very long swim in the Northwest Branch of the Anacostia River. It seemed to me not quite warm enough for a plunge, but I hoped for her sake the sun would soon appear. I had no idea the widow lady had never learned how to swim.*"

At that point I was beyond observing the reaction of caring Alice or curious Robert. My sore eyes were lowered, and they stayed that way as my face dropped softly into my plate of half-eaten tongue.

I must say the Wright house beat any hospital for atmosphere and treatment. I wanted to recover, of course, but not so fast that I would have to leave too soon. I had a room to myself because the twelve-year-old son, Bobby, temporarily moved in (voluntarily or not I do not know) with seven-year-old Elias, five-year-old James, and two-year-old Charles. Mrs. Wright, full of well-developed motherly and nursing instincts, kept me nourished, even going so far as to bring me my meals in bed. Her assistant was ten-year-old Clara Belle, who was as efficient at her mother in caring for the patient but accompanied every action with a wide assortment of giggles. Alice Wright tucked me in for three straight nights as if I were the oldest of her children, though at age twenty-six she was just four years older than me. Even after thirteen years of frontier living and five little Wrights under her chemise, she was still a kind, generous, rosy-cheeked, and vivacious woman. If she ever felt weary, she did a good job of hiding it from me.

"I can't pay you for food or shelter," I admitted to Alice on the third night.

"You will be able to before long," she said. "You won't stay sickly under my care. You'll be able to get out of bed and work."

"Great," I said, with forced enthusiasm.

The next morning, Clara Belle brought me fresh eggs in bed, describing how she had collected them herself from the family chicken coop. She then told me, while giggling of course, that I would have to get dressed because it was moving day. She must have read the concern on my face. "Don't worry, Mr. Harry," she said. "You'll still be seeing me and the rest of the Wright family."

She was right. She and her mother took me down the street to the general store and ushered me to a cot in a storage room amid barrels of everything from flour to sugar, pickles to potatoes, crackers to candles. Fortunately, no stinking hides were kept there. Clara Belle bounced playfully on the cot and declared it too hard for a child but just right for a man who wasn't too tall or too particular. That fit me, all right. Alice then gave me a tour of the well-stocked shelves in the store itself.

"You'll be working soon," she explained. "Don't look so excited."

"Sorry. Do you mean here?"

"Yes. Bob likes the idea if you promise to show up every day and are willing to learn the business. And I tell you, business is booming. You'll stay busy. In time you'll meet Bob's partner, Charlie Rath. He'll go along with the hiring. He is absorbed with the hunting, freighting, and marketing of the hides, not the store personnel."

"This is some store. I never worked in a store before. I'll do my best."

"Don't fret about it. I'm sure you'll be a conscientious clerk in no time."

Clara Belle, with a serious face, had worked her way behind us and began tugging at the back of her mother's dress. "Tell him, Mama," she whispered.

"Yes, yes, dear," Mrs. Wright said. "And if you don't mind, Harry, Bob and I may call on you on occasion to watch over the children for us, babysitting if you will."

"I'm not a baby" declared Clara Belle, still as serious as an undertaker.

"All right. Will you, Harry, when called upon, be willing to look after our four boys and this little girl and keep them out of mischief?"

"Sure. I'll do my best. Someday I might want to have a passel of my own."

Clara Belle stepped out from behind her mother clapping her hands. She gave me a quick hug and then backed away, clapping again, and slipping back into the giggling mode.

In the morning I swept and mopped the general store floor under the watchful eye of Robert Wright. I had done such things as a swamper at a saloon in Lawrence, but my new boss still corrected the way I maneuvered the push broom and took hold of the mop. He then got busy out back conferring over hides with partner Charlie Raft, but he told Bobby Wright, all of twelve and going on eighteen, to make sure I did things the right way. The boy was obliging since he was tired of doing the sweeping and mopping himself. He also proved as bossy as his father, but I took it well. My belly was full, I was sleeping indoors at night, I would be making money soon, and the sweet-smelling woman who had nursed me back to health was still very much on my mind and in my nostrils. Alice Wright showed up at noontime with the rest of her brood and a picnic basket, from which she served cold chicken and warm cornbread as we sat on the floor under an open window. A sunbeam struck me directly in the face, so I had to shade my eyes as I chewed. Clara Belle was full of giggles as she watched me intently, and her brothers Elias and James picked up on that, laughing so hard they spit bits of cornbread. That in turn caused the youngest, two-year-old Charlie, to squeal with delight.

"Nothing is that funny," their mother scolded. "And don't laugh with your mouths full."

"Crumbs everywhere," said Elias, wagging a finger at me. I suspected he was mimicking past action by either his mother or his father.

"He will need to sweep up the crumbs this afternoon," said older brother Bobby.

I just kept chewing, while squinting in exaggerated fashion at each child in turn. Five-year-old James declared, "He funny man."

As it turned out I did no more sweeping or mopping that first day. My mouth was still full when their father took me out back to meet his partner, Charles Rath.

"You ain't afraid of a little hard work, are you, Larry?" Mr. Rath asked.

"Not at all, sir," I replied for he didn't look like a man who would accept a qualifying response. I didn't even bother to tell him I was Harry, not Larry.

I spent all afternoon and part of the evening helping Mr. Rath transport hides to AT&SF freight cars. That left me exhausted and wanting a bath. I settled for splashing water on my face and chest before collapsing on my cot. Robert Wright found that amusing. "Hides do get heavy, Harry," he said. "You won't be doing that for Charlie regular. Tomorrow, I'll introduce you to the rest of the business. Clerking ought not prove nearly so strenuous for you. Sleep well."

My mind was racing, and my shoulders and arms were aching, so I didn't fall asleep immediately. After some tossing and turning, I settled on lying on my stomach. That did it.

But shortly after drifting off a firm hand on the back of my neck awakened me, though my eyes remained shut. "Yes, Lizzie," I said, because Elizabeth Pepper used to go for the neck whenever I wasn't showing her the attention she demanded. A female voice followed, whispering, "I'm sorry." I figured I must be dreaming because during my six months with Miss Pepper, apologies from her were as rare as mountain goats in Kansas. When the hand moved from my neck to my left shoulder, I not only turned to the side but reached out. My own hand touched something that was not a neck, and I reached out further, hooking my arm around a warm body and drawing it on top of me. My half-asleep action was not unprecedented. Elizabeth Pepper liked to be on top.

It was a wonder to me that Alice Wright did not scream or dig her fingernails into my face. Instead, she asked, rather calmly at that, "Have you become delirious, Harry?"

That opened my eyes, of course, but instead of releasing her immediately, I stared into her soft, sympathetic eyes for a moment. I was apologizing even before I let go. She slid off me with surprising grace and held up a little basket. "I thought you might like a bite to eat," she said as she pulled a chicken wing out of the basket. When I didn't reach out to take it right away, she pressed the wing against my lips until I began to nibble.

An awkward silence followed, and I was tempted to pull a blanket over my head while I chewed. But she came through again and talked to me as if I had done something, even if wrong, that wasn't worth making a fuss over. She inquired about my health and my workday and then told me a little about herself. She had been only thirteen, just three years older than Clara Belle, when she married nineteen-year-old Robert, who happened to be her first cousin.

"I'm not saying all marriages are made in heaven, but a good marriage can be," she said. "Bob and I have a very good marriage. I love children, he loves his work, and in between we love each other, which means we on occasion need a break from the kids and the general store. That's where you come in — if still willing to watch the little Wrights for us from time to time."

"Of course. Nothing has changed."

Something had changed, though. I had grabbed her. It had been an accident, of course, but then I had kept her on top of me for too long. I vowed to make amends by watching her children whenever she wanted and keeping my eyes as well as my hands off her. Furthermore, I would work hard every day at the general store and never make her husband regret hiring me.

"Thank you for the chicken," I said without looking at her face or any other part of her beautiful being. "And I'm sorry about . . ."

"Sbhhh," she said. Out of the corner of my eye I saw her press a finger to her closed lips. "Say no more about it. I shall do the same. Now go back to sleep. Days begin early at the general store."

"Yes, ma'am," I said.

She smiled, turned away abruptly, and headed for the door. I wasn't going to watch her go, but she was swinging the empty basket like a child would a pail, so I couldn't help myself. Going back to sleep didn't prove easy. All kinds of improper thoughts popped into my head, and they were still there the following morning in broad daylight. I knocked them out by beating my head against a sack of Wright flour. My mother after all had been a Christian woman who aimed to raise me right — to fear God's wrath as well as my father's beatings. I wasn't sure if her suicide was a sin or not, but under the circumstances it was certainly forgivable.

On my second workday Robert Wright showed me everything the general store had on its shelves, basically a repeat of the tour his wife had given me earlier. Afterward he stressed that to be an excellent clerk (and he expected nothing less from me) I must not only be familiar with all the merchandise but also treat customers the right way (cordially but not as family looking for handouts and special deals) and know how to handle the cash box and transactions (paper money, coins, gold all accepted, but only he could extend credit, accept payment in kind, and barter). Whatever he wanted was fine with me, including whatever salary he cared to pay me. It was my intention to hold onto this job (unlike my previous three in eastern Kansas), become a respectable citizen, and grow with Dodge.

I didn't see Alice Wright or the children all day, but at quitting time, the wonderful mother appeared at the store and asked me to look after the five children that very night since she and Mr. Wright were having a supper meeting with other founding businessmen at the home of Frederick and Matilda Zimmerman. She apologized for the short notice, explaining that there had been some confusion about the date and whether all the wives were to be included in this gathering.

"If you are too exhausted or have other plans, you can be excused from this duty," she said.

"Of course, he'll do it," said Mr. Wright.

And, of course, I did. I delighted all the children except the oldest (Bobby) and the youngest (Charlie) with a long not-quite-bedtime story about a flying buffalo herd and green-skinned hunters from Mars who rode turkey vultures instead of horses. Bobby told me he had never seen a flying buffalo, ignoring the other fantastic elements I had created just for the Wright children. He only wanted to hear true tales like the ones his father told, such as how young Abe Lincoln was born in a one-room log house and split rails for his daddy and how little Georgie Washington couldn't tell a lie to his daddy and admitted he had chopped down the cherry tree. Charlie just wanted to cry for his missing mama. But the other two boys thought that the green-skinned hunters were mean and the turkey vultures scary and clamored to hear more about them as well as about Mars. Clara Belle was relieved that the bad guys from Mars mounted on turkey vultures couldn't catch the harmless flying buffalo. I knew almost nothing about Mars, but I took them all outside and pointed to something in the night sky that might have been a planet. By the time their parents returned, all the children were in bed except Bobby, who fell asleep in a chair.

Alice rewarded me with a pat on the head, and Clara Belle climbed out of bed to kiss me on the forehead. Robert Wright told me I could report to work the next day a half hour later than usual.

Chapter Three

It was the morning after my night with the Wright children that I first met Wyatt Matters in person. I was hard at work, climbing on a barrel so I could hang pots, pans, and washboards from hooks in the ceiling. Mr. Wright didn't like to leave any space empty.

"I see you're getting up in the world," said Mr. Matters, as if he somehow knew how down I'd been since Elizabeth Pepper left me and I left the grain mill in Atchison.

"Yes, sir," I said but didn't laugh because Mr. Wright had his eye on me.

"Leave the help alone," said Mr. Wright. "There's work to be done here."

"In your narrow-mindedness, Mr. Wright Can Do No Wrong, there is always work that needs doing." Mr. Matters then introduced himself to me, but I already recognized him by reputation. Mr. Wright had warned me about this most peculiar man in a top hat and purple bowtie. Of course, I didn't mention that. I told him my name and said I was glad to meet him. After squatting on the barrel top, I still needed a long reach to shake his chubby little hand. Not even that top hat gave him much height.

"So, new to Dodge City, are you? Of course, everybody and everything is relatively new in Dodge City."

"Yes, sir." My knees cracked when I stood up.

"How do you like our little town so far, Harry? Oh, excuse me. Trader Bob and the other entrepreneurial elite consider it *their* town."

"I suppose, as usual, you are *not* going to be a customer today," said Mr. Wright. "Just here to criticize and complain, complain and criticize, and bother . . ."

"No bother. Just go about your business, Trader Bob."

Wyatt Matters dismissed my boss with a wave and then whispered to me, "Mr. Wright Can Do No Wrong would no doubt love to hang me from that hook next to the washboard."

"I heard that," said Mr. Wright. "You'd only rot up there. You'd never sell."

Mr. Matters shrugged, ran his fingers over staves of the barrel as if trying to determine what was inside, and then began talking to me, rather to my ankles. "As a newcomer to Dodge, Harry, you might not realize that the so-called founders, a prejudiced group that refused to recognize me, wanted to call it something else — Bullburg, Buff City, Bufflerville, Queen of the Buffalo Hides, Stinkiest Little City in America. Actually, I just made that last one up, but you catch my drift. Bisonville would be more correct since the proper name of the Great Plains animal is bison, not buffalo. People here just don't accept that hard fact."

"Like I said, always complaining and criticizing," said Mr. Wright.

"Shames me to say it, but the town's creation was all about Trader Bob and the founders wanting to profit from the humpback shaggy-haired beasts and deny Plains Indians their main source of food. In case you were unaware, Harry, bison hunting is the fundamental activity in the economy and society of all the Plains Indians."

All I knew was I couldn't land a job with the non-Indian buffalo hunters and that despite exhausting myself carrying all those heavy hides for Charles Rath the other day, I was glad to have a position at the general store. I didn't know quite what to say as I had never come across any wild Indian of the Plains. It didn't matter. Mr. Matters wasn't waiting for me to respond.

"I went in a different direction as far as the naming game. I suggested calling the new town 'Flagitious Frontier Folly,' which confounded the founders even after Mr. Wright Can Do No Wrong got out Noah Webster's dictionary and found out that *flagitious* means marked by scandalous crime or vice, having been derived from the Latin noun *flagitium,* meaning shameful thing. But don't get the wrong impression, Harry. I was not against a new town forming on the prairie. I was against the *wrong* kind of town forming on the prairie. I want to settle down and make my home here, but the way things stand, I see where it will be necessary for me to oppose the crime and vice that is the prevailing condition. I'm sorry to report, Harry, that we've had some needless killings in town already."

"That's enough, Mr. Matters," said Mr. Wyatt, striding over to the barrel. "You are scaring him and confusing him with your nonsense."

The adversaries were now on each side of me as I stood between them and above them. I had no more items to hang on the hooks, but I kept my arms raised as if standing between two duelists. Fortunately, these two men were unarmed and only dealt in words.

"Don't be absurd," Mr. Matters said. "My capacity for perception is limitless."

"You know very well we named ourselves Dodge City because we are here in no small part to support Fort Dodge, which was named for a U.S. general. And you know equally well that once we had carved a place for ourselves on the Plains only two men have been shot — one a hard case who didn't live here and had a beef against the railroad and the other an anonymous Negro."

"The victim was Tex. A good, peace-loving man from Galveston, Texas."

"My point is two is not too many."

"Two is too much."

They were both leaning heavily against the barrel, which caused it to rock slightly even though the sugar inside weighed twice as much as me. I lost my balance and dropped to one knee to keep from falling off. I did notice that both men appeared ready to catch me, which I took to be a good sign.

"Don't get your back up, Mr. Wright Can Do No Wrong, I'll be pressing on," said Mr. Matters. "I have more important business at Zimmerman's store."

"Frederick Zimmerman can't stand your

meddling any more than I can. And his store does carry pistols and rifles."

"I'm not going there to see Mr. Grimmerman or his plump wife. It so happens that . . ."

"That's Mr. Zimmerman. And I'm Mr. Wright. Keep up that kind of disrespectful talk and someone will one day knock that top hat off your head and maybe your head to go along with it."

"Or shoot me between my big blue eyes, right, Trader Bob? Violence happens, especially in Dodge."

"I don't appreciate being called Trader Bob either."

"As Ralph Waldo Emerson says, 'A man is what he thinks about all day.' "

"And what do you think about all day? All you do is loiter about town making a nuisance of yourself. You don't seem to have a family or real home or do any kind of work or . . ."

"I think. That happens to be the most important thing man can do; thinking is what separates us from the birds and the bison. Wealth and position, things you strive for, do not bring about true power or happiness. The great thinkers dwarf the mighty warriors, the highfalutin politicians, the sanctimonious proselytizers, and most definitely the proficient profiteers when it comes to making the world a better place. Gaining knowledge and high thinking make for the noblest of occupations."

"Just go, you vagabond!" Mr. Wright made several guttural sounds and started to walk away. But he soon stopped to address me. "And you get down from there before you break a leg."

Mr. Matters didn't go immediately. He took hold of my left ankle and gave it a firm squeeze. "Such a caring shopkeeper," he said. "But do be careful, Harry. I want you to know I am no vagabond. I live in a fine, broad tent that is my home, my permanent residence. Should you ever need anything, come see me in my tent on the wrong side of the AT&SF tracks. It may be just a lowly tent in the eyes of the big bugs who want to build and build some more, but it suits me fine. I bid you adieu for now, but I shall be seeing you." He patted my shoe, tipped his top hat, straightened his purple bowtie, and took a leisurely stroll to the door.

As soon as I hopped off the barrel, Mr. Wright shouted at me: "Enough time has been wasted. Now get that barrel off the middle of the floor."

I didn't know what to make of Wyatt Matters after that first meeting. He came back to the store the next day, top hat, bowtie, and all, only to confuse me further. "Fear not," he told Mr. Wright. "I am a customer today." He pointed up at the shiny frying pan I had hung from the ceiling the day before. "I want that one. Sorry to inconvenience you."

To reach the pan I needed to stand again on the barrel, which had to be maneuvered out of the corner and into position. I struggled mightily while he watched until finally Mr. Wright came over and lent me a hand. This seemed to amuse Mr. Matters, who kept giving us directions: "No, no, not like that. You're veering to the left. Over this way a little. He's pushing, you pull. Don't let it get away from you now. That's it. A little more. A little more. Excellent. Just a little more to the right and we'll be all set."

"You could have bought it yesterday when he was already up there," said Mr. Wright as he paused to hold his back.

"Didn't need such a big pan yesterday. I'm having an important guest over tonight and I'm cooking."

"You could have at least lent a hand with the barrel."

"You expect the customers to do your work for you, Trader Bob?"

"Never mind. Sell him the pan, Harry.

Don't let him talk down the price. The price is fixed."

Mr. Wright removed himself to the other side of the store but kept a steady gaze on me as I wrapped the pan in brown paper, twice being corrected on my technique by Mr. Matters. I then awkwardly tried to tie it with a string. After I retied four times, the customer was satisfied.

"Forgive me," he said. "I don't wish to make your mundane job more difficult, young man. My only intent is to cause the bumptious shopkeeper over there a little further annoyance. In fact, to make it up to you, I'll give you twice the fixed price, but you must pocket half of it."

"I can't do that. Mr. Wright wouldn't approve."

"Exactly. There are more important things in life than gaining the approval of a shopkeeper. But let's turn our backs to him to make our transaction, shall we? His disapproving eyes are as fixed as his high price."

We pulled it off. I had a few extra coins in my pocket and, or so I believed, guilt all over my face. He assured me I had done nothing against the law and that Robert Wright might own the store but did not own me. "I've had my eye on you, Harry Hannum," he said. "You have eyes like mine, the color of the Big Blue River."

My young blue eyes caught his bigger blue eyes over our conspicuous noses. I was transfixed. Not only did his eyes have depth but they also had waves of energy swelling and dying away as if they were reading my every thought. I suspected my eyes must seem shallow to him for the only thing they were saying was: *For someone with such interesting eyes you sure are ugly.* But then, out of the blue, I thought of Elizabeth Pepper, who was anything but ugly. I was always telling her how stunning she looked from blond hair to pliant toes, but one time she gazed into my eyes and surprised me by saying it was like looking into pools of blue water. In retrospect I suspect she was seeing her own reflection in those pools. It occurred to me now that this extended eye contact with Wyatt Matters might be something like that — this unsightly man of twice my age was seeing a younger version of himself. That didn't please me at the time. I abruptly turned my head to see if Mr. Wright was still watching us from across the room. He was.

"Forget the Big Blue River," Mr. Matters said. "I only mentioned it because of its geographic proximity. Let's have a better look at the blueness." He put a hand on my cheek and gently turned my head so that he could study my eyes again at even closer range. "Got it. The bridges of our grand noses are the Strait of Gibraltar connecting you, the Mediterranean Sea, with me, the Atlantic Ocean. Together, as short as we are, we stand tall like the Rock of Gibraltar."

I had never heard of that rock and furthermore I resented being compared to any rock, especially one that resembled him. For the first time I noticed the hairy strands protruding from both his nostrils. I was secretly delighted when Mr. Wright came over, disingenuously thanked Mr. Matters for purchasing the pan with hard cash, and then showed the unwanted customer to the door. It was time to move the barrel again.

On the following day, Wyatt Matters made no appearance at the general store. I spent my day putting things on and off shelves and satisfying customers and Mr. Wright as best I could while watching for the man in the top hat the way my mother used to watch for my drunken father to came home from the tavern. It wasn't that I didn't harbor good feelings about the attention he had shown me, but I knew Mr. Matters' presence greatly displeased my employer. I was also apprehensive about having those deep blue eyes on me again. For what purpose? How did I warrant that kind of attention let alone those extra coins he slipped me?

After my duties for the day were done, I went out for fresh air instead of retreating immediately to my room in back. I walked down Front Street, which was busier than ever. On occasion I was jostled by men moving twice as fast as me. I found myself apologizing for being there and forcing these people with places to go to make detours around me. I passed the Wright house with a certain longing, perhaps for a good-cooked meal or another chance to watch over the children or something else that I needed to expunge from my head. I absentmindedly drifted away from the crowd and crossed the railroad tracks without looking in either direction. On Locust Street, thinking I was alone, I paused to take some deep breaths of the night air. It was October and temperatures were beginning to fall, but instead of picking up any scent of autumn, I was struck by a harsh, hot breeze carrying the smell of stinking buffalo hides.

"You never know when the wind will shift, young man."

I turned and didn't see anyone at first, but then I spotted a man in a top hat waving a book at me. He came right up to me and practically shoved the book in my face. The title was *Travels into Several Remote Nations of the World,* by Jonathan Swift.

"I'm rereading it for the third time," Wyatt Matters said. "On his first voyage, the shipwrecked Lemuel Gulliver has landed among the Lilliputians whose small size is mirrored by their small-mindedness. These little people have silly customs, petty perspectives. They have tied him up because they fear such a large, educated man is dangerous and at the very least will ridicule them for their foolishness."

"Is it a true story?" I asked.

"No, no, my boy. Knowing as many facts as possible never hurts, but we mustn't forget the wonderful creative works that are fiction, in this case a savage satire mocking the English customs and politics of the time, which happens to be early last century."

"Oh," I said because I didn't know enough about what was going on then or now in England to mock anything. "I like to make up stories sometimes." I was mostly thinking of my tale for the Wright children about flying buffalo and green-skinned hunters from Mars. I was pretty sure it wasn't a satire, just a story about fantastic creatures having an adventure.

"Wonderful. Making up things does take

some original thinking. What Swift gives us, though made up, is a great slice of truth. I wasn't shipwrecked, of course, and I didn't arrive here at this island in the prairie by accident, but I do feel very much like Mr. Gulliver and the citizens of Lilliput have many similarities to the men of Dodge. I'm sure you can readily see that men like your Robert Wright are doing their best to restrain me."

I shrugged, not wanting to criticize my boss even this far from the general store. I didn't want to see more of Mr. Matters, but as I tried to move away, he restrained me by taking hold of my wrist. It was not a severe hold, and I could easily have broken away, but then he spoke in such a melodious tone that I had to listen: "So nice of you to come see me, young man, and glad you have arrived as sober as a judge and not bearing arms. You clearly are a decent, reliable, law-abiding, wide-eyed sort, one worthy of my consideration. This way to my tent."

He led me by the wrist all the way down Locust Street to a lot that would have been empty except for an unusual tent with a rectangular base and the pointed top of a tepee. It was spacious and warm, with a central fire going and the smoke rising through a flap on top. On one side of a long side table were kitchen utensils, including the frying pan he had recently purchased and was now blackened from use, and on the other side were a stack of books and a higher stack of newspapers. He had me sit on one of the three chairs while he chose to hop up on one of two leather trunks with straps, buckles, handles, and dome tops. His legs didn't reach the ground. Behind him was a coat stand on which hung many articles of clothing, including what looked like two backup purple bowties. Beside the stand was a buffalo robe draped over a pile of colorful blankets.

My curious eyes surveyed the room until I realized he was following my eyes with his own. "Like a home," was all I could think to say.

"Since Mr. Wright Can Do No Wrong called me a vagabond, I'm sure you believed I couldn't possibly be living in such style. My home is part tent, part tepee, which allows me the space I need and the convenience of having an open flickering fire. The Plains Indians know what they're doing. The smoky air weighs less than fresh air and hence floats high and out of the tepee top while the fresh air floats in. Of course, one must still mind a fire like one would a red-cheeked lover to keep the flames at a constant low level without letting them burn themselves out. Ah, you blush when I compare a fire to a red-cheeked lover. You are temperate, peaceful, and diffident around the ladies."

I wasn't sure what diffident meant but it didn't sound good. "I just about got hitched with a yellow-haired beauty just a few months ago," I said. Yes, I was exaggerating how close Elizabeth Pepper and I had been to matrimony, but I felt I must defend my honor as a woman-loving man.

"When did she leave you?" he said.

"Who said she left me?"

"Never mind."

"OK. She did leave me. But I had nothing to do with it. I mean it wasn't my fault."

"I wouldn't think so. You were just being yourself."

"I suppose so."

"Of course, oneself can always be improved. See all those books over there. They can help. And I can help you with my experience if you are willing."

"Are we still talking about women?"

"Oh, I see why you might think so. Pardon me. I was thinking in broader terms. I was talking about the uncompromising process of becoming an educated, high-thinking man, a Renaissance man if you will, not unlike yours truly. But now that you mention it, I was wondering what kind of women a respectable, unsophisticated young fellow like yourself takes a shine to. For instance, you don't limit yourself to well-formed fair-haired ladies of a deceitful nature, do you?"

I had lost his drift, was still focused on the word "unsophisticated," the meaning of which I did know. "I'm not that young. I'm twenty-two."

"Not too old to fulfill a purpose, Harry. I am forty-two, though some say I could pass for fifty." He flashed a smile but then snorted and went back to his solemn face. "I am a man of much experience and learning. That you can be assured of."

"I don't doubt it."

"You, on the other hand, are like a babe in the woods, rather like a babe on the treeless prairie, seeing as this is southwestern Kansas. I not only have been studying you but also have inquired about you from the obliging Alice Wright and her suspicious husband."

"Oh." I crossed my legs and my arms, probably to keep from fleeing the tent. I didn't appreciate being likened to a babe anywhere, and I couldn't help but wonder if Mrs. Wright, whose hair was brown and with a few streaks of gray, had told Mr.

Matters about my attraction to her. But I remembered she hadn't told her husband about my inappropriate advance, and when my host didn't mention her name again, I relaxed somewhat.

"Tell me Harry Hannum, are you interested in learning more?"

I was still thinking about Alice Wright, so I had no immediate answer.

"Well, young fellow, are you?"

"I don't want to go to some college, if that's what you mean."

"No, it is not. I would be your teacher, so to speak. You require my guidance. I don't say this lightly. Most of the reckless young men around Dodge refuse to be guided and are doomed to misspent lives and early deaths."

I shivered though it was plenty warm with that little fire holding its own. My father hadn't taught me much of anything. But he set an example all right. I didn't want to be anything like him; I wanted to be somebody who was even slightly significant. "Nobody wants an early death," was what I managed to say.

"I can't totally guarantee that, Harry, but I can give you the information you need to not only live long but also to live well. And by that I don't mean possessing a lot of gold, silver, and banknotes or to own large houses and big businesses like Trader Bob and Mr. Grimmerman. Aristotle told us the importance of educating our minds and our hearts. It so happens that I am not a poor man. But I have chosen to live in this tent because I'm happy here away from the hustle and bustle of Front Street and the crowd of money- and pleasure-seekers. It was my wise choice not to make my life meaningless by displaying my wealth and pursuing *more* money. I have a nobler purpose — in short, to educate my mind."

"You do seem mighty smart. What about your heart? Is that educated, too?"

"Oh, yes. Do not be fooled by me living alone. I have not ignored my heart. I have loved and have had lovers. I know about their hearts, too. I have studied love and romance through the ages. I shall not go on about myself. My story doesn't matter to most people. Perhaps one day, if I think it matters to you, I will tell you more. Let me just say I once suffered from restlessness, what Baudelaire called *le grande maladie de l'horreur du domicile,* which essentially means 'the great illness caused by a horror of home.' I used to travel to get away from my home, no matter how stately others perceived it to be. But those days are over. I am so much older and wiser now. Here in Dodge, I have found my heart and my permanent home, though I must say my home has much room for improvement. I believe if anyone can make Dodge City and environs a better place, it's men like me and eventually you, too, if you have the right disposition."

He had given me a lot to digest. I had some trouble picturing him with a lady love, yellow-haired or not, but I supposed some women were more attracted to minds and manners than faces and bodies. I was surprised he had plans for an extended stay in Dodge, considering how he had all those run-ins with town founders and such. I thought I wanted to stay in Dodge longer than I had in Lawrence, Elgin, and Atchison, but I figured it mostly depended on my keeping my job at the general store. I knew I needed to make some money to live — like most people. Wyatt Matters certainly wasn't like most people. It was easy to *not* be a money-seeker when you already had money to spare. I wondered how he might have obtained his, but before I could ask, he threw out a question that made me forget about money, women, and Mr. Matters' secretive past.

"So, Harry Hannum, how would you like to be my protégé?"

I'm sure I must have looked bewildered

because he quickly explained that *protégé* was derived from a French word meaning "one who is protected." Of course, that hardly cleared things up for me. He continued, "And you need protection, young fellow. Who doesn't like to be protected?"

"Protected from what?"

"From two things: the dull, impoverished minds of shopkeepers for one, and secondly, but not because it is of lesser importance, the wild frontier, dangerous Dodge City. As we speak our town is full of people who will lie to you, steal from you, assault you, and even shoot you."

"Mr. Wright doesn't believe Dodge is really so dangerous."

"The avaricious shopkeeper speaks. Robert Wright, like so many people in this world, feels he is right even when he is dead wrong. Such people are most concerned with profit and loss and their own comfort, to the extent they won't always show you their true faces. They have no use for me. As for Charles Rath, I have felt his wrath simply because I told him he was a ghoul for profiteering from death."

"Oh, you mean those buffalo hides."

"Tons of bison hides. The hunters and skinners of bison are pretty much filthy devils who are among the biggest troublemakers on any given night in Dodge. What's more, the bison belong to the Plains Indian and . . ."

I interrupted by pointing emphatically to the pile of blankets with the buffalo robe on top.

"There's a difference. That robe was given to me by a Kaw, or Kansa, subchief whose name I have written down somewhere in this trunk but means 'The One Who Runs Down Bison.' I hid him in my blankets from eighteen Pawnee raiders, and he later awarded me with this fine robe prepared by his sister, Yugije Mi, whom I fell in love with, but that's another story."

"Land's sake! You've known Indians, an Indian maiden even."

"I never said Yugije Mi was a maiden. Her name means 'Female Who Presses the Hard Corn with Her Hands.' She had pressed much corn through the years. She won my heart but died of a white man's disease — smallpox. She . . . There you go again, getting me off the subject. You have left my question unanswered." He slid off the trunk, scurried up to me, and repeated his question, "Do you, Harry Hannum, consent to be my protégé?"

It sounded like something he should have asked the Kaw woman.

"I'm not sure what it entails," I admitted.

"Listen and learn. Listen and learn some more. That's the gist of it."

"I can do that. But I'll have to keep listening to Mr. Wright. I work for him."

"I understand. You don't have to quit the general store to become my protégé. Listen to Trader Bob but don't always believe what he says. Know that he can be wrong."

"I know that anybody and everybody can be wrong."

"That's a start, my protégé. Even I, your mentor, can be wrong on rare occasion." Mr. Matters' sedate demeanor suddenly changed. He broke out with a surprisingly high-pitched laugh, accompanied by a hardy pat on each of my shoulder blades.

I must have given him another puzzled look.

"*Mentor* comes from Homer. Athena disguises as Mentor and guides Odysseus' son Telemachus in his search for his father. So, you see, I'm your guide, your teacher, your confidante."

"Why me?"

He laughed again but kept it brief. "Why anybody? I am an excellent judge of character. You are worth saving, molding into a well-educated, thoughtful man, like I once was. But now I'm old, past forty. I must think of the future. We both must, mentor and protégé. Along with everything else I have thoroughly studied the goings-on in Kansas since it became a territory in 1854. I foresee many changes. Dodge won't stay this way forever. There will be more shootings, more violence. But the lawmen will come, the killings will stop; the buffalo will disappear, the cattle will come; the cattle will go, the farmers will prevail, probably some of the shopkeepers, too, but that can't be helped. You see, I am not only your mentor but also a visionary. I will see you through all the turmoil ahead in Dodge. We shall persevere."

We left it like that. I can't say I truly believed in his vision or in his ability to guide me. I was a clerk in Dodge City now, but there was no certainty it would last. Tomorrow I could be a humble clerk in Emporia, an overaged messenger boy in Junction City, a lowly stable boy in Hays City, or a vagabond back in Atchison. My vision wasn't much. I couldn't even see my lonely heart becoming educated any time soon. I kicked the rails as I crossed the tracks and told myself to pull myself together. I wasn't picturing his fat little face with the big nose, nor his top hat, Sunday suit, or bowtie. What flashed repeatedly in my head was that word *Original* on his oversized silver belt buckle. By the time

I was walking along Front Street and hearing piano music, vociferous singing, shouts, screams, and at least one gunshot, I had stopped talking to myself. I was shuffling through the dark general store to get to my sleeping quarters when I convinced myself of something: While Wyatt Matters was a strange bird indeed, it wouldn't kill me to give the position of protégé a shot.

Chapter Four

Over the next several weeks I listened as best I could to both Robert Wright and Wyatt Matters. Mr. Wright liked to instruct but preferred to correct. I couldn't help but believe the boss enjoyed telling me I had filled an order wrong, had treated a customer with too little or too much respect, or had swept the floor worse than his twelve-year-old son. Mr. Matters once corrected me on my listening (shouldn't be done with eyes half-closed and hands over ears) but otherwise was all about instructing. He bombarded me with facts and commentary about historical happenings — from keystone events like the Lewis and Clark Expedition and the California Gold Rush to groundbreaking events like the inventions of dynamite and typewriters — and his assessment of books, including the unfamiliar Leo Tolstoy's *War and Peace* and Gustave Flaubert's *Madame Bovary,* as well as one I had heard of (but hadn't read), James Fenimore Cooper's *The Last of the Mohicans.* I wondered how any of this had anything to do with Dodge City, Kansas, or me improving my station in life. I didn't question my mentor or complain, but during one session in his tent, he suddenly half-scolded me with this statement: "You can learn how to shoe a horse and become a farrier and you can learn how to shoe a man's foot and become a cobbler, but to become a Renaissance man you must patiently walk in the shoes of everyone from Prince Bagration and Natty Bumppo to Sacagawea and Emma Bovary."

"I see," I told him, though I was not acquainted with the names he dropped.

"No need to say you see when you don't see," he said. "Nobody gets educated overnight. It takes hard work and patience. And right now, you are wondering where all this education will lead you."

"I wonder, Mr. Matters, if besides being a mentor and a visionary you are also a mind reader."

"I figured you might ask me that, son. Reading minds is a magician's trick, featured as early as 1781 by Philip Breslaw in London's Haymarket Theatre. But it is no trick for me. I read your various verbal and silent signals, as when you just said *I see* while tugging your ear, which happens to be something I do when trying to figure something out. Who to best read the thoughts of a protégé than his mentor?"

"I suppose you're right, Mr. Matters."

"Of course, I am, son. I can give you an uncommon tutelage that will allow you to achieve great heights, but it isn't something that happens suddenly like a blow to the head. *'Rome ne fu pas faite toute* en *un jour'* to quote from the twelfth-century French collection *Li Proverbe au Vilain.*'"

He had lost me. I wasn't certain what *tutelage* meant, and I didn't know any word in French except *merde,* which had also been the only French word my father had known. I found myself studying Mr. Matters' hairy ears while resisting an urge to tug my right ear. I changed the subject.

"I've noticed of late that you've started calling me *son,* Mr. Matters."

"True enough, son. It just seems so natural considering our age difference, my desire to see you grow, and how much time you've spent at my home listening or half-listening to me. No need for you to call me *papa,* but you might try out Wyatt instead of Mr. Matters."

"All right, Mr. Matters."

"Wyatt. I sense you are unsure about me referring to you as *son*."

"Not really. I don't know. My father never called me *son*. Several times when he was angry at me or more likely at my mother, he called me a *son of a bitch*."

"Your father never called you *son*. That's not the end of the world. I figure you have the right to be called somebody's son. And I am somebody, son. As my protégé, I shall educate you and protect you as any decent father would — only better."

"I called him *Horrible Hannum*," I mumbled, my thoughts lodged in the house with the boarded-up back door in Bladensburg, Maryland.

"Admirable alliteration. Your birth father was no account, either beating you or ignoring you. He is long gone. He offered you nothing then and can offer you nothing now. I can offer you the world. Isn't that what you always wanted, son, to amount to something?"

He was exactly right. I wasn't sure how he knew it unless it was more of his mind reading. I had skedaddled for the West to become a man, a better man than my father for sure but that didn't figure to take much effort. So far, I hadn't beaten anyone, but then I didn't have a son. I hadn't abused or tried the patience of a wife, but then I didn't have one of those either. I had only been drunk once (after Elizabeth Pepper left me in Atchison). I hadn't held down a job for any great length of time so far, but I aimed to do better at the Dodge general store. I had traveled by train to reach this railroad town. No way in hell I was going to blindly cross the tracks and let a steaming locomotive smash me to unrecognizable bits.

"Never mind too much what has come before," Mr. Matters said. "By sticking with me, son, you'll earn the nickname *Honorable Hannum.*"

"Does anyone call you *Honorable Matters*?"

"Fair question. Your Mr. Wright Can Do No Wrong" and his kind surely don't. They don't know how to deal with an unorthodox and independent-minded man or woman. But I take pride in who I am, thus my purple bowtie, my top hat (it also makes me look taller, right?), and this." He pointed to the word *Original* inscribed on his belt buckle. "Through the years, though, I have indeed been called *honorable* by both men and women, more so by men and women who are blacker or redder than the pale-faced greedy shopkeepers and small-minded clerks who populate . . . Ugh! That was a most regrettable faux pas. A thousand pardons. You are an exception, son. Certainly, you are not small-minded, and by the time I'm through with you, you'll be such a broad-minded, original, honorable freethinker that you won't be able to recognize your old self."

"There must be other small-minded young men in Dodge you could help?"

"Drinkers. Drifters. Carousers. Shooters. Greedy, selfish, hot-tempered, trigger-happy fools. You are none of those things. Don't sell yourself short, the way Trader Bob does. You have promise, son, potential excellence. I have been around. I know. You will be receptive and benefit from my sagacity."

"Huh?"

"My experience. My wisdom. My honorableness." He hooked his thumbs in his *Original* belt buckle.

"Mr. Wright says a man *must make it on his own hook.*"

"Yes, it is possible to do it that way, just look at me. But the fact is that while a man might make it on his own, almost all will fail to make it in the right way. Do not be discouraged. You'll find, under my guidance, that a man *must* rise above his circumstances to become a Renaissance man. I'm not saying it's easy or else more people would do it. Like I've told you, it'll take continuous hard work, but I know you can accomplish a grand transformation."

"I could disappoint you and myself."

"Won't happen. You came West. You came to Dodge City. You met me. What is still to come will be history. You can't go wrong. You are my protégé. People will come to respect you and remember you — if you are willing to be guided, instructed, *fathered.*"

"All right, Wyatt. I was just checking."

I stayed plenty busy through October, sweeping, mopping, lifting, stacking, and sometimes clerking at the general store because it was, like Dodge City as a whole, a hopping place. Each day dozens of train cars carried away valuable hides (the kind Wyatt Matters frowned upon because they were the products of white hunters) while dozens of carloads of grain, flour, sugar, and other provisions arrived. Wagons often lined Front Street. Supplies came in most any hour. I had to work hard to keep up with Robert Wright, who was constantly ordering supplies from Kansas City and still had trouble keeping up with the demand. Through it all, he managed to stay amiable with most of his customers, even Wyatt Matters, who showed up daily but made purchases only every two weeks. Mr. Matters mostly came to see me, and the few times Mr. Wright was short with me were after those "aggravating" visits.

"He's a loafer," Mr. Wright complained to me one afternoon after Wyatt had interrupted my work by reminding me for the thirtieth time that while a man's physical labor was necessary at times, developing the mind was the most important aspect of human existence. "Only thing not lazy about him is his tongue. Well, his hands, too. He waves them about as he rattles on about unpractical things. And did you ever look at those hands: They are soft as a lady's but not even the fat lady in a circus has thumbs that enormous."

"Yes, sir," I said, but then I found myself defending Wyatt Matters since I was his one and only protégé. "But, you see, his brain is always working. He knows so much. He believes strongly in education, well, self-education since I am not sure whether he ever went to any school. Mind over matter — that's his . . . eh . . . philosophy."

"I think Mr. Matters is out of his mind and a damn nuisance."

"He thinks I have potential."

"To be as crazy as him? Don't fool yourself, Harry. You're a regular sort of fellow from Bladensburg, Maryland, just like me. He will lead you astray. The old bachelor lives in a tent, for goodness' sake. It's no wonder he doesn't have a wife now, if he ever had one. And Alice tells me you do well with most of our children and would like to have some of your own someday. First, of course, you must find yourself a good wife. Stick by me, follow in my footsteps, and you'll become an upstanding citizen of Dodge City, Kansas, instead of an outcast in our growing community."

Mr. Wright put a firm hand on my right shoulder and pressed down until I felt lopsided. He asked me if I understood the situation, and I nodded my head solemnly like a level-handed common laborer whose goal in life was nothing more than to fit in and serve his betters and one day earn enough money to support a family. To think otherwise, I decided (though I wavered on this every day), would be fooling myself. I'd be giving in to Wyatt Matters' outlandish notions about me and my future. There was no money in being a protégé, and I doubted my ability to retain all the historical and literary information he relentlessly fed me, not that knowing such things would help me find a wife. I couldn't totally distance myself from a man who called me *son* and seemed to have my best interests at heart. I would have to be a false protégé for the time being. That might not be honorable, but, in a way, it was because I didn't want to hurt Wyatt's feelings. On my darkest hours lying alone on my bed in the storeroom, I would see everything clearly: If I kept sincerely listening to Wyatt Matters, I would become a lonely social outcast like him, but while he was a brilliant social outcast, I would always remain a dullard, lacking even the imagination to become a town drunk like my old man.

By month's end, Wyatt Matters was going about town telling men, women, and children that Dodge City must change its ways if it intended to grow in the right way. He argued that the town had been established by evil men who wanted to enrich themselves by providing the sinful services denied by the military at Fort Dodge — specifically, watered-down whiskey, crooked games of chance, abused soiled doves, price-gouging store owners, bison hides practically stolen off the backs of poor Indians, and a free reign to every kind of lawbreaker, including gunslinging murderers. He put before men, women, and children, whether they could write their own names, or not, a petition to the governor to mandate reform. It was not a way for a man to make friends in a town he supposedly wanted to settle into for life, and I doubt more than a handful of citizens scribbled their names on the document. Wanting to be a regular sort of frontier fellow, in other words someone who was not above having a few mild vices, I avoided signing the document myself by stating that if I did so, Mr. Wright would surely learn about it and promptly boot me out onto the street. Mr. Matters came to the store with pen in hand three straight mornings, and I put him off each time, but he was persistent.

"You ready to sign?" he asked upon his return on the fourth afternoon with the petition and yet another nickname for my employer. "Or does Bobby 'Money is Might' Wright have you bamboozled? There's more to life than working for wages, and you don't make much of that in the work you do here. The slaves were freed seven years ago, son."

"I knew that without you telling me," I said. "I'm kind of busy here."

"Yes, with me. I'm a special customer."

"Mr. Wright says you just talk and talk and hardly ever make a purchase. He isn't sure how you get the money to buy anything when you do decide to buy."

"None of his business. All Trader Bob needs to know is I've never been like Jesse and Frank James robbing banks and trains and such."

"He believes you are lazy. He says a man

who doesn't work for a living isn't living, that in fact he is nothing!"

"You know better. I *am something.* That's an unadulterated fact. Look at this proboscis of mine. That's *something.* Look into my enlightened blue eyes. *They are something.* And consider my brain, which you can't see, but you know is there, working night and day. It is *really something.* Knowledge has value, son."

"I know, I know," I admitted, becoming discomposed. I couldn't look at his face. "But how do you live? I mean, you have your tent in the vacant lot on Locust Street, but how do you get your money for food and clothes and the wine you offered me that one time."

"Oh, I see. It isn't just Trader Bob who wants to know the source of my wealth. I'm sure he wants to get his hands on more of it. But you aren't greedy like him, are you?"

I looked around the store to make sure Mr. Wright was still out back talking hides with partner Charles Rath. I then shook my head. Fact was, I just wanted to make enough money to survive. Alice Wright still brought me food at times, and I could eat all I wanted when I looked after the children. I slept on a cot for free in the storeroom. I felt almost blessed.

"Of course, you aren't greedy like him. How could you be? You're my protégé. Do you think he is someone you should emulate?"

I wasn't sure what *emulate* meant. "Mr. Wright is all right," I said weakly.

"If he doesn't say so himself. Or maybe it is the lovely, motherly Alice Wright who you hold in esteem. I know you spend a lot of time with her."

"I do not!" I was sorry I had ever mentioned Alice Wright to him." I looked for a cloth to wipe imaginary dust off a shelf. "I look after the children as a favor to both Wrights. And I don't do it for money. I like to play with some of those kids."

"Admirable. You want to work for and play with Wrights your whole life?"

"No. If I had my own wife and kids, then . . ." I stopped talking because his grin was so wide, I began to feel foolish talking about such matters.

"I'm glad to hear it. I was just making sure that Alice Wright doesn't have you under her thumb." Wyatt wiggled both of his enormous thumbs under my nose, which was nearly as large as his, so at times his fingernails accidentally brushed against my nostrils. "As human beings have been telling each other since the sixteenth century, *There are other fish in the sea.* Or here in western Kansas we might better say, *There are other Jack rabbits and Jill rabbits on the prairie.*"

"I don't have a one-track mind, you know," I said. "I'm not looking for another woman."

"Besides Alice Wright you mean?"

"No. I don't mean her at all. I mean another woman after the one I knew in Atchison."

"Right. Elizabeth Pepper, the well-formed fair-haired lady who proved herself untrue and broke your heart."

Wyatt Matters not only knew a lot but also remembered everything you told him. "My heart isn't broken," I insisted a little too loudly. Mr. Wright had returned and was scowling as he crossed the room to check the cash box as was his habit many times each day. I thought he trusted me well enough but maybe not with Mr. Matters in the store as a corrupting influence.

Wyatt carried on as if Mr. Wright wasn't there. "I want you to know, son, that learning, gaining knowledge, and going through your time on earth as an enlightened man does not preclude having a good, thoughtful, tender, supportive lady in your life."

"How many women like that live in Dodge?"

"You'd be surprised. Of course, there are women who are in Dodge to get what they can as fast as they can, but that doesn't make them any different than most of the men who have come here. But not all women are hard, and you are too young to be hard-bitten."

Mr. Wright now spoke up. "Are you a buying customer today, Mr. Matters, or are you just looking to pester my help?"

"Just having a little discussion with my son about the mysteries of the opposite sex."

"Not on my time. Hey, wait a minute. What do you mean by son? Nothing biological, I know. Like me, Harry is from Bladensburg, Maryland, and his old man was hit by a train."

"Calling Harry *son* speaks of our relationship. It isn't something you'd understand, Trader Bob."

"Think not? I have four sons and all of them are legitimate, not to mention a little girl made of sugar and spice." Mr. Wright left the cash box, brushed past the unwanted customer, and placed a meaty hand on my shoulder. "Now, son," he said. "Make like a good boy and fetch some firewood for the stove." He then turned to Mr. Matters. "It feels downright chilly in here this morning."

I ran out back to the woodpile and soon returned with two short pieces of cottonwood that I carefully fed the cast-iron stove, which was toward the rear of the store. Mr.

Wyatt told me I must keep the fire going in the stove now that winter approached but I should never overload it because trees were mighty scarce around Dodge and cottonwood burned quickly. He did have the biggest woodpile in town behind the store and never resorted to buffalo chips for fuel.

My boss and my mentor were preoccupied with each other. I kept behind the stove and listened to their verbal battle.

"You have no business suppressing Harry's mental development and expression, Mr. Wright Can Do No Wrong. Stop treating him like a slave."

"A slave? He earns wages, has a free room, many free meals, the joy of play with my children, and the security of practically being part of the Wright family."

"Practically a slave."

"You, Wyatt Matters, are a troublemaker, an agitator. You kindle discontent. You are a firebrand."

"Firebrand. Excellent word. Calls to mind John Brown, the abolitionist firebrand who waged a war on slavery."

"A madman. As unstable as a three-legged table."

"Yes, he has been called a 'monomaniac' but also a 'saint.' By the way, he was also once a businessman like yourself, engaging in tanning, land speculating, sheep herding, and a dozen or more other business ventures, most of which failed."

"What's your point? I am a successful businessman by anyone's standards. More than that I am a leading citizen. You'll find no greater advocate of Dodge than me. And what are you? A bit of a nuisance, somewhat of an outcast, a discontented mischief-maker."

"I prefer firebrand. I can tell you what I'm not. I'm not a money grabber, a demagogue, a Bible-thumper, or a hypocritical social reformer. At the same time, since this seems to be a boastful atmosphere, I am no common man. I have the knowledge and insight to reach higher level of existence on the wild, lawless frontier. In a word, I am perspicacious."

Mr. Wright drew silent and pinched his cheek. Clearly, he didn't know what *perspicacious* meant any more than I did. He started to circle Wyatt like a pugilist sizing up his opponent. The fight was still on, though I knew that neither man was one to throw a punch, first or otherwise. Mr. Wright stopped abruptly as if he had run into a wall and pointed a finger at his adversary.

"No point in name calling," he said. "The bottom line is that you have no business, no work of any kind, and do nothing of a positive nature. You denounce, censure, and lambaste our town and our good citizens. If Dodge was full of men like you, the town would die before it even got going."

"I beg to differ, Mr. Wright Can Do No Wrong. If not for me, Dodge would go to hell. It may go there anyway unless you and your money-grabbing associates don't start listening to me and heeding my advice. I have as much stake in Dodge as you, just not one because it would gain me a pecuniary advantage. *Our* community is full of vice, and crime shall surely run rampant and ruin us unless we nip in in the bud."

"I'm as much against crime as you or any man. You exaggerate. When one looks deeply enough, of course one will see certain things of an unpleasant nature in a frontier town. I call them growing pains."

"It doesn't seem to pain you at all. What are you doing about the shootings in the saloons and on the streets? Dodge is bound to see more murders unless my petition results in civilizing ordinances and, dar'st I say it, a more enlightened viewpoint on frontier living." He pointed a finger that if it had been another inch longer would have poked Mr. Wright in the eye. "Sign my petition if you care."

"I care to let Dodge grow, a natural process that can't be forced. We all have the best interests of Dodge at heart. Things take time. You can't go around like a Cotton Mather waging a holy war against the forces of evil by tracking down and eliminating every man who has a little too much to drink and shoots off a gun or two and every saloon gal intent on providing various services to the mostly male population."

"You throw out the name Cotton Mather. And while Mather sounds a lot like Matters you are off the mark when comparing me to him. I do not glorify New England's Puritan past or believe in witches. We need to deal with the real killers, not alleged witches."

Mr. Wright looked ready to bite Wyatt Matters' finger, but instead he stepped back and looked all about as if trying to spot me. "How long does it take someone to fetch wood from a woodpile," he muttered.

"You seem to have an interest in history," continued Mr. Matters, who apparently couldn't resist educating a non-protégé. "Allow me to tell you about some earlier newly formed settlements with so-called growing pains. In the 1820s, New York City was plagued by street gangs — the Forty Thieves, the Plug Uglies, the Dead Rabbits, and the Roach Guards. Gold Rush–era

San Francisco was marked by lawlessness, including duels and murders in broad daylight, mostly by young, intoxicated males. Denver was founded in November 1858 and in its first year of existence a dozen men were murdered. Down in Texas four year ago, John Wesley Hardin shot down his first man, a former slave; J.W. was just fifteen at the time. In Springfield, Missouri, on July 21, 1865, an argument over gambling debts turned deadly, and Wild Bill Hickok bested Davis K. Tutt in a shootout in the public square. You want to hear more?"

"No thank you. I will not deny that humans can be aggressive and violent, but we can also be cooperative and supportive. And really, how many of us are actual killers?"

"Too many do kill and too many more become disposed to killing, especially when they are young men loaded with whiskey and carrying loaded guns. Closer to home, I'm sure you've heard about what happened just last year in the brand-new cow town of Newton, Kansas. The Santa Fe Railroad got there, and the saloons, gambling parlors, and brothels sprang up like prairie fire. The general shooting massacre started in a saloon and when it was over five men were killed and three wounded. You want the bloody details?"

"No, thank you. Anyway, Dodge City is a buffalo town, not a cow town."

"That's even worse. Bison are wilder than steers. Our town has already started off on the wrong foot. In no time at all, unless things are done right, we can turn into another Newton."

"I suggest you take your petition to Newton. Now where the heck is Harry?"

"Over here, sir," I said. I had slipped out from behind the stove and was vigorously working the push broom near the front of the store.

Normally, Mr. Wright would have asked me what I was doing or why I was doing it. But instead, he addressed Wyatt Matters. "I do believe, sir, your son is showing you to the door."

Mr. Matters, with petition in hand, left without the last word.

Chapter Five

My mentor and my boss had different ideas about what kind of person I should strive to be — an enlightened, independent thinker was the ideal for Wyatt Matters, an obedient hard worker was what Robert Wright expected. I was caught in the middle of their expectations, which caused me endless stress until I determined I didn't have to choose — I was young enough and flexible enough to be both. Each in his own way did seem to genuinely care about my welfare. Despite their different philosophies on life and argumentative tendencies, they also cared equally about Dodge City's future. The two men saw eye to eye on law and order. For Mr. Wright, curbing gun violence, as well as assaults and thievery, was necessary to protect not only the lives of his wife and five children but also his sizable investment in the general store and the future of the settlement. For Mr. Matters, making every effort to establish a safe, peaceful town was a noble undertaking like past endeavors by such utopian idealists as Plato in ancient Greece, the Shakers in New England and beyond, the Transcendentalists in Massachusetts, the Rappites in Pennsylvania, and the Icarians in Texas. He told me about all of them. I had heard of Plato before, mostly because Elizabeth Pepper used to talk endlessly about Platonic love (sometimes she was all for it, other times dead set against it).

After hearing about and opposing Mr. Matters' petition for "civilized ordinances," Mr. Wright and friends petitioned the governor to recognize Dodge and the surrounding area — Ford County — as qualifying for self-government. As it was, the new town was under the political and legal jurisdiction of Ellis County, but that put the nearest sheriff and judges one hundred miles away. Six hundred inhabitants were necessary to qualify, so saddle shop owner Isaac Young began collecting names. I provided my name for the census and so, too, did Mr. Matters, since Dodge was his chosen home. That didn't keep him from calling the citizens foolish for rejecting his call for ordinances, because only these regulations could make a Ford County sheriff and judge effective.

In November, while Mr. Young was taking a census and Mr. Matters was continuing to complain and argue, violence again raised its ugly head in Dodge. It happened at the Kelley and Hunt dance hall, where a scheduled "respectable" dance took place. I elected to break out of what Wyatt Matters called my "outgrown shell" to attend. I never had been one for dancing, but where else could I hope to meet someone of the opposite sex who offered me something I didn't have to pay for? It had been months since Elizabeth Pepper had abandoned me in Atchison, and in Dodge City the only woman I knew was the appealing but very married Alice Wright. For some reason I didn't tell Wyatt of my plans even though he had identified my social shyness and surely must have known that a man could find many ways to be enlightened.

When I walked into the dance hall trembling like a cottonwood leaf, I got my first big surprise of the evening. Wyatt Matters was lodged in a chair along the far wall, and he waved me over as if he hadn't seen me in years instead of a day and a half. The chair next to him was empty, so I felt obliged to sit down. He then told me that he had been saving it for someone, but it was no problem because she was otherwise fully occupied.

"Did I hear you right?" I asked. "Did you say *she*?"

"You did." He was tapping a foot to the fiddler's lively tune, and since I had never seen Mr. Matters sitting anywhere except inside his tent, he looked totally out of place. The hall was crowded with men, a few of whom had partnered up to twirl around the floor together, and enough young women, respectable or not, to keep things interesting. I looked past the dancers to the punch bowl table where I spotted a dumpy, gray-haired lady dipping into the bowl. I might have guessed she was a librarian, but Dodge City didn't have a library.

"Is that her?" I asked, trying to direct Wyatt's attention to the punch bowl.

"Who?"

"The one you were supposed to save this chair for."

He laughed. "That's Mrs. Amanda Ames, a seamstress who married a soldier when she was eighteen, became a widow at nineteen, and now at age thirty-nine going on fifty is a professional widow. But Lord knows she savors her punch, especially when it has been spiked. Looks like you might need a patch sewed on the elbow of your coat. She's the one to see for all your sewing needs, son."

"Oh. But who's the one you are seeing now?"

"Seeing is right. I'm an observer not a dancer. How about yourself?"

"I might try to dance, but I hope it won't be with Mrs. Ames."

"Alice Wright and husband aren't here in case you are wondering."

"I know that. If they were, I'd be looking after the children. I'm wondering who was warming up this chair before I sat on it."

"Follow my eyes, son, follow my eyes."

I did. And when I caught sight of what he was looking at, I nearly fell off the chair. She was that stunning, a rare beauty in motion. I stretched my neck left and right and finally stood up trying to keep track of her, an auburn-haired lady in shimmering red whose long glistening silver earrings danced along with her. She was perhaps too thin but of nice form and was so light on her feet that I suspected a tempestuous wind could carry her clear to Wichita. Nothing about her reminded me of Miss Pepper, who had satiny yellow hair, round cheeks, a plenteous bosom, and a tendency to tip forward when dancing or otherwise moving too fast. Each time the young woman in the red dress swung around so that I could see her wide-eyed, rose-colored, delicately modeled face again, it was as if I were seeing it for the first time — and each time I was enchanted.

I forgot my mentor was there until he placed a clammy hand on my wrist and pulled me back onto my chair. Before I could ask him how he managed to get such a young, practically flawless woman to sit beside him, he began to carry on about the history of dance, which he said originated 9,000 years ago in India and was a big thing for both entertainment and religious reasons in Egypt 5,300 years ago. Nothing much else registered. I didn't care a lick about ancient dances. I just wanted one dance with the beauty in the red dress.

"You look at her as any man would look at her, especially those two Texans bucking out there like wild horses." Mr. Matters said. "I suppose I shouldn't have expected anything more."

"How do you expect me to look at her? Who is she?"

"A lady, a real lady. Those Texans aren't showing her enough respect. She must be getting weary."

"She doesn't look tired. I suppose you wouldn't know her name."

"Jane Hankin."

"Jane Hankin, I think I love you."

"Silly boy. No, I shouldn't say that. You are

just a young man, and young men are foolish. I heard a couple of those Texans say the same thing. What do any of you know about love? It's so predictable. I knew what was in store. She wanted to come here, though. She can't be hidden away forever."

"You really know her?"

"I am her escort."

That didn't sink in right away. In my mind I was already on the dance floor moving in perfect rhythm with Miss Hankin, dazzling every observer, even some who weren't present. Yet, I stayed put as if nailed to the chair. "Jesus Christ!" I called out. "She's an angel."

"Those Texas boys have been drinking more than the punch," said Wyatt Matters, standing now as if in protest. "And look. They're both armed, armed to dance. Can you believe it? They'll be trouble. I know it. Those fools, those young fools!"

"Maybe so, but she keeps smiling at them." I wondered if angels ever smiled exactly that way, as if they knew what heaven was all about.

"She's being polite."

I didn't argue with him. The motion before me was making my head swirl. She seemed to be reveling in all the attention, though of course unaware of mine. In that sense she wasn't so different from Elizabeth Pepper, who would flip her loose yellow hair around as if waving a welcoming flag to the world. But somehow this auburn-haired Jane Hankin was different. She had to be different. How badly I wanted to find out just how different. I wondered how much of that spiked punch I'd have to drink to work up the nerve to cut in on those bucking Texans. Their lean, unshaven faces made them look dangerous even before I noticed a few knives stuck in their belts along with those pistols. It was a wonder they didn't accidentally stab each other. I almost wished they would.

"Damn their hides!" shouted Mr. Matters. "The scamper juice has made them all budgy! Mark my word, there'll be a fight before the night is out. It's the same old story, year after year, decade after decade, century after century, millennium after millennium. Spoony young sons of bitches, with no offense intended to their mothers, getting violent — a timeless tale indeed!"

"Quiet, Wyatt, please. They can hear you."

"They think they've invented this form of social debauchery and dissipation! Little do they know that the revelry of alcohol, song, and dance has been going on since the ancient Greeks and Romans were celebrating their wine gods Dionysus and Bacchus.

Even whiskey Gods are nothing new. Certain Indians have built actual temples to the whiskey-drinking god Bhairon the Terrible, a disgusting deity who drapes a snake around his neck and angrily stomps about the world of mortals carrying in his four arms and hands the severed head of a demon, a bloody war club, a bottle of whiskey, and a bowl of meat, no doubt containing forbidden buffalo meat. Over there, they really are *buffalo,* a different animal."

"I don't think these fellows care to hear about Indian gods."

"Well, they had *damn* well better listen. I have nothing against a little wine, the thinking man's drink. To wine and dine lifts the spirits. Whiskey makes young men nonthinkers — at least to not think straight — which causes them to be angry and aggressive and not care about the consequences. But the consequences can be tragic! Hear me, you Texas Terrors!"

"I heard that," said the brawniest of the Texans, who took a swig from a bottle he pulled out of his coat. He tried to hand the bottle off to the one of his kind who was currently the one dancing with Jane, but that fellow didn't want to let go of his partner. The brawny Texas took another swig, then staggered over to us and held out the bottle.

"Drink with me," he said. It wasn't clear if he was addressing Wyatt or me, but we both declined at the same time. "Drink, Shorty!" he said, thrusting the bottle toward Wyatt's mouth. That *proboscis* got in the way and there was a collision, but Wyatt stood perfectly still, merely snorting once. "Where I come from it's an insult to not drink with a man," the brawny Texas continued.

"He's sorry," I said. I was prepared to tell a lie, that my old friend was advised not to drink whiskey on his doctor's orders. It wasn't necessary.

"I'm not here to drink, dance, discuss my height, or do wrong. I'm talking here with my son."

"I know that." The brawny Texan took a pull on his bottle. "I heard you talking. There's something you ought to know about Injuns, Shorty. Injuns is Godless creatures, especially the Comanche. They believe they were created by wolves and a variety of other dumb, cruel beasts. And I believe them."

"The Indian god I was talking about is known in the large south Asian country of India, where humans arrived from Africa 55,000 years ago. I was not talking of an American Indian god. While the Comanches don't have a creation god per se, most American Indians believe in a

Supreme Being, the Great Spirit, who is called Wakan Tanka by the Sioux, Maheo by the Cheyenne, Chebbeniathan by the Arapaho . . ."

"God damn it. Shut your trap. You can't tell me anything I don't know about Injuns. Not less than a dozen years ago when I was knee-high to a horny toad, Chief Peta Nocona's band of Comanches stole our livestock and killed my daddy along the Pease River in Parker County, Texas."

"I know that. I mean I never knew about your daddy or his livestock, but I knew about Chief Peta Nocona, his wife Cynthia Ann Parker, and their son Quanah Parker, who today seems to be an up-and-coming leader among his people."

"To hell with him!"

"Maybe you didn't know, Mr. Texas, that when threatened, horny toads have the ability to gulp air to quickly inflate their bodies and also to spurt blood from their eyes."

"I bet the Comanche can do the same. Those Godless savages! Those . . ."

The brawny Texan had worked himself into a frenzy and suddenly toppled backward as if Wyatt Matters had pushed him (he hadn't even touched him). He clutched the nearly empty bottle tightly on the way down and it did not break. As I helped him to his feet, he offered me the last swallow, while Mr. Matters talked to me as if the drunk couldn't hear: "Look at him. The whiskey may as well be filling his empty brain cells. Drunkenness is the enemy of moral insight and self-knowledge. You see, son, living well is about ascertaining truth and understanding the nature of the good. This man represents the nature of the bad in man. He and his fellow dissipated Texans command the dance floor because of their anger and aggression, but what have they accomplished? They are fools I tell you — addle-headed young fools! Each and every one of them, down to the very last drop of whiskey."

The brawny Texan, now slouched in my chair, did not respond. He was staring straight ahead but his eyes were blurry. "How 'bout that?" he said. "There's two of her now. Two red dresses. Two . . . but four legs. Four of the most splendiferous . . ."

"He has double vision," Mr. Matters said matter-of-factly. "It's a common effect brought on by heavy drinking."

I was glad I was not a whiskey drinker. Two of Jane Hankin? That would have been too much for me to handle. Seeing one of her was too beautiful for words, more than enough for one man to want to grasp. But my vision was impaired by the actual man grasping her — a tall Texan who hadn't even bothered to take off his spurs.

"He's an octopus!" declared Wyatt Matters. "He can't paw her like that."

Wyatt Matters started to walk out onto the dance floor, and I let him go, using the excuse that someone had to keep watch on the brawny Texan. Disgusted with myself, I collapsed next to him in Mr. Matters' chair and watched like something worse than a wallflower.

Wyatt and the tall Texan were going face-to-face or would have been if Wyatt were a foot taller. Objecting to being called a fool by the small Kansas man, the tall Texan pressed a thumb against Wyatt's nose as if trying the impossible task of flattening it. At least he had released all of Jane Hankin except for her left wrist. "That's a fighting offense where I come from, Grandpa. If you weren't such a mossback and shorter than shortgrass, I'd . . ."

"You'd what? Beat a man twice your age to an inch of my life? Shoot my eyes out? I'm not worried. I can tell you that the average life expectancy of a white male in Kansas is only 42.6 years and I have only .2 of that time left anyway."

"Stop your jabbering. I never said I wanted

to kill you, you babbling Jayhawker. I'm fixin' to teach you some manners, though."

"How can you do that when you have no manners yourself? I see the way you're treating that young lady. Despicable! Don't they pay homage to Lone State womanhood in 'The Yellow Rose of Texas'? What's wrong with you, man. Unhand that young lady at once!"

"She's a Kansas woman," the tall Texan said, but sheepishly, and he did let go of the auburn-haired Jane Hankin's delicate wrist. She examined her wrist as if inspecting for bruises or broken bones.

"You are free, Lady Jane," Wyatt said. "Perhaps you'd like to sit this one out. Please take my chair."

"Thank you, Wyatt. I shall."

It didn't strike me that he was calling her *Lady Jane* and she was calling him by the first name until later. At that moment she was walking right toward me because I was occupying Mr. Matters' chair. In my chair, the brawny Texan was almost himself again, siting up nearly straight, waving his empty whiskey bottle over his head, and singing, "There's a yellow rose in Texas that I am gonna see/Nobody else could miss her, not half as much as me." I was transfixed — by Lady Jane's approach, not the singing — but still managed to jump up and offer her the chair.

"No thank you, sir," she said, ever so politely, before bowing her head. "I didn't like dancing with that man earlier, and don't care to sit beside him."

I immediately considered my chances of removing the brawny Texan without getting myself thrashed or even shot in front of the woman I loved. But the odds got worse when the tall Texan left the dance floor to confront me. He falsely accused me of punching his pal in the belly. "Grandpa was too old to fight, but you sure as hell ain't, you stinkin' Kansas Red Leg."

"I'm a mild-mannered man from Maryland."

That did nothing to pacify the tall Texan, but it did cause Jane Hankin to take a second look at me, and with nothing close to contempt. Maybe she assumed that being from the East I was kinder and more educated — her kind of man.

"You ain't carrying no pistol, mild man. You best go get it."

"Don't own one," I said, which caused Jane Hankin to almost smile at me.

"He turned down my whiskey, too," said the brawny Texan, interrupting his own singing.

There's no telling what the pair would have done to me had not Wyatt Matters come over to tip his top hat to Jane and reclaim his chair. "Here's one for you Texas boys," he said, and just like that he began to forcefully hum a tune that he later told me was *"El Degũello,"* a song of hatred and merciless death played by the Mexican bands of Santa Anna before they stormed the Alamo on March 6, 1836. It was small wonder that the tall Texan took offense. He knocked off Wyatt's top hat, twisted his purple bowtie, and threatened to punch him in the nose no matter how old he was or where he happened to be from — anywhere but Texas wouldn't do.

"Ah, you remember the Alamo! You have something going on upstairs." Wyatt reached high to tap the tall Texan on the forehead. "At least you have some sense of historical perspective, no matter how distorted. Those Texians defending the Alamo with forty-nine-year-old David Crockett were young fools, but they were brave as bulls, willing to die in a slaughter, all for a cause — freedom, which to young men like you and your amigo here means endless unrestrained dancing, hard drinking, and shooting off your mouths and guns to no end."

I figured Mr. Matters was asking to be

punched, but the tall Texan lowered his hands to his sides. He seemed memorized by Wyatt's words, unsure of whether, as a diehard Texan, he was being savaged or saluted by this babbling Jayhawker. He looked up to his friend for guidance, but the brawny Texan was rubbing his forehead as if the whiskey had gotten to him, too.

"My old friend is all for Texas, before and after the Civil War if not during," I said, as if Wyatt Matters needed me, his protégé, to speak up for him. I picked up Mr. Matters' top hat, brushed it off, and placed it squarely on his big head.

"That's my boy," he said. "The truth be known, and it should be known, I admire Sam Houston the hero of San Jacinto for remembering the Alamo and whipping the Mexican dictator Santa Anna but also for fervently arguing that Texas must *not* secede from the Union and refusing to take the oath of the Confederacy."

The tall Texan and brawny Texan didn't know whether to stand up for Sam Houston or not. They exchanged a look that suggested *why bother with this old fool and cowardly kid from Maryland; they ain't worth the trouble.* Indeed, the brawny Texan merely stood up and, once he got his balance, walked away with his pal toward the punch bowl.

There was now an open chair for Lady Jane, and she might have taken it had not a string bean in a Sunday suit moved in as soon as the two Texans departed. His hair was slicked back so it shined, but he still applied some spit to a cowlick on the back of his head as he bowed to Jane, introduced himself as Timothy Swan, and requested a dance. Wyatt started to answer for her, something about how tired she must be, but Jane accepted the hand of the Swan and they floated back to the dance floor together.

"You were a mite slow, son," said Wyatt Matters, stating the obvious, which I didn't appreciate. I sat down and crossed my arms. I watched Jane move with her surprisingly sure-footed partner while thinking I'd get up at any moment and cut in on this fellow who seemed even more mild-mannered than me.

Wyatt must have read my mind or maybe my pout. "She's out there with that farm boy for one reason and only one reason only," he said. "She loves to dance. She'd dance with you, too. All you have to do is ask."

"I know that," I said. "What else do you know about her?"

"Lady Jane is a fine young lady. She's not one to be manhandled by Texans or anyone else."

"I know that, too. You called her Lady Jane."

"I do. Name seems to fit. There was a noblewoman named Lady Jane Grey who in her teens became queen of England for nine days in the sixteenth century. That Lady Jane preferred academic studies to hunting parties and such. Oh, and she read Plato. She felt mistreated by her harsh parents, and later she was stuck in the Tower of London by the supporters of Queen Mary and, sad to say, her head was eventually put on the chopping block and severed with one clean stroke of the executioner's ax. It is my learned belief Lady Jane died an innocent victim of the men plotting around her."

"Awful," I said, and much to my horror I imagined a sharp blade slicing through Jane Hankin's long white neck and then those silver earrings still dangling from her severed head.

"No worries. I'm here to see that *my* Lady Jane avoids the same fate. I am guiding and protecting her."

"You mean she's a protégé like me?"

"Not exactly."

"Well, tell me more. She's not married or anything like that, is she?"

"Why do you ask that?"

"Because I feel one should stay away from

married ladies, and I wouldn't want to stay away from Jane."

"Does she act married? Not that she acts improperly. She is striking in that red dress."

"You said it, Wyatt."

"The bodice is cut perhaps a little low."

"I wouldn't say that."

"Of course, it really isn't shocking attire for a dance in Dodge. There's one thing you should know — she's no dance hall gal. She's simply attractive. She can't help that."

"I can see that. Why did she come to Dodge of all places?"

"She was at Fort Dodge first in a rather unpleasant situation. But that doesn't matter. She is here now — that does matter."

"I agree. But she couldn't have been in the Army, could she?"

"Of course not. She's a woman. She abhors weapons."

"Why was she at Fort Dodge then? How could she stand it?"

"Fort Dodge has a laundry where she worked. That was no small undertaking. The other laundresses were jealous of her, and the men were . . . well, you know how soldiers get."

"I can imagine. You were there protecting her?"

"Something like that."

"Did she fall for any particular soldier?"

"Look, let's drop it. It already feels like ancient history. Anyway, I don't know *everything,* son."

That was a rare admission for him, but I needed more information. "You must know what she does in Dodge City?"

"She works at a store like you do. You apparently haven't stopped by the new shop near Hoover's saloon."

"I haven't even stopped by Hoover's saloon. What store is it?"

"The overpriced one owned by the enterprising German couple, Frederick Zimmerman and his plump wife. She's a halfway decent person. Fred is rapacious and grim and thus known to me as Grimmerman. He was born in the Black Forest, you know, that part of southern Germany famous for its oppressive canopy of evergreens, watchmakers, and cuckoo clocks."

"I'm not sure."

"The most intriguing Black Forest city is Freiburg im Breisgau, which picturesquely sits on the western slopes, where the Dreisam River flows into the Rhine Valley. The city has only been around since 1120, which does make it slightly older than our Dodge City."

I wasn't interested in the Black Forest or,

at that moment, Dodge. “What about that store where Jane Hankin works?”

“You must have seen it. I don’t know how you could miss the larger-than-life buffalo gun on a pole in front of the building and the big sign reading ‘Guns, Pistols, Ammunition, Hardware, Tinware, and Lumber.’ ”

“Oh, that place. But I don’t understand. Jane Hankin sells guns?”

“Not her. Grimmerman handles that side of the business, along with the agricultural implements and lumber. But one side of the store features jewelry, pocket watches, and clocks. Those are most of the things Lady Jane sells. In fact, that’s where her silver earrings come from. No, she didn’t steal them. She’s an exemplary clerk. Like you, she seems to want to work.”

“Most of us don’t have much choice. You know something, Wyatt, I’ve always wanted to have a pocket watch of my own.”

“And then you’ll never be late for work, and Mr. Wyatt will raise your salary one penny in a year or two.”

“Maybe I’ll just save my pennies and buy one.”

“You’d better visit Grimmerman’s store before then. By the time you have saved enough money to buy the watch, you’ll be wearing a top hat like me to hide your balding head."

"It's not that bad. Anyway, I can always go to the store and just look."

"I'm sure you will. The allure of gorgeous women is timeless — from Delilah to Helen of Troy, from Cleopatra to Messalina, from Nefertiti to Marie Antoinette, from Hester Prynne to Madame Bovary, from Adah Isaacs Menken to Lotta Crabtree. But do me a favor and do *not* ogle dear Lady Jane."

"I'd never do that."

"I trust you won't. R-e-s-p-e-c-t. That's what she deserves — your utmost consideration. She dances so well, doesn't she? And that Mr. Swan is awfully smooth on his feet for a farmer, certainly no clodhopper."

"I hadn't noticed."

"Right. No doubt at the farm he mostly dances around the livestock and the manure."

"I don't care about him."

"I understand. You should know that to me Lady Jane is infinite love and a beam of the divine light, as the thirteenth-century Persian poet known as Rumi said of such women. Rumi further states *she is not the being whom sensual desire takes as its object. She is a creator, etc.*"

I had never heard of this Rumi, but I felt a blush coming on, so I wiped my face with my sleeve without taking my eyes off the splendid face and neck above the red dress. "Sounds like you know Miss Hankin quite well, Mr. Matters."

"As a matter of fact, I do."

"Has she . . . eh . . . seen your tent?"

"Everyone in Dodge has seen my tent. But I've said enough."

Still, Wyatt told me more, tastefully describing the faces and bodies of alluring women of all ages, though mostly young, from all ages of recorded human history. But then he saw fit to start lecturing me on how Renaissance men were wrong for believing that beauty on the outside was always a sign of beauty on the inside and that Sir Thomas Overbury was right when he wrote in a 1613 poem, *All the carnal beauty of my wife is but skin-deep.* At some point I stopped listening because Miss Jane Hankin looked so inviting. I stood up to better survey the room. Only Mrs. Ames the seamstress was at the punch bowl. I heard some whoops, which allowed me to spot the two Texans. I was relieved to see them leave the dance floor and retire to the back room, where Wyatt said poker games were always in progress, though he had given up the game long before coming to Dodge. I was ready to make my move.

"Go for it," said Wyatt Matters, again taking on the role of mind reader. "I know you will be respectful. When you get to be my age, you'll start to regret the things you didn't do far more than the ones you did. That's why I'd like to see you do *more* in Dodge City."

When I cut in on Timothy Swan, he immediately frowned but made no fuss. He bowed to his dance partner, thanked her, and went to the punch bowl as a condemned man walks to the gallows. I felt superior to him, but now had to replace him, and I remembered how Elizabeth Pepper had often criticized my "stiff motions" on the dance floors of Atchison. Jane Hankin made things somewhat easier by looking me over and smiling as if she liked nothing better than blue-eyed men who were no taller than her and possessed big noses, pale skin, and attached earlobes. I marveled at her glow; it was as if she had lit a candle under her delicate chin. Her teeth were perfect, as white as beer foam, I thought, not because I liked beer any more than I did whiskey but because I remembered several times when beer-loving Elizabeth Pepper had her fun applying the foam to my teeth as if it were a whitening powder.

"I'm sorry," I said because I had caught myself ogling.

"Why's that?" she asked, not losing her smile. "Did you forget my name?"

"No ma'am. Miss. Miss Jane Hankin."

"And you are Mr. Harry Hannum. Wyatt has told me a lot about you."

"He has?"

"Not really. He says you clerk for Mr. Wright and like buxom women with hair the color of goldenrod. He commented that you blush easily. I can see that for myself."

I thought I should hide my face, but I didn't want to turn away from her. Instead, I tried to cover her eyes with my right hand. She giggled, sounding not unlike ten-year-old Clara Belle, and then held my hand for a too-short moment before pushing it aside. "What does Wyatt tell you about me?"

"Not much. Nothing before tonight. He says you sell jewelry for Mr. Zimmerman and like to dance. But I could see that for myself with those Texans and that Swan fellow with the bear grease hair."

"The Texans were fun for a while. Then they danced too hard and frightened me. Sometimes while they wildly swung me around, their guns would bump against me. I told them I didn't like it, but they wouldn't stop. Their hands were everywhere, too. And then I thought they might try to hurt

Wyatt and maybe you, too. I wouldn't have liked that."

"Neither would I. How about Mr. Swan?"

"Nice fellow. Danced a little soft, though. Can I count on you to dance just right?"

"I wouldn't do that if I were you. I've been told I dance stiffly."

"By the woman with hair like goldenrod?"

"I never compared her hair to a goldenrod or a sunflower or anything else. Wyatt Matters made that up. Anyway, she was just a girl I once knew, long gone. And I'm glad."

"It's not so easy getting rid of lovers and such."

"It so happens she rid herself of me. But it's for the best."

"I believe you but tell me why."

"Well, 'cause I'm meeting you."

"I'm not all that interesting."

"Yes, you are. I mean that's hard to believe. I'm sure you're very interesting. You're so . . . so . . ."

"Yes?"

"I'm not so good with words, not like Mr. Matters."

"Then hadn't we better dance rather than stand out here in the open trying to think of words to say to each other."

"Of course," I said, but I waited for her to put her left hand on my shoulder before I touched the middle of her back. Then I took her other hand.

The touch was magic as we covered ground slowly, mostly in circles, and in silence. Females are supposed to be the ones who swoon, but I thought I'd surely start swooning. She was stronger than she looked, though, and seemed to hold me up.

"It's true then, you don't talk nearly as much as Wyatt," she said.

"Does anybody? He's a nice gentleman, kind of old, though."

"I wouldn't call him old, Harry. He's experienced, mostly smart. He knows so much about everything."

"I know. He's funny that way. Sometimes he'll be telling me something and interrupt himself to quote Socrates or one of those other Greek guys. You know Socrates, right?"

"No. I've lived in the West all my life."

If she was joking or funning with me, I missed it. "I understand," I said, holding her a little tighter. "What part of the West?"

"Mostly Kansas."

"Tell me more."

"I have some bad memories. I'm in no mood to talk about it."

"Sorry. I'm from Maryland and have my share of bad memories, too."

"Guess that happens everywhere — Kansas, Maryland, Greece."

"Truth is, I didn't hear much about Socrates growing up in Maryland. It was Mr. Matters who told me about that Greek philosopher and what he once said: *The only true wisdom is in knowing you know nothing.* But I do believe Mr. Matters prefers this other Socrates quote: *There is only one good, knowledge, and one evil, ignorance.*"

"Could be I'm evil then, Harry Hannum. For instance, take what we're doing."

"Just talking."

"And dancing. You would think that Wyatt, who says his dancing days are over, wouldn't know much about the subject. But he does. I had no idea that Germans were waltzing in Venice back in the thirteenth century and that in the beginning it was considered scandalous. Imagine that!"

I immediately thought of scandalous activities but admitted, "I don't know how to waltz."

"There's no waltzing here, silly. Swinging each other around the dance floor is good enough for me. I can happily report to you that the woman with the goldenrod hair was wrong. You don't dance like a stiff."

"Thanks. You're so light on your feet you don't let me step on your toes."

Then, of course, the fiddler switched to a livelier tune, and I immediately stepped on one of her feet and then the other. But her unrestrained giggles thrilled me so much, I began to laugh — at myself and with her.

Too soon, though, our bliss was rudely interrupted by three or four gunshots from the back room. All dancing stopped, and Jane Hankin trembled so hard standing still that her silver earrings began to flutter and, under that fetching red dress, her knees commenced to shaking. I took her into my arms without thinking, but she didn't pull away. She buried her face in the hollow of my neck and wept. Some of the dancers were moving toward the sound of the shots, others headed for the front door. Wyatt Matters churned his chunky little legs as he raced to us and positioned himself between Jane and the now open door in back that led to the gambling tables.

"I bet it was the Texans," Wyatt said.

"Doing the shooting or getting shot?" I asked.

"We'll have to wait and see on that. How are you holding up, Lady Jane?"

"I'm not," she said, and she started to sink in my arms. I squeezed harder but couldn't stop her from sliding down to her knees. Wyatt helped her stand back up, but she cried out as if we were striking her and then bolted in a panic toward the front door. Before getting there she accidentally knocked Timothy Swan to the floor and then caused Amanda Ames to spin out of control and spill a full cup of punch. It might have been humorous but not under these circumstances.

"She couldn't wait to escape," said Wyatt. "I'm afraid, son, that shows you just how alarming firearms can be for the poor girl. She nearly jumped out of her skin. It's bad enough she works all day in a store that sells guns and sees men on the streets carrying guns but now she must be subjected to guns going off at night in a dance hall."

"Should I go after her, Wyatt?"

"No point. You'll never catch her. She'll run all the way home and lock herself in the house. I don't hear any more shooting, but she'll be safer there. I had a premonition that something like this would happen. But Lady Jane needed to dance."

"I feel like I should, you know, do something."

"Nothing either of us can do except go to that back room and see which of the poker players are still standing."

"No thanks," I said. "I'm inclined to go back to my room at the general store."

"Almost girlish in your squeamishness?"

"I'm no doctor. And I'm not going out of my way to see bloodshed and suffering."

"I've dealt with plenty before. It's not going to go away by itself. We need to face up to it. Anyway, I get a sense nobody is suffering back there now. The dead don't suffer."

"You face up to it, Wyatt. I'm sure you'll tell me all about it in the morning."

Indeed, I got the deadly facts early the next day at the general store. Wyatt gave them to both Robert Wright and me after the father had sent two of his visiting sons, Elias and James, out of the building. "Play pirates outside, boys," he told them. "You don't need to hear this." I didn't either. But I listened anyway. The two Texans, the brawny one and the tall one, had accused local gambler Matt Sullivan and his partner Billy Brooks, former marshal of Newton, Kansas, of cheating. Sullivan and Brooks naturally denied it. The Texans just as naturally refused to accept the denial. They decided it was only fair to make off with the large pot on the table. A third Texan, who was neither brawny nor tall, lent them his gun hand because he had lost money earlier. The only shot he fired missed the mark while the brawny one and tall one never even cleared their pistols from their holsters. Sullivan and Brooks did not miss their targets. The two accusers would never dance again, let alone get back to Texas, not unless someone decided to transport them in a pine box. Their ally was dangerously though not fatally wounded. Wyatt predicted that as soon as possible this third man would get out of Dodge by train and seek further medical attention in a safer place.

CHAPTER SIX

Wyatt Matters, who always thought most highly of himself, rose to another level in his own estimation after the dance. He had talked his way out of a confrontation with those intoxicated young Texans, which made him feel proud even if it was nothing unusual for him. He was even prouder of his accurate prediction — that those hotheads would fight before the night was out. "It reinforces the two points I have been constantly stressing, son," he said two days after the dance hall tragedy when he caught up to me standing on the street in the shadow of the oversized buffalo gun model that topped the pole in front of Frederick Zimmerman's store. "Number One: Youth, whiskey, and guns don't mix. Number Two: Dodge City is in desperate need of law and order, and it will only get worse as the year plays out like a Shakespearean tragedy."

He was showing little concern for the two

men who needed to die violently to reinforce his two points. I must admit, though, since I never saw their dead bodies stretched out in the poker room, they were hardly occupying my mind. Not that they necessarily deserved to be shot, but they had no business harassing Jane Hankin that way at the dance.

I stopped hearing Wyatt when I fell deep in thought about the only Shakespeare work that I was remotely familiar with, *Romeo and Juliet,* featuring those star-crossed lovers and their feuding families. I began thinking of myself (luckily, I was far from any looking glass) as Romeo Montague despite the fact the Hannum family was past feuding with anyone — what with the cholera having taken my two sisters and brother, the railroad my father, the river my mother. It was easier to envision Jane Hankin as Juliet Capulet. She was young (though perhaps no younger than me), lovely (no one could top her in all of Dodge as far as I was concerned), respectable (a good dancer did not a dance hall girl make), and unattached. I wondered if the Hankin family was anything like the Capulets.

Mr. Matters tapped my shoulder and laughed when I winced. "Did I interrupt something?" he asked. "Thinking about dead Texans, dead bison, dead soldiers, dead presidents, or dead family?"

"Family in a way, but nothing dead. I was thinking about the Capulets and Montagues. But I suppose they are dead if they ever existed. I guess more about the Hankins."

"They've gone the way of the Capulets and Montagues. All dead except for Jane."

"How do you know that?"

"I just know. We talk."

"About her past? And your past, too?"

"Forget it. Let's dwell in the present, shall we?"

"I need to know more."

"About many things, yes, but not about where I come from."

"Fine. I'd rather know about where she comes from. I mean I know it is somewhere in Kansas, but she wasn't more specific. She said she had a lot of bad memoires."

"That's true. The Hankin family was from St. Louis. She was three years old when Kansas Territory was formed in '54 and the Hankin family moved from St. Louis to Lawrence, which was founded by the New England Emigrant Aid Company in no small part to keep the territory free of slavery."

"Lawrence? Really? I lived briefly in Lawrence in 1870 but didn't even know that

— about the slavery thing. Not about the Hankin family living there, either."

"They were long gone by 1870, son."

"Hey, wait a second. Didn't you tell me that the deadly Rebel guerrilla William Quantrill raided Lawrence during the Civil War?"

"I did. You *are* retaining some things I tell you. The raid began at 5'oclock in the morning on August 21, 1863, to be exact. Quantrill and his Number One Bushwhacker, Bloody Bill Anderson, wanted to bring hell down on those abolitionist Jayhawkers."

"My God! Jane was there?"

"Yes, twelve-year-old Jane was in bed along with the rest of the Hankin family when the raiders descended on the sleepy village. Jane, naturally, hates to talk about it."

"But what happened?"

"Lawrence was left in ashes, two hundred men and boys killed, including four of the Hankins. That's the story in a nutshell."

"And Jane?"

"She's here, isn't she?"

"I know but was she hurt?"

"Not so you could notice on the outside. It's a historic event that every American should know about, but you now know all you need to know on the subject. Let's drop it."

"Jane told you all this just like that?"

"I know. Now get back to the present, son."

"But Jane . . ."

"Life goes on."

"For some," I said, thinking more about the dead members of the Hankin family in Lawrence than the two dead Texans in Dodge.

"The people had sure rebuilt Lawrence by the time I got there. To think I was in the same town where Jane grew up."

"Yeah. That's growing up the hard way."

"Where'd she go after Lawrence?"

"Unimportant. She stayed until she needed to leave. What's important is her residing in Dodge City today."

"Yes, yes, by way of Fort Dodge, but I can't help but feel sorry for her."

"She needs protection from the past and the present."

"OK. I'd do anything for her."

"Sure you would, but how long have you been standing out here, Romeo?" Wyatt asked, no doubt eager to change the subject.

"Huh?"

"More than an hour, I'd say, ever since Trader Bob let you off work early."

"Then why'd you ask?"

"Why haven't you gone in? Grimmerman

is grim but he doesn't bite. Matilda, the wife, might even pinch your cheek, giving it some color, and say: 'Welcome, *Vögelchen.* They let you out of your cage.' *Vögelchen* means 'Little Bird.' "

"Huh? Why would she say that?"

"Never mind. She's German. Why haven't you gone in?"

"Could be I'll wait to see her till she's done working for the day. Or doesn't that meet with your approval?"

"You didn't ask to leave work early just so you could stand out here waiting like a nervous schoolboy. What has you afeared of going inside?"

"I ain't afraid. You want me to go in?"

"Suit yourself. She's a fine young woman. What's holding you back?"

"I couldn't think of any pretense. You know I'd never go buy a gun or jewelry for that matter. I don't need a plow. I can't afford to buy a pocket watch. I have nothing to say to Mr. and Mrs. Zimmerman. Anyway, I don't really want to bother Juliet . . . I mean Jane. It's likely too soon for me to go a-courting. The double shooting was just a few days ago. She took it hard. Those Texas boys really shook her up on the dance floor, and then they shook her up even more getting themselves shot dead by that Billy

Brooks and Matt Sullivan, who are still on the loose."

"As they shall remain since we lack law and order. But never mind those shootists. You aren't like that. Don't want to bother her? How do you know she doesn't want to be bothered by the likes of a fine peace-loving fellow like you?"

"You really think so, Wyatt?"

"For the love of Shakespeare! What if Romeo had taken that attitude with Juliet, Adam with Eve, Paris with Helen, Mark Antony with Cleopatra, Napoleon with Josephine, Queen Victoria with Prince Albert?"

"I suppose you know everything about true love like you know everything about everything else."

"Not all true love is true."

"All right. Do you want me to go in or not?"

"Look, you're my protégé but that doesn't require you to remain standoffish to an upstanding representative of the opposite sex."

"She likes you. You talk to her. I was kind of wondering what she is to you?"

"To me? You're imagining things in that silly young head of yours. The last thing in the world I want to do is show my age by standing in the way of young romance. And the way I see it, nobody else does stand in the way at this time, unless of course somebody happens to . . .”

“You don’t mean Timothy Swan the farmer, do you?” I kicked at the street, raising a little dirt and dust.

“Farming is an honorable profession for dullards. That won’t do for Lady Jane, even if Mr. Swan is polite and probably wouldn’t even shoot a skunk in his chicken coop.”

“Let me get this straight. You’re saying Jane doesn’t like wild men with guns but on the other hand doesn’t go for dull men who labor in the field day after dreary day? What about clerks working indoors day after dreary day? Would she disapprove of my work the way you seem to do? In other words, Wyatt, where do I stand?”

“With her, you mean? Right now, I’d say you’re on the outside looking in. Only you can change that. Girls — I should say young ladies — don’t always listen to the advice of wise old men.”

I tried to kick the street again but accidentally banged the toe of my boot against a hitching post. “I . . . I’ll talk to her later.” *Sometime when you aren’t around bothering me,* I thought but did not stay. I hurried back to the general store because being a dull clerk seemed easier than acting like a suiter or a protégé.

■ ■ ■ ■

It took me a week to work up the nerve to visit the Zimmerman store. It was just my luck that Jane Hankin wasn't there, but I pretended to be pricing various items — silverware and pocket watches, not firearms. Matilda Zimmerman watched me closely with a half grin. She wasn't fooled. She didn't pinch my cheek, but she was friendly. She asked if the amethyst ring I was eyeing was for myself or for my betrothed and agreed that a timepiece would be useful so I wouldn't be late for my own wedding. When I started to set her straight about how I was more than content with bachelorhood, she burst out laughing so loudly that her husband came out of the back room waving around a six-shooter. I instinctively held up my arms, took a step back, and prepared to duck a bullet.

"Aren't you the nervous type," Frederick Zimmerman said. "I never shoot customers."

"It's a girl, not a gun that has made Harry Hannum as uneasy as a hen in a fox's den," Matilda Zimmerman said, as if I wasn't even there. "He is looking for a ring in case he finds a delicate finger that will fit it, though he is trying so terribly hard to deny it. No doubt it's a new experience for the young man. We mustn't frighten him away, Fred."

I couldn't speak. I disliked being compared to a hen instead of a rooster, and I was startled to find out Mrs. Zimmerman knew my name. I wanted to blurt out all the manly things I had done *with* and *to* Elizabeth Pepper of Atchison but then, since I was an honest fellow, I would have had to tell how fickle Miss Pepper had latched onto that railroad man and left me to stew in my own juices.

"It's a new Colt Open Top," said Mr. Zimmerman. He steadied the revolver right under my nose and then began spinning the cylinder to show me it wasn't loaded but had a six-round capacity. "No cap-and-ball weapon this. Chambered for .44-caliber metallic cartridges. Interested? Or are you a tried-and-true percussion man opposed to newfangled developments in firearms?"

Unlike Mrs. Zimmerman he kept a straight face. I could sense he knew that I didn't carry a pistol now and never had done so in my life, which made me in his eyes a bloody fool, one likely sometime soon to be the victim of some Dodge City hard case.

"I was just looking," I said, backing toward the front door.

"Indeed," said Mr. Zimmerman. "The girl

you are looking for has been feeling under the weather lately. We sent Jane back to her room in the Essington House. She's ill but I'm sure it's nothing terribly contagious."

"Love sickness is no laughing matter, Fred," said Mrs. Zimmerman but then she laughed again, so I tipped my hat and stumbled out into the street like a humiliated drunk tossed out of a saloon.

I stood in front of the Essington House half that night before retreating to my quarters at the general store. I couldn't square in my mind the idea of courting a sick girl even if I was lovesick. The next day, Jane was feeling better but not well enough to report to work. That information came from Wyatt Matters, who insisted after my own workday was complete that he escort me to the Essington to inquire further into Jane's condition. When we arrived, we were confronted in the lobby by a man fairly young and highly inebriated. He waved a hammer at Wyatt Matters in lieu of a gun while yelling vulgarities about Wyatt's mother, whom he assumed was unwed; Wyatt's breeding, which he assumed occurred in the slums of New York City; and Wyatt's haughty disdain for the building, which the hammer man himself had built, as well as the meals and rooms offered there.

"Get the hell out," the man said as the hammer swished down through the air, missing the tip of Mr. Matters' nose by inches.

"You say that as if we are well acquainted."

"You're Matters. We don't need the likes of you pimping interlopers from the East."

"You have no idea where I'm from, sir, for I've never told anyone in Dodge. I have every right to be here."

"Not in the Essington House. I'm Essington. Not only am I part owner but I'm also the carpenter." He raised the hammer again, nearly striking his own chin with it.

"Watch it, my good man. I've never in my life seen a carpenter employ a hammer in such a careless manner. You are doing no credit to your profession."

"And you're no credit to mankind. I've heard you ranting. You been condemning the Essington. I take it personally. The Essington House is me!"

"Allow me to quote President Abe Lincoln: '*We are not enemies, but friends. We must not be enemies. Though passion may have strained, it must not break our bonds of affection.*' "."

"To hell with Lincoln. To hell with U.S. Grant. To hell with you. I'm from Virginia."

"Yes, I did detect a slight Southern accent. I

assure you, sir, I have no particular grievance against Virginians or your establishment."

"You're a flannel-mouthed liar. You've been spreading discouraging words about the entire Essington House — the way I made it, the way I operate it, the way I treat customers, the way I breathe!"

"I have simply told people that I prefer to live in a tent and prepare my own meals. I am sure the Essington has a lot to offer certain people, one of whom is a young woman named Jane who occupies a room on the second floor and does take her meals here when not feeling sick. Right now, she does feel sick, and we are here to see about . . ."

"Are you saying the food at the Essington made her sick?"

"No, sir. The cause of her sickness could be one of many things. I am *not* a physician."

"Well, it might have done just that. Sure. That would figure. The son of a bitch cook is incompetent."

"You don't say. Why don't you let him go?"

"The food he makes is enough to gag a dog off a gut wagon. The Injuns ain't right when they say they use every part of the buffalo; there are parts that should never be cooked and eaten by civilized men and women. Yes, I'm full as a tick, but who made me that way — that confounded cook. He'd drive a parson to drink. Damn him to hell. He's poisoning the customers!"

"We aren't customers, so we aren't complaining. Perhaps you'd like to put down that hammer or else find a nail?"

"I'd dismiss the bastard in a second if I only could find . . . Say, does either of you two Johnny-come-latelies know how to make a buffalo stew using only the good parts?"

"Like I've told you, sir, I cook only for myself and at times for my friends," said Wyatt. "And the correct name for the animal, dead or alive, is *bison.*"

"I already have a job," I said.

"Then get the hell out!" Mr. Essington shouted, but he didn't show us to the door. Instead, he ran in the opposite direction while hammering away at the stale air and cursing the cook. Next thing Wyatt and I heard was a loud bang from somewhere in the back, most likely the kitchen. We froze and stared at each other.

"Could a hammer make that sound?" I asked.

"I doubt it, not even when employed by a carpenter in his cups," said Mr. Matters.

"What do you think it was?"

"A shot."

"But Mr. Essington wasn't carrying a gun."

“Right you are. I suppose we should go back there and take a look.”

Wyatt Matters went alone. I didn’t feel up to it. I took a seat on a stool in the corner of the lobby and sat uncomfortably for a long time before Wyatt returned with a concise report of what happened: “The owner was making such a fuss that the cook shot him, right in the head. Mr. Essington died instantly.”

“I can’t believe it.”

“Go look for yourself if you like, son.”

“Murdered just like that. I don’t have to see it.”

“I wouldn’t say murdered. A hammer in the right hands can be a dangerous weapon. I would say it was a clear-cut case of self-defense. Nevertheless, the cook has fled the scene in case Mr. Essington has any friends in town.”

If Jane Hankin had heard the shot, it didn’t cause her to get out of her sickbed. Even Wyatt suggested it would be better to inquire about her health at another date. I left the building about as quickly as the cook, while Wyatt stayed behind to handle the inquiries of any interested party that came along in the absence of any law officer.

Jane Hankin was back on her feet the next day, but I was too busy to call on her. After a long day at the general store, I did some children watching for Alice Wright. She was ever so grateful as usual, and I confess that though she was an older married woman and the love of my life was down the street selling jewelry at Zimmerman's store, I was tempted to wrap my arms around those full, but not too full, hips. There was nothing to be done except condemn myself for thinking such thoughts about my employer's wife, but it did keep me from immediately pursuing the now healthy Jane. Mr. Matters asked me in the morning if I feared young women in general or just ones who worked in gun stores. I reminded him of my recent heated relationship with young Elizabeth Pepper, formerly of Atchison, and added that Jane had been more fearful than me of those gun-toting Texans at the dance hall.

"But you're a man, son, and she is in many ways like a delicate flower," he said, never one to let things just lay low.

"What about yourself? You don't wear a gun and are against gunplay."

"No such thing as gunplay, son. It's always potentially deadly business. But we're not talking about standing up to another man with a weapon. We are talking about standing before a woman unarmed, unafraid, and mindful of her feelings."

I was all set to agree with him when he propounded the idea that I might be looking for a new mother since my real one had to be fished out of the Northwest Branch of the Anacostia River. I found that to be in poor taste, especially since he was constantly trying to be my new father. He then had the nerve to bring up, for reasons not at all clear to me, an ancient king of Thebes who went by the name of Oedipus and unwittingly killed his father and married his mother, who then hanged herself when the truth of their relationship became known. It of course made no sense, since a B&O steam engine had run over my father and my dear mother had drowned herself before I could even see her again, let alone suggest she remarry. (While I thought Mr. Matters was off his nut to bring Oedipus into the equation, it might be argued that Wyatt was ahead of his time and brilliant, because twenty-seven years later a self-proclaimed psychoanalyst named Sigmund Freud introduced the Oedipus complex to the world. My feeling now, though, is that Dr. Freud, who is still alive, is as nutty as the late Mr. Matters.)

The bottom line is that at the end of the year 1872 I neither acted on my lingering fascination for Mrs. Alice Wright nor my burning love for Miss Jane Hankin. I knew

I would hate myself more if I succeeded with the former or failed with the latter. Mr. Matters, even if he thought he was being helpful, made matters worse. First, he saw fit to elaborate about Hester Prynne's committing adultery with her minister Arthur Dimmesdale in Nathaniel Hawthorne's *The Scarlet Letter* and Emma Bovary's pursuit of an adulterous relationship in Gustave Flaubert's *Madame Bovary.* I was out of my element, but I did respond that the women I had encountered in the James Fenimore Cooper's *Leatherstocking Tales* all seemed genteel and beyond reproach.

Not satisfied with admonishing me for the immoral thoughts he imagined I had, he cornered Alice Wright and worked into conversation the importance of wedding vows, telling her that "to have and to hold from this day forward, for better, for worse, for richer, for poorer" dated back to Thomas Cranmer's *The Book of Common Prayer,* originally written in 1549. He went on to point out how her working partnership with Robert Wright exemplified how social stability and moral behavior were possible even in a place like Dodge City. Mrs. Wright was no doubt confused by Mr. Matters' out-of-the-blue talk (was he attacking her or commending her?), since she didn't need the strange man or anyone else to tell her the value of a good marriage. She went to her husband to possibly shed some light on the subject. Mr. Wright rolled his eyes and replied, "Jupiter! Thunder! A têtê-à-têtê with a lunatic!" Fortunately, Wyatt Matters at least had the sense not to bring my name into his conversation with Mrs. Wright and neither she nor her husband made the connection with yours truly. Thus, I still had my job at the general store and was not relieved of my children-watching duties.

I had trouble trying to figure out Wyatt Matters' exact relationship with Jane. He was worried about her, telling me that the shooting of the brawny Texan and tall Texan followed by the shooting of Mr. Essington had unsettled her. I concurred because she was my true love, but I really had no idea if Jane seemed settled or unsettled. I thought it best to leave her alone until my mentor declared her "settled."

While Wyatt was intent on making sure my interactions with married Alice remained Platonic, he made a heavy-handed attempt to bring me, his protégé, and the lovely but fragile Jane, his I-wasn't-sure-what, closer together. Without consulting me, he visited the Zimmerman store at a time when Jane was out running an errand for her employer.

Wyatt carried a dried sunflower bouquet in my name that he handed to Matilda Zimmerman. I had seen the sunflowers strung together and hanging upside down to dry in a dark corner of his tent, but I had assumed they represented his idea of Kansas frontier decoration. Along with the dried sunflowers, my mentor provided a card with short verse that was anything but Shakespearean:

Dearest Lady Jane:
You light up Dodge City like a prairie fire
While gunfire brings you
close to girlish tears
But I go unarmed and you
have me fully charmed
I pray these preserved
flowers last for years.
—Your dance partner and ardent admirer,
Harry Hannum

Matilda Zimmerman placed the bouquet on the counter and eyed Wyatt Matters suspiciously. She knew her husband, who sold guns for a living, disliked the man for coming around and preaching gun control and for trying to get him to sign a petition to prohibit the carrying of firearms within the city limits. Wyatt was even less welcome in the Zimmerman gun store than he was in the Wright general store. At least in the general store he on occasion made a purchase. I wasn't there, of course, but Wyatt later detailed his visit with Matilda.

"You best go, Mr. Matters," Mrs. Zimmerman had advised him. "Bringing Fred flowers won't make him change his opinion of you."

"The flowers are intended for your faithful employee, Miss Jane Hankin."

"Oh, is that so?"

"Yes, it is so. If you would be so kind as to hand them to her when she returns, Matilda my dear, I would be most appreciative."

"I don't understand. You are giving a girl half your age flowers?"

"The female of the species adores flowers, especially receiving them, no matter the age of giver or receiver. But I'm sure you, being of the same species, must know that."

Mrs. Zimmerman scratched her chin and finally stopped watching the non-customer as if she suspected he might be intent on grabbing a diamond necklace or worse a pearl-handled pistol. She opened the card attached to the bouquet and began to read it aloud.

"Why this isn't even from you," she said.

"Absolutely correct, Matilda. Nor is it *for you*. But had I suspected you liked dried sunflowers so much, I would have brought you a similar bunch."

She now regarded him again, this time in horror as if he were a blowhard trying to make a mash on a respectable married lady. "You best hobble your lip before Fred hears you . . ."

"I understand, Matilda. I shall leave you to your work and to your husband. But please see to it that your young hardworking Miss Hankin, whom we all adore, gets the bouquet and reads the card from the young, overworked Mr. Hannum."

When Mr. Matters spun around and moved toward the door as if he were late for an appointment, Mrs. Zimmerman shouted after him. "I never gave you permission to call me Matilda, you old goat!" At the same time, Frederick Zimmerman emerged from the back room on the run, and when Wyatt abruptly stopped in the doorway and glanced back, he noticed the gun store owner's face was red and practically smoking like a recently fired pistol. "Did that loco son of a gun give you those dead flowers!"

Wyatt didn't linger to hear Mr. and Mr. Zimmerman discuss the matter, but Jane Hankin eventually did receive the bouquet and read the verse. She was *not* fooled. She knew that I would never address her as "Dearest Lady Jane," recognized the handwriting on the card (having seen Wyatt's gun-control petition a half-dozen times), and strongly suspected that I didn't know what the word "ardent" meant. She avoided coming to the Wright store to question me on the matter. Instead, she showed up two days later at Mr. Matters' tent and demanded to know why he had taken upon himself to act on behalf of a young man who could not act on his own and why he wanted to cause her to feel "dreadfully awkward" around her employers.

"Oh, dear," said Wyatt. "You didn't like the sentiment expressed in the verse?"

"That's not the point. You signed the card *Harry Hannum.*"

"I have no doubt I was expressing the sentiments that Harry actually holds close to his heart but was unable to express because of his shyness and lack of experience in such matters."

"Just look!" From behind her back Miss Hankin produced the crumbling dried-out bouquet. "They were already falling apart like this by the time I got them!"

"How disappointing for you, Lady Jane. Matilda and Frederick Grimmerman should have handled them more carefully. Dried sunflowers are more delicate than live ones. They should have known better."

"Mr. Zimmerman thought you had brought them for his wife and . . . never mind."

"That's right, Lady Jane, never mind the Grimmermans. This isn't about them."

"They're the *Zimmermans,* the people I work for. I must mind them."

"Of course, for work. But what do they know about young passion? This is about young Harry. Despite the state of the bouquet, you must realize that he meant well and that fresh flowers are impossible to come by in Dodge City, Kansas, in late November."

"Does Harry Hannum even know anything about these old flowers? Does Harry Hannum even know what you have done? I haven't heard a word from him since I danced with him that horrible night in the dance hall when the Texans . . . I don't even like to think about it, and I have certainly *not* been thinking of him."

"Shyness can be a curse, Lady Jane. But you've heard from him now."

"I heard from you. It's . . . it's too amazing, seemingly impossible. Like a dream."

"But not a bad dream, not really. Harry, bless his heart, was too shy to tell you of his ardent love himself so I, as a far more experienced smart old fellow, saw the need to step in and advance young romance."

"It didn't work, Wyatt."

"Just because the dried flowers crumbled?"

"No, no. You don't understand."

"I've never seen you so angry before, Lady Jane."

"I'm not angry at you. I'm . . ."

"It hurts me to see you angry as much as it does to see you sad. You know that. We have this most incredible connection, something rare and beautiful and as natural as a babbling spring."

"Oh, Wyatt. Stop. Please stop. I told you I'm not angry."

"Flabbergasted then? A little discombobulated maybe?"

"I don't know. I don't know those words."

"If I've done or said anything wrong . . ."

"Do you have to be so good with words! The truth of the matter, Mr. Matters, is that I am captivated by older men with big noses and big brains. There, I've said it."

"Heavens to Betsy! I am not easily shocked, but . . ."

"Nobody ever brought me flowers before, dried or otherwise. Could it be, Wyatt, you are the actual man enchanted by me?"

"Enchanted, yes, but not in the way you think."

"The flowers speak for themselves. And the verse expressed your sentiments."

"You know, Harry has a fairly large nose himself."

"I must tell you I am *not* charmed by young, shy men."

"He hardly drinks whiskey and doesn't carry a firearm."

"Neither do you, Wyatt. Does our difference in ages really mean that much? I think not."

"Most people call me unsightly while Harry is considered by some a sight for sore eyes."

"I don't consider him at all. My eyes aren't sore when I look at you. I'm a firm believer that handsomeness is in the eye of the beholder."

"Hmmm. A nice turn of phrase. Phrasing like that warms the cockles of my heart, but what you're saying can't be. I have found that most young people are warmed by the cockles of other young hearts."

"Pshaw! I don't care about young people who don't care the way you do. You are a kind man. Kindness trumps everything else. I feel romance comes upon us and knows no bounds!"

"There are bounds, Lady Jane. It may not seem that way at times on the frontier. But there must be bounds if we are to be considered civilized people. If there weren't any bounds, people would be shooting people all the time — even more so than in Dodge City. You wouldn't like that, would you, dear girl?"

"Now you're calling me a girl. I'm not. I'm twenty-one. You're only forty-one."

"Forty-two. But there are other considerations, young lady."

"You don't consider me desirable? You don't think I could cook for you or live in a tent? You think I care that you don't dance? I know I could never in a million years be as smart as you, but don't we have some wonderful, intelligent discussions?"

"Yes, but this isn't one of them. What I mean to say is our friendship is something solid. You don't want to ruin that. You don't want to do anything to damage that, and it would, it surely would. Maybe you can't see that clearly now but in time you would regret . . ."

"You . . . you don't love me."

"Wrong. The love I feel for you is like the love a . . . It's just a different kind of love."

"Yes, yes, different from all other loves. We have a love that is extremely unique."

"Actually, *unique* means one of a kind so comparatives and superlatives should not be used to modify it. Something is unique or is not unique. Do you understand? It's absolute. You can't say *extremely unique.*"

"Very well, Professor Matters. But our love is *very unique.*"

"You've missed my point. But never you mind. Now, the truth is that my good young friend Harry has a different kind of love for you. Perhaps you don't feel the same way, but Harry's love is . . ."

"Stop. Stop. I know he's your friend, but I don't need to hear about Harry. Not right now anyway."

"I understand. I'll stop for the moment. We'll both stop. I think you had better get back to the store, young lady. Frederick and Matilda Grimmer . . . Zimmerman . . . must wonder where you went off to in the middle of a workday and are no doubt worried sick about you already since Dodge City remains in a barbarous state."

Wyatt Matters then quickly ushered Jane Hankin out of the tent and sent her on her way. He told me all this about a week later, but unfortunately only after I had finally tried to "act" toward *his* Lady Jane. Much later in life, long after my Dodge City days were over and my mentor was long dead, I read Edmond Rostand's 1897 play "Cyrano de Bergerac" about a shy young Frenchman named Christian de Neuvillette who is only able to seduce young Roxane with the help of beautiful love letters written by Cyrano. It naturally called to mind what Wyatt Matters did for me twenty-five years earlier in Dodge. Of course, there were differences. For one thing I never enlisted Wyatt's help to win over Jane Hankin, and for another, Lady Jane recognized the ruse right away. Still, I can safely say that Cyrano de Bergerac and Wyatt Matters did have something very much in common — grandly oversized proboscises.

CHAPTER SEVEN

On a Sunday night, the first of December, Alice and Robert Wright went to dinner with Dodge newcomers George and Amy Cox at the Essington House. Mr. Cox had seen golden opportunity and purchased the place after the old owner, Mr. Essington, had gone after the cook with a hammer and been shot dead for his outburst. The town's principal hostelry was under renovation, scheduled to reopen with a whopping thirty-eight rooms in early 1873, but the dining area was already in fine shape and Amy was a grand cook. Entertaining the influential Wrights made good social and economic sense since the leading citizens of Dodge — neither I nor Wyatt Matters came close to qualifying for that group, of course — had formed a pact and stuck together like the flat, fleshy pads of the pricky pear cactus.

Anyway, while the Wrights were breaking bread at the Essington House, I oversaw their four youngest children — baby Charles, James, Elias, and Clara Belle. Twelve-year-old Bobby Wright, who wanted people to start calling him Robert, was off by himself playing buffalo hunter and Indians. Mrs. Wright came home right after dinner to make sure the little ones were in bed. Mr. Wright had gone with Mr. Cox to Hoover's saloon for a nightcap or two. The young Robert Wright noisily protested being put to bed early, and he ended up shooting his mother from behind with a long stick rifle fashioned from a cottonwood branch before retreating at last to his bedroom when she warned him that she would tell his father.

"You boys are relatively easy to handle until you turn twelve," Alice Wright told me when we went out the back door to get a breath of fresh air.

It was a dark night without a trace of a moon. She could have led me out the front door, where we might have been seen by passersby, but we were out back, where I couldn't make out her fine figure and could just barely see the whites of her eyes. I assumed she had taken wine or some other alcoholic beverage at the Essington House. For those reasons, as well as the state of my mind and body, I had the courage to ask something totally out of character: "How

’bout us twenty-two-year-olds, Alice? . . . I mean Mrs. Wright, sorry, but I really would like to know if you can handle someone of that age . . . you know, a young single man?”

“Such as yourself, Harry?”

“Well, I suppose. After all, I’m the only young single man around . . . that is to say, in the immediate area.”

“You weren’t drinking in front of the children, were you Harry?”

“Me? No. Wyatt Matters shares his wine with me on occasion. That’s it.”

“Stone sober, eh? Well, my head is spinning a bit. That’s why I needed the night air. You think I lured you out back with something else in mind?”

“What? No. I wasn’t thinking at all.”

“I’d be lying if I said I didn’t expect something like this sooner or later from you, Harry. I don’t believe it will get to the point where I find it necessary to slap your face. I am right, aren’t I, Harry?”

“You’re so right . . . for me.”

“I don’t doubt you can only say something like that because you can’t see my face.”

“I . . . I see it in my dreams, Alice.”

“If I tried to slap you now, I would likely miss your face. I can’t even see your . . . no, no, don’t get any closer.”

I froze and looked at the sky. I couldn't find a star, let alone the moon.

"Good boy," she said. "What ever happened with that young single woman employed at the Zimmerman store? Joan, isn't it? I thought something was developing there."

"No, no development. Her name is Jane, not Joan. She . . . she isn't for me. She likes older men and maybe farmers, too. I don't know. All I know is I . . . I need you, Alice."

"Stay," she said, as if talking to a pet dog. "You know what's right."

"You, Alice, you."

"It is me — Mrs. Wright. I suggest you go back to calling me that. It's a sign of respect to one of your elders, particularly one who also happens to be a married lady."

"You're only four years older than me, Alice . . . Mrs. Wright. Mr. Wright is six years older than you. Age doesn't matter when two people . . ."

"What matters is I am nothing like a dance hall girl or a prairie nymph or whatever you care to call them. The good Lord knows there are enough fallen angels in Dodge. Wedding vows are important, Harry, perhaps above all else. Mr. Wright is a good provider, a good husband, and solid as a rock. Our marriage represents social stability and moral behavior — qualities that should be valued everywhere, even in a largely untamed buffalo town like Dodge."

I couldn't believe my ears. She was virtually repeating things Wyatt Matters had once said to her. I covered my ears with my closed knuckles and shook my head. I was glad I couldn't see her face, and I no longer wanted to be able to hear her. But I could smell her by no means cheap perfume, maybe something French that Mr. Wright had imported from the East along with the sacks of flour and sugar. And I still ached to touch her, but not as much as I still longed to touch Jane Hankin, even though it seemed probable the auburn-haired coquette had allowed herself to be filled with the wine of Wyatt and then to be seduced by that sweet-talking old conniver. I folded my arms at my chest, took two steps backward, and tried to locate the back-door handle.

"I'm sorry," I said. "I'll be going. I enjoyed looking after your children and minding the store, but I won't be bothering you again. I lost my head. I'll . . . I'll go out on the prairie and look for buffalo bones. Tell Mr. Wright that I appreciate his hiring me but that I had to leave, tell him I . . . I . . . I don't know what."

"I'll tell Bob nothing. You'll come to work tomorrow morning as usual. Nothing has changed here, not really — nothing has happened. I'll say nothing to my husband and nothing more will be said by you or me about any of this. Is that a deal, Harry?"

"Yes, yes." I reached out as if to shake on the deal but decided it was inappropriate and withdrew my hand and then myself. "Thank you, thank you. I'll let myself in and then out the front door." Inside the house I heard the chatter of children coming from upstairs. I raced through three rooms to reach the front door, and once standing outside the Wright house, I took a deep breath of air that was somewhat fresher.

The next day I continued my rash behavior. I went to the Zimmerman store, still sober, and right in front of the owners I asked Jane Hankin if she would like to have dinner with me sometime. Naturally, I thought she would turn me down, and once she did, I was prepared to write off my true love forever and even tumble headfirst into the bitterly cold Arkansas River.

As she nodded her head in the affirmative, her silver earrings danced delightfully on both sides of her neck, which looked longer and more graceful than ever. In my mind I compared her to a white trumpeter swan I once saw visiting my neck of the woods in Maryland.

"Are you saying you will?"

She nodded more sedately this time.

I now wondered if she had become a *mute* swan.

"Are you really sure?" It was a dumb question, but I really needed to hear her voice.

"Yes," she said. "That would be nice."

"Tonight?"

She shook her head.

"Tomorrow night?"

"Saturday night. That's only four nights away. Afterward we can take a walk and talk. We should do that. There'll be more moonlight then."

Now, no words came from my mouth. Wild thoughts were pounding through my head and weighing down my tongue while four Zimmerman eyes were fastened on me. Still mesmerized by Jane's slightly swaying earrings, I nodded my head to her jewelry while wondering how I would ever survive until Saturday night. Finally, I started for the door.

"She lives with us now," said Matilda Zimmerman. "That is to say she is staying in our outbuilding, which Fred fixed up mighty nice. That's where you'll find her if she isn't here at the store."

"Thank you, ma'am. And thank you, too, Mr. Zimmerman."

"She's a good girl," he said.

"Yes, sir. I . . . I know."

I was near the front door when Jane called out to me, "You know a good place to dine, Harry?"

"Eh . . . well, the Essington House is under renovation as you know, and I'm not certain the dining room is officially open to the general public."

"I don't want to eat there. That's where the cook shot Mr. Essington."

"Sure, I understand. I do know of a few other spots that serve . . ."

"Never mind. I know what we'll do."

"You do?"

"We'll ask Wyatt Matters to dine with us and we'll have our marvelous meal right inside his roomy tent. I'll help with the cooking, and you can do the dishes. Doesn't that sound grand?"

I wanted to protest, for I believed I had already learned all I wanted to know about the old man and my true love and didn't want to think about them together ever again. "I don't know about . . ." I stopped talking because the Zimmermans were still peering at me, no doubt taking in every single word. I left with only one last word, "Grand."

■ ■ ■ ■

We were having bison tongue, but Wyatt Matters said it was all right, because a Cheyenne trader at Fort Dodge had given the tongue to him in exchange for glass beads and a porcelain teacup. "A fair trade," said Wyatt. "The beads were of no significance to me but the teacup had been in my family for two generations." I asked about the teacup, but Wyatt had nothing more to say about it. He washed the bison tongue, covered it with hot water, seasoned it, and simmered it for nearly three hours, which made for a late dinner but gave him plenty of time to talk about food and drink through the ages. He mentioned a Greek philosopher named Epicurus, who apparently was devoted to fine food; a Greek god named Dionysus, who loved wine, the so-called nectar of the Gods; and a Greek cook named Mithaecus, who wrote a cookbook in the fifth-century BC. And that was just for starters; then came his revelations about what Jesus and his disciples ate at the Last Supper, the skewering of hogs in Middle Ages spit roasts; the feasting on peacock, swan, and goose by nobles of the Renaissance; and the savoring of French cuisine during the Enlightenment. I'm sure he continued in the vein, since Jane

Hankin was enraptured by his every word, but my resentment was building along with my hunger, so I excused myself and left the tent to get some fresh air. I'm sure I wasn't missed. I returned just in time to see Wyatt peel skin off the tongue, slice it, and serve it hot to Miss Hankin, who hovered over his shoulder in her bright blue gingham dress like an enthusiastic but nervous blue hen.

"I've never tasted anything more appetizing in my entire life," she said. "Thank you, kind sir."

"My pleasure, Lady Jane. It's a specialty of the house . . . eh tent."

He laughed and she laughed with her mouth full.

"Next time, I'll cook you up something. It wouldn't be as good, but . . ."

"Nonsense. You're every bit the cook I am, Lady Jane. And it is my belief that *Two cooks are not too many to spoil the broth.*"

"Might I have a bite?" I asked.

After the meal, which I admit wasn't bad, I was eager to leave and not to leave Jane behind. She was ready to go all right, but she asked that both Mr. Matters and I escort her home as she would feel doubly safe that way. She had us each take an arm. As we sauntered along Locust Street and then across the tracks, it felt as if we were a monster with three heads, only the middle of which wasn't grotesque. Her three-room outbuilding, which looked freshly painted in midnight blue, stood about fifty feet behind the substantial Zimmerman home on Walnut Street, but we didn't make it all the way there. She got the notion to continue the stroll because she found the cold air invigorating and wanted to see how growing Dodge City looked at night. I suggested that Wyatt could go back to his tent if he felt tired, and he might have done so except Jane blurted out: "Why spoil a perfect evening. Let's all go."

We were passing Tom Sherman's dance hall by the railroad depot and about to turn around when Jane got another notion: She'd love to dance again. I saw that as a good sign because she had danced with me before and Wyatt had let her know that while he studied the history of dance from the acrobatic dances in ancient Egypt to the quadrilles in French high society, under no circumstances would he himself dance. Of course, he gave her no reason — I suspected he knew that all the dance knowledge in the world couldn't make him less stiff and awkward on the dance floor — but he promised to watch. Yes, I was no picture of manly grace, but his position boosted my confidence. For perhaps the first time since I met Wyatt and certainly for the first time that evening, I felt I had the advantage over him. I didn't have a wealth of words like he did. I was, in fact, what Wyatt had once called "a stifled, maladroit young man" when it came to women. Now, though, I saw myself as something more — someone who didn't need to express his passion in words. I was a gallant knight, strong and silent but ready to dance and defend her honor all night. She would have had to have been blind not to see how heartfelt and unabated my feelings were toward her. *I don't need you now, old man,* I told myself as the three of us entered Tom Sherman's dance hall.

No sooner did Jane and I take the dance floor than things went sour. The hall was full of drinking and carousing soldiers from Fort Dodge, and the worst of the lot was a Private Hennessy. He kept bumping into me as if looking to fight a civilian, but I showed restraint, even when he pushed me out of the way and began to dance with Jane. For one thing he was twice my size and wore the uniform of our no-longer-divided nation, complete with his service revolver. I'm sure Jane didn't want to dance with this armed drunken soldier, but she did so as not to put herself or me at risk. I joined Wyatt, who stood near the door, thinking he might think of a way for me to get Jane back without aggravating Hennessy. But Wyatt wasn't paying any attention to the dancing activity. He was in the middle of a nose-to-nose talk with gambler Charley Morehouse, who two months earlier had seriously wounded Johnnie Langford in a gunfight. Morehouse was trying to make it a heated conversation by accusing Wyatt once again of being a friend of Langford's. Heavy whiskey drinking hadn't impaired Morehouse's memory.

"You're looking for revenge, ain't you, old man?" he shouted.

"I'm not even looking for a dance," Wyatt replied.

"You're no innocent bystander. You were in on it with Langford last September."

"Didn't know Langford from Adam or you. Of course, innocence is a relative thing. Ten years ago during Montana Territory's gold rush, road agents were considered heinous for killing and robbing innocent miners, yet whenever a road agent was arrested, he would boldly declare, 'I am innocent!' In fact, the gang of outlaws up that way became known far and wide as the Innocents."

"This is Kansas, you bottom-feeder, and you're as ugly as a mud fence."

"In the Southwest, people make beautiful

walls out of mud. Actually, it's mud and straw mixed and dried to form adobe, the Spanish word for mudbrick."

"What are you talking about? I already told you this is Kansas."

"Thank you. As you probably know, Kansas was admitted into the Union as a free state on January 29, 1861, just in time for the Civil War."

"Talk straight. Was you a Bushwhacker or a blue belly?"

"Does it matter?"

"Didn't fight, eh? A yellow belly!"

"Call me what you like, but roll these figures around in your head, friend: 360,222 Union dead, 258,000 Confederate dead. Most of those war casualties were anonymous pawns who weren't fighting for or against slavery. The war was stupid; violence is stupid. Someday, this country will outgrow violence, my friend, and that, by the way, shall include Dodge City, Kansas."

"Them is fighting words, windbag. Dodge is my home, and I ain't stupid."

"Excellent. Then there's nothing at all for us to fight about, is there? We're quite a bit alike, you and me, both wanting the best for Dodge City. We both want peace! Am I right, friend?"

Mr. Morehouse clawed at his beard. "I

don't know, could be. As long as the gambling is good, I'm happy here."

"Fine. I do not consider peaceful gambling a sin. In fact, as you no doubt know, the Bible does not specifically condemn gambling."

"Yeah, sure. I know that. What about fighting?"

"The Bible doesn't say fighting is wrong in itself. It can be either noble or sinful, depends on the situation. Fighting someone like me would be sinful because I am a small, peaceful man who means no harm to you or any other man, woman, child, or baby yet unborn."

"Right. And you're ugly, too. But, you know, I got to fight a noble fight, goddamn it!"

Mr. Morehouse turned abruptly and crashed right into me. I fell backward, said it was all my fault, and apologized humbly and lavishly. He kept giving me the evil eye, so I added, "I assure you, sir, I am as peaceable as Mr. Matters. I'm here to dance, not fight."

"Then why aren't you dancing?"

Even while falling back, I could smell the alcohol on Morehouse's breath. "Well, sir, I sort of lost my dancing partner. See that soldier dancing over there with . . . eh . . . my girl."

"Hennessy, huh?"

"I believe that's his name. The gentleman cut in on me."

"Gentleman my ass. He claims to be the upper dog at Fort Dodge. One of his comrade in arms told me Hennessy was so mean he'd fight a rattler and give it the first bite. But look at him out there, all fancy-free and pawing your girl. He don't look all on fire to me."

"A curly wolf soldier like Private Hennessy is no doubt itchin' for a fight," suggested Wyatt. "Dancing and drinking are never enough. The young lady wants no part of him."

"Yeah, you got something there, old man. He shouldn't have busted into a private dance uninvited. Don't fret none, young feller, Hennessy needs to be taught a lesson, and I'm the one who can do it. I ain't afraid to fight the son of a bitch. And, by God, it'll be a noble fight."

I shrugged. He was implying that I wasn't the kind of guy who could teach Hennessy a lesson, and he was right. Of course, at first, I didn't think that fighting would be a good teaching tool. But when I looked to the dance floor, I saw that one of Hennessy's large paws lay flat and comfortable against the seat of Jane's blue gingham dress.

"That bastard," I blurted out. "What nerve."

If that wasn't enough to get Charley Morehouse out onto the dance floor, Mr. Matters gave him the final verbal push. "Sometimes when soldiers come to town, they think they can push citizens around and do whatever they want with the women. But I'd watch yourself if I were you, Mr. Morehouse, the private is armed."

"Well, so am I, old man, so am I."

While Wyatt and I expected a verbal altercation and perhaps some fisticuffs, things on the dance floor escalated with the speed of a charging bison bull. Angry words and swinging arms were quickly followed by drawn weapons and gunfire. Other soldiers and citizens jumped in, and a melee ensued. At the sight of the first exposed gun, Jane rushed into the arms of one of the two men who brought her to the dance. Not me! Wyatt Matters escorted *my girl* from the premises. I, though, remained in place, in what I suppose was a frozen state brought on more by her leaving with my mentor than the violence they left behind. I can't say how many shots were fired, but a couple of the last ones resulted in the death of Private Hennessy ("Good riddance," Wyatt later said) and the mortal wounding of Mr. Morehouse. Me, an innocent bystander, eventually walked out of Tom Sherman's dance hall unscathed but unhappy.

I didn't go to Jane's outbuilding home on Walnut Street or Wyatt's tent home on Locust Street. In fact, I didn't even go to my room at the Wright store on Front Street. I wandered over to Boot Hill, which was just then getting started, and for half the night contemplated the uncertainties of life and randomness of death. I reached no great conclusions except that death was certain and thus was more *inexorable* (yes, another word Wyatt had added to my vocabulary) than random. I also felt much regret. It was like what one of the newspapers said about the shooting affair a few days later: "We are assured that the respectable law-abiding portion of the community regret the circumstances very much and are determined to prevent a repetition of such outlawry." But I felt I had far more reason to feel regret than most because, as I saw it, my words, along with those of Wyatt Matters, had triggered the whole deadly melee.

That wasn't the end of shooting trouble that year in Dodge. Billy Brooks, who with Matt Sullivan had eliminated two of those troublesome Texans at the Kelley and

Hunt dance hall in November, was anointed "Bully Brooks" by Wyatt Matters — and there was a lot of truth in that nickname. Brooks liked to play lawman in Dodge and order citizens about even though there could be no official badge wearers since the town wasn't yet legally organized. More about Mr. Brooks and shootings in a moment. But first I must mention that Miss Jane Hankin still occupied a certain mostly warm spot in my brain, especially during the coldest Dodge days and nights. A few days before Christmas Mr. Matters walked with me along Front Street explaining to me that his feelings for Jane Hankin hadn't changed despite her vowed love for him and her several visits to his tent when I wasn't present.

"Lady Jane is a fine person, but she is complicated," he said, his stride steady. "She's intelligent with the propensity to think, act, and form opinions without outside influence."

"Sort of like you, huh?"

"How true. Of course, there are differences, the obvious one being she's a beautiful young woman and I'm a — shall we say — an odd-looking old man."

"I never noticed."

"She's also sensitive, as fragile as a flower — something I've pointed out to you several times before but perhaps hasn't yet registered in your head. She has been through a lot of hurt in her twenty-one years, and they'll be more hurt ahead no matter how much you and I try to protect her."

"Because of the violence we've been seeing in Dodge?"

"That doesn't help. But hurts happen anywhere in this world, as you well know from your childhood in Bladensburg, Maryland, and she knows from her childhood in Lawrence, Kansas."

"What about your childhood, Wyatt? Where did that happen again?"

"Not again. I've never said. And I don't intend to. It's best forgotten."

"Too much hurt for you back then?"

"Not hardly. I'd call it an unconcerned childhood. Now let's get back to the subject at hand — our beloved Jane Hankin."

"Would be glad to. How beloved she is to you has been of some concern considering how she feels about you."

"I have made it clear to Lady Jane how things must stand between her and me. She understands or is at least nearing understanding. The kind of love we have for each other shall never die. Now, don't start pouting, son. It isn't at all like the kind of love you have in mind."

"What do you mean? My kind of love for her won't ever die, either."

"Glad to hear it. Naturally I wish her to find a good young man, one with a bright future, one who chooses turning the other cheek over showing off his gun hand, sobriety over intemperance, and the rebirth of Renaissance thought over a return to Middle Ages mentality. In short, son, in my mind I continue to envision you and Lady Jane together."

"Really and truly?"

He stopped walking, so I did. "You know I am no liar. If there is something that I don't want you to know, I'll simply not say it. I'm not going to lie about it. You believe I think of you as my son. I know that. Now trust that I think of her as my . . . my son's potential wife."

"You hesitated there for a second. Are you sure?"

"It's too cold standing still. Of course, I'm sure. He who hesitates is lost and I am never lost."

He resumed walking. I shrugged and wiped my dripping nose with the back of my hand. But then I followed. I had been having my serious doubts about Wyatt Matters, but now I was pretty much convinced he had my best interests at heart. Of course, he had won me over with words, and he was a man whose word knowledge I figured must match that of the late Noah Webster, publisher in 1806 of *A Compendious Dictionary of the English Language,* followed up by 1828's *An American Dictionary of the English Language* (Wyatt kept a copy of the latter in one of his trunks but didn't need to call upon it often). Still, I took him for his word. A fellow had to trust and believe in somebody, and my self-confidence was still a work in progress. Fact was, Dodge City didn't feel like home yet, and without my mentor around I would have felt lost.

As we walked on, we talked about Christmas — actually, for a change, I did most of the talking. I told him I had only disturbing memories of Christmases past in Bladensburg. My mother had believed in hanging stockings over the fireplace in theory but did it only once. Usually, she forgot all about it by Christmas Eve or else decided she had nothing "good" to put in a stocking. The one exception was when I was five or six and she put up four red stockings — one for me and the other three for my deceased sisters and brother. Inside each was a three-inch candy stick. For a short while I was delighted because, as the only living child, I was able to devour all four sticks. But I broke a tooth on the fourth one (God's punishment, I believed) and found myself locked in the root cellar on bread rations for two days and one night (my mother's punishment for my greed and selfishness). Much later, as a drunken trick, my father hung a stocking that belonged to a woman who was not my mother. Inside were two marbles that appeared to have been blackened by fire. My mother didn't find that amusing, but then I don't remember her ever being amused. Wyatt had nothing to say about his Christmases past except that he did get stockings and that they were always overflowing with edibles and shiny objects. He then quickly brought Christmas to the present.

"I wonder what kind of special gift Lady Jane would like for Christmas," he said in such a way that he didn't sound anything like a potential father-in-law.

"I'll get her something special," I said. "You can count on that."

"Good for you."

'You think I can't? I'm making good money now at the store. I'm not so greedy and selfish to spend it all on myself, you know."

"Good for you."

I couldn't think of what to get her, though, and as I started to ask Wyatt for suggestions, I bumped into Billy Brooks, who was walking toward us as if he owned the street. I would have apologized to whomever it was, but seeing as it was Mr. Brooks, I practically begged his forgiveness. He acted as if he usually shot people for less but finally accepted my humble apology.

"Just watch where you're going next time," Mr. Brooks said. "The both of you."

"You are hard to miss, my good man," said Wyatt. "This meeting is most fortuitous. I've been meaning to talk to you for some time."

"Yeah? What for?"

"I know you have been a lawman of sorts elsewhere in Kansas, but I wanted to remind you that here in Dodge you have no official law-enforcement capacity. Perhaps you don't realize, we have no officials, elected, or appointed or . . ."

"What's it to you? You trying to make trouble?"

"I never try to make trouble, Mr. Brooks. I just thought you needed a gentle reminder from a peaceable man. We need law and order in Dodge, but it must be the right kind."

"I don't need a reminder from you about anything. Anyway, some of the saloon owners pay me to keep order among their rowdy patrons. That makes me official."

"This is the public street not a saloon. And

neither Harry Hannum nor I is in the least bit rowdy."

"Just shut your bone box and step aside, you and your Harry."

I wished Wyatt hadn't introduced my name into the discussion. I took three large steps to the side. Mr. Matters did not. Instead, he decided to stand his ground and lecture Mr. Brooks about his bad habit of intimidating and domineering folks whom he viewed as vulnerable.

"Law and order will one day come to Dodge, but it can't come from a bully who actually causes death and disorder."

Even I thought Wyatt had stepped over the line by not moving and then maligning this known gunman. Mr. Brooks gave Wyatt's purple bowtie a tug, a small act that many men, bullies or not, found irresistible. Wyatt only adjusted his bowtie and smiled. That angered Mr. Brooks further, and with one swift hand gesture knocked off Wyatt's top hat. He then called Wyatt several names, "rantankerous bag of wind" being the nicest.

Wyatt looked even more vulnerable than usual standing there with a bare, mostly bald head, so I picked up his hat. I thought if my mentor made any movement, sudden or not, Mr. Brooks would pull his pistol and fire in a blur.

"Rantankerous," said Wyatt, and then he said it two more times.

"That's what I called you all right. Want to make anything of it?"

"It's a most interesting word. I'm not saying it isn't a proper English word, just that I have never used it myself. I suspect it is an alteration of *cantankerous,* probably after either rancorous or rant."

"What the hell are you talking about?"

"Nothing at all. Words fascinate me."

"Like I said, a bag of wind."

"Not necessarily. I do on occasion talk at length, but things I say often have value."

"I say shut the hell up." Billy Brooks took out his pistol, though he did so in no hurry and then just twirled it with two fingers in the manner of a bored person twiddling his thumbs.

"Go ahead and shoot me dead if you must," Wyatt told him. "That will surely cause the good citizens of Dodge to rise up and demand law and order from duly elected officials. The end result would likely be you, my friend, hanging from the highest tree, and a better Dodge, with justice for all."

"Yeah, and you'd be deader than dead and lying six feet under on Boot Hill."

"There was an apostle named John, maybe you've heard of him. He said, 'Greater love hath no man than this, that a man lay down his life for his friends.' "

"What church you belong to, Reverend?"

"Morality doesn't come from one's church or religion, my friend. The Bible is complex, full of beliefs and moral implications that can be interpreted in many ways. Somewhere in there, you'll also find this: 'To do righteousness and justice is desired by the Lord more than sacrifice.' "

"Just a lousy Bible-thumper then!"

"I don't thump anything or anyone. Jesus says, 'I desire mercy, not sacrifices.' "

At that point, Bully Brooks must have been perplexed on how to proceed. He first holstered his six-shooter, but then must have had second thoughts because he suddenly yanked it back out. For the first time he pointed the gun at Wyatt's chest. "Go ahead then, you blamed bloviator, and start begging for mercy."

"*Bloviator, one who bloviates.* That's quite the entrancing word, Mr. Brooks, and totally unexpected from you. The verb 'bloviate' is a pseudo-Latin alteration of blow, expelling air through pursed lips. The noun form is bloviation, and . . ."

"Didn't I tell you to shut your bone box. I don't need to hear you bloviating about bloviation. And neither does your Harry."

Their conversation had taken a strange turn and I was now the one perplexed, but I was relieved when Mr. Brooks once again returned his weapon to his holster. Mr. Matters kept on talking, continuing in a similar vein by suggesting that along with *bloviator,* another word that Mr. Brooks might find interesting was *rigmarole.* I found the word equally unfamiliar. Mr. Brooks, though, had stopped paying attention to Mr. Matters and pushed by him to face a new adversary, one whom he clearly considered more worthy.

The fellow's name was Brown, whom Wyatt later told me was a yardmaster back in Newton when Brooks was a lawman there. Not even Wyatt knew what triggered what happened next. But Mr. Brooks did draw his revolver, as did Mr. Brown and Mr. Brown's assistant. At least six shots were fired. Mr. Matters and I heard all six shots, but the last three from a distance as we had both run down the street and taken cover in the general store. We would later learn that Mr. Brooks suffered an inconsequential wound while Mr. Brown took a ball to the head that unexpectedly did not prove fatal. In the general store, Mr. Matters was breathing hard, and no doubt I was, too. I know that after the last shot, I could hear my heart pounding.

"What just happened?" I said. "I can't believe it."

"Just another typical day in Dodge," Wyatt said after taking another minute to catch his breath.

"Typical? We could have been shot!"

"When bullets fly that's always a possibility. Too bad about how things went out there. I thought my conversation with Mr. Brooks was starting to get interesting."

"Huh? Like you said, he's a bully. He would have gone on bullying."

"Perhaps. But a man who can use a word like *bloviator* can't be all bad."

"What about a man who isn't even sure what the word means?"

"Well, allow me to edify you, son. A bloviator tends to employ big words and orate in a pompous style when articulating, elucidating, and going into a long rigmarole about right and wrong, etiquette and impropriety, courteousness, and effrontery on Front Street."

"Oh, I see. Does that sound like anyone we know, Dad?"

"I am not saying that Mr. Brooks was entirely wrong to call me a bloviator. I am not without self-awareness. I do mean well. And isn't it far better to bloviate on occasion than to blow somebody's brains out without so much as a single word?"

"Yes."

"Very well. I rest my case. In any case we are reasonably safe from flying bullets in here."

"It's you two again," said Mrs. Wright, who rose from behind the counter with two-year-old Charlie cradled in her arms. "Mr. Wright is down the street on business. I heard shots."

"Just Bully Brooks down the street on *his* business. You'll be happy to know that nobody touched a hair on Harry's head."

Charlie began to bawl.

"You had the day off, Harry," Mrs. Wright said. "I thought you were back there on your cot fast asleep."

"No, ma'am," I said. "My apologies."

"No harm done. Does Mr. Matters wish to purchase anything?"

"Not today," said Wyatt. "Thank you for your hospitality. We'll be on our way unless you need the services of Harry."

"I do not. I'll say good day to you gentlemen. My baby needs his nap."

We watched Mrs. Wright duck down again behind the counter where she no doubt had blankets laid out for her youngest child.

"Nothing like a baby in a mother's arms to make one wish for peace on Earth, including Dodge," said Wyatt, who was rocking back and forth as if listening to imagined music. "Naturally, though, the mother must one day give the child up, and the child is bound to be disappointed."

"Maybe I should stay and help, at least till Mr. Wright gets back."

"He should be here at any moment. He must have heard the shots. All of Dodge must have heard them. Didn't Alice Wright look afraid?"

"Who can blame her with all that gunfire coming from the street."

"Yes, but she was looking at me with horror, as if I had fired the shots, me a man of peace and law and order."

"I thought she was looking at me."

"Seeing you was reassuring after she saw me. Without doubt, like her husband, she has no use for me and would prefer I never invaded the sanctity of the general store."

"Maybe she was just afraid you'd approach her and go into one of your rigmaroles."

"Excellent, son. Despite another shooting in Dodge, you've learned a new word or two today and made them part of your vocabulary. Hey, since we are here, why don't we look for that special Christmas gift to give our Lady Jane."

Chapter Eight

The place to get Jane Hankin a special Christmas gift should have been her workplace — either a derringer to help her get over her fear of aggressive men with big guns or a silver brooch so that she could smartly fasten the collar flaps of her proper white blouse. Instead, Wyatt Matters led me around the Wright general store, picked out a three-piece silver-plated mirror brush and comb set, and had me purchase it with the hard-earned money I made at that store. The man Wyatt called "Mr. Wright Can Do No Wrong," "Bobby 'Money Is Might' Wright," and "Trader Bob" did not give me an employee discount, but later Alice Wright secretly slipped me some of my money back. She first laboriously explained that it wasn't because she wanted to in any way deceive or go behind the back of her husband but because she recognized how little he paid me, as well as my own sincere effort to respect her marriage vows and to pursue an available well-groomed female whose youthful vanity made a handheld mirror, brush, and comb essential to her existence.

I initially resented the fact Wyatt didn't shell out a penny, even though he had plenty of money reserves hidden on his person or somewhere inside his Locust Street tent. Sensing my resentment (he always claimed he could read me like an eighteenth-century novel of sensibility), he reminded me that he never barred me from his tent and gave me his worldly-wise advice free of charge and, furthermore, that giving a coveted young woman a Christmas gift I didn't have to pay for myself would distort my moral compass and set me on a path of *parasitic dissipation,* whatever that was.

As it turned out, Jane Hankin did not answer the door of her small blue house when I arrived with the wrapped gift in hand on Christmas morning. She wasn't at the Zimmerman store either or back at the tent where Mr. Matters was sleeping in (yes, I felt a little guilty that I went back there to check).

I fetched from the pocket of Wyatt's coat his leather-bound notebook and tore out a blank sheet from the back. The notebook was part diary about the doings in Dodge, part commentary about the state of mankind in general, part poetry, and part vocabulary list. While Wyatt was snoring with a hint of a self-satisfied smile on his unattractive mug, I couldn't resist taking the opportunity to read some of the entries, including a few written in verse. Yes, I felt slightly wicked about invading his private words, though I mostly felt a combination of disappointment and relief that he barely said anything about me, his protégé, and only mentioned Jane once or twice in passing. Law and order seemed to be the predominant theme. His vocabulary list mostly included strange words that had no meaning to me and for which he provided no definitions — *absquatulate, lickspittle, flummox, dubersome, conglutinant, fuddled.* At a nearby vacant lot I sat for a long time trying to compose a rhyming note to attach to my gift.

It was well after the noon hour that I finally finished this first attempt at a poem. Mr. Matters was an old hand at producing verse (on paper in his notebook but also out of thin air in the middle of one of his lectures), and he would quote lines of classic poetry off the top of his head as part of my education. All that stuck with me were the first two lines of "Ode to a Nightingale," written by a young, apparently sober Englishman named John Keats: "My heart aches, and a drowsy numbness pains/My sense, as though of hemlock I had drunk." My heart was aching for Miss Hankin, but I couldn't bring myself to put such a notion down on paper. Wyatt told me that nightingales, especially the males with their melodious song, had inspired writers throughout history, including the ancient Greeks as well as another old Englishman name of Mr. Chaucer. But Wyatt also told me that every single nightingale lived across the pond, meaning the Atlantic Ocean.

Anyway, I didn't feel capable of writing an ode to anything or anybody, and when I considered Jane, I thought of myself as a red-tailed hawk and her as a passenger pigeon. So, I came up with "A Gift from Saint Nick," not that I thought of myself as any kind of saint, let alone a poet, but it was the best I could do. It went like this:

A Gift from Saint Nick
Did you happen to see Father Christmas
Otherwise known as Saint Nick?
Well, he's been a-watching you
And brought you this present right quick.

It's something for you to believe in
Something you can hold in your tiny hand
And something that will confirm the fact
You're the fairest maiden in the land.

I was hardly satisfied and plenty embarrassed — no doubt if I had opened her gift myself and looked into the handheld mirror, I would have seen a crimson face. Still, I figured if she was there when I got back to her house, I could always stuff the rhyming note in my pocket and tear it to pieces later in a back alley.

Well, Jane still wasn't home, so I left the package and note on the doorstep and ran away to take a quiet walk on Boot Hill. It was two days later — two days without as much as a thank you from my true love — that I learned some shocking news — from Wyatt Matters, who else? Miss Hankin had been seen in the arms of Matt Sullivan on a dance floor and more than once arm and arm with that gambler right out in the open on Front Street. I found that hard to believe since Mr. Sullivan, like most men in the dangerous gambling profession, carried a gun and, along with Mr. Brooks, had dispatched those two troublemaking Texans.

"Your information must be false!" I told Wyatt in the middle of my pout in his tent.

"Don't kid yourself, son. I don't spread rumors or falsehoods."

"It's just gossip, Jane doesn't like men who carry guns." That didn't sound strong enough. "In fact, she *unequivocally abhors* them!" I shouted, using two vocabulary words Wyatt had recently taught me.

"I do, as the great Socrates did, and keep away from the gossip of people. He stated that *rumor* was an evil thing. 'By nature,' Socrates added, 'she's a light weight to lift up, yes, but heavy to carry and hard to put down again. Rumor never disappears entirely once people have indulged her.' Yes, son, I heard things about Lady Jane and Sullivan the gambler, but I went out and had them confirmed by more than a handful of reliable sources, including Mr. and Mrs. Zimmerman, and George Flinger the drugstore man. If you can't trust your druggist, who can you trust?"

I sat down on his tent floor and went back to pouting. I didn't know who I could trust. I wasn't sure I could unequivocally trust Mr. Matters, let alone his reliable sources. I sure as hell didn't want them to be right. In fact, I didn't think I could bear it. It had bothered me when I got the idea Wyatt was romancing her behind my back. I was so relieved when he cleared himself, which had opened the door for me. And now Matt Sullivan was slamming the door in my face.

"Why him?" I asked. "Why not me?"

"I myself was in the dark about Mr. Sullivan. This romance must have developed quite suddenly. Mr. Sullivan must have moved like lightning. I understand your hurt, son. Don't think this thing hasn't affected me as well. I'm constantly checking the pulse of activity in Dodge, but I had no idea about this development. Lady Jane has not confided in me on matters of romance."

"It's like a punch to my belly."

"I heard Mr. Sullivan doesn't like to punch. Doesn't want to hurt his delicate hands. Needs them operating smoothly for dealing cards."

"A kick in the teeth then. He holds guns in those hands. He kills. How could *she*!"

"Women are often harder to figure than men. Women are more complicated."

"You're so smart. You say so yourself. You must know why she did this to me. Why, why, why!"

"It is my educated guess, son, that you waited too long to actively show a commitment to our Miss Hankin. If you don't act in a male-heavy community such as Dodge, you know some other man certainly will. Young, innocent, and beautiful women are a precious commodity hereabouts. This is a perfect time for me to repeat a proverb I've brought to your attention several times previously: *He who hesitates is lost.* I have traced it all the way back to a 1713 play called 'Cato,' in which a character states, 'The woman that deliberates is lost.' But the saying applies to men, especially young ones like yourself."

"Hey, wait a minute. I *acted.* I gave her that expensive Christmas gift with a card. I wrote my own verse. That's not rumor; it's fact."

"Yes, an unsigned card with eight lines of verse that follow an ABCB rhyme scheme as Coleridge used in 'The Rime of the Ancient Mariner.' "

"She could have at least thanked me. Not a word."

"She knows I am the rhyming man here in Dodge. She thought I wrote it."

"And you let her thank you!"

"Certainly not. I would never take credit for a poem like that."

"You didn't like my poem?"

"It wasn't bad for your first try. You are learning . . . rather slowly, but . . ."

"You did tell her the gift was from me, then?"

"I was *totally* honest. I told her I picked out the gift but that you bought it."

"If you told her that, why didn't she come to me and . . ."

"Are you starting to doubt me, son?"

I wasn't *just* starting to doubt him. "You

didn't let me finish. Why didn't she come to thank me if she knew the truth?"

"In two words: Matt Sullivan. She has been preoccupied. I wonder what he gave her for Christmas."

"Damn him. He's gun crazy!"

"The other day, Mr. Sullivan walked into the Zimmerman store, handed Frederick Zimmerman his hide-away gun, and told him he was not *there* to acquire a replacement, and in fact had decided to never carry a firearm again unless out of town hunting."

"How'd you hear that? More gossip?"

"No. Matilda Zimmerman is a reliable source. Matt Sullivan's handing over his gambler's weapon that way struck a nerve with Jane. Afterward, he ambled to the store's jewelry department and asked our Lady Jane to go to a dance. She accepted."

"Just because he turned in his gun? I've never even owned a gun."

"She saw his act as a noble sacrifice. Here was a strong, self-assured, and not unattractive young man who had voluntarily given up his guns *for her* and he promised it was *forever.* She was unequivocally moved. And he loves to dance."

"So do I. With her! Even without a gun, he's still a gambler. Do women prefer gamblers to store clerks? Is that it?"

"Hard to say, son. Like I've been telling you, Lady Jane has a mind of her own. Oh, one other thing I heard. I almost forgot. Matt Sullivan is no longer just a gambler. He now keeps his own saloon. All his gambles must be paying off."

"And I never gamble. Are you saying I should?"

"All I'm saying is *He who hesitates is . . .*"

"Pained!" I yelled. I stood on my tiptoes and seemed to tower over him That wasn't enough for me. I wanted out of his tent. He wasn't blocking my exit, but I shoved him anyway. I hadn't shown any strength for so long that I forgot how much I possessed. My mentor went flying backward, and his top hat flew off and hit the ground before he did. He landed hard and didn't flop, but he wasn't knocked out

"The horror!" he screamed. "Violence from a most unlikely source!"

I couldn't argue with that statement. I stormed out of the tent and retired to the same vacant lot where I had written my unappreciated verse for Jane Hankin. I stomped on the dirt for a minute or two and then dropped to my knees. From there I looked to the sky as if begging for forgiveness. In all the years I'd spent at home in Maryland taking my father's abuse, I had never once dared strike back at him. And then the B&O engine flattened him, and my chance was lost forever. Fact was, I had never been in a grown-up fight either, not that pushing down an old man constituted any kind of fight. I couldn't stand Matt Sullivan at that moment but no more than I couldn't stand myself.

Wyatt showed me something by tracking me down to the vacant lot and stooping to pick me up off my knees. He then bent down again to brush the dirt off the knees of my trousers. I thanked him and then apologized to him, over and over, as if asking forgiveness for a hundred other sins besides my inconsiderate shove.

"I don't know what got into me," I admitted. "It wasn't me who pushed you. I mean it wasn't like me. It was like . . . I don't know, like I was pushing my father, the real one."

"Forget that sorry excuse for a man. He's long gone."

"I know. I know. I hardly ever think of him. It's just . . . I just don't know."

"Let's stick to the present time for now. Matt Sullivan stepped into her life. Nothing you or I can do about that. You must at least realize now that nothing happened between Jane and me like what is happening now between Mr. Sullivan and her. Furthermore, it could never happen."

"Yes, I'm sorry to have thought that . . . you know."

"Never apologize for thinking. It is thinking that separates us from the beasts, along with speech, fire, and the ability to hate people we have never met. It's not me who has pained you, son. I just happened to be standing there. It is Mr. Sullivan you are angry at."

"I know that. How could he do it . . . so fast?"

"A gambler takes chances, puts himself on the line. A clerk only waits — for customers, for orders."

I no longer felt like being apologetic. I pulled away from my mentor and crossed my arms. "All right, I'm a clerk who waits on other people. Maybe it's not as exciting or rewarding as being a Dodge City gambler or saloon owner, but it's honest, respectable work. I thought you wanted Dodge to be a place full of honest and respectable people."

"To a degree. But so many of the so-called respectable people conceal evil. No, they don't go around shooting people or brawling in saloons or even shoving anyone, but they are loaded with greed and hypocrisy and capricious judgments."

"Not me! I bought her that expensive Christmas present."

"So, you've reminded me a half-dozen times."

"I care for her and respect her, really and truly. I wasn't pretending when I wrote that poem for her. Perhaps I exaggerated when I called her *the fairest maiden in the land.* But, as far as I'm concerned, she is at least the fairest maiden in Dodge City . . . Lawrence, Elgin, and Elk City, Kansas, too . . . and, I'd say, a hell of a lot *fairer* than Miss Elizabeth Pepper, formerly of Atchison. What do you say to that?"

"I say that you were using the word the way the Grimm Brothers did in 'Snow White' when Snow's evil stepmother asks, 'Mirror, mirror, on the wall, who's the fairest of them all?' "

"If it was good enough for the Grimm Brothers, it's good enough for me."

"The trouble is, by fairest, they meant most lovely, most beautiful. Their *fairer* does sound like a poetic word but, alas, it is also archaic."

"Huh?"

"The meaning of the word has shifted in modern times. Today 'fair' means one who is pale and blond, and while Lady Jane has nearly alabaster skin from spending all her time working in the store and dancing in various indoor venues, she is clearly auburn-haired. What's more, particularly if she hasn't read 'Snow White' lately, she is likely more familiar with 'fair' meaning something between poor and good and thus your *fairest* was not complimentary. In other words, the beautiful lady might have thought you were calling her something less than beautiful, something like *fair to middling.*"

I uncrossed my arms and threw them in the air. "You forget she didn't think I was calling her anything. She thought it was *your* 'fairest' on that card."

"A fair point, son. But it was just a word on paper, no match for many words spoken face-to-face."

"Sure, all your words spoken to her. Everyone knows you are ponderously garrulous."

"Excellent. Two vocabulary words you didn't know until you met me. You could have chosen a better adverb, however. I prefer to think of myself as knowledgeably garrulous. In any case, the words I spoke to her — which, I might add, were always in your best interest — were easily cast aside. 'Twas the blandishments of the gambler and saloonkeeper Matt Sullivan that won over our Lady Jane."

He hadn't taught me the word "blandishment" yet, but I got his point anyway. I decided to hate Matt Sullivan for as long as I lived — rather to dislike him intensely, since Wyatt had almost convinced me that hate was self-destructive and never solved any problem. "I really dislike intensely that honey-tongued greedy hypocrite!" I ended up saying, which made Mr. Matters smile. I really didn't know Matt Sullivan at all.

On Saturday night, December 28, 1872, Mr. Matters got tired of me moping around his tent, acting as if I were alone even in his company. I had yet to see Jane Hankin in the company of Matt Sullivan, so I was denying to myself that anything was going on between the two unlikely lovers. It wasn't working so well, though, so I continued to mope as if it were my favorite pastime.

"You need to get a hold of yourself, son," he said. "All of Dodge knows about them now. It does you no good to think about them when I'm giving you so much else to think about. You weren't even listening when I explained the Ku Klux Klan Act passed last year that allows the president to deploy the military or any other means to stop the KKK and other vigilante groups from threating and harming the freed slaves in the South."

"I heard you, but this is Kansas."

"The Negroes of this state need the equal

protection under the law just as the Negroes do in the former Rebel states. And that goes for Dodge City, too."

I yawned and curled up on the buffalo hide that had been a gift to him from the Kaw subchief. I clutched my knees to show him I had hold of myself. He was not impressed.

"You try my patience, protégé. But I must remember what Aristotle said: *Patience is bitter, but its fruit is sweet.*"

"The bitterness part I understand completely. Waiting patiently for Jane to come to her senses has made me bitter. She used to be so sweet. I know sooner or later she will be sweet again."

"Let's go. Get up."

"You don't like me lying on your dead bison?"

"You need a dose of reality." He reached down, grabbed both my wrists, and pulled me to my feet. Then he held his back. "You're heavier than you look."

"All that knowledge you've fed my brain has added great weight to my head."

"Put your coat on. We're going to Mr. Sullivan's new establishment."

"You mean his saloon?"

"On Saturday nights it is more like a dance hall." He tugged my arm as if I were a child reluctant to see the doctor about a bellyache.

"And you know how much Lady Jane loves to dance."

"That doesn't mean she'd go there," I insisted but not really believing it myself.

"We'll just go and see."

And so we went. Through the smoky window of Sullivan's place, I could make out some swirling bodies. Upon pressing my nose to the glass, I spotted the exquisite body that belonged to Jane. She filled out a red dress enough to dazzle the eyes but not so much as to cause you to believe she worked in such a place. Her auburn hair looked soft and neat, and I imagined her an hour earlier in her little blue house making extensive use of my expensive Christmas gift.

"That's her all right," said Wyatt, who had opened the door to look. "She reminds me of a cardinal, although it is the male of the species that is bright red, while the female bird tends to be a bit drabber, reddish but browner."

"Is that him she is dancing with?"

"Who else? He's not the kind of man that would let anyone cut in on him."

"I can't go in."

"You need to see the truth."

"I've seen enough from here."

"Don't be a coward, son."

"You want me to be the kind of man who will try to cut in anyway?"

"I want you to be a man who can deal with the current state of affairs instead of hiding away and pretending things aren't as they are. And then to be able to move on with his life."

"You don't even seem to mind that Matt Sullivan has moved in on Jane."

"I mind. He has a past as we all do. He has participated in violent acts. But a man has the right to reform, to become a better man, the kind of man that suits Jane."

"And I'm not the kind of man Jane wants. Is that what you're saying?"

"I'm saying we should see what they're like together. I want to get a better reading on both their feelings."

"And then you'll move on with your life, too?"

"I'm not moving on. I'm sticking with Dodge City and Lady Jane."

"Well, I can do that, too."

"If you say so, son. Shall we descend among the dancers?"

"Let's. I feel like I could use a drink."

Wyatt and I kept our eyes on the inseparable couple as we wound our way through the crowded room. Mr. Sullivan was a slick-haired dude in a frock coat who seemed more intent on staring at his partner than moving his feet. He had no reason to look our way, and Jane didn't notice us either. The music was still going strong when Matt Sullivan stopped swinging his partner and bowed deeply to her, which made her smile. When he lightly pressed his trigger finger to her nose she laughed and blew him a kiss. I disliked him more intensely than ever. He held up a finger as if to say he'd be back in one minute and moved over to the bar. The bartender was asking him something while pointing at the piano player. I saw my opportunity. Jane was standing alone on the dance floor.

"I'll just go ask her to dance," I said to Wyatt, but I didn't move right away. It was as if I needed his permission.

"I wouldn't if I were you."

"Of course, you wouldn't. You don't dance."

"It's not that. I'm reading her face. See for yourself how she is looking at him talk to the barkeep. It's clear she has eyes for only one man."

"I don't see that. She's probably wondering why he left her standing there."

"That's not how I read it. She'll not want to dance with you. And he won't want you to. Others here know it. Nobody else is asking her. Can't you see it, son? *L'amour*!"

"What makes you pass such a discouraging word? I bet you a week's pay she'll accept my polite invitation to have the next dance. I mean I would bet you if either of us were a betting man. What's the worst that can happen? You said Matt Sullivan gave up his guns, so he can't shoot me down in cold blood."

"I think a *no* from Lady Jane would hurt you just as much. But go for it if you must. We both want to learn the truth about the nature of their relationship."

I couldn't back down now. But I took only two steps when a popping sound and the crash of glass caused me to stumble. Out of the corner of my eye I saw a man fall at the bar and it wasn't the bald bartender. Mr. Sullivan went down, and the music stopped just as abruptly. Maybe other patrons screamed, but the only scream I heard came from the auburn-haired beauty in the red dress. Confusion followed as patrons scurried about, some moving toward the dead, unarmed body, others backing as far away from it as they could get without leaving the room. Jane did neither. She froze in mid-floor, mid-scream.

I wanted to continue toward her, but Wyatt cut in front of me as if to shield her. He pointed to where the deadly shot passed through the window I had been peering through earlier. A couple of men went outside to look. Wyatt took Jane in his arms, his back to the window and the door. "You are safe now," he told her. Her legs looked like they had gone limp. The little old man was somehow holding her up. He called me over. "Take her, son," he said. "I have something to do." I couldn't imagine what he possibly had to do, but we made the exchange smoothly. Jane was now in my arms.

Jane's face was pressing hard against my chest, about where my heart must be. Over her shoulder I saw Wyatt kneeling by the head of the dead man. He was examining as a doctor might or, to be more exact, a coroner. He stood up shaking his head. "That's a bloody big hole," he announced to the crowd around him. I heard. Jane heard. I must have loosened my grip on her. But instead of rushing to her man stretched out on the floor, she slipped through my arms. She had fainted. I managed to drop to my knees and keep her head from striking the dance floor.

Wyatt didn't notice Jane lying there with her head in my lap. He had already moved away from the bar to the door to question a buckskin-clad stranger who had just entered the saloon. I saw people crowding around them as if they suspected Wyatt had caught the killer. Somebody tapped me on the shoulder and asked if my girl had been shot. I said no, then he and another man helped me carry Jane to a room in back. It turned out to be Matt Sullivan's office, and the late Mr. Sullivan had already been carried there. His body took up the couch, so the bartender directed us to place Jane on the most comfortable of three chairs.

Jane was still out of it and I was helping to keep her in a seated position when Wyatt finally arrived in the office. He checked her breathing and shook her shoulder until she opened her eyes. "It's me," he said. "You're perfectly safe." Someone who announced he was a physician but was known more as a horse doctor appeared and took over, but Wyatt made a fuss and kept it up until the dead man had been transferred to the floor and Jane was comfortably stretched out on the couch, lying on her back with legs raised on cushions. "Nothing can be done for the dead," Wyatt told the doctor. "Our concern must be for the living."

Wyatt was also concerned about the identity of the shooter. He had determined it was not the buckskin man, who turned out to be a buffalo hunter just off the hunting grounds. Wyatt told everyone present what he had found out. Under questioning from

Wyatt, the observant hunter had provided valuable firsthand information. There had been a man at the window with a Smith & Wesson revolver. The man had hard, accusing eyes, a drooping mustache, a high-crowned hat, an unbuttoned, brown-checkered vest, and a smaller pistol protruding from his blouse. The man had climbed onto a dun horse with dark tips on its ears and zebra stripes on its legs and had ridden off proudly as if at the head of a Fourth of July parade.

"Hell," said the bartender. "That sounds a lot like Billy Brooks."

"Weren't they partners once?" said someone else.

"Sure thing, gambling partners," replied the bartender, now the only one still hovering over the late Mr. Sullivan. "But that don't matter. They had a falling out some weeks ago. They threatened to shoot each other on sight."

"Looks like Bully Brooks saw Matt Sullivan, but Sullivan didn't see Brooks," said Mr. Matters. "And Bully Brooks got Mr. Sullivan in his sights with a .44-caliber Model 3 Smith & Wesson."

"Billy has one of those for sure," said the bartender. "He also has a mean streak a mile wide."

"What did the Bully and your boss squabble about?" Wyatt asked.

"A couple of things. I remember there was this cardsharp that Mr. Sullivan caught with an ace up his sleeve or something along those lines. Billy Brooks wanted to shoot the man on the spot, but Mr. Sullivan insisted on escorting the sharp safely to the city limits."

"Doesn't sound like much of a reason to take up arms," said Wyatt. "But this is Dodge."

"It wasn't just that. There was this other matter between them."

"What matter was that? You see, I'm Mr. Wyatt Matters and I'm aiming to see that these needless shootings stop occurring in our fair city."

Despite my concern for Jane, I found myself wondering exactly what "fair" meant in that sentence.

"That right?" said the bartender. "You some kind of lawman?"

"No, just a citizen who believes in law and order. These killings will be stopped!"

"That's possible, I reckon. Too late for poor Mr. Sullivan, though. He wasn't even carrying a gun no more."

"I'd heard that."

"It was her doing. She was the cause."

"What are you talking about?"

The bartender pointed to the couch where Jane Hankin suddenly opened her eyes. "She got him to lay down his arms, even his emergency self-defense pistol. Billy Brooks called Mr. Sullivan a henpecked milksop. Billy took a shine to the lady in the red dress, too, you betcha. As partners they used to share things, including their women, fifty-fifty. Mr. Sullivan wouldn't have none of that no more, not with this fine woman, and that got Billy all riled up and filled with resentment. You ain't seen angry till you've seen Billy enraged. Poor Mr. Sullivan. 'Tis a pure shame. Sure hope she's all right, though. She seems like a sort of decent young lady."

Chapter Nine

It turned out Bully Brooks was serving some of Dodge's founding fathers as a "private lawman," and none of the town leaders held him accountable for shooting Matt Sullivan, who had never been viewed as a solid citizen. It didn't seem to make any difference that the deceased had been unarmed and had supposedly put away his guns to please the woman he reportedly was intent on marrying. Wyatt Matters, though he barely knew Mr. Sullivan, was up in arms about the situation and as usual was not shy about telling every merchant in town how a man like Brooks only compounded Dodge's urgent problem with gun violence.

Jane Hankin was not up in arms, but she was so devastated by the shooting that she was laid low. She had managed to get off that couch in the late Mr. Sullivan's office on her own and walk back home with Wyatt on one side of her and me on the other, both watching for any sign of a sudden relapse. It was only after we had gotten her back safely to her narrow bed in her little blue house that she collapsed. After that, we saw no sign that she wanted to get off that bed anytime soon.

Frederick and Matilda Zimmerman, who owned the house, were good about everything. Jane could stay there as long as she wanted and could return to her clerk job at the gun and jewelry store whenever she was ready. It would clearly take some time. She was too afraid to even go out to the outhouse, let alone to work or to the dance halls or to the Wright general store or to Mr. Matters' tent or to Matt Sullivan's funeral.

Jane didn't want to eat, only to sleep or to cry or to cry in her sleep. Her nervous condition was so alarming that after just two days, Matilda Zimmerman called for Dr. Thomas L. McCarty, who had arrived in Dodge City in November. His treatment, beginning on New Year's Eve, would include bloodletting, purgatives, morphine, and other drugs and medicines from his impressive stock. The results would not be good: scream-inducing nightmares, bellyaches, headaches, and lethargy only increased as the days went by in 1873.

"The unfortunate young woman still has the brain of a young girl — soft, vulnerable, and prone to influence from any and all sources," the doctor pronounced while none other than Mr. Matters was interrogating him in Jane's tiny kitchen four days into the new year.

"What do you mean by that, Doc? Jane is an intelligent young lady with a mind of her own."

"I assure you, sir, there is no demonic explanation for her condition. She was so attached to that gambler that when he took the fatal bullet to the back of the head, she felt as if the same bullet had penetrated her own cranium and caused brain damage. Of course, that is not physically possible, yet when one's head is so malleable at her age, there could be a very real root problem. Possibly she has lesions or other abnormalities on the brain, but it would take an autopsy to determine that."

"Any more of that excessive bloodletting and you will surely kill her."

"I understand your impatience, sir. But healing takes time. It might not seem that way to you at this difficult moment, but the girl is not a lost cause."

"I know that. I can't say the same for some of your treatment methods."

"Are you a physician? I think not. I know what's best for the patient."

"She doesn't need all that morphine either, Doc. For the love of Hippocrates, I don't want her to become morphine dependent."

"All your concerns are understood. But I have seen some good signs. I can tell you that though her heart palpitations are worrisome to her and others such as yourself, they are harmless. Although it is not readily apparent, she has plenty of life left in her. Rest assured, I shall continue to treat her, but what she needs more than anything is the will to live and to love again."

"I do concur with your last statement, Doctor. However, if I might suggest . . ."

"Yes, yes," I said. "If only Jane would live and love again. I am so willing to help her, if only she would let me. I would do anything."

"And who are you again, young man?" Dr. McCarty asked.

"I'm . . . I'm the man the patient *should* love."

"I am sorry she doesn't seem to acknowledge you. Has she no relatives?"

"She has us, Harry Hannum and me," said Wyatt. "Now as I was saying, Doc, I know you are a druggist at heart, but I would say it is unwise to overdo it with the drugs, let alone the bloodletting and purgatives."

"What may I ask is your profession, sir, to question me in this manner?"

"I am a man of many professions and none in particular. If you want a label, make it Renaissance man."

"Renaissance? In 1873 Dodge City? If you're worried about my credentials, I'll have you know I graduated from the Jefferson Medical College in Philadelphia, Pennsylvania, class of 1870."

"Experience is valuable, Doctor. I began my own study of medicine when you were still in short pants."

"Where? In your own home?"

"Sometimes. Sometimes at the better libraries. Sometimes in the field."

"Pre–Civil War, I presume."

"Frankly, my background and your background don't matter in the least. What matters is what's happening here and now. You have injected the patient with morphine as if it were a newfangled wonder drug."

"It did wonders back in St. Louis for those female patients I treated for menstrual cramps, morning sickness, and diseases of a nervous character."

"I wonder if you fully realize morphine's addictive properties. The truth is while it can relieve pain temporarily, it can cure little, certainly not the patient's agoraphobia."

"Agorawhat?" said Dr. McCarty, pressing

down on his bushy beard until it all but covered even his lower lip.

"Agoraphobia, the irrational fear of leaving one's own home and finding oneself in large, open spaces or crowded places from which escape is difficult."

The doctor mulled that over for some time, while I wished to escape Jane's kitchen, but not to go outside. I wanted to open the door to her bedroom and tell her how my love could save her if she would only love me back. It was funny but while I had considered her my true love for many weeks, I had never realized how much I truly loved her until now that she was sick and nobody seemed able to make her well again.

"Is that a legitimate term?" the doctor finally asked. "I paid strict attention at all times while attending Jefferson Medical College, and not once did I hear such a phobia mentioned by one of my professors or read about it in a textbook."

"Understandable. You would have needed some after-school study. It was just last year that pioneering German psychologist Carl Friedrich Otto Westphal coined the term in his article *'Die Agoraphobie, eine neuropathische Erscheinung.'*"

"That's a mouthful," the doctor said. "I suppose you know the cure, too?"

"Nothing is a sure thing, as you should well know. But a better bet than morphine and all the rest that you prescribe is *moral treatment,* which emphasizes spiritual development and requires healers and others who come into contact with the patient to show kindness and an optimistic spirit."

"You don't say, Mr. Renaissance Man."

"In this particular case, improper external conditions — to be specific the wanton use of guns and the overall violence in Dodge City — have induced what derangement we see today in this otherwise healthy young lady."

"What I don't quite understand, sir, is your stake in my patient's welfare? I know you aren't kin and I also know you're too old to be her . . ."

"Watch what you're saying, young doctor. Shooting off at the mouth can be a fatal disease in Dodge."

"Do I perceive any kind of threat in that last remark?"

"From me? Absolutely not. Not only do threats inevitably lead to trouble but I am also too peace-loving and too old for physical confrontations."

I'm not too old, I thought. But in my mind the doctor was doing the best he could. He was no specialist in whatever illness this special woman had. I finally asked the question that had been spinning inside my head since Wyatt and I arrived at the blue house to meet the doctor. “Can she receive visitors at this time, Doc?”

“She needs her rest after my examination. But I won’t object if you go in for just a moment . . . alone. You don’t talk *too* much.”

As eager as I was to open the bedroom door, I waited for permission from Mr. Matters. But he stepped in front of me when I tried to advance, not really to impede me but so that he could again challenge the doctor — with words, of course. “When you gain some valuable experience, Dr. McCarty, perhaps you’ll realize your shortcomings and heed my warning about the danger of morphine addiction.”

Dr. McCarty did not take the bait. He was about done talking . . . and certainly done listening. “I’ll be going,” he said, clutching his black bag of drugs and syringes to his chest. “Dodge has a horse doctor or two and at least one Renaissance man but for now is essentially a one-doctor town. And I am it. I’ll check back on the patient in a couple days. In the meantime, should her condition worsen, look me up at my office in the drugstore at the northwest corner of Second and Front Streets.”

"If her condition worsens, Doctor, your audacious treatment will be to blame."

No harm done. Wyatt was shooting off at the mouth again, but he was dealing with an unarmed professional man trained to cure people, not bury them. I made sure the doctor was leaving and then approached the bedroom door. Wyatt got there first.

"Remember — kindness," he whispered as he opened the door. "The moral treatment."

Yes, his comment annoyed me. When had I ever been anything less than kind to her or, for that matter, anyone else in Dodge? Although Jane wasn't eating much, I was the one who most often brought her food, usually the broths made by Matilda Zimmerman. And that wasn't all. It was me who brought her water and, when she wasn't up to swallowing, an occasional piece of crushed ice to munch on. It was me who took her chamber pot out both before and after work. What's more I didn't overtax her with excessive talk, as was the wont of Mr. Matters.

As usual, Jane lay in bed staring at the ceiling, more like trying to stare through the ceiling at the birds, the stars, the heavens above. I had darted around Wyatt to present Jane with a few leftover dried sunflowers I had found hanging inside his tent. When I held them under her nose, she sniffed, but it might have only been because her face was wet from a recent crying spell (probably the result of her hearing some of the word noise from the kitchen).

I accidentally dropped the small bunch of dried sunflowers on Jane's chest. "Later, when you are well, I'll give you fresh ones," I told her, but her face remained a blank, as if she didn't recognize me or even an act of kindness.

"That is hardly encouraging, son," said Wyatt. "It's January, and Kansas sunflowers don't even bloom until mid-August."

More than ever, I felt like a schoolboy who had just been reprimanded for bringing the teacher a rotten apple. And Mr. Matters, who must have been reading my mind, wasn't done yet. "You forgot to bring her one of those savory apples Mrs. Zimmerman had cached in her storage shed for winter." What's more, I saw a hint of a smile on Jane's face when Wyatt removed the dried sunflowers from her person and touched her forehead, I suppose to see if it was warm.

"You're going to be all right," he told her. "You have all the time in the world to get well. The demand for jewelry in Dodge isn't so great that you can't take a little time off, and Mr. and Mrs. Zimmerman have no other use for this building. I'll keep coming by to see how you are doing. And tomorrow, Harry will bring you one of Mrs. Z's apples . . . if he doesn't forget."

"Who?" said Jane.

"Why Harry Hannum, of course, the young man standing right here in front of you."

"Yes, Harry. And you are dear Wyatt, my friend. I must be a terrible bother."

"Not at all dear Lady Jane. You've been through a nightmare. But let's not dwell on the past. Let's talk of the future. We are into the new year, and you'll be picking spring flowers in a few months, picking those sun-loving sunflowers in late summer, picking out prime bison meat and choice corn for feasting in the fall . . . in short, picking up all the pieces in your life."

He was stealing my sunflower thunder, but it did get her to raise her head slightly off her pillow. For the longest time she stared at Wyatt as if she was trying to make sense of his oversized nose but then surprised him and me by freeing a hand from under the covers and blowing the old man a kiss just as she had done for Matt Sullivan on his last night on Earth. But then her head fell back, and she brought out her other hand. Slowly she folded her arms, crossed her hands on her belly, and closed her eyes. She was now perfectly still as if she had been laid out for her funeral and she was beyond pain. I wasn't.

"Please, please get well, my love," I pleaded. Her eyes stayed shut.

"I think that's enough talk right now," Wyatt said, a rare admission for him. "It wouldn't be kind to keep her awake when she clearly needs to rest."

I hesitated, so Wyatt took hold of my wrist and pulled. But I freed my arm. "I did forget the apple, but I didn't forget the poem."

"You wrote another poem? I didn't see you stick a piece of paper in your pocket."

"You don't see everything," I said. "Anyway, I didn't write the poem down. I did it all in my head and kept practicing it until the right moment came along."

"I'm impressed but are you certain this is the right moment? I'm not sure she'll be able to hear you."

"But you aren't sure."

"That's right. Let's see what effect it has on her. Recite away, son."

I cleared my throat and moved in closer to the head of the bed. It unnerved me when Jane's eyes suddenly popped open, but I looked up toward the ceiling, licked my dry lips, and spoke my piece in ABAB verse:

There was a man you thought you knew
You went so far as to call him Matt
He gave up his firearms just for you
And then his poor brain went splat.
What is a beautiful young lady to do?
Should she go to bed and lay flat?
Or should she change her point of view
And cry out, "There'll be no more of that!"

I don't know what I was thinking. It hadn't sounded so bad when I practiced it alone. It didn't go well. Mr. Matters threw up his hands, accidentally knocking off his top hat. He then covered his ears, but he couldn't have missed hearing Jane; she cried out that loudly: "Splat! Splat! Splat! Billy Brooks is a bully rat!" Under different circumstances, her words might have sounded like part of a nursey rhyme. But as it was, she followed it up with a scream and a wild waving of her arms as if protecting her face from a swarm of bees. Wyatt sent me into the kitchen and began the difficult task of trying to calm the patient. I sat on a stool and pouted miserably but at least did show great patience. Wyatt finally came out after nearly half an hour. He didn't say a word. All the way back to his tent he gave me the rare silent treatment.

"Need I say a word?" he asked at the flap of his tent.

"Splat," I said, bowing my head.

"That's right. You'd better go to your room at the general store and think about what you did tonight. I can only hope that it didn't set Lady Jane back too much."

"Amen," I said.

He let me have that last word. Think I did on the long walk to the store and the long time I spent lying with my eyes wide open on the cot in back. I could not excuse myself. I told myself that, yes, poetry could be beautiful in the hands of the masters, but that in the hands of amateurs it could be in terribly poor taste. I vowed to never rhyme again. And maybe ten minutes later I found myself repeating the first two lines of the only lullaby I remembered my mother ever singing to me:

Twinkle, twinkle, little star
How I wonder what you are

It is hard to say whether Wyatt Matters or I showed a greater concern for the welfare of bedridden Jane Hankin. We were both attending to her regularly, usually at different times, sometimes bringing food, sometimes helping her eat that food, and often reassuring her that her nervous condition was only temporary. The words, of course, came easier for Wyatt, and I admit that while she once or twice almost smiled when Wyatt visited, she was prone to frowns when I showed up. I suspected she was worried I might decide to share another dreadful poem. I became discouraged at her lack of responses to my gestures of kindness, but I persevered. Jane Hankin had become my *cause* even though not before or after the harrowing shooting had she showed me one-quarter the attention she gave the late Matt Sullivan. I admit I was jealous of her memory of Mr. Sullivan and her near smiles for the smooth-talking Mr. Matters.

Because poor Jane occupied so much of our attention, Wyatt and I let the cold days of January slide along with little commitment to our mentor-protégé relationship. During my day job at the store, I had to fight my wandering mind to think about customers instead of the ailing Jane. One morning, though, a buffalo hunter called "Prairie Dog" Dave Morrow (apparently, he once raised those little barking beasts) pulled up in front of the store and caught not only my attention but the attention of most of Dodge. It wasn't him so much as what he was carrying in the wagon bed — the carcass of a white buffalo. Mr. Wright paid $1,000 on the spot to take possession of the rare beast. I don't know if anyone ate the meat rare or otherwise, but my boss had the head mounted and shipped to Kansas City for display. The only one around who found this business offensive was Mr. Matters. He had long argued that eliminating the great herds of bison was the greatest sin being perpetuated by the white man against the Indian. And now he claimed to anyone who didn't run away from him that shooting a single white bison and turning it into a spectacle was dishonoring every Plains Indian who had ever lived.

"The white bison," he told Mr. Wright, "is sacred to all the tribes. The hide of a white bison is a revered talisman, a possession beyond price."

"In the civilized world, Mr. Matters, everything has a price," my boss replied. "I thought it was quite generous of me to give the great head away so the American public can marvel at it. As for the white hide, I paid hard cash for it, my wife thinks it is gorgeous, and it shall hang proudly on a favored wall in my home."

I refused to take sides in the matter, though I didn't turn down an invitation from Alice Wright to come to the Wright house for a look at the prize wall hanging. And afterward, I raved to Jane Hankin about the brilliance and softness of the hide and told her that while I rarely longed to be rich like my boss, I wished now that I could have purchased the hide as a gift to her. She issued a tortured groan as if I had done the shooting and slaughtering myself. I'm sure it had something to do with Wyatt Matters' influence over her along with the fact that the killing of any kind of man or beast tended to make her wail like a windstorm across the Plains.

As January moved along with several blasts of north wind, it was clear that despite our best efforts and the treatments of Dr. McCarty, Jane wasn't improving. Without stating the obvious, we had both resolved to never abandon her. But on January 13 as we stood inside his tent before his fire pit with wine glasses in our hands, Wyatt insisted we make New Year's resolutions even though it was two weeks late. He credited the Babylonians with making the first New Year's resolutions as part of a twelve-day ceremony during the reign of Hammurabi during the eighteenth-century BC, and how could I or any other living soul in Dodge City challenge that? But on this night, I was in no mood for ancient history. As far as I was concerned, his "BC" stood for *beyond comprehension.* I didn't even like to think back to my own "BC" — *Bladensburg childhood.* He befuddled me. Here was a forty-two-year-old man whose head was full of timelines through the ages and historic facts from around the world, yet he had nothing to say about his own history — where he was born and raised, how he came to know so much, how he could afford to live without any visible means of support, and what had turned him into such a proponent of law and order.

"It seems silly to make resolutions now," I said, because I couldn't think of anything except to be of service to Jane Hankin every day, and I was already doing that even though she never rewarded me with a smile or a thank you.

"Titus Livius, better known to us as Livy, wrote in his 27 BC *History of Rome,* 'Better late than never.' Of course, he said it in Latin, but I'd have to check my notes in my trunk to give you the accurate phrase, something *sero quam* something."

"Don't bother. I believe you."

"Much later, 1386 to be exact, Geoffrey Chaucer said it in English in 'The Yeoman's Tale' from his *The Canterbury Tales.* I do recall Mr. Chaucer's exact wording: *For better than never is late; never to succeed would be too long a period.*"

"Well, I'm sorry, but I think it's too late in January to make a resolution."

"Never say it is too late. I'll go first." Wyatt cleared his throat, took a sip of wine, and then held his glass up to the smoke swirling upward. "I resolve to within ten years create a Dodge Utopia with me as mayor, you as vice mayor, and Lady Jane as director of dance and peaceful assembly."

It sounded wonderful but at the same time pure whimsy. Wyatt, though, was not one to indulge in nonsensical fantasy. We clanked glasses and drank to his resolution.

"A utopia, you say. Right here in Kansas?"

"Why not? I've been stressing utopian ideals all along. You don't remember me mentioning the one that existed in Indiana back in the twenties — New Harmony?"

"Sure. I mean I do recall you speaking of *harmony,* but . . ."

"Social reformer Robert Owen wanted a community where social equality — for women, too — would flourish and its members could study science and natural philosophy without the encumbrances of capitalism. Many of the settlers traveled by boat to get to New Harmony, so they referred to their journey as a 'Boatload of Knowledge.' Doesn't that sound ideal? Of course, here on the Kansas prairie we'd have to call it a

'Wagonload of Knowledge,' or a 'Train of Knowledge,' but you get the basic principle. In time we'd change the name of Dodge City to New Honesty, and we'd fill *our* utopia with people who go against society's grain in that they pursue knowledgeable gain instead of monetary gain."

I could safely say that Mr. Matters went against society's grain by pursuing limitless knowledgeable gain, but he must have at one time pursued monetary gain because he was sitting pretty in his tent without having to labor, gamble, steal, borrow, or beg. As for me, I didn't so much go against the grain as get buried underneath it.

"If I want to fit in at New Honesty," I said, "I'd better increase my knowledge tenfold."

"Keep listening to me with both ears and you can't go wrong. How'd you like Mr. Wright Can Do No Wrong to stop calling you Harry the Lowly Clerk and start addressing you as The Honorable Vice Mayor Hannum?"

Mr. Wright had never called me *Harry the Lowly Clerk,* but I wanted to hear more.

"And Jane would really have a position in the governing of your New Honesty?"

"In *our* New Honesty. You better believe it. You don't think she'll hold that desultory position in bed forever, do you? She'll be directing and dancing up a storm, a peaceful storm. They'll be no guns in New Honesty — you can count on that."

"I sure hope she'll be dancing with the vice mayor."

"No doubt. As vice mayor you'll be working hand in hand with the director of dance and peaceful assembly in curbing all wicked behavior and criminal activities."

His vision of the future was too good to be true. He must have known that. He was just saying things I wanted to hear. Dr. McCarty had all but given up on his beautiful bedridden patient. I had started to wonder myself if she would ever dance again with anybody.

I felt heavy in the head and tired in the legs. The fire was suddenly producing too much heat and the tent was becoming smoky. I set my glass on the ground and moved away from the fire pit. I sat slouched against one of Wyatt's valuable trunks and watched him tend to the fire and smoke.

"Whatever happened to that place in Indiana, that New Harmony?" I asked.

"Never mind that. What is important is that it lasted four years and we can improve on past utopias."

"But with all that knowledge, why couldn't those New Harmonians make it work?"

"Amid internal disputes over money, the community collapsed. But that is neither here nor there because money matters would be of no concern in New Honesty."

"But money always comes up. Store owners like Mr. Wright and Mr. Zimmerman earn money by selling goods, and people like me get a drop of it by helping to sell those goods. Likewise, the hunters earn money by shooting bison, the farmers earn money by planting things, the gamblers earn money by betting on things, saloon owners earn money by serving drinks, the sporting girls earn money by engaging men, and you earn money by . . . I'm not sure."

"I catch your drift, son. But now it is time — past time, actually — for you to make your resolutions just as men and women have been doing since ancient Babylonia!"

"More than one?" I asked, my mind still a blank, most likely because I lacked resolve.

"One for starters. You do want to improve yourself, don't you?"

"OK. I resolve not to drink whiskey or carry a six-shooter."

"You hardly imbibe now and are gun-shy. That doesn't work. You need to resolve to *not* do something you are now doing."

"OK. I resolve *not* to write any more poems and certainly *not* to give any to Jane if I do."

"Weak. Let me help you. On your feet and pick up your glass."

I obeyed mindlessly.

"Repeat after me: I, Harry Hannum, resolve to put my full trust in Wyatt Matters and never again doubt his motives for educating me and for turning me into a knowledgeable citizen of Dodge City and in time into an enlightened vice mayor of New Honesty."

I did so, though I couldn't remember all the words and he needed to repeat some of them for me. Once I was done saying all *his* words, I sighed heavily as if I had just made my vows at a shotgun wedding. Wyatt gave me a quick pat on the back and then broke open a second bottle of what he called "native viticulture" — red wine that he said was grown along the Missouri River near Kansas City. He carefully refilled my glass, as if spilling one drop would create an explosion. We touched glasses and they stayed touched because he didn't make a toast right away.

"To the absolute recovery of Lady Jane," he finally said.

"Absolutely," I said, but I held my glass below my chin and pictured poor Jane Hankin lying in that bed, just a shell of herself.

"Go ahead, young man. Drink up. A second glassful is all right. It's a far cry from the reckless whiskey drinking conducted by the young louts of Dodge."

I scrunched up my face as I swallowed, but it went down smoothly.

"Now we can begin working to transform Dodge into a better place," he said between sips. "Let's get to work, son."

"At this hour? I'm fixin' to go to bed. It's an early workday tomorrow at the general store."

"Ah, yes, working for Trader Bob, one of those merchants, bison hunters, gamblers, hucksters, pimps, and other greedy men on the make who moved west with the tide to swim in the sea of sin and clever deceit that is today's Dodge City. But you are probably right. Not much we can do tonight."

With that pronouncement, Wyatt refilled our glasses. He had worked himself up a mite, and as we began our third round of wine, he didn't have the patience for just sipping.

Chapter Ten

On January 16, 1873, Isaac Young presented a copy of the completed Ford County census to Wyatt Matters and me. It showed 609 valid citizens. Wyatt believed that only nine or ten of them had the necessary character to qualify as citizens of future New Honesty. He considered himself a *Man on the Remake,* virtually the antithesis of all those *Men on the Make,* but he did have something in common with some of them — a desire for law and order.

The next afternoon, as he was coming out of Jane Hankin's place shaking his head and I was heading in with a pot of Matilda Zimmerman's bison bone broth, he spoke to me as if announcing his candidacy for public office: "I have no political, religious, or self-righteous reasons for wanting law and order in Dodge, and guns don't scare me to death as they do the unfortunate Lady Jane and to a lesser extend my young protégé, but how can there be education, enlightenment, harmony, and honesty in our community when too many thick-skulled hard cases are loitering about and wantonly shooting off firearms this winter as boys would firecrackers on the Fourth of July?" I guessed that the name of the murdered Matt Sullivan must have come up in his conversation with Jane.

I gave him a quick nod but then rushed past him into the house, only wanting to feed Jane Hankin, not to listen to another lecture on law and order — a topic that Wyatt had beaten to death to me in the tent and to Frederick Zimmerman, Robert Wright, and the other founding businessmen of Dodge. For the first time, I was able to get Jane to sit up in bed so that I could sit on the edge and more easily spoon-feed her the broth. As she seemed more at ease with me, I began to tell her manufactured stories about my childhood in Bladensburg, Maryland, such as how my father used a cat-o'-nine-tails to frighten away a man who had been bullying me, how my mother rescued a puppy from drowning during a flood, and how I once won a prize in grade school for my flawless recitation of Alfred Lord Tennyson's poem "Tears, Idle Tears," which I in truth was unfamiliar with until Mr. Matters recited it from memory two days before.

Jane could listen as she slurped, which I saw as major progress. She was getting better and getting to know me at the same time — or so I thought. I wasn't really the idiot who wrote about Matt Sullivan's head going *splat.* I was the gentle soul who was helping her cope with her condition and was considerate enough to never again mention Mr. Sullivan or his violent end.

"You are looking good, Jane," I said, holding back the spoon so I could study her wet lips without the slurping. "I mean you're looking better; you've always looked good."

She reached out as if to grab the spoon, so I went back to work. I noticed on her dresser my Christmas gift to her — the three-piece silver-plated mirror brush and comb set. I considered fetching the mirror and holding it up to her face so she could see just how much better she looked than a month ago. And that's not all. I imagined myself brushing and combing that loose auburn hair. It seemed too risky, though. It was something a lover might do, not that I thought the gambler Matt Sullivan had ever once combed her hair. I decided it would be better to talk about something else.

"Since I've told you a few things about my childhood, maybe you'd like to do the same," I said. "All I know is you had a kind of rough time growing up in Lawrence, Kansas, which must have been an unsettling place throughout the Civil War. Naturally, if you don't want to talk about those days, I completely under . . ."

Jane's hands jerked in the air as if in a spasm. The left one clipped my left ear. The right one knocked the spoon away, causing broth to splash over her and run down her chin. At first, she allowed me to dab at the wetness with a towel kept at bedside for just such an accident. For the first time I got a good look at her chin dimple, which was more substantial than I realized. I paid special attention to it with the towel.

"What the hell are you doing!" she screamed.

In my shock, I dropped the towel. I had seen plenty of her melancholia since she became bedridden but never her anger. She wasn't done. She put a hand on my Adam's apple as if to fend me off or else choke me — I couldn't tell which.

"I'm . . . I'm . . ." I couldn't remember what I was doing.

"You aren't my husband."

"That's right, Jane. I . . ." It crossed my mind that Jane had either secretly married Matt Sullivan or intended to and was already considering him her husband. "You do know who I am, don't you?"

She rubbed her eyes, poked me gently in the nose, and then let her head fall back on the pillow. "Sorry," she said. "I thought you were my . . . somebody else."

"I'm Harry, Harry Hannum."

"You aren't him. Where is he?"

"Your . . . your husband?"

"No, no. Forget I even mentioned him."

"All right. I can do that."

"You aren't the nice man. Where is the nice man?"

"I am the nice man."

"You can't fool me. You are *not* him. He was telling me the story of Joan of Arc, how she was the savior of France. But he never finished because I fell asleep. Whatever happened to Joan. There was something about a fire."

"You must mean Mr. Matters. He never told me that story. But I'm sure it must have a happy ending. He'll probably be back tomorrow to tell you the rest."

"There are no happy endings. We all die horrible deaths."

"You're not going to die, Jane." My hands hovered close to her face for a minute before I dared brush away strands of auburn hair from her eyes. "Now you can see who I am, right?"

"Don't touch me! You are just like him."

"Mr. Matters?"

"No, no! My husband. Wyatt is my dear friend."

She looked too good to be delirious but what other explanation was there? I didn't look anything like the late Matt Sullivan. The only thing I had in common with him was our interest in Jane. I didn't dare try to get clarification. I didn't even dare remind her I was Harry Hannum or to ask her if there was anything else that I could do for her. She might take it the wrong way.

"I'm glad he is not here now," she blurted out.

"You mean Wyatt Matters?"

"My husband!" She closed her eyes.

"That's it, Jane. Get yourself a good sleep."

She said nothing more. I took a seat on the only chair in the room and waited to see if her eyes would open. It was a Friday night in Dodge City, but there was nowhere else I wanted to be. For a while I just watched her breathe. When my eyes grew tired, I closed them and pleasantly imagined her dancing in her red dress without a partner. But not for long. Gunshots woke me — distant shots but not too distant, from the nearest dance hall, I guessed. Jane must have heard the shots, too, because her head jerked off her pillow and she screamed as if her loose auburn hair had caught on fire. When I went to reassure her that the shots were distant, she screamed again even louder. "I'm Harry," I said over and over, but that important information didn't seem to register in her confused head.

It was man about town Wyatt Matters who brought the news; he had been in the middle of it. After visiting with Jane, he had decided to make the rounds in Dodge's saloons and dance halls to assess the excess of unruly behavior so he could make his report in the morning to the city founders. The latest shooting affair involved half a dozen young men who had been doing more drinking than dancing. Wyatt had urged them to do less of the former and more of the latter or else they might end up shot down in the prime of life just like Matt Sullivan and so many others. Two in the increasingly disorderly party took offense, believing the dandy in the top hat and purple bowtie was threatening them. Both drew on Wyatt, who smiled, tipped his hat, called them almost sons to him, and then quoted an ancient Chinese general named Sun Wu four times in succession: "He will win who knows when to fight and when not to fight"; "The greatest victory is that which requires no battle"; "Who wishes to fight must first count the cost"; and "It is easy to love your friend, but sometimes the hardest lesson to learn is to love your enemy." The six-shooters wavered in the hands of the belligerent pair as they considered the hardest lesson to learn and perhaps sought to identify their real enemy. "It's not me, fellows," Wyatt told them. "Listen to the advice of General Sun and we all shall live to enjoy another moon."

"Damned if I will," said the smaller of the two, but he holstered his Colt. "We don't want no Chinamen in Dodge."

"That's a fact," said the other. "We come from Idaho. The celestials been overrunning the territory."

"Listen, fellows. The white man can live in peace with the yellow man, red man, and black man. No need for trouble if we treat all men alike, live by the same laws, deny no man the liberty to go where he pleases. You see where I'm coming from?"

"We know where you're going, dandy man!" shouted the taller one, who still had his gun out. "Git!"

The smaller but bigger shouldered of the two began to push Wyatt toward the door. "You belong out there with General Moon, you damned Boot Hill dodger."

"Hey, I'm not Sun or Moon. This is Wyatt Matters speaking. This isn't Idaho.

It's Kansas, and Dodge is my hometown. Why, I'm one of the original citizens. I have your best interests at heart. I am no man's enemy."

"You ain't no man at all," yelled the pusher.

Wyatt kept talking, quoting himself instead of Sun Wu, but he also kept backing toward the front door, ready to call it a night. Some young men were just too roostered to reason with; he'd give it another try some other night.

"Leave grandpa alone," shouted a dance hall regular named Barney Cullen who had previously heard several of Wyatt's impromptu lectures on Front Street. "If anyone gits, it'll be you, Southers."

And just like that gunfire filled the dance hall. As was often the case in such drunken affairs, nobody was sure who fired the first shot. Before backing out the front door unscathed, Wyatt saw Cullen, Southers, and a third man, Edward Hurley, go down. It wasn't clear whose side Hurley was on, but he apparently was the only one who never got up again.

Despite the late hour, Wyatt came back to the blue house to check on Jane. She was wide awake now, having screamed herself to hoarseness while rejecting my attempts to comfort her. It was as if I were a stranger who had invaded her sanctuary and made himself at home. Yet, she welcomed the old man. Wyatt and I were standing in the doorway between the kitchen and bedroom when he told me in a half whisper about Dodge's latest shooting affair. I wasn't sure how much Jane heard from her bed, but she stayed calm, as if she were listening to a tall tale that she had enough sense not to believe. Afterward, Wyatt went to sit beside her on the bed.

"I am not afraid," she told Wyatt. "If I stay under the covers, nobody can hurt me."

Wyatt was obscuring my view of Jane, but I didn't dare get any closer because I wasn't sure how she would react. I wanted to shout out to her: *For God's sake, I'm no stranger! I am Harry Hannum, the man who loves you most.* Although Wyatt had convinced me he was not after the hand of Jane, I felt queasy when he soothed her brow with his two chubby but soft hands. There hadn't been much time to get jealous about Matt Sullivan, but there was no denying that the green-eyed monster (introduced by William Shakespeare in 1604, according to Wyatt) was lurking inside me.

I finally edged in closer to better hear what they were talking about. Wyatt was carrying on about ancient times, how an ancient

Athenian named Thucydides said that an armed society was a lawless and backward one and that *not* bearing arms differentiated civilized Greeks from barbarians. "Let me just add my dear Lady Jane," Wyatt continued, his voice seeming to soothe her as much as his soft hands, "that Thucydides possessed an evolutionary — and might I add optimistic — view of history, believing that one day even the barbarians of the world would refrain from carrying weapons. And so sweet child, do not despair. There is hope yet for the people of Dodge City, Kansas. Even the oafish louts amongst us — the descendants of Bully Brooks and his like — shall in time recognize the error of their ways. They may even lay down their whiskey bottles along with their six-guns. Meanwhile, dancing will continue to be, as John Dryden once remarked, 'the poetry of the foot." But dance halls will be transformed into decent safe artistic places where fun-loving but sober dancers, young and old, can offer the truest expression of a people. Jane Austen correctly observed that 'to be fond of dancing was a certain step towards falling in love.' You, my dear, shall dance again, shall fall in love again, shall live a full fulfilling life. In short, as difficult as it is to realize at this moment, the tragic, underhanded death of Matt Sullivan is *not* the end of your world or of mankind's evolution."

Her head popped up and her eyes were open wide in astonishment. I expected the mention of Mr. Sullivan's name to give rise to another screaming session. Instead, she offered Wyatt more than half a smile — no doubt her most expansive one since the Sullivan shooting — and allowed him to plant a kiss on her forehead and caress her cheek.

"May he rest in peace," she said, closing her eyes and purring like a cat curled up by a fireplace. Wyatt finally gently lowered her head as if placing a baby in a cradle. When her head reached the pillow, she wore a look of utopian contentment.

I was impressed by Wyatt's performance. I had to admit I had never showed that much tenderness toward Jane or anyone else, not even Elizabeth Pepper of Atchison. Even though I had bombarded Miss Pepper with what I judged to be affectionate kisses, it had never soothed her. I never had the words she wanted to hear. But she was more to blame. Had she ever understood why I was dissatisfied with my work at the Atchison grain mill or why I couldn't find anything good to say about my childhood? She had never permitted me to cry on her shoulder and then she gave me the cold shoulder, running off with the railroad man. I wanted to slap my own face as I thought: *Why the hell am I thinking of that false-hearted woman when Jane Hankin is right in front of me.*

"She's asleep now," Wyatt whispered.

"Good," I said, now hovering over Wyatt's shoulder for a better look at my true love. "You should have heard her scream when she heard those shots from the dance hall. Maybe she thought Matt Sullivan was getting it all over again."

"We need her to get out of this bed, of course, but I have to say it's a good thing she was here and not dancing with that Ed Hurley tonight. That might have been *too* much for her. She was acquainted with him, too, you know. Mr. Hurley used to play poker with Mr. Sullivan."

"Really? Dodge is a small world."

"Small and violent, much too violent. We'll have to keep handling Lady Jane with kid gloves."

I nodded even though I imagined handling her, with and without gloves. Considering her condition, it made me feel guilty. "Sometimes she doesn't even seem to know who I am," I admitted. "I've done all these things for her, yet she . . ."

"Stop. Are you feeling sorry for her or for yourself?"

"I better go to bed."

"Right. Work in the morning as usual?"

"As usual. You going to your tent?"

"No, I'll stay. She's at peace now. But I want to be here should she wake up screaming."

Jane Hankin didn't wake up screaming — as far as I know — but she did wake up the next morning, and I assumed Wyatt Matters was still there, though I didn't try to confirm it. Jane was still my *cause,* but the way she responded so much more to my mentor, I decided to back off a little and just bring her food with only a few sympathetic but unthreatening comments and no touching whatsoever. The general store work kept me busy enough during the day, and at night I made my deliveries to Jane, listened to Wyatt's lectures, and once a week sat with the Wright kids while Robert and Alice socialized with such other leading citizens as the Zimmermans and the Coxes, who had reopened the former Essington House, now calling it the Dodge House.

In the wake of the dance hall shooting that cost Edward Hurley his life, Wyatt Matters picked up his campaign to bring law and order to Ford County and Dodge. He had the time since he didn't have a job and wasn't looking for one and couldn't spend every waking moment educating me or soothing Jane. In fact, on the night of January 30 while I was entertaining the Wright children with marbles, spinning tops, and dominoes, Wyatt was pressing upon the Dodge House crowd that the killing of Hurley and wounding of Cullen and Southers was the last straw.

As usual he was going about it at the wrong place (the Wrights, Zimmermans, and Coxes were trying to enjoy their bison tongues and livers) and in the wrong way (accusing this orderly crowd with feasting every night while the body count in Dodge kept mounting). Finally, George Cox, tired of listening with his mouth full, had two employees escort Wyatt out of the Dodge House.

Undaunted, Wyatt moved down the street to Alfred Peacock's billiard saloon. Later he filled me in on what transpired there. Men manipulating cue sticks for money were not inclined to hear him out either, but Wyatt was persistent in getting his point across, paying special attention to a skilled player named McDermott. Wyatt, though he claimed to not know one end of a cue stick from the other, bested the man in a billiards game in a ten-dollar wager, all the while lecturing him on fair play and lawbreaking.

Mr. McDermott was fighting mad and demanded a rematch. Instead, Wyatt led him over to the corner and accused him, based on his own personal investigation, of having been the one who shot down Hurley during the dance hall melee thirteen days ago.

"Maybe I did, maybe I didn't," McDermott said. "What's it to you?"

"It wasn't a fair fight. You shot Hurley when he wasn't looking."

"That's right. He was looking at Nellie River, the dance hall queen. He thought she was his girl, I thought she was my girl, and I don't know what Nellie thought except maybe it would be all right if two men fought over her."

"I see, so there were extenuating circumstances?"

"I don't follow you. If I didn't shoot Hurley, he'd of shot me sooner or later. That's the way it was."

"Maybe so. All I'm saying is it didn't have to be that way."

"Not if Hurley would have released his hold on Nellie."

"That's not what I mean, young man. What I mean is if nobody had brought guns to the dance, nobody would have been shot at all. Guns and whiskey and dance hall girls don't mix well."

"That's pure fool talk. And again, I ask you, what's it to you?"

"I was there that night. I saw Hurley go down. Only later did I learn from a fellow who called himself Scotty that it was you who shot down his friend."

"So you were there. Hurley couldn't have had too many friends. Who are you, Hurley's daddy or something?"

"Never saw the man until the night he was shot. What interests me is making Dodge City a safer, better place. I'm not a lawman so I can't do anything about what happened that night. But I can tell you Dodge needs lawmen like a bottle of good wine needs a cork, and those lawmen need to enforce an ordinance that prohibits the carrying of guns within city limits. And young men like you need to . . ."

"Shut the hell up. I don't need you to tell me what I need to do. You come in here telling me it wasn't a fair fight when you don't know your ass from a hole in the ground. You must be plain loco."

"Not so plain, Mr. McDermott, and there's no doubt I know far more than you will ever know even if you lived to be eighty — which is about as likely as seeing a kangaroo in Kansas."

At that point, McDermott decided to

point his six-shooter at Wyatt, just to scare him out of the billiards parlor perhaps or maybe to force him to engage in a rematch. It is doubtful he would have pulled the trigger on a man twice his age who had only been talking. In any case, he never got the chance. A man with a cue ball face came out of nowhere and stepped between them, his six-gun already out. Without a word he plugged McDermott in the chest and watched his victim fall. "Code of the West," said the gunman, showing no immediate need to flee. "A man's got to avenge an injustice done to a friend. Ed Hurley was my friend."

"I understand, Scotty," said Wyatt. It was no time to give a lecture.

Chapter Eleven

Many members of the Dodge business community who hadn't viewed McDermott's shooting of Hurley as the "final straw," now suggested John "Scotty" Scott's revenge shooting of McDermott was indeed "the straw that broke the horse's back." The thinking went that some friend of McDermott's would eventually shoot Scotty, and then a friend of Scotty's would be out to kill Scotty's killer — a circle of merciless retribution that could go on indefinitely. Mr. Matters said it was more proper to say *the camel's back,* based on an ancient Arab proverb about overloading those desert beasts of burden, but he didn't fuss over that minor point. He was too delighted that Dodge was finally listening to him and seemed on the verge of bringing in official lawmen to curb the violence.

Among those convinced that the deadly atmosphere in Dodge must change was

Frederick Zimmerman, whose thinking was much influenced by his wife and by the alarming condition of their bedridden employee, Jane Hankin, if not by Wyatt Matters' endless lecturing on the subject. On February 9 Mr. Zimmerman scurried into the general store and right past me to confer with Robert Wright on the necessity of more law and order.

"So far," Mr. Zimmerman said, "it has been mostly bad men killing bad men, but not always, and sometimes innocent bystanders have been terribly damaged by the recklessness. We must put a stop to it, just as the Army has put a stop to Indian raiding and murdering."

"I tell you, Fred, we aren't going to get any help from the boys in blue out at Fort Dodge," said Mr. Wright. "It's up to us to act! We have no other choice, my friend."

"Act? In what way?"

"By organizing a vigilance committee. Look what the Montana vigilantes did less than ten years ago at the gold mining towns of Virginia City and Bannack. They hanged a couple dozen road agents over a two-month period and stopped the violence."

"Oh. That sounds rather drastic. And Dodge isn't a gold-mining boomtown."

"But we are booming with buffalo hides

and our businesses are flourishing. Bad men come into Dodge every day. We have to protect our property and our profits, my friend . . . and naturally our fragile women."

"Ah, yes. Miss Hankin still shutters at any loud bang, whether from a firearm or not. Matilda and I are worried sick about the poor girl. It's been more than a month since the murder of the man she hoped to marry."

Hoped to marry. Those words stung. I couldn't wait to get off work and relay that overheard conversation to Wyatt Matters. He had nothing to say about Jane's former hopes or her current seemingly hopeless condition. Instead, he provided more details than I wanted to know about the Montana vigilantes of the 1860s as well as the San Francisco vigilantes of the 1850s. His conclusion, based on those two historic examples, was that vigilantism did not translate to justice and that taking the law into one's own hands was never justified. I offered no opinion. But Jane was on my mind, and I was sure she wouldn't tolerate hangings any more than she could shootings. I excused myself from Wyatt's tent to see about Jane's Sunday evening meal

On my way there, I saw Front Street in an uproar because a gang of roughs were impeding the movement of citizens and occasionally firing their pistols into the air. I was confronted by two men carrying half-empty whiskey bottles. They introduced themselves as "Texas" and "Antelope" and demanded to know my name and whether I was part of the dirty, rotten vigilantes who had ordered them out of Dodge. I said I knew nothing about any vigilantes in this neck of the woods and for some reason told them to call me either "Kansas" or "Prairie Chicken." My response not only pleased them enough not to rough me up or shoot me but also amused them so much that they wrapped their arms around me and tried to corral me so that we could become better acquainted at Tom Sherman's dance hall. There had been plenty of trouble before at Sherman's and I expected more of it right soon, so when the pair of rowdies got distracted by a passing lady carrying two hat boxes, I broke free and ran toward Jane's place behind Walnut Street. I felt fortunate not to take a bullet in the back.

Indeed, there was big trouble at the dance hall that night, but, as Wyatt later suggested, it wasn't brought on by Texas and Antelope. The recently formed vigilance committee, twenty in number, again ordered the pair to leave town, this time backing their demand with an array of six-shooters, rifles, and shotguns. Texas not only refused to holster his gun but also waved it around like a Lone Star flag. A shot was fired, then another and another, and maybe fifty more after that. Texas died on the spot. The wounded Antelope dropped dead while in flight. The newspapers said that twenty balls were found in each of their bodies, and identified the vigilante victims as Charles Hill, alias Texas, and Ed Williams, alias Antelope.

The identities of the vigilante committee members, who had made vows of secrecy for their mutual protection, were never revealed. Wyatt suspected, since Matilda Zimmerman was so distraught afterward, that her gun shop owner husband had handed out weapons to the vigilantes who needed them and might have even been at the scene of the shootings. Wyatt also told me that Alice Wright told him she was proud of her husband for leading the effort to rid Dodge of desperadoes. All I know is that I was at Jane's place at the time and couldn't keep her from hearing all that disturbing gunfire. Trying to cover her ears with two of her pillows backfired on me. "It's all right, Jane," I said, wondering if my voice could ever sound soothing. "Nobody will hurt you. You need a nice long rest." She dreadfully misinterpreted my words. She screamed and tried to hit me with one of the pillows. "Murder!" she yelled and then she screamed some more. "Leave me alone! Don't touch me! I know why you are here! You had no right to come find me! Get out of my house! I shall not be killed! Murder, murder, murder!"

I realized what was happening in her distressed head. She had no idea that I was Harry Hannum. She believed that not only were there many men outside her door trying to shoot each other but also one madman who had broken into her house and was attempting to smother her. Helpless to help, I fled to the kitchen and waited until I heard no more screams. When she began to murmur, I figured she'd survive the night without me, and I fled the house.

Dr. Thomas L. McCarty came around the next day and pronounced Jane Hankin had suffered a major setback in her recovery. He made three admissions. One, he had never seen a case like hers in his life. Two, he could not explain what had triggered this far-fetched fear for her life. Three, he had no idea how to treat a head that was wounded inside.

Wyatt Matters was incensed by the vigilante action of February 9. Wyatt believed — and he wasn't shy about telling the whole town about it — that Dodge had taken a step back in its development as a community with the extralegal killings of Texas Hill and Antelope Williams, even though sanctioned by the so-called best citizens. Since he was so incensed and I was under his influence, I became slightly incensed, too. But I drew the line when he told me that because Robert Wright was among the foremost vigilantes I should as a matter of principle quit my job at the general store. The truth was I didn't dwell too much on the vigilantes or the vigilante victims. I thought of Jane Hankin, more wretched than ever and no longer open to my thoughtful visitations because I terrified her as much or more than any gun-toting son of a bitch. I confessed about my involvement with Jane's pillows. Dr. McCarty, as baffled as he was by Jane's condition, verified her new fear of being smothered rather than shot, while even Wyatt suggested I lay low for a while as not to drive fragile Lady Jane to a premature grave.

For the next month my life became unbearable. All I did was work and work some more at the Wright general store and listen and listen some more at the Matters tent. Half the time I was in a numb state and the other half in an agitated state from missing Jane. I strongly considered taking up whiskey drinking, visits to liberal-minded soiled doves, and even target shooting to occupy my time in manly fashion. I did none of that, in no small part because I believed Jane would think ill of me, or rather *iller* since I was already the man who smothered instead of soothed.

In my absence from Jane's life, Mr. Matters took to visiting her more frequently. The fact that she worked (well, not for some time) for the vigilante supporter Frederick Zimmerman and lived rent free in the Zimmerman outbuilding did not seem to bother Wyatt. He said that she was a child blessed by the angels and above the self-serving and illicit deeds of mankind. I kept visualizing him sitting on the edge of her blessed narrow bed, his hands all over her to make her well, and her responding to his golden voice and Midas touch. It made me ill, at least in my head. I didn't know if the numbness or the agitation was worse. How I kept going to work day after day I do not know. I suppose I didn't want to be numb, agitated, and unoccupied.

Robert Wright's general store not only was the largest on the High Plains of Kansas but also served as a bank. He lent money to other businessmen, homesteaders, buffalo hunters, and even the occasional gambler who needed a stake — everyone but Wyatt Matters, who always had enough cash to get by without ever explaining how he did it. I personally had little use for money myself; my work pay wasn't much but I didn't need much. My needs were incredibly simple — that is what I thought until one cold evening in early March when I went over to Wyatt's tent to continue our regular discussions about Jane and had my own revelation.

"Dr. McCarty says the illnesses of the head are a mystery to medical science," I told Wyatt as we sat at the center of the tent around his recently improved sunken oven, a two-foot-deep pit walled with stones. "He says we know no more about the brain than we do the far side of the moon — both being more parts imagination than real."

"Yes, Lady Jane's problems are all inside her head," Wyatt said. "But I would not label her condition *madness.* In the ancient world of Greece and Rome, madness usually meant wandering and violence. Jane goes nowhere and is absolutely nonviolent. In ancient Mesopotamia, madness was believed to be caused by deities, so one mental trouble was known as the Hand of Ishtar and another as the Hand of Shamash. Elsewhere, disorders of the mind were attributed to sorcery or witchcraft or the wrath of God.

And for many years hence, madness was still being attributed to divine, diabolical, and magical influences. Even during the Enlightenment, madness in humans could no more be explained than the nature of wild beasts. Madhouses were born. The so-called mad were restrained with chains and given treatment with whips."

Wyatt was getting carried away by history as usual. I squirmed in my layers of clothes, accidentally knocking off the wool blanket that covered me from the knees down. I didn't bother to retrieve it. "We were talking about, Jane . . . in modern times — today," I reminded him. "Chains and whips have nothing to do with her. Anyway, you said she wasn't even *mad*!"

"Such impatience in the young. But I suppose you want to get to bed early so you'll be fresh for another workday with Trader Bob, who might be better called Traitor Bob for fermenting the vigilante movement that turned law and order on its proverbial head."

I could only sigh deeply. "Never mind Mr. Wright. I want to know about Miss Hankin. I don't even get to see her anymore, but I want to help her more than ever. Why doesn't she get better, especially since you say it isn't madness? What is it?"

"Extreme nervousness. Not brought on by

deities, devils, or dark magic but by our gun-crazy frontier society. Simply put, son, Lady Jane has become alienated from society and fearful of its destructiveness, of violent sudden death, if not death in general. Perhaps not rational — for even hermits are part of society and death is inevitable no matter how one behaves — but *not* lunacy."

"All right. I mean not all right, but it has been more than two months now since she was *right*. What the hell do we do about it?"

"I like your show of passion, son. But we must show patience. Her nervous condition is not as simple as recovering from a broken arm or even a broken heart. As I've told you, Dr. McCarty, the Zimmermans, and any other mildly concerned parties out there, we must faithfully continue our moral treatment, in which we are guided by optimism and kindness."

"She won't even let me be kind, and my optimism wanes by the minute."

Of course, Wyatt needed to say more, and he denounced pessimists such as the German philosopher Arthur Schopenhauer, who apparently wrote that there was no meaning or purpose to existence, that life was essentially suffering, and that suffering was evil. I told him I was no Schopenhauer and that I believed existence, whether in wild Dodge

City, Kansas, or tame Bladensburg, Maryland, beat nonexistence any day of the week. He awarded me with a pat on the head and then talked about the beauty of optimism, quoting Alexis de Tocqueville, a French observer of American life: "Most Americans seem to believe that the future can be better and that they are responsible for doing their best to make it that way."

I stood up and began to pace in a wide circle around my relaxed, bundled-up mentor who kept looking at the flames inside his little fire pit as if he not only knew everything there was to know about the past but also could see into the future.

"The thing is," I finally said, rubbing my cold hands together or perhaps it was more like wringing them, "the only future I want to make better right now is that of Jane Hankin."

Wyatt then began to lecture me about my own state of mind. "Your proclivity for thinking constantly of Lady Jane might be viewed as admirable on the surface, but there is a certain deep danger in it when you consider your predilection for pessimism and a proneness to your own paralysis. I know she is pretty and pleasing and pure when healthy but your peculiar pensiveness regarding her frankly has me puzzled."

Those were a lot of big "P" words that I didn't fully understand. I didn't feel like admitting to my limited vocabulary once again. "Your moral treatment just doesn't seem to be working, Wyatt, not when gunfire and such keep happening all around her. There must be something more to be done."

"Not in Dodge, probably not anywhere. Few individuals have true insight into the conditions of the mind or soul."

"You sound like Doc McCarty. He only knows about necks and below."

"At the risk of smothering what little optimism you have left, I suggest that the great mind doctors of the future are only now being born."

"Are you saying that nobody will be able to cure Jane until she is as old as you?"

"I am not. If you and I don't falter in our love and understanding, she has a good chance

to rise out of bed any day now and plunge back into the world."

"I heard Mr. Wright tell Mr. Zimmerman that Jane would be better off in a lunatic asylum. Mr. Zimmerman replied that Mrs. Zimmerman would never permit that."

"Matilda is wise on that score. All around the country there are now *insane asylums,* which in the mind of the officials sound better than lunatic asylums. But the bottom line is the people put in those places are asylum inmates and, while chains and whips are no longer used as far as I know, chances of recovery in them are about as low as a convict being rehabilitated in our state prison at Lansing"

"But Kansas does have one of those asylums?"

"The Topeka Insane Asylum opened last year. It's hard to know what goes on in there or what kind of treatment they give the inmates, but I heard it's already becoming overcrowded."

"So, it must be a pretty popular place?"

"Probably not so much with those confined inside, but no doubt the institution has been welcomed by the families and friends of the lunatics."

"Maybe they could help Jane."

"I told you she is *not* a raving lunatic."

"I know that. So maybe it would be easier for them to help her than it would be the really mad people. I'm trying to be optimistic here."

"Maybe so, but you mostly sound crazy, son."

"I do? I wonder."

"Look. Don't let yourself slip away to the other side."

"You mean the other side of my brain?"

"I'm simply saying, give whatever ideas you have going on inside your own peculiar head a long-needed rest."

As instructed, I was prepared to give my big idea a rest (i.e., do nothing about it, which was my usual style in those days anyway). But then in the second week of March there was more vigilante action and more trouble, not only for the men targeted but also for Jane Hankin. First a fellow named McGill — who was called a desperado, but I think must have been a lunatic — walked the streets of Dodge amusing himself by shooting through windows of whatever house he passed. For some reason he passed up the Zimmermans' main residence on Walnut Street but fired into the only outbuilding window facing the street. The slug passed through Jane's kitchen and an interior door and broke the lamp next to Jane's bed. That random shot did get Jane out of the bed but then to hide under it. Her screaming woke up Mrs. Zimmerman in the main house. Whatever moral treatment Wyatt Matters was giving her had been instantly nullified. Dr. McCarty came by and gave her laudanum to allay her panic and produce sleep, but it took more than an hour to coax her out from under the bed. A half-dozen vigilantes caught up with McGill and riddled him with bullets but that didn't make Jane feel any safer. It was still gunfire, and no matter who created it, she considered it evil. She possessed a brittle brain, and Dodge was not the place to find healing, what with its overabundance of gun-toting young men prepared to blaze away for practically no reason at all.

That became abundantly clear the very next night. It turned out McGill had a younger partner named Burns, who was in a dance hall, either mourning McGill too much or not enough. Burns got into an argument with a blubbery dance hall owner, Tom Sherman, who, according to Wyatt Matters' investigation, was one of the vigilantes who had filled McGill with lead. Sherman gave Burns the same treatment upon catching up with him next to a hog shed in a dead-end alley. The next morning Burns' body was discovered with eight bullet holes in it, while a high shot had scattered his brains in his hair. I saw that for myself because I was enlisted by my civic-minded employer, Mr. Wright, to be part of the burial detail. He lent me a shovel and I followed several other shovel carriers, as well as the two men carrying a pole to which the body was fastened. On Boot Hill, three of us began digging, but I was told to stop much sooner than expected. The grave was barely three feet deep, but the others said that was good enough. Once Burns' body was freed from the pole and dropped into the hole, I was ordered to fill it up. All the others, except the late Burns, of course, left before I was done.

Sometime after the burial, Wyatt made one of his daily trips to the general store — to speak, not buy. With Robert Wright scowling at him from the other side of the counter, Wyatt told me that Jane had been awakened by the late-night shots fired by Sherman into McGill but had believed them to only be part of a frightening dream. So, she hadn't hidden under her bed again, but that hardly eased my head.

"I need to go out back and see about supplies," Mr. Wright announced. "Try to keep your visit reasonably short, Mr. Matters. We do get real customers in here."

"Go forth and multiply your riches, Trader Bob. Predatory merchants must prevail!"

"I'll be gone ten minutes. Don't be here when I get back unless you intend to buy a hammer and nails."

Wyatt waved goodbye to my boss. "That man is after me to build myself a house. Doesn't think a tent has a place in a growing city. At least he didn't go vigilante on me and order me to leave town."

"Jane isn't getting any better," I said because the only thing on my mind was her. On Wyatt's advice, I had forced myself to stay away from her (supposedly for her own good) but her condition had only worsened. If it got much worse, I envisioned her resorting to suicide. Certainly, she would never in a million years find a gun and shoot herself. Since she never left her home and rarely her bed, drowning seemed most unlikely unless it was possible for one to drown in their own tears. After her misconstrued *experience* with me, she would never try to smother herself, even if it were possible. Too much laudanum might do the trick, though. I hated myself for thinking the worst about Jane.

Wyatt, seeming to read my mind as easily as he did one of his dense books, rolled his eyes. He was tired of my pessimism. But he didn't help matters, not by a long shot. "About the time you were burying that Burns boy, Lady Jane had an actual dream — a rather astonishing one at that," he said as he went to the corner stove, either to warm his hands or for dramatic effect. I controlled myself for as long as possible and didn't ask him to continue, knowing full well that he would. Finally, I gave in.

"You plan to tell me about this astonishing dream of hers?"

"Don't be alarmed, son," Wyatt said, turning away from the stove.

I was instantly alarmed.

"As unpleasant as it may be, I have to tell you, son."

He always had to tell me something.

"Remember what I'm about to tell you is only a dream."

"I know, an astonishing dream."

"Yes, but more so a disturbing dream."

"What is it? Did she dream of flying bullets?

"Deadly bullets. In the dream she was back at her old home in Lawrence. Confederate guerrilla 'Bloody Bill' Anderson rode up on his large steed, trampling the family vegetable patch. When her mother and father stepped out of the house and complained, Bloody Bill shot them both dead."

"Horrible. What really happened that day?"

"Jane's mother sobbed and begged one of the Bushwhackers, probably not Bloody Bill, to spare her husband. The guerrilla showed no mercy to the quiet man, firing point-blank into his chest, but spared the weeping woman."

"Her dream then was worse than what actually happened in 1863."

"Not sure how a dream can be worse than reality, but anyway the dream continued, and Bloody Bill shot Jane in the breast. And then he burned down the Hankin house."

"No! But in real life Jane wasn't shot at Lawrence, right?"

"That's right. Afterward Jane and her mother had to carry on without the male Hankins — the father and Jane's three brothers — and a smoldering house."

"How did they manage?"

"They got help. A new house was built."

"In the dream or in real life?"

"In real life. In the dream, Jane entered the smoldering house and lay on her bed."

"The bed didn't burn with the rest of the house?"

"Dreams aren't always logical. Anyway, while she is lying in bed, a Union soldier shows up saying he aims to kill Bloody Bill. But that can wait. Instead of remounting and giving chase, the Union soldier takes out a handkerchief and tries to mop up the blood trickling from the girl's breast. It seems like the proper thing to do even if he is a cavalryman and not a doctor, but he gets carried away. You get the picture? I mean he gets *really* carried away and commences to forcefully violate her. As she desperately and unsuccessfully tries to fight him off, she awakens, alone in bed of course."

"You mean that happened to her after her family was shot to pieces?"

"That's right — in the dream."

"She told you all this?"

"Yes. You see I have started trying to interpret her dreams."

"Interpret? I don't understand."

"It gives me insight into her mind — her deepest thoughts and fears. It's not an exact science and I'm new at it, but in the case of this dream, not much interpretation was necessary."

"Yes, it seems rather straightforward . . . and, like you said, disturbing."

"More than you know."

"What do you mean?"

"I may as well tell you the rest, son. Jane described what that Union cavalryman looked like. He had blue eyes that matched his uniform, a large nose, and earlobes that were not free but connected directly to the head. She identified him as you."

"Me! She hardly recognizes me anymore, but I show up in her bad dreams?"

"It seems that way, son. Can't be helped. Dreams are figments of the imagination."

"I wasn't even in the Civil War. I was

born in 1850. I was too young. Hey, wait a minute. You got pretty much the same eyes, nose, and ears as me. That despoiler in her dream could have been you."

"No, no. I'm practically bald. The Yankee soldier had a full head of light brown hair, like you. Plus, he didn't say a word all the while he was abusing her."

"Sure, sure. You would have talked all through it, telling her about all the raping being done in the very old days by Zeus and the other Greek gods."

"Harry. Do you hear what you're saying? One might think you were out of your head."

"Maybe I am. I once dreamed I was the conductor on a train that ran over a man who didn't look anything like my father. For one thing, he wore a top hat. It was you!"

"How disturbing that must have been for you."

"But how easy to interpret!"

"You feel angry at Jane for having you surface in her awful dream and resent me for telling you about it. But I felt I must, if only to show you where things stand between you and her. She obviously requires a lot more healing, and you need to be more understanding and . . ."

"I need to get to work, Wyatt, as ludicrous

as that might seem to a totally sane man like yourself."

I had gone beyond apologies. There was no telling what I might have said next, but an actual customer walked into the store. It was none other than then the blubbery vigilante who had sent McGill and Burns to early graves. Tom Sherman was looking to buy long johns, as his old pair was holey and wouldn't last him through the winter, and some plum preserves to please his sweet tooth. He brushed me aside and said he was a big customer and only dealt with the big boss. He began hollering for Mr. Wright. I tried to tell him the owner was busy, but Sherman kept yelling. I raised my voice but remained polite. My voice was not heard.

Mr. Wright returned red-faced, stomping his feet, and waving his arms. Instead of asking what was going on or asking Mr. Sherman to calm himself, he shouted at Wyatt Matters, "What in damnation have you said to agitate a paying customer!"

"Where the hell you been, Bob," Mr. Sherman said. "When I come to buy, I demand service!" He was already serving himself, though, pulling from a high shelf the largest pair of long johns I'd ever seen in my life. "Just right," Mr. Sherman said, holding the undergarment johns up to his proud belly. "Fit for a king."

"Oh, it's you," said Mr. Wright, as if he no more wanted Tom Sherman in his store than he did Wyatt Matters. "No reason to shout. The boy could have helped you."

"Bosh. I come for the other. It was overdue!"

"Just came in yesterday." Mr. Wright reached under the counter and pulled out a jar of plum preserves.

"Ah, royal purple," Mr. Sherman said, licking his fleshy lips as he grabbed the jar. "Nothing but the best for the noble keepers of public safety!" He pried open the jar and stuck in his thumb, which he then gave a good lick and a noisy suck.

Wyatt of course couldn't let that comment pass. He marched right up to Mr. Sherman and stood on his toes to put his nose within inches of Mr. Sherman's chin. "There is nothing noble about you, sir. You shoot down two men in twenty-four hours and think only of your belly and your ass."

Mr. Sherman smacked his lips, set the jar down on the counter, and squeezed his wool long johns as if choking a sheep. "You're asking for big trouble, little man," he said. "Why do you let this riffraff into your store, Mr. Wright? He has no respect for the committee's long hours of vigilance."

"You shot down Mr. Burns for no other reason than he was a partner of Mr. McGill, who you shot down earlier."

"I am upholding law and order, just like Mr. Wright and all the good fellows who serve on our committee."

"You are holding up law and order."

"I am enforcing the will of the committee. And you are a worthless vagrant. Tell him, Mr. Wright."

Mr. Wright began looking behind the counter, as if there might be other jars hidden there.

"I suggest, Mr. Wright," continued Mr. Sherman, "that our committee take action against this man and his young associate."

"I work for Mr. Wright," I insisted.

"But you associate with this ne'er-do'well, and quite frankly you strike me as being an equally shady character, part of the rabble. What say you, Bob, should we at the very least run this pair out of Dodge?"

Mr. Wright gave the evil eye to Wyatt and seemed to be considering Mr. Sherman's suggestion, but then he surprised me by coming to my defense.

"Harry Hannum is conscientious if on occasion absent-minded. If you have some specific problem with him, I want you to spell it out. You can't just go making unsubstantiated charges against anybody and everybody."

"Sure, we can forget the boy for now, until he gets out of line. It's the little man with the big hat we need to get rid of."

"Wyatt Matters is an irritant, without doubt, and I have at times personally wanted him out of my hair, but he carries neither gun nor knife and cannot be labeled a dangerous man."

"Just an ass then," said Mr. Sherman, flapping his long johns as if he were a one-winged bird, a turkey vulture perhaps.

"All mouth I'd say."

"We don't have to take his mouth, Mr. Wright." Mr. Sherman bunched his long johns into a ball and took two lumbering steps toward Wyatt. "Get out!" he shouted, pointing to the door with his free hand.

"When did you purchase the general store from Mr. Wright?" Wyatt asked. "I'd like to be cast out by the proper owner."

Now it was Mr. Sullivan's turn to go chin to nose with Mr. Matters. "You're in over your head, little man. Nothing I hate worse than an agitator who doesn't have the belly for strapping on a shooting iron."

"You, sir, have the belly to be everything offensive in a human being," said Wyatt.

Mr. Sherman dropped his long johns and

took a step backward, even as he reached for his belt. He wasn't too fast, but of course didn't need to be against an unarmed man. He never got his gun out, though. Mr. Wright caught him by the wrist and glared at the weapon. "Not today, Tom Sherman, not today."

"All right, Bob, all right. Maybe this isn't the time or the place." He holstered his gun, but to show he still meant business he used a thumb and a forefinger to imitate pulling a trigger. "Bang! Better watch out for me tomorrow, little man."

"Tomorrow things will be different in Dodge." Wyatt said, but I'm sure he didn't literally mean the next day. "Ford County will have formalized legal institutions, create courts, and elect sheriffs. A man like you will have no place in the community. You shall be declared an outlaw, a vile serpent."

Mr. Sherman broke away from Mr. Wright's grasp and I thought for certain he was going to deliver a blow on behalf of fat snakes. But he stopped short when Mr. Matters unleased a series of words that on the surface might have sounded conciliatory.

"You are an incredible product of your frontier environment, Mr. Sherman. Your acts of moral turpitude are unsurpassed here in Dodge. Clearly, you have a tremendous capacity for ignis fatuus. I dare say that folie de grandeur rules your very existence. In short, Mr. Sherman, calling you a rapscallion doesn't do you justice. You are a malefactor of the first order — a veritable king of vindictiveness like King Henry VIII of England or an emperor of eradication like Caligula of ancient Rome."

While Mr. Sherman was digesting those words, Mr. Wright handed him the jar of plum preserves, draped the long johns over the vigilante's shoulder, and showed him to the door. "Your credit is good," Mr. Wright told him. "Pay me later."

After Mr. Sherman had cleared the door, Mr. Matters slapped his hands together as if brushing off dirt and clapping at the same time. "Bully for you, Mr. Wright," he said. It was the first time I'd heard Wyatt call my boss something other than *Mr. Wright Can Do No Wrong, Bobby "Money Is Might" Wright,* or *Trader Bob.* "I don't think I ever enjoyed myself being called an irritant so much in my life. Anyway. Mr. Wright, you stood up to that monster on behalf of Harry and me. I thank you."

"No need. Tom Sullivan has about worn out his welcome. He supposedly joined our organization for the public good but almost right away he empowered himself. He had his own grievances with Burns and McGill and shot them for his own selfish purposes. What he did was an outrage on common decency. Hard bad men like him keep creeping into our organization."

"Still, you gave him his plum preserves and fat long johns."

"He has always paid up."

"And Burns and McGill paid the ultimate price."

"The organization does not sanctify shootings."

"Perhaps not. But your Dodge City Vigilance Committee has become a farce and an outrage on common decency."

Mr. Wright was clearly mulling over Mr. Matters' words. Finally, he gave a heavy nod but crossed his arms at the same time and grunted. "I've heard enough," he said.

"It will be hard to boot out men like Sherman, Mr. Wright Can do No Wrong. Your best bet — and the only decent thing to do — is to disband the entire committee. Vigilantes are not the answer to Dodge's problems, especially when the Shermans of the world have infiltrated a committee that never should have formed in the first place."

"You go too far, Mr. Matters. Don't push your luck."

Chapter Twelve

In April 1873 Robert Wright, Frederick Zimmerman, and the other founding businessmen of Dodge City toasted themselves at Alfred Peacock's saloon and then again at George Cox's Dodge House when Kansas Governor Thomas Osborn declared Ford County organized. But the group congratulations ceased when other Kansas officials called Isaac Young's census into question. Apparently the required six hundred names were listed, but there were some repeats and a few that could not be linked to a living human body. I didn't understand the politics in the situation, but Wyatt Matters said that the Atchison, Topeka & Santa Fe Railroad was behind the protest, because it figured to bear most of the tax burden of a new county government. The state Supreme Court wouldn't decide on the legality of Ford County until June, which Mr. Matters considered a personal slap in the face even though the founders still considered him eccentric, an outsider trying to nose into the town's inner circle.

"You know what this means?" he said to me as we sat on the only two cottonwood stools in his tent, a bottle of half-empty red wine between us.

"No, sheriff," I said, as I gulped my second glass. I had undoubtedly become less reverential toward my mentor, if not downright flippant at times, but he never admonished me for it. He could tolerate me acting like a spoiled child as long as I didn't become one of those disorderly young Dodge men prone to violence.

"More vigilante action, that's what. You just wait and see, and I doubt you'll have to wait long to see what a blow this is to the good, peaceful people like Lady Jane."

He refilled my glass. He'd been doing that a lot lately mainly because Jane Hankin's lingering lethargy and seeming dismissal of me as a friendly human being had also set me back as his protégé. I was numb to new learning and had started to drink whiskey on desperate occasions to deal with my state of despair at not being able to help her or myself. He gave me wine so that I wouldn't resort to the red-eye found in saloons. While pouring me wine, words poured from his mouth about ancient Greeks — how their poets extoled the virtues of certain wine, how physician Hippocrates used wine to cure fevers and other conditions, how these most knowledgeable and civilized people drank unmixed or undiluted wine to separate themselves from the barbarians. I drank Wyatt's undiluted wine but still felt like a barbarian. I told him neither Hippocrates' wine nor Wyatt's wine could cure Jane's mysterious condition. I suppose I was becoming a bit unmanageable, perhaps even unruly, during our tent sessions.

"You know something," I said, but my speech was slurred, so I held my tongue.

"A thing or two," he said. "But you tell me: What do I know?"

"Nothin'."

"Go ahead, son. You have something on your mind."

"You're not so . . . so ironodrastic as you think."

"*Ironodrastic?* That is not a legitimate word; it's the wine talking. The word I taught you is iconoclastic. It describes me perfectly. I'm innovative, nonconforming, questioning, critical, dissenting, radical. and all together . . ." He finished his sentence by thrusting his belly toward me and tapping the word *Original* on his belt buckle. "But why the frown? As I have often stressed to you, being an iconoclast is something to strive for whether you are in the Deep South challenging the plantation system, in New York City challenging the Tweed Ring, in California challenging the railroad tycoons, or in Dodge City, Kansas, challenging the state and local government."

"Is Robert Wright an ironoclast?"

"The word is iconoclast. And no, he is not one. He is the opposite. Your boss is a traditionalist, a conformer, a stick-in-the-mud, one of a herd, a frontier tycoon, a money-grubber."

"You are *not* so different."

Wyatt took my glass away with only a little fight. His usually wan face was starting to take on the color of the wine. "You've had enough, son," he said. "When you start thinking I am like Mr. Wright . . . well . . . you aren't thinking straight."

Only a month or two ago I wouldn't have challenged anything Mr. Matters said. He could have told me the sun revolved around the earth or that dinosaurs lived in Dodge City and I would have believed him. But now I felt argumentative.

"Mr. Wright is rich, works hard for his money, and is stingy about handing it out. I don't know how rich you are, but you seem to have enough to get by without working and you're obviously on the miserly side."

"I invite you to my tent for some fine wine, and you insult me. Like the ancient Greeks, I believe strongly in hospitality, pleasing my guests with beverages, meals, accommodations, and other standard comforts like the custom-made stool you're occupying. But it's late and I'm none too pleased that no law and order has come to Dodge, so perhaps I should bid you goodnight."

"There you go," I said. "You the *iconowhatever* want a Ford County sheriff and Mr. Wright the traditionalist wants a Ford County sheriff. Not different at all."

"In the meantime, he is one of the vigilantes who are operating illegally right under our noses."

I rubbed my nose, thinking with some degree of satisfaction that my mentor's nose was much bigger and uglier than mine. "So maybe you're the traditionalist, he's the iconowhatever."

"I usually encourage thought, son, but I believe you are overwrought from too much thinking and too much wine."

I wasn't thinking now. I was just talking. "Mr. Wright and you both go for younger women. He married Alice, six years his junior. But you are far outdoing him. You're forty-two. Jane is my age."

"One and a half years younger than you to be exact. What of it?"

"You know what of it."

"I thought we were done with that nonsense. You still think I have designs on that young woman, marry her perhaps?"

"She's in no condition now. Maybe when she gets better, if she ever does."

"She will. And she won't marry me or anyone else. She's . . ."

"She's sick in the head. She must be to even think of marrying you."

"She is not thinking of marrying me. Marriage is not in my head or her head. I believe the wine is having the same effect on you that whiskey would. You are beginning to aggravate me."

"Yeah, well you've been plenty aggravating. You know everything but you don't know how much you aggravate. A lot of people have told you that. Good old Bob Wright for one. But do you listen? No, no, no! You just talk and talk, nothing but aggravating talk. Some mentor you turned out to be."

"Goodnight, son."

"Damn it. I don't like it. But maybe marriage is the honorable thing to do . . . or will be. Then you'd have to share all your hidden wealth with her like any honorable husband would. It might even be the law in Kansas. With all that money, she could put up with all your ugliness and aggravation."

"My wine has made you crazy. I never thought I'd see it. Clearly, you aren't seeing anything straight."

"No matter. Love is blind."

"And you're out of your mind."

"You once said you wanted me and her to be together . . . and now this."

"Now what? She's a sick young woman. I'm caring for her."

"In sickness and in health!"

"Flummadiddle! You're my protégé and naturally I'm concerned about your mental state, but I'm in no mood for dealing with it at this late hour. I had no idea that wine would have this kind of effect on you — that is if it is the wine and not something more. You're acting like a sick young man. You've made an ass of yourself tonight. I've never said this to you before, son, but now I am: Get the hell out of my tent!"

Wyatt Matters was right. It wasn't just the wine speaking. My rebellious state carried over to the next day and the day after that and on and on into May. I acted not only like a poor protégé but also like a poor employee. I, in fact, acted like I was out of my mind. I told general store customers not to bother me with their stupid inquires, yelled at several of the Wright children for getting in my way, and called Mr. Wright a *nefarious skinflint* (it wasn't original; Wyatt Matters had called him that a time or two). The boss finally took me aside on the day I refused to help Mrs. Wright find her missing shawl, but instead of getting angry or even asking what was wrong, he told me I had been working hard, which he appreciated, but now it was time to take a break and go somewhere to clear my head. I told him I couldn't afford to buy a getaway horse or a train ticket back to Bladensburg, Maryland (my old hometown had just popped in my head; I didn't really want to go back there while I was alive).

"It'll do you a world of good to get out of Dodge for a few days, or longer, if need be," he said during a rare nighttime visit to my bed in his storeroom. "Alice suggested that very thing to me this morning when you came over for breakfast and snapped at Clara Belle for trying to sit on your lap. You made her cry."

"I made the giggler cry. Damn me. Please extend my apologies to the little one."

"She'll soon forget it, but we can't let it happen again, can we?"

"Hell, no, not if I can help it." I spoke without conviction. I felt like crying for making Clara Belle cry.

"Good, good. I think Alice's suggestion was a darn good one. She found the paisley shawl she misplaced, by the way. It was on a hook under my heavy coat."

"Good old Alice. She wants me to get the hell out of Dodge?"

"Not permanently."

"I have no place to go."

"Why not visit the capital?"

"I don't wish to see Washington, too swampy, too close to Bladensburg."

"I meant our capital — Topeka, Kansas."

"Right. Home of the Topeka Insane Asylum."

"Yes, there is that. There is also the new Capitol, where the legislature meets. The building is a work in progress, though. You might like a visit to the Keith & Meyers Dry Goods Store. You could send those gentlemen my highest regards, and . . ."

"Ugh!" It escaped from my mouth like a belch. I was sick of working day after day in Wright's general store and the last thing I needed was to see more dry goods. I jumped out of bed, startling the boss because I had gone to bed naked. I began pacing the room, holding both of my temples as if to keep my head from bursting open.

"You aren't yourself, Harry."

"Huh?" I looked down at my nakedness. "If Alice could see me now."

"Hop back in bed, Harry my boy."

I did, covering myself with blankets up to my chin. It was the first time Mr. Wright had called me his boy. He had enough real sons, and even though we were both from Bladensburg, Maryland, and were both attracted to the mother of his real children, and saw each other almost every day, we were anything but close. He was into making money, dictating, being the boss, authoritarianism, and ridiculing Wyatt Matters and my relationship with the man he called Dodge City's most obnoxious blatherskite. I was into making Jane Hankin better, worrying, being a halfway decent employee, submissiveness, and, until lately, listening to the many words of Mr. Matters (who had been impressed that Robert Wright knew the word *blatherskite,* let alone *obnoxious*).

"You feel all right?" Mr. Wright asked. He started to check my forehead to see if I had a fever, but at the last second pulled his hand away. Like me, maybe he figured that was something motherly Alice Wright should be doing.

My head wobbled as if it couldn't quite nod yet wasn't ready to shake. It gave me a stiff neck. My legs felt weighted down or else I might have climbed out of bed again and run naked out onto Front Street screaming the sky was falling or at least that a Kansas twister was coming.

Mr. Wright now felt up to placing a moderately heavy hand on my shoulder. "Get ahold of yourself, Harry Hannum," he said. "Alice tells me you have been anxious to get your hands on some books?"

"There's not even eyeing them these days." I wasn't sure if I'd have access to Wyatt Matters' stack of books ever again — or if I'd want to, seeing as I now considered us officially estranged.

"We sure enough are in short supply of books here in Dodge. Alice and some of the other local ladies who read are working on changing that situation. In the meantime, I can tell you that in the capital city, the Keith & Meyers Dry Good Store has opened its doors to the Topeka & Shawnee County Public Library, recently founded by the Ladies' Library Association over there. Maybe they have a book that will do you some good. I have none to recommend myself, but Alice is partial to one called *Little Women,* written by a woman back East of course."

I suspected that Mr. Wright wouldn't be caught dead reading such a book, even if his wife liked it. Wyatt Matters had mentioned *Little Women* and the author, Louisa May Alcott. It was about four sisters and offered the themes of family life, work, and true love. I knew nothing much about family life (at least the good kind), a bit more about work (at least the drudgery kind), and believed I knew a powerful lot about true love, albeit the unappreciated kind in Atchison with faithless Elizabeth Pepper and now the unrequited kind in Dodge with the troubled Jane Hankin. Mr. Matters had also recommended the book to me (even though I had no living sisters, let along brothers), but lately I'd become far more interested in another book he recommended, one written by a man, and no common man — pioneering English psychiatrist Henry Maudsley. Wyatt liked Maudsley's conviction that passion and selfishness could cause criminality and madness and that anger, religion, and love were the three most dangerous passions. What struck me, if not Wyatt, was that Jane was neither an angry nor religious person, so her current problems must revolve around love. In fact, Wyatt told me that back in

1863 Dr. Maudsley wrote, "The ardor of love is a temporary insanity."

"I wonder if that library has Maudsley's *The Physiology and Pathology of the Mind,*" I blurted out, forgetting that I wasn't alone.

"The what?" said Mr. Wright.

I repeated the title. I was glad Mr. Wright didn't ask me what *physiology* and *pathology* meant. I had this deep notion that if anybody could help Jane it was Dr. Henry Maudsley.

"What kind of book is that?" Mr. Wright asked.

I suddenly remembered another reason Wyatt liked Dr. Maudsley. The doctor had once spoke of the "single minded pursuit of riches as a cause of moral and mental degeneracy." I got flustered. My boss didn't need to hear such talk.

"Never mind. sir. My mind is on other things. I must be going."

"In the middle of the night? Where to?"

"To Topeka."

"Really?"

"Why not. To Topeka or bust!"

"Fine. I'm glad you are taking my suggestion. But don't get out of bed just yet. It can wait till morning when the trains are running, can't it?"

"Yes, I suppose it must. But no longer than that. I must do something in Topeka!"

"At the Topeka & Shawnee County Public Library, I presume."

"Yes, that will be one of my stops."

My first morning stop, with train fare for two in hand, thanks to the generosity of Robert and Alice Wright, was the outbuilding that Jane Hankin lived in and still called her little blue house, thanks to the generosity of Frederick and Matilda Zimmerman. I hadn't seen my true love for a long time, maybe only one or two brief visits since that horrible day on the ninth of February when she suspected I was trying to smother her with a pillow. I had stayed away, as painful as it was, on the advice of both Dr. McCarty and Mr. Matters, who asserted that my presence in her room might cause her to go into hysterics — and they didn't mean laughter. I suspected that the doc didn't know what the hell he was talking about, and that Wyatt had ulterior motives. Still, I obliged them, not wanting to chance jeopardizing Jane's speedy recovery. *Speedy?* What a joke. It was the previous year, December 28, that Bully Brooks had triggered Jane's collapse by murdering Matt Sullivan. In the first two and a half months of 1873, Dodge had seen at least a half-dozen more killings and during that time I'm not sure Jane ever got far enough outside to see Front Street.

I entered the house without knocking and merely cleared my throat before advancing into her bedroom. It was early, but she wasn't in bed. She sat in a white nightdress on a stool and was gazing into the handheld mirror I'd given her for Christmas, back when she could look at herself and see a healthy, happy woman. I had no idea what she thought of this sad, sick woman before her now, but I was glad to find her alone. No Wyatt Matters bringing food and futile talk. No Dr. McCarty scratching his head and offering nothing but platitudes. No Matilda Zimmerman wondering why the hell I was harassing the poor girl. It was up to me now to do something not at all like myself — to be bold and forceful and willing to gamble. I had it in my mind that her only chance and my only chance was waiting for us in Topeka.

She caught sight of me in the mirror but didn't scream. Her look was one of indifference or unresponsiveness or maybe both. She swept a comb through her auburn hair, licked her lips, and continued looking in the mirror. I had the two train tickets in my hand and felt foolish standing there waiting for the woman I loved to say something, but

I was working up the nerve to say something myself. It was as if I had left my boldness outside her bedroom door. One of the tickets slipped out of my hand and dropped to the floor. When I bent to pick it up, she suddenly pivoted on the stool, extended her long legs, and struck my left hip with surprising force.

"Excuse me," we said at the same time. That made her laugh, which took the sadness right out of her brown eyes.

"You laughed," I said. "It's been so long."

"It's you. Isn't it?"

"I think so."

"I knew you'd come back."

"You wanted me to?"

"I didn't recognize you at first. You aren't so short. You look younger. Has your nose shrunk?"

"I didn't grow, and my nose is the same. Maybe you are mistaking me for Wyatt Matters."

"I certainly am not. Look." She took the mirror off her lap and held it in front of me until she was satisfied that I had thoroughly examined my face. "See what I mean."

"No. I see bags under my eyes. I haven't been getting much sleep lately."

"Poor, Harry. I've been sleeping very well of late, though I'm getting mighty tired of it."

"You said my name. I wondered if you'd even remember it."

"Don't be ridiculous. You are Harry Hannum, friend of Wyatt Matters."

"Protégé is the word, or was. But never mind him. Do you remember that I am your friend, the friend who gave you that mirror and that comb, also a brush?"

"I comb in the morning and brush at night. It's just the way I am." She turned away to lay the mirror and comb on her dresser.

"That's fine with me. You have such nice hair."

"You have more hair, Harry, than Wyatt does."

"Naturally. He's an old man. It's nice to see you out of bed."

She looked startled for an instant. Quickly she raised her collar and held it tightly closed so that it covered most of her neck. "You wouldn't do anything bad, would you?"

"Never." I prayed she had forgotten her baseless fear of me. "I'm a very good friend, remember?"

"Yes, Wyatt's friend."

"Your friend, too."

"I want you to leave, Harry Hannum."

"Leave? But I . . ."

"I need to get dressed." She stood up, released her collar, and walked to the closet door. She opened it and sang out, "Everything is here, but what to wear, what to wear!"

"You must be feeling better to want to get dressed . . . I mean in an outside kind of dress."

"One must be dressed to go outside. That's what I intend to do today. Would you step into the kitchen and promise not to peek until I'm ready?"

"Yes. This is wonderful news. You see, Jane, I would like to take you out."

"Like to a dance? I'm afraid not. I'm not up to dancing just yet. I'm a little afraid."

"Understandable . . . I mean you have done nothing for so long and it will take time for your body to . . . I don't want to dance either. I want to take you on a little trip."

"Me?"

"Don't you feel up to it?"

"I haven't shed a tear in two whole days. There's no noise going on inside my head right now. I've been hearing so much loud noise and unpleasant voices. Today, though, it's quiet up there, too quiet, like a graveyard. That's why I want to go out, need to go out. Will you take me to Wyatt's tent?"

"I'd rather not. I have greater plans than that."

“To the store? Mr. and Mrs. Zimmerman have been so very kind to me. But I’m not ready to go back to work. I’m a little afraid.”

“That’s fine. No dancing. No working. Not for me either. Mr. Wright has given me time off, as much time as I need. How would you like to get away from Dodge City?”

“What? No, I couldn’t do that. Dodge is my home. Wyatt would hate that.”

“I’m sure he would. But I don’t mean permanently. Mr. Wright tells me that Topeka is a nice place to visit. It’s the capital of Kansas, you know.”

“I didn’t think that changed while I was lying in bed. But why would I go there?”

“They have a library, and the new Capitol going up, and peaceful politicians — things like that. Maybe it will help you to go there and see the sights.”

“With you?”

“Certainly, with me. We’ll catch a train together at noon. You aren’t afraid, are you?”

“Of course not. I’ve ridden many trains.”

“Good. You get dressed now and pack a few other things for the road. A small bag will do.”

“Where’s your bag?”

“I’m fine. We won’t be staying that long. Just want to see if I can get this book by a guy named Maudsley and get to the bottom of a few things that have caused me a great deal of anguish and bewilderment."

"Poor, Harry. We can't have that. Now into the other room with you. I've found the dress I've been looking for. It's red." She took it out of the closet and held it out under her chin. "Do you like it?"

I did. I had seen her wearing it before. It was her dancing dress. In fact, I was almost certain it was the dress she was wearing the night Matt Sullivan was shot.

She packed a small leather bag, and we went. She was willing to go, not even questioning why we were going or my sanity. It was as if she had stored up so much energy while in bed that she felt she could go anywhere short of China or do anything short of taking part in a gunfight. Within seven hours the Atchison, Topeka & Santa Fe had taken us east — the same direction all those bison hides and bones traveled — to the station in Topeka. A half hour later, Jane and I were eating crackers and cheese and drinking coffee, compliments of the owners of the Keith & Myers Dry Goods Store.

Because of book growth, though, the library had moved to rooms over the Blake & Halm hardware store. We bid farewell to Messrs. Keith and Myers with mouths still full, and I quickly led Jane to the new library quarters confident we would gain insight from Maudsley on not only her condition (an extreme but improving nervous state of mind brought on by gun violence and helplessness) but also mine (an increasingly unstable state of mind brought on by love madness and helplessness). We were greeted in a room full of overloaded bookshelves by a most pleasant and knowledgeable (Mr. Matters might have even agreed) old librarian, Alice Griffith. I took as a good sign the fact she had the same first name as Mrs. Wright and that Mrs. Griffith proudly stated we were standing in one of the finest free libraries west of the Mississippi. She led us through two other rooms with similarly stacked shelves.

"In the past twelve months we've acquired four hundred volumes," she said. "Our library now contains six hundred and one books. I have read six hundred in their entirety. I was unable to get through Thackeray's *The Virginians,* which as far as I'm concerned is the worst historical novel ever written."

I figured she must be more than a match for Wyatt Matters when it came to literary cognizance. "I can't imagine reading that many books in my lifetime," I told her. "At this time, I am not interested in any novel. In fact, I have a particular book in mind, an extremely serious book by a Henry Maudsley. I don't suppose you've heard of it, Mrs. Griffith, but . . ."

"*The Physiology and Pathology of the Mind,* published by Harvard University in 1867."

"Land's sake. How'd you know?"

"Dr. Maudsley's style is vigorous and clear, not infrequently crisp, though he uses several faulty expressions. For instance, I question whether the verb *to crave* should be employed intransitively as he does in his sentence, 'Unsatisfied appetite craves for more nutriment.' And then there is this sentence: 'A stranger conversing with her would not have discovered that she ailed anything at all.' I don't believe the verb *to ail* can be employed transitively with a personal subject. But don't get me wrong. I loved many of the things the doctor says and recognize him as a visionary, a seeker of the truth. Such brilliance, faulty expressions aside, deserves to be quoted, which is something I often did."

"My God! I know a man in Dodge who has quoted Dr. Maudsley to me. It doesn't seem possible there can be two people who do that."

"In my case, *The Physiology and Pathology of the Mind* came out when I was a war widow working at the Harvard Library, the oldest library system in the United States. What is your friend's background?"

"I guess I don't really know. He's secretive about it. I do know Mr. Matters knows just about all there is to know and has read *The Physiology and Pathology of the Mind*."

"I might like to meet your Mr. Matters someday."

"Yes, ma'am. But like I said, he's back in Dodge. What I'd really like now is to get my hands on *The Physiology and Pathology of the Mind*. What luck that you know it so well. In which of your rooms can I find it?"

"I am sorry to disappoint you, young man, but we do not have in house a copy of Dr. Maudsley's *P&P*. Sadly, I left my personal copy back in Cambridge, Massachusetts, when I . . . Are you all right, young man?"

I had dropped to my knees and was trembling uncontrollably. The odds of finding the desired book in Topeka must have been incredibly slim, but here was Mrs. Griffith with this amazing connection that seemed like fate. I had believed I was destined to open Dr. Maudsley's book and in short order discover not only the roots but also the cure for Jane's condition. When I burst into tears, Jane knelt beside me trying to wipe my face with the sleeve of her red dress. Mrs.

Griffith was not without sympathy. She offered me smelling salts from a small blue bottle made by the Boston and Sandwich Glass Works Company. I accepted. The harsh fumes filled my nostrils and probably prevented me from fainting.

"I'm sorry," I said, wiping my nose as Jane helped me to my feet. "I don't know what got into me. I wanted that book so badly. I thought . . . I don't know what I thought. You see Jane here has been feeling poorly in the head for some time and . . ."

"Don't fret yourself, Mrs. Griffith," said Jane. "My mind is doing much better now anyway."

The two women guided me unsteadily from the third room to the first room, where we sat at a corner table with two books in front of us. To my amazement the thickest of the two turned out to be one of the personal favorites of Mr. Matters — *Zell's Popular Encyclopedia: A Universal Dictionary of English Language, Science, Literature, and Art*. Mrs. Griffith said she kept it handy for quick reference to things she might not know off the top of her head. She opened the book to the M's.

"As I suspected, no entry for Henry Maudsley," she reported, snapping the book shut. "Never fear, young man. I have something here that should interest you more."

She opened the second book on the table, a leather-bound volume with no title or author's name on the cover. Inside, though, was a handwritten title page that read "Quotable Quotes Found Notable by Alice Griffith."

"That's me," she said, leafing through the well-worn pages of neatly written quotes, the elaborate quote marks all looking like the wings of angels. "I started this while at the Harvard Library. Here you go. Listen to this one, children: 'The sorrow which has no vent in tears may make other organs weep.' "

Mrs. Griffith read in the kind of soft, tender voice I imagined a mother should possess. I immediately checked under my eyes to make sure no tear stains remained.

"How beautiful and so true," said Jane. "Who said that?"

"Your Dr. Henry Maudsley."

"Not really my doctor. I never heard of him until Harry mentioned him. He does sound like he might understand why a woman gets teary-eyed, more so than Dr. McCarty of Dodge."

"Anything else from Dr. Maudsley?" I asked. "Anything about insanity?"

"Let me see," said Mrs. Griffith, who did not act as if there was anything unusual about my request. She turned pages slowly, licking her fingertips with every other turn.

"Well, would you look at this. Here's a longer Henry Maudsley quote, which I note here is from his 'The Emotions' section of *P&P,* page 130. I almost forgot. I'm not sure what possessed me to include this quote. I suspect I was having an emotional moment at the time. Should I read the quote to you?"

I gasped and leaned forward, accidentally causing the little table to wobble.

"You'd better," Jane said, "or Harry's heart may explode out of his chest."

Alice Griffith, in the same gentle voice, read the following: "One of the earliest symptoms of an oncoming insanity, and one that is almost universally present as the expression of a commencing deterioration, howsoever caused, of the nervous centres, is an emotional disturbance, upon which follows more or less perversion of judgment."

This time, I took it like a man — dry-eyed and stone-faced. Jane Hankin did not. She started to weep, then stopped suddenly and asked Mrs. Griffith to read the moving quote again. The old librarian hesitated, but then reread the passage, using an even gentler voice, the kind I imagined an angel should possess. Jane lowered her head onto *Zell's Popular Encyclopedia* and sobbed. I put a hand on her left shoulder and told her everything would be all right and there was no reason to cry. Miss Griffith gently lifted Jane's head to free the encyclopedia so it wouldn't get wet. She then put a hand on Jane's right shoulder and spoke like an angel's mother: "That's it, my dear. Let it all come out."

Ten minutes later, the droplets finally stopped running down Jane's face. She folded her hands on the table and sat up straight like a schoolgirl trying to impress her teacher. "You see, Mrs. Griffith," Jane said. "I had one of those terrible emotional disturbances. The man I was engaged to, Matt Sullivan, gave up his guns for me last December, and then one night, right before my eyes, I saw him shot down in cold blood, his brain matter splattered on the dance floor. I was devastated and am still in the process of recovery."

It was the first I'd heard Jane talk about the shooting, and it was the first I'd heard that Matt Sullivan and Jane had actually been engaged. If Wyatt Matters knew, he'd kept it from me. I grinded my teeth and clenched my fists in my lap until all the sadness in me was gone. I was glad that Mr. Sullivan was out of the picture now. I still vaguely saw Mr. Matters, as old as he was, as a threat to my romantic aspirations. But if not him, I envisioned younger rivals emerging once

Jane went back to work and felt like dancing again. I had her to myself now in Topeka, Kansas, but we'd have to return to Dodge. Thinking of Jane with any other man, dead or alive, was driving me crazy right there in the library in front of my true love and the old woman whose brain seemed the female equivalent of Wyatt Matters' male noggin. I thrust my fists upward into the underside of the table, rattling it and causing both women to stare at me. I didn't want to hear another quote. I didn't want to stay seated another second. I paced about, tearing at my hair.

"I see that Dr. Maudsley's quote has also affected you, young man," said Mrs. Griffith. "I'm so sorry I read it to you and your young lady, but it was my intention to be of service to readers like you two, in my mind the principal purpose of a good librarian."

"You mustn't blame yourself, Mrs. Griffith," I said. "In fact, I believe you have hit the nail on the head. Jane's confinement to her bed in Dodge was a clear case of perversion of judgment following her emotional disturbance. I believe Jane would agree."

"Yes, I wholeheartedly concur. But it has helped immensely to bring it out in the open here. You are a very good librarian, Mrs. Griffith."

"Think nothing of it, dear girl. Think of

nothing else but getting well and restoring your judgment."

"Yes, indeed," I said. "You seem reasonably sane, Jane." I paused and then quoted as best I could a Dr. Maudsley's sentence that Mrs. Griffith had earlier mentioned from memory: *A stranger conversing with her would not have discovered that she ailed anything at all.*

"What about you, young man?" Mrs. Griffith asked.

"What about me?"

"You seemed upset about something a moment ago. How do you feel now?"

I couldn't answer her. I felt terrible — as if Jane was nearly all right again while I was slipping into my own oncoming insanity. I asked Miss Griffith for directions to the Topeka Insane Asylum.

Chapter Thirteen

The asylum at 143 Kansas Ave. was much more than I imagined. We introduced ourselves to a Dr. Brown, who worked in the administration building in some capacity under the superintendent. He looked at Jane first, then me, then her again. I could tell that he was wondering which one of us was insane. All the while he kept up a stiff smile, but he seemed like a nervous man, the way he constantly tapped his cleft chin while his eyes appeared to almost blink separately. He showed us to his second-story office, which had artistic furniture and three barred windows overlooking a vast lawn streaked with lingering, pure-white snow. As we looked out a window, the doctor explained that the architects had paid special attention to creating a sanitary arrangement of the buildings in the shape of a great womb. I couldn't see it but said nothing. Jane, though, readily agreed with him, adding that all the embryos looked hale and hearty. I thought that an interesting observation on her part, but Dr. Brown seemed troubled by her words and the way Jane pressed her fingertips to the windowpane.

When he sat down at his large carved desk and then suggested we all sit down, Jane didn't budge. I took one of the small hard chairs across from his desk. "I'm glad there are bars on the window," he whispered to me. Clearly, he had determined that I was the normal one and that it was the woman who was to be admitted. I tried to straighten him out, saying that we had both been questioning our respective sanities but were now just looking over the lay of the land.

That caused Dr. Brown to scratch his head and then run a finger in repeated circles over his chin. "We are relatively new here," he said, "but nobody to my knowledge has voluntarily admitted himself."

"Let's not jump the gun, Dr. Brown." I replied. "We took the train in from Dodge. This visit might be only exploratory in nature."

"How so?"

"I am a person desiring further information on . . . you know, insanity."

"I see. We here at the asylum, from the superintendent on down to our last attendant, no longer regard insanity as the extinction of the mind, as hopeless and incurable."

"Nice to know. Not sure, though, if you can be of any help to me . . . us. How do you feel around here about Henry Maudsley?"

"I'm not familiar with the name. He must be one of our new patients."

"Not likely. I believe he lives in London and is quite the opposite of a patient. He wrote *The Physiology and Pathology of the Mind.* They don't have a copy over at the Topeka free library, but I figured you could have it here at the asylum."

"Not that I'm aware of. We have a day room where our patients sit and read, but we generally select certain books. In at least one instance here the cause of insanity was novel reading."

"What he wrote was new, possibly groundbreaking, but was no novel. I'm mostly interested in facts, Doctor, you know, knowledge. Would you say most of your patients are pleased to be in your asylum?"

"Pleased?" Dr. Brown adjusted his position in his cushioned chair several times. He collected his thoughts at his own leisure. When he at last spoke again he sounded like a man trying to sell a mansion or perhaps membership in a secret society. "I can tell you that our rooms here are roomy and cheerful, and from the glazed windows all have nice views of the countryside and the town — some even of the new Capitol. We strive to treat our patients like normal people and to help them have social and active lives. We don't lock anyone away in a dark room and apply the outdated practice of 'out of sight, out of mind.'"

"What about out of mind, out of insight?"

"Excuse me?"

"Sorry, Doctor. I was just thinking out loud, muttering if you will."

"Do that often, do you, Mr. Hannum?"

"Actually no. I am usually silent in my sorrow and frustration."

"I see. And what might be the cause of your overbearing sorrow and frustration?"

"I'm not sure it is always overbearing."

"I see. But still there is a cause, is there not?"

"Jane's delicate condition. Trying to fulfill my . . . my mentor's enormous expectations. My work at the Wright store. My life in Dodge City. The remoteness. The violence. The . . . I don't know."

"And that is why you have made this long journey in search of our asylum?"

"You might say, I don't want to dodge my feelings any longer."

"I see. And you suspect certain physical causes have disabled your brain?"

"Disabled? No nothing that extreme. I think all the time. I've just been wondering if my thinking might be what one would call unbalanced. It could be that I am madly in love."

"I see. Among the causes of insanity in our inmates, we find three cases of disappointed love and two of domestic trouble. But all five are of the female sex." He glanced over at Jane, who had finally turned away from the window but was now focused on the doctor's fancy wall clock that had been carved out of wormy walnut. "And, tell me, Harry — you don't mind me calling you Harry, do you? — is that lovely woman madly in love with you?"

"Ah, Doctor, that is the question. It remains to be seen. If she is so inclined, she doesn't know it yet."

"You think her thinking unbalanced as well?"

"Perhaps it was. Her nervousness was always there to a degree, but it rose to a new level because of a tragic incident — the violent death of the man she thought she loved. Her nervousness led to despair and idleness. She couldn't get out of bed for the longest time. But look at her now, Doctor — standing in your asylum at least 270 miles from home looking with the utmost fascination and curiosity at your timepiece."

The clock chimed on cue. It was five o'clock. The doctor jerked in his chair, though he surely should have been used to that sound unless someone had only recently given him the clock.

Jane turned away from the wall and approached the doctor's desk with a bounce to her step and a smile that could more than match his. "Time heals all wounds," she said cheerfully.

Those four words were all it took for Dr. Brown to determine that Jane was sane. He also must have figured my mad love for this woman wasn't enough to make me a candidate for residency. In fact, I suspect he had determined it was understandable if I were even halfway normal.

"Excellent," he said, clapping his hands so hard it made me jump.

I followed his lead and stood up.

"It is?"

"It is getting late," Dr. Brown said, still smiling. "I have my rounds to make before the evening meal."

"I feel I could eat a horse," said Jane, rubbing her belly.

"Excellent," the doctor said again. "You'll be my guests for supper. We appreciate healthy appetites at the asylum. One of our female inmates believes she has been condemned by God and therefore is without hope. She is tired of life and seeks every method to conceal any instrument that could open a vein or an artery. Oddly enough, although she wants to destroy herself, she refuses food, because she fears that it may contain poison. For six months she has taken our constant and incessant attention. We won't let her starve to death."

"Poor woman!" said Jane.

"Indeed. Hers is a great distress of mind brought on by the loss of her husband, struck down by a rabid Southern sympathizer four years after the late war."

"I understand, though it isn't the loss of a husband that always brings great distress. Sometimes having a husband can be more distressful. Will the poor woman be joining us for supper, Dr. Brown?"

"No, no, the widow Knapp takes her meals alone in her room for her own safety. But after we've eaten our meal, we might pass by her room if you're interested in a quick tour of our institution."

"I'd love that, Doctor," Jane said.

The doctor clapped his hands again. "And following the tour, I'll find you some excellent accommodations."

I must have had a puzzled look now because the doctor's smile broadened at least on one side of his face, and he explained: "We can't possibly expect you to return to Dodge tonight even if there is a late train running. Not only do the inmates receive the best of care at our asylum but also our non-residents receive our closest attention."

The three of us sat at a corner table in a dining hall with a half-dozen attendants. Because inmates howled like wild animals, stole food from others, threw their food, and generally lacked table etiquette, they mostly ate in their rooms like Mrs. Knapp. Jane didn't eat a horse, but she polished off a plate of pork, yellow squash, carrots, and buttermilk pie and took a second helping of fresh-baked bread. Dr. Brown admitted the inmates didn't eat as well as us in winter because the asylum gardens were dormant and fresh meat wasn't always available. I asked about all that buffalo meat in Kansas, but he said nobody thought to provide it to the institution.

During the quick tour of the asylum, we heard after-dinner howling, along with some wailing and considerable moaning. The widow Knapp was in no condition to receive visitors. She had tried to strangle herself with one of her stockings and then was stopped at the last second from plunging a fork into her neck. For her own good she had been bundled within the folds of a heavy blanket with a cord tied around it to confine her hands and limbs. Dr. Brown hurried us along to our adjoining rooms, whose small windows looked out at an empty, fenced-in courtyard. My room smelled strongly of medicine but then my sleeping quarters at the back of the Wright general store had various disagreeable scents, including musty flour, bear grease, and tobacco smoke. Jane remarked that her bed was narrower and harder than the one she slept in at home. She ended up pulling her three blankets onto the floor and tossing and turning in them all night.

When I went to her room to wake her up, she was already sitting on the bed in her white nightdress. I must say her auburn hair was pointed in all directions, and she looked ready to scream. It didn't make me want her any less. When she crossed her legs, I sighed.

"I kept hearing loud moaning all night," she complained, as she took the comb I'd given her for Christmas out of her bag and went to work.

"Some of it could have been from me," I confessed. "I was dreaming . . . never mind."

"And I kept thinking of poor Mrs. Knapp, suicidal and restrained."

"You know, Dr. Brown didn't even show

us the wild wards where the violent men are kept. One of the attendants told me that bloodcurdling sounds often come from there. I suppose the good doctor wanted to spare you, you being a . . . you know, woman and all."

"I suspect to spare you as well, Harry. Anyone can tell you are a sensitive, tender man."

"Thank you, I think."

"Sometimes I wonder, though, if all men are intrinsically violent, whether they are sane or not."

"Don't ask me. I don't even know what intrinsically means."

"Did you know at the far end of the courtyard they have already started a cemetery. I made out two markers. Some of these patients will never get out alive."

"Nobody gets out of this world alive."

"Who are you quoting, Dr. Brown, Henry Maudsley, or Wyatt Matters?"

"I think it dates before their time. Probably Jesus Christ said it first. Anyway, Jane, we can at least leave the asylum this morning, can't we? Hard to believe that I came here thinking it might be right for . . . you know, you and me. I'm convinced Dr. Brown doesn't consider us as legitimate candidates for residency."

"Right you are, Harry. To choose to live here would be insane. I welcome the return to Dodge City. It isn't perfect by any means, but it is my home."

"Mine, too."

When the Atchison, Topeka & Santa Fe pulled into Dodge, we were surprised to see Wyatt Matters standing on the platform grinning at us like a man who had won a huge poker pot with a pair of deuces. He gave Jane Hankin an exuberant hug — his most emotional display ever witnessed by me. She allowed him to take hold as long as he wanted, which was too long in my opinion. Finally, he broke it off and gave me a stern look while laying a soft hand on my head as if I were a disobedient dog who had run off after an elusive deer and had finally returned home to get fed. In his own sweet time, he explained his presence. His sources had seen me leave Dodge the previous day with a woman, and Mr. Wright had told him I had likely gone to Topeka for a short break from work. When Wyatt found Jane's bed empty, it confirmed his assumption that the woman was Lady Jane. Who else could it have been? Certainly not Alice Wright. Next, he sent a wire to someone he knew in the capital city who then watched us get off the train and proceed to the free library. At Wyatt's request, this same fellow, who happened to be a reverend and former mayor of Topeka, had then tailed us unseen to the asylum and telegraphed several reports back to Wyatt in Dodge.

"You care so much about me, Wyatt," Jane said.

"Yes," he said. "About the both of you. I'm just thankful you're all right."

"You mean you were spying on us?" I asked.

"The Reverend Josiah B. McAfee is one of the best," Wyatt said. "We see eye to eye on so many things. He founded the Leavenworth Collegiate Institute, the state's first education institution of any consequence, preached against lawlessness and slavery, was nearly lynched for his views, served in the Union Army and then as private secretary to the governor. While mayor of Topeka in 1870 and 1871 he and his handpicked policemen were a terror to evildoers. During his administration no saloon man got a license with which to debauch the citizens of Topeka. He was also one of the men who pushed for the creation of the Topeka Insane Asylum. That's the kind of brilliant man we need to make Dodge City a better place."

It was the first time I had heard my mentor speak in admiration of any man who was still living. And it reminded me that I still knew absolutely nothing about Wyatt Matters' past.

"So, you must have spent quite some time with the Referend McAfee," I said.

"As you know, son, unlike him, I have no religion. I *do not know* there is someone up there watching over us, thus I am an agnostic. But the Reverend McAfee never preached to me. And there was little I could teach him. We have had the most extraordinary conversations about past worlds, our frontier world, and other worlds."

"I can imagine. And you met him in Topeka?"

"No, no. We met when the border ruffian war raged in Kansas, and I was . . . Hey, what's happening here! I did not come to the tracks today to speak of myself. I'd like an explanation. Why did you take the train to Topeka? If Trader Bob was right and you needed to get away, why did you choose Topeka and why did you take Jane?"

"I thought I might have business there . . . that is that *we* might."

"At the Topeka Insane Asylum?"

"Yes," said Jane. "And we passed the test."

"At the free library, too," I quickly said,

not wanting to dwell on the asylum visit. "I wanted to learn a few things."

"Always admirable."

"We met this amazing Mrs. Griffith, an old librarian who has probably read as many books as you and answered all our questions."

"You don't think I could have done that?"

"I wanted to locate a copy of *The Physiology and Pathology of the Mind.* Unfortunately, the library didn't have it. But Mrs. Griffith knew the book so well. She had her own book with quotes from Dr. Maudsley that she wrote down when she was in Cambridge, Massachusetts, working at the Harvard Library."

"How nice for her. Copies are hard to come by west of the Mississippi. My only copy is no doubt at the bottom of the Ohio River. I made the mistake of lending it to a fellow I was traveling with on the sidewheel steamboat *Wild Wagoneer.* He turned out to be quite insane. He read for maybe half an hour before he flung the book into the rushing water. And then he flung himself in. Neither his body nor the book were recovered."

"How awful," said Jane. "The poor fellow might have done better in an asylum."

"So, Lady Jane, you were impressed with the insane institution in Topeka?"

"It was architecturally sound and comforting in its form. The food we were served was surprisingly good, too. But I could have done without the constant wailing and moaning. And that strange bed didn't fit me right. How are doings in Dodge?"

"Nobody got himself killed while you were away. What about you, Harry?"

"I didn't get myself killed in Topeka."

"Or put in the asylum, eh?"

"It wasn't for me," I said.

"So glad to hear it. Of course, I could have told you both that. In fact, I did tell Harry that asylums are not right for folks with temporary ills. It is a mistake *not* to listen to me. I don't say things just to hear myself talk."

"Don't blame Harry. I wanted to go with him."

"But why? You'd been long in bed and hadn't even been seeing him."

"Harry wanted me to go with him so badly. I was ready for a change of scenery, and I guess I owed Harry something for giving me that silver mirror, comb, and brush last Christmas."

"That was two and a half months ago."

"I know. I wanted to thank him. I sort of lost my way."

"A lot has happened to you this year, that's for sure. But I was worried all to pieces. You departed so suddenly, and you didn't bother to inform me."

"I'm sorry."

"I'm not," I said. "You don't have to know everything, Mr. Matters. Sometimes people need to find out things for themselves."

"And what pray tell did you find out in Topeka besides the fact neither of you is out of your mind?"

"Yes, there was that and . . ."

"And what, son?"

"That . . . that we're in . . . I mean I'm in . . . you know, in love."

Jane might have blushed. It was hard to tell because I couldn't look her squarely in the face. Mostly I was studying the tops of my well-worn shoes.

"What do you have to say about that declaration, Lady Jane?"

"Well, it isn't so crazy, is it? I've felt that all along from him, well, most of the time except when I thought he was trying to kill me with the pillow."

"And how do you feel about our Harry?"

"I can't say just yet. I am still getting used to being normal again."

"Anything you two need to tell me about the night you spent together at the asylum?"

"We don't have to tell you everything," I said.

"Nothing happened. Dr. Brown gave us separate rooms. I couldn't sleep all night. Harry moaned a lot. I guess the walls weren't as thick as they seemed."

"The Zimmermans were terribly worried about you, Jane. Perhaps you'll want to apologize to them for getting up and leaving that way."

"I shall apologize. And I'll thank them, too, for all they've done for me. I feel I may be ready to return to work soon."

"No need to be in a sudden rush, Lady Jane. The important thing is we are together again back in Dodge. This is where we belong — the three of us."

"We sort of reached the same conclusion," said Jane

For me, Wyatt Matters hadn't been part of the equation. But I didn't say anything. I had displayed quite a mouth in the last few weeks, especially since stepping off the train. I was talking too much and not listening enough, hardly the way for a protégé to act.

Chapter Fourteen

I'm sure Wyatt Matters hadn't given me up as a lost cause just because I had taken Jane Hankin out of Dodge for a couple days and upon my return had talked back to him like a malcontent. Still, he stopped stopping by the general store, even though I was back to clerking and cleaning for Robert Wright six days a week. Nights, I again lent my child-watching services to Alice Wright. Even though I had awkwardly announced my love for Jane at the train platform, I didn't press my luck. She had gone back to selling hardware, tinware, and jewelry at the Zimmerman store but only part-time and told me twice she wasn't ready yet to start mingling with the masses, which I took to mean men, of which I was one. I vowed not to become frustrated and sorrowful, at least not to the extent that I started questioning my sanity again. It was some consolation that she didn't appear to be seeing much of

Mr. Matters either. But the spring was racing toward summer, and I was spending the days and nights without my true love.

Three different times I passed by Wyatt's tent with the idea of restoring our mentor-protégé relationship, but I admittedly also wanted to make sure Jane wasn't there. She never was, though each time he had a visitor — a man. I heard the man's gravelly voice — though, of course, Wyatt was always doing most of the talking — and listened in the shadows, but never went inside to identify Wyatt's mysterious visitor. Although I dedicated much time to the task, it was hard to piece together the bits of conversations I overheard. The primary topics discussed were Bloody Kansas, John Brown, Frederick Douglass, the Civil War, Reconstruction, Harriet Tubman, Shakespeare's *Othello,* the color of Jesus Christ's skin, Southern food such as okra stew and jambalaya, the Dodge City Vigilante Committee, and the upcoming election to decide Ford County's charter public officials.

I suspected that Mr. Matters had found himself a new protégé if not a replacement protégé. I still didn't barge into his tent, since that seemed a little crass — like a man barging in on his wife whom he suspected of having an affair. On my fourth spying mission to his tent, I hid behind a woodpile until the *other* man emerged. I was startled to see that he was neither young nor white. I recognized him as one of Dodge City's few black businessmen but couldn't recall his name or exactly what he did. To refresh my memory, I followed him. He walked fast for a short man (somewhere between Wyatt and me in height) as if making up for lost time. At Railroad Avenue he rushed into a hole-in-the-wall restaurant called Taylor Made. Next door was an unoccupied two-horse wagon with three rows of seats in the back and a painted sign on the side reading "Fort Dodge Express." I had seen the wagon passing by the Wright store many times, usually loaded with soldiers either arriving with enthusiasm from Fort Dodge or headed back to the fort and looking none too sober. I recalled now that the usual driver of that wagon was dark-skinned, and that Mr. Wright had called him a cocky colored civilian named Taylor who was employed by Lieutenant Colonel Richard Dodge, the commanding officer at Fort Dodge.

The door of Taylor Made was locked, and I thought the restaurant was closed. But when I started to walk away, the door chimed as it swung open. A thin mahogany-skinned woman in an apron stood there with her hands on her slim hips. She stared at my face with such intensity I imagined her trying to read my mind the way Wyatt did. I instantly admired her high cheekbones, and then looked past her to size up the small dining area. I saw only two or three tables, and no customers.

"You open?"

She pointed to her open mouth and then to my mouth. She made a throaty sound that wasn't close to a real word. I wondered if she was an escapee from an asylum.

"No, no food, Miss," I said. "I'm looking for someone, a Mr. Taylor, I believe."

She crossed her arms and pursed her lips.

"I saw a man come in here who I believe is him."

She shook her head and made motions as if I should back up out the door.

"All right," I said, pointing to my mouth. "Eat."

She still hesitated, but then a man called out from somewhere behind her. "It's all right, Monique. He isn't one of them. He's Mr. Hannum, Mr. Matters' friend."

An instant change came over this Monique. Her cheekbones rose even higher with a grand smile, and she stepped aside to wave me inside. I was delighted that she was sane. She lit a candle on the corner table and pointed to a chair. As soon as I sat, she pointed to my mouth again and then patted the left side of her chest as if demonstrating a beating heart. Next, she tapped my belly with one finger, apologized with her soft brown eyes, and then ran off into what I assumed was the kitchen as if I had ordered something.

The owner of Taylor Made, who was about twice as dark and three times as wide as Monique, appeared before the food did. He confirmed that he was Mr. Taylor, first name William, the sole owner of the restaurant and the man who ran the Fort Dodge express shuttle service for Colonel Dodge.

"I'm impressed," I said.

"You bet. Not bad for a former Missouri slave who was worth less than a Missouri mule. Most of those soldier boys I bring into Dodge City are here to drink and frolic in the saloons and dance halls. But some eat, and I call the regulars who take the meals at my place the 'Gumbo Guys.' Tonight, though, jambalaya is on the menu, not that we have a menu."

"Sounds . . . eh . . . different."

"Won't find the likes of it anywhere west of St. Louis. Rice, beans, ham, more rice, fowl, crawfish, salt, peppers, more rice. Cooks get creative with it. I first met the dish in New Orleans about ten minutes after I met Monique. She figured since she couldn't talk, she may as well cook me a good old Creole meal. She's been cooking for me ever since, and now for the Taylor Made customers to boot. But I must apologize for her."

"No need. It doesn't bother me she's a mute."

"Yes, she fell off a New Orleans balcony and hit her head when she was six. But I wasn't talking about that. She was rude to you at the door, afraid to let you inside when you asked for me. Lately she's been as skittish as a prairie dog with a buffalo herd approaching."

"I understand. I know a woman who's been full of fear. She's getting better."

"Monique has plenty of reason to be afraid I suppose . . . for me that is. She's not nearly so worried about herself. Great gal. Loves her man. Never talks back."

William Taylor broke into a deep laughter that seemed to cause the entire table to shake. Monique appeared, scowling not smiling, and placed a full plate of jambalaya in front of me along with a fork and knife. I started to ask them to join me, but Mr. Taylor told me that they both were mindful of knowing their place and thus never sat down with customers, not even Wyatt Matters, his best customer. Monique nodded and put her hands on those narrow hips that swayed just enough to attract one's attention.

"I didn't know Mr. Matters came here to eat," I said.

"Oh, yes. The wise old man who lives in a tent."

Monique put her hands overhead and drew in the air the outline of a top hat.

"Mr. Matters discovered Taylor Made some time ago," Mr. Taylor continued. "On occasion he takes the Fort Dodge Express wagon to tell Colonel Dodge on how to run the U.S. Army. The wise old man has an opinion about how soldiers, civilians, Indians, and the U.S. government should behave."

"Sounds like him. I didn't know you even knew him."

"He's by far my biggest supporter in town, besides my wife, of course. Since Monique can't speak, I probably visit that wise old man in his tent more than I should. But never in my life have I been so engaged in invigorating conversation with another human being."

"I know what you mean. But I mostly just listen to him."

"And you listen well. He speaks highly of

you as his . . . eh . . . pupil. Is that the right word?"

"Protégé."

I hadn't yet taken more than half a bite of jambalaya. Monique uncrossed her arms, stepped closer to the table, and did some pointing — to my plate, to my fork, and to my mouth. I quickly took a forkful, and even while chewing I took another large bite. I rubbed my stomach, closed my eyes, and smacked my lips as if the meal she had cooked was beyond words. Maybe it was. I considered it superior to bison tongue or anything else I'd eaten in Kansas. Monique seemed satisfied with my response. She managed the squeak of a small animal before scurrying back to the kitchen.

"She's delightful," I said as I put my fork in fast motion. William Taylor remained standing, with his back to the wall, watching me with what appeared to be amusement. As I filled my belly, I thought of Jane Hankin and all those meals she had taken in bed. I promised myself that in the next day or two I would ask her to dine with me at Taylor Made, which seemed like a nice quiet place for one recovering from a nervous condition.

"As a pupil — I mean protégé — of Mr. Matters, we are happy you came, Mr.

Hannum," the owner said. "I take it you are of the same mind as him about political matters."

"We don't talk much about current politics. Sometimes he tells me things about the government in Athens and Sparta and such."

"I was thinking more in the lines of race."

"Never have seen him race. He mostly takes his time going where he wants to go."

"You must know Mr. Matters was a great abolitionist."

I half nodded as I worked my fork. Wyatt hadn't told me directly, but it didn't surprise me. I always figured he was one who favored the underdog — such as Indians and buffalo and peaceful men and women.

"Of, course now he is an exceptional advocate of Negro participation in business and all walks of life. Not everybody in town appreciates us, you know."

I hadn't really thought about it, but I nodded more forcefully as I chewed away. I didn't ask him to expand on that statement, but he did.

"Some of the soldiers from the fort have Southern leanings and when they ride into town on the Express wagon, they aren't shy about calling me names and putting me in my place, rather the place they think I ought to be. Likewise, I am not particularly liked by the townsfolk, and some of Dodge's finest wouldn't be caught dead walking into Taylor Made for a meal. However, I have demonstrated sufficient respectability to be allowed to live and work in Dodge. It helps that I have the Colonel Dodge connection, that I have mostly kept my mouth shut, that I can produce a marriage certificate, and that Monique doesn't flaunt her natural beauty on Front Street."

I kept nodding and chewing until I had finished my last bite, after which I patted my belly and complimented the chief and the owner on their hospitality. As if her name had been called, Monique reappeared. She set my plate aside and, in its place, served me another treat from New Orleans. Mr. Taylor called it a king cake but added that some people called it a *three kings cake* in honor of the three wise men who visited Jesus after his birth.

"During Christmas time, celebrators like Monique's family down in New Orleans are known to put a hidden trinket inside that can represent Christ or some other person," Mr. Taylor said. "But go ahead and take a bite of cake, Mr. Hannum. Monique hasn't put anything Christ-like in her king cakes for years. As for me, my mammy raised me to believe Jesus was the same race as us, and we never ate cake."

The cake was loaded with sugary purple icing, and I savored two pieces. Mr. Taylor also ate two pieces, while standing. Monique smiled at both of us and then agreed to take one small bite before she returned to the kitchen carrying dirty plates and utensils.

"She's so skinny sometimes I think if she stepped outside into the Kansas wind, she'd blow away clear back to New Orleans," said Mr. Taylor. "Sometimes I wonder if that might not be best. And for me to follow her on a fast horse."

"You mean leave Dodge?"

"Keeping my mouth shut hasn't been so easy lately. Mr. Matters tells me I have as much right as any other American to have my voice heard and the freedom to protest injustice. How can I disagree with that? Trouble is when I do speak my mind among the diners here or when I'm driving the wagon those five miles between the town and the fort, it tends to set off certain men in town, men who possess the lynch mentality."

"Really? It's 1873 and this is Kansas. You have right on your side. How many of those bad men can there possibly be in Dodge?"

"Hard to say. But they all have guns."

"Even though he hasn't heard about a

shooting in Dodge in more than two months, Mr. Matters still insists that we need lawmen and ordinances against carrying guns in town. All of that could be coming to Dodge soon, what with the June elections in less than a week."

"Yes, Mr. Matters has said the same to me . . . more than once. It's not only about shootings or even the saloon brawling. The change can't happen soon enough, Mr. Hannum. None of those bad men frequent my restaurant or have any use for me. What frightens Monique the most is that some of those rowdies are active members of the Dodge City Vigilance Committee."

"Mr. Matters has his issues with the vigilantes, too."

"Yes, sir. That wise old man supports me all the way."

"That's fine by me. Hope you and Monique do stick around."

It was hard to stay one step ahead of Wyatt Matters. Before starting work on the first day of June, a sudden burst of confidence sent me dashing over to Jane Hankin's house with every intention of asking her to dine with me that evening at Taylor Made. She wasn't home. I couldn't imagine where she might be. As I trudged to the general store, the only possibility I could think of was Mr. Matter's tent. I'd be late for work if I checked to see if she was there. That was my excuse. If she was there, engaged in conversation or something else, I didn't think I could stand it.

I tended to customers all morning as if I valued them, but in my head, I blamed them for invading my space and interfering with my thinking — all of which centered on the missing Jane. Long about noontime, I was sweeping customer dust and shooting back with my broom at a couple of shootists using cottonwood sticks — seven-year-old Elias Wright and five-year-old James Wright. I had finally gotten Jane out of mind. So, of course, that's when she walked right into the general store behaving like any normal customer.

"The Zimmermans have a short list of things they need — a hammer, a box of wire nails, two pounds of dried fruit, and a bolt of red calico," she said, ignoring the *bang-bang-bang* of the boys. "Can you help me?"

I could only stare at first. Instead of the scoop-necked, tight-fitting red dress she wore when I closed my eyes and imagined, she wore a loose-fitting brown calico dress with high collar and long sleeves minus any ruffles or ribbons. This was her workday dress, not her dancing dress. She also wore what looked to be a new broad-brimmed sunbonnet that hid most of her appealing auburn hair. But when she turned and spotted nails for sale on a shelf, I saw delightful auburn curls cascading down the back of her head.

"Well," she continued. "I see the nails. Can you help me with the rest?"

"Happy to help," I said.

But first I had to play dead on the floor to provide the Wright boys with a satisfying conclusion to our shooting game Their father allowed me to carry Jane's purchases to the Zimmerman store, where she had gone back to work full time. That explained why I hadn't found her at home earlier. I was relieved. Better for her to go to work than to Wyatt Matters' tent. The new sunbonnet, though, was a gift from my mentor and her old admirer.

"Now that I'm going to and from work and spending more time outdoors, he wants me to have the proper protection for my fair-skinned face and fragile little head," she said. "Not that I think of my head as little. Of course, Wyatt's head is awfully big."

I couldn't argue with that. I wished it was me, not Wyatt, who had first thought to buy her a sunbonnet. When we arrived at the Zimmerman store and stood under the oversized "Guns, Pistols, Ammunition, Hardware, Tinware and Lumber" sign, I held out my arm to keep her from walking in right away. In so doing, I dropped the bag of dried fruit but managed to hang on to the rest. I apologized twice, and she accepted both times. But then she asked me to be more careful, and my natural shyness returned like a recurring bad dream. I couldn't say what I wanted to say to her. I only managed to brilliantly announce how warm it was for June and how there figured to be many hot, sunny days ahead.

"The sunbonnet helps," she said. "I'd better go in. I'm committed to being the kind of reliable working girl Mr. and Mrs. Zimmerman want. And you had better put those things inside and get back to work yourself or Mr. Wright might think you skedaddled with me like that time you took me to Topeka."

"I . . . I remember that time fondly."

"Topeka was nice, I suppose. As I recall, we never did get a close look at the new Capitol."

"I . . . I had you to myself."

"Come on, Harry. I'll thank you for helping me when we get inside."

"I have something to ask you outside first. You can thank me by saying *yes*."

"You want me to say yes without hearing the question?"

"Yes . . . I mean no. I wanted to ask you, now that we are both back to being normal people living our normal lives in Dodge City, if you'd be so kind to take a meal with me after work."

"Tonight?"

"Yes, you see I discovered this out-of-the-way but pleasing little restaurant that . . ."

"Can't tonight. I'm eating with Wyatt."

"In his tent?"

"No. He says his new friend has a place that serves succulent food. The friend's wife does the cooking."

"Creole food perhaps? The new friend is a Negro? The wife doesn't say much?"

"Oh. You know William and Monique Taylor, too? Wyatt didn't tell me."

"Wyatt doesn't know I know." I brushed past her now and tried to open the store door myself. Of course, I dropped something again — two things in fact, the hammer and box of nails. The hammer made a bang like a gun going off. Jane jumped. The box broke open and the nails scattered across the boardwalk. She rescued the calico bolt and dried fruit from my arms and entered the store. I let her go without a word. I knelt carefully to retrieve the nails and began muttering under my breath — calling Wyatt Matters names and using the same names for myself.

Everything seemed to work out. Once I had restored the nails to the box, I went inside and apologized to her and to Frederick Zimmerman. After exchanging cordial goodbyes, I told Jane I'd probably see her sometime that night at the Taylor Made since there were only three tables. That prompted her to invite me. She said that Wyatt Matters would welcome my presence since he had the impression that I was displeased with him and had been avoiding him. I told her that it was my distinct impression that Mr. Matters was avoiding me and preferred to lecture the *old Negro*. But we both agreed that William Taylor was a fine not-so-old fellow and that as a meal maker Monique beat the Dodge House cooks hands down.

The meal went well. Monique served up hot, steaming cups of what had become her specialty after she and her husband moved to Kansas — "buffalo gumbo." Wyatt had eaten it before, and this time Monique put in crushed red peppers with vinegar and salt to add extra spice to the dish. It was so good that Wyatt never suggested it be called *bison gumbo*. As expected, he did most of the talking, but he made a point of never leaving me out of any conversation, nor anyone else either, including the mute cook, whom he asked questions that required only a nod or shake of her pretty head.

"You sure can pick 'em, Wyatt," Jane said as she finished off her gumbo and picked the napkin off her lap. As she wiped her mouth, I thought how much I wished to be that napkin — going from her lap to her lips and soon back to her lap again. "I can't remember ever eating a finer meal. I thank you and the Taylors for making this evening possible."

'And let's not forget *our* Harry," Wyatt said. "He has contributed his share to the wonderful dinner conversation."

At first, I thought Wyatt was being sarcastic, though he had rarely ever resorted to saying the opposite of what was true to make me look foolish. I couldn't think of any of my spoken words as being memorable that night, but I let the matter drop after I gave him a half-hearted nod of appreciation.

"If all the citizens of Dodge were like you folks, Monique and I would never want to pack up and make tracks out of Kansas."

"Please, Willie, no talk of leaving us," said

Wyatt. "You got to give Dodge a fair chance. As a town we can only get better."

"That's what they said about New Orleans, but after the war things got worse there, not just for freed slaves but for Negroes who never knew slavery. The South is the South. Kansas is the North. We migrated here expecting to buy into a better life."

"You own this restaurant, don't you? And you run the wagon service between here and Fort Dodge, don't you?"

"We feed mostly colored folks here and a Chinaman or two. I wouldn't have the Dodge City Express if not for a condoling Colonel Dodge out at the fort."

"Hell, that's something. I don't think Colonel Dodge likes the way I advise him now and again on how to run his Army and improve life at both the fort and the city."

"I can't count the times wagon passengers and men on the street have called me a black son of a bitch for no reason at all. Pardon my French, Miss Hankin."

"We're on your side, Mr. Taylor," Jane said. "The Hankins were Jayhawkers, and we never owned a single slave. We lived in peace during the border war, and we were still living in peace in 1863, that is until Quantrill and Anderson struck like the devil, like two devils."

"Yes, Mr. Matters told me," Mr. Taylor said. "The Lawrence Raid was a horrible thing — one of many horrible things that occurred in that war against slavery. Monique and I were in New Orleans, but we could feel the pain all the way down there. We're grateful you survived, Miss Hankin."

"I was twelve. Most of the women and children survived. My daddy and my three brothers did not. I saw them fall. The Bushwhackers pulled them out of their blankets and shot them as easily as one might swat flies on a sunny day. And then they burned our house. They burned the town. I saw Bloody Bill light a match."

"I'm sorry," William Taylor and I said simultaneously.

"That wasn't the end of it. Mama never was the same again. Nothing was ever the same again. I'm the one who should apologize. I brought up this unpleasant mealtime topic."

"Quantrill was not a reasonable man and Anderson was insane," Wyatt said. "It was a time of unreasonableness and horror on both sides. As President Lincoln said in Philadelphia on June 16, 1864, 'War at the best is terrible, and this war of ours, in its magnitude and its duration, is one of the most terrible.' We can all count as a blessing the fact that slavery and war are a thing of the past."

"Amen," said Mr. Taylor. "But unreasonableness is not. The other night, very late . . ."

Monique interrupted him by noisily setting a tray down in front of him. She had made plum pudding for dessert. Before serving, though, she put a finger to her lips, as if telling her husband to say no more. He patted her hand and continued. "As I was saying, one of my drivers who can pass for white received a beastly beating from passengers he was taking out to the fort. They did so for no other reason than he was driving the wagon for a self-important colored cuss — yours truly."

"I respect your opinion on that, Willie," Wyatt said. "But my take on it is that the young men who did the beating and shot off their mouths about you had been doing some heavy drinking. When they get on a whiskey bender like that, they are just as likely to get violent with their own kind as they are with men of a different color."

"I always respect your opinions, Mr. Matters. Allow me to point out, however, one thing about the meanness of white men. They can drink whiskey and be mean to anyone, but they don't need to touch a drop of the stuff to kill a colored man."

"None of us here are mean," said Jane. She tasted the pudding and smacked her lips. "Now then, let's talk of something more pleasant, like friendship. The way I see it, William Taylor, you have no better friend in Dodge than Wyatt Matters. Wyatt Matters, you have no better cause in Dodge than Willie Taylor. The pudding is delicious, Monique. Tomorrow, I aim to tell Matilda and Frederick Zimmerman and everyone else I know what a fine table you set at Taylor Made. Thank you. Thank you."

William Taylor thanked her and looked at his wife, who was beaming and began offering plum pudding seconds. Wyatt accepted, and so did I. Jane said she couldn't eat another bite but would be back for more another evening and would pay next time. She stood up and gave Monique a hug. "I'll help with the cleanup," Jane said. "No, no, I insist. I feel so at home here."

Monique made some signs that her husband understood.

"Monique accepts your kind offer," said Mr. Taylor. "But first she wanted me to ask you something, Miss Hankin."

"Anything," said Jane.

"She wants to know if you are engaged?"

I dropped my spoon. I looked at Wyatt and he looked at me.

"Engaged?" Jane said. "Where did that come from?"

I didn't doubt that she, Wyatt, and I all had the name "Matt Sullivan" circulating in our heads. I shuddered, even though the man had been laid to rest more than five months ago.

"My wife has been observing you three. Usually, she can tell exactly where everyone stands or sits. She can see you are all good friends and the special way that Mr. Matters and Mr. Hannum look at you. But she has been unable to decide which one of these gentlemen has asked for your hand in marriage."

Jane laughed and tapped Monique on the chin to get her attention. Next, Jane began to point, first to her own hand, then to Wyatt's big nose, then to my confused face. As soon as she was done with that exercise, she shook her head so vigorously that her auburn hair danced on her shoulders.

"Please tell your wife, Mr. Taylor, that she is under the false impression that I am engaged to one of these gentlemen," said Jane.

"No need," said Mr. Taylor. "She understood you quite well, Miss Hankin." Monique then made some more hand gestures to her husband. "My wife apologizes for having had the false impression."

The room fell strikingly silent. There was no more conversation at the table. Soon we were all standing and saying our goodnights and telling each other how much we'd love to do it all again real soon. Jane suddenly remembered she had volunteered to help with the dirty dishes, but Wyatt told her how late it was and reminded her about her work at the store in the morning.

"I'd like to say one more thing that I believe is important," Wyatt said as we all stood at the doorway. "It is my not-so-humble opinion that you, Monique, and you, William, are exemplars of the kind of blissful married life I have never known and never shall. I'm glad that my young friends Jane and Harry were able to witness this atmosphere of happy domesticity in Dodge City. You see ever since I introduced them last November at the Kelley and Hunt dance hall, I've believed they were a good match, one that I have been encouraging ever since. So far there has been no engagement but an old man who believes in young love can only hope."

Jane lowered her face, which was showing a brilliant blush. I wasn't sure if my own face was showing color, but I was all choked up and began shuffling my feet like a schoolboy singled out for giving his teacher a shiny red apple.

"It has been a delight, but I must be going," Jane said. "I'm not used to being out so late. It is far past my bedtime. I . . . I must go."

"As does Harry," Mr. Matters said. "Perhaps you wouldn't mind escorting Miss Hankin home, son."

I could have kissed the wise old man.

Chapter Fifteen

I told myself I must not get a swelled head from Wyatt Matters' apparent encouragement of a romantic relationship between Jane and me. Not that I doubted his motives . . . well, perhaps just a little. No matter what he said, it was up to Jane to reciprocate my affections toward her. As I walked her home, we were silent. I was putting together words in my head, and I imagined she was both bone tired and deep in thought about the late Matt Sullivan, whether they had officially been engaged or not. By the time we arrived at the blue house I had a little speech ready about how lucky William Taylor was to have Monique and how I hoped my luck would change soon. Jane, though, didn't give me a chance, thanking me for seeing her home safely and then quickly darting inside as if I'd been chasing her instead of escorting her.

I was not totally discouraged. Overnight

the words that ran through my head were the three encouraging ones spoken by my mentor, *A good match.* In the morning, before my eyes fully opened, I envisioned her and me seated at a table for two at Taylor Made. I planned to ask her at noon with a flower in my hand. Alice Wright maintained a small rose garden on the sunnier side of the general store. If I plucked only one, I figured it would go unnoticed. Still, I couldn't do it, hardly a criminal act but unworthy of an honest man in love. I went to the Wright home to ask her permission. I was glad to see Robert Wright had already gone to the store.

"You want a single rose, Harry?" she asked while busy scrambling eggs for her large brood.

"It's a beginning," I said. "I'm in love, truly in love. I know it now."

"Are you saying you want to give me a flower from my own garden?"

"What?" I suppose I should have expected such a response considering my past mildly inappropriate behavior toward Alice. "I'm sorry, ma'am. I should have been more specific. The rose would be for Jane Hankin."

"Oh, I see. Of course, you have more sense than to ask an old married lady like me for a flower to present to me. It's been a hectic morning, Harry."

"You know you aren't old, Alice, just five years older than Jane."

Saying that got me thinking in amazement how close the two women were in age. Alice seemed so much older, especially when she began calling her children to the breakfast table.

"Jane Hankin, you say? That makes perfect sense, her having the distinction of being the only young female store clerk in all of Dodge. It's taken you quite some time getting around to it, hasn't it, young man?"

"I suppose. This will be the first flower, but we have spent time together already."

"I almost forgot. You had some strong competition. Wasn't she madly in love with Matt Sullivan?"

"I've heard the rumors, but he's dead."

"Yes, for some time. Didn't she stay home in bed for the longest time mourning his loss — lovesick you might say?"

"It's not something I dwell on. Anyway, she is free of him now."

"As I was telling Mr. Wright the other day there is nothing to be done about young love. It's as natural as spring and spring flowers. And now summer nears. Where are those kids!"

"Well, I'd better go now. Thanks for the flower."

"I sense you're a little afraid, Harry, uncertain about what falling in love means now and down the road. I suspect the reason you are telling me about your strong feelings toward Jane Hankin is because you are nervous, at a loss on how to proceed."

"No, ma'am. I just wanted the flower to give her."

"Don't call me ma'am, Harry. What about Wyatt Matters?"

"What do you mean?"

"That old nonworking busybody has an opinion about everything. How does he feel about your young love? I ask because it is common knowledge that he has paid a great deal of attention to the much, much younger Jane Hankin in both her home and his bachelor's tent."

Talk about busybodies, I thought. I didn't want to admit that I had until recently been plagued by the same suspicions. "No worries," I said.

"As you know, Mr. Wright and I consider him a suspect character, one who can't be fully trusted to have the best interests of Dodge City or anybody living in it but himself at heart."

"Mr. Matters is often misunderstood. He has my best interests at heart. He is all for Jane and me. He cares about her the same way he cares about me. He is a caring man. Really, he is. You and Mr. Wright just don't see that side of him. But I've seen how much he cares for a thirty-seven-year-old black man with a mute wife. Everything is fine with Wyatt."

"Well, Harry, I am all for you and Jane, too, even if it means agreeing with *that* man."

"Thank you, Mrs. Wright."

"Alice."

"Thank you, Alice. Jane is sensitive and sweet, the best woman I've ever known, present company excepted, of course."

"You're sweet, but no need to say that. I must ask, though, if you are positive that she isn't another Elizabeth Pepper?"

"Oh, you remember me telling you about Miss Pepper. I had about forgotten her. I never asked Miss Pepper to marry me. In fact, we were never officially engaged."

"Right. She ran off with the railroad man before you got the chance to make it official."

"You don't forget anything I tell you, do you, Alice? But this is different. I really love Jane. It wasn't this way with Elizabeth Pepper. Elizabeth wasn't a good woman."

"Not in retrospect anyway. Is there something I can help you with, lover boy, perhaps some advice on how to make Jane's love for you blossom? She does love you, doesn't she?"

"Oh, yes. Well, I'm pretty sure. I don't really need advice. Just the flower."

"In that case, why not go full hog. Take three roses or four. Make it a bouquet."

"Thank you so much, Mrs. Wright. I'll gladly pay you. Mr. Wright can take it out of my pay."

"No need to go that far. Just let my husband know that I said you could take the flowers. And do go back to calling me Alice."

"Thank you, Alice."

Clara Belle was the first of the Wright children to appear. She skipped into the kitchen, but instead of sitting down at the table, she danced around it, pointing at me. "Harry has a girl; Harry has a girl!" she cried. Her mother told her to stop that rude behavior. "Harry has a lover; Harry has a lover," the precocious child sang out. Her mother couldn't stop her. But Clara Belle's incessant giggling finally did.

Jane Hankin couldn't go to dinner on June 3 because she had promised to be the "fourth" in a night of whist with Mr. and Mrs. Zimmerman and Alice Wright. Robert Wright wasn't a card player — at least not the no-betting kind of cards — and anyway had work to catch up on at the general store. Since Jane agreed to go to Taylor Made with me alone the next night, I was in a good enough mood to volunteer to help Mr. Wright pour flour from barrels into sacks and rearrange the shelves.

While working late my mind was only partially on my menial tasks. The rest of it was loaded with anticipation at the prospect of seeing Jane twenty-four hours later wearing her red dancing dress and me handing her those three roses to match. I imagined a kiss or two would come with the exalted occasion. Before the night of June 3 was through, though, I had cause to recall how Wyatt Matters had more than once quoted a bit of advice from Benjamin Franklin's *Poor Richard's Almanack:* "Blessed is he that expects nothing, for he shall never be disappointed."

As he later told me, Wyatt Matters had spent the day of the third out at Fort Dodge assessing the quality of the soldiers and conferring with the commanding officer, Lieutenant Colonel Richard Dodge. Wyatt expressed his belief that the honorable William Taylor deserved a pay raise for running the Fort Dodge Express so efficiently and deserved the patronage of more soldiers at his superlative restaurant in Dodge City. Colonel Dodge readily agreed and divulged that Willie had been his private cook for a while at the fort until he found out that Willie's wife was the real cook in the family and that they wished to start their own restaurant.

"I can vouch for the Taylor Made food, even if Monique Taylor makes most of it," he said. "Unfortunately, I'm unable to get into town often to partake of it. As for the men, I can't control where they go or what they do during their off-duty hours. I can only punish those who come back late or unfit for duty due to drunkenness."

"I understand, Colonel Dodge," said Wyatt. "After all, you stopped the sale of alcohol at the fort and keep the men well regulated, but to make Dodge City totally off-limits would no doubt result in desertions and mutinies."

"Something like that. I can't promise anything, but I'll see about Willie getting a slight increase in compensation. Now, what else can I do you for, Mr. Matters?"

"The important matter of the bison, sir."

"Ah, a noble beast the buffalo. I'm an avid buffalo hunter, you know."

"Yes, I do. Last fall you took three Englishmen on a three-week hunt and you killed 127 bison, more bison than would have supplied a brigade. And I heard you plan a similar hunt this year."

"And you would like to come along, is that it?"

"Absolutely not. As a matter of fact, I want you to call it off."

"Say what?"

"I want you to leave the bison alone as much as possible. As you said they are noble beasts, and the Plains Indians need them far more than the white man does."

"I can't argue with that. But they are expendable."

"The bison or the Indians?"

"Look, Mr. Matters. I thought by now, you'd have adjusted to the way things are."

"Never when things are wrong."

"I fail to understand why any of this has to do with you, but U.S. Army officers have a rich tradition of taking time out from their duties to direct hunting parties, arrange competitive hunts, and get buffalo in their sights for shooting practice."

"Your survival on the Plains hardly depends on such activities."

"Western Kansas abounds with buffalo, thus the invasion of swarms of hide hunters. Shooting buffalo is their livelihood. And for many officers in the field, shooting buffalo is a source of pride. Colonel Cody once proved his skill by personally slaying forty-eight buffalo in thirty minutes."

"The waste! He was killing twelve bison a day for a year and a half and killed more than four thousand bison in one eight-month period. How much skill could that take?"

"Plenty to be that productive. Why are you condemning Cody? He was just doing his job. He was employed as a hunter for the railroad, and he kept the workers well fed. They don't call him Buffalo Bill for nothing."

"And what about you, Colonel Dodge? Is it not true that half a dozen years ago General John Pope, commander of the Department of the Missouri, requested a dozen bison tongues and you detailed a squad of marksmen to scour the Plains for the shaggy beasts and the soldiers returned with a wagonful of tongues, far more than General Pope needed?"

"Could be. Everybody savors the taste of buffalo tongue. You should try it some time."

"I've had it but never again. My point is that it isn't just the bison hunters doing the damage. You and other officers serving our country feel justified in killing hundreds of two-thousand-pound animals for nothing more than their two-pound tongues. No wonder the Indians are up in arms."

At that point, according to Mr. Matters, Dodge threw up his arms and gave him a look that suggested the colonel would have liked nothing more than to cut out the tongue of his uninvited guest.

When Mr. Matters finally departed to the great relief of the colonel and no doubt others at the fort as well, he went back to the city in the Fort Dodge Express. William Taylor was the driver, making what he hoped would be his last run of the day before turning to his restaurant business. Wyatt was his only passenger. The two had just pulled up next to Taylor Made and were chatting away about how Plains bison tongue stacked up to New Orleans ham and chicken gumbo when five intoxicated would-be passengers stepped up to greet them with drawn six-shooters. Behind them, either looking bored or else giggling, were a half-dozen dance hall girls.

"We all been waiting to go out to the fort for hours, you black son of a bitch," said one of the men, pointing his pistol in Mr. Taylor's face. Wyatt recognized the gunman as Scotty Scott, who had shot down Mr. McDermott back in January and was now not only a business partner in Alfred Peacock's billiard saloon but also a not-so-secret member of the Dodge City Vigilance Committee. "There's a dance going on out there and I'll be damned if some damned Negro makes us late."

Mr. Taylor started to apologize, but Mr.

Matters interrupted. "It's all fine, fellows and gals," he said. "The dance can't start without female partners, can it? Looks like most of them are still here in town. There was no action yet out at the fort when we left it."

"I know you. You're nothing but a vagrant and a troublemaker. You been trying to close our saloons, take our guns away, and stop us from killing buffalo."

"Not at all. I like a good glass of wine now and then, believe guns are sometimes necessary for self-defense out in the wilds, and that sometimes hunting, even a bison on occasion, is necessary to put food on the table — and by food I don't mean just the tongues."

"Shut your bone box!" Scotty Scott now pointed his six-shooter at Wyatt, holding it so close it scraped Wyatt's nostrils. "You're asking for a little vigilante action."

"Leave my friend alone," said Mr. Taylor. "It wasn't him who made me late getting here."

"Ain't that sweet," said Billy Hicks, another vigilante, a stubby fellow with a gaping mouth whom Mr. Matters said reminded him of a sawed-off shotgun. "A black son of a bitch sticking up for a low-down pale-faced bastard."

"Amen, brother," said Petey Hicks, who was Billy's actual brother. "Which one should we shoot first?'

"Next one who opens his trap!" shouted Scotty Scott.

William Taylor wiped his mouth with the back of his hand and then revealed lips pressed so tightly together that they protruded forward. Wyatt Matters, though, put a finger to his closed mouth as if he were considering speaking but had not yet made up his mind. William snorted and shook his head vigorously, as if saying, *Don't risk it with these bad boys.*

But Wyatt's tongue pushed its way through his lips and began to flap. "We are no threat to you, boys," he said "Don't let the whiskey tell you otherwise. We're all good Americans here. And as good Americans you fellows surely must support the very first amendment to the U.S. Constitution that guarantees freedoms concerning religion, expression, assembly, and the right to petition. The relevant part here is that the First Amendment states that Congress shall make no law abridging freedom of speech. Of course, that doesn't give anyone the right to say things that incite imminent lawless action, but I'm sure we can all agree that me citing the First Amendment shouldn't incite you boys to get trigger-happy. You see even in Dodge City on the Kansas frontier, where men drink too much and take offense at the slightest slights, the U.S. Constitution must be upheld, and we all must be diligent in our effort to . . ."

Wyatt kept on talking as he put an arm around the dumbfounded William Taylor and tried to direct him to the front door of the Taylor Made restaurant. The two friends had taken maybe five steps together before the first shot was fired. That got Wyatt to close his mouth, but he wasn't the one shot. The slug hit Mr. Taylor on the left side and in its course passed through his kidneys. Mr. Taylor stayed on his feet but did not try to get into the restaurant, perhaps fearing that these men weren't above following him inside and putting Monique in danger. Instead, he turned and fled in the opposite direction. Another four shots followed, directed at Mr. Taylor's backside, but Wyatt believed that all but one missed. Two of the dance hall girls were screaming while the others were in a daze, except for a fleshy blonde named Lottie who appeared to be laughing, over what Wyatt couldn't say.

In any case, Scott, the Hicks brothers, and the other men were slow to follow. One of them asked how they would get to the dance at Fort Dodge now. Scotty replied that he'd drive the damned wagon himself if need be. Meanwhile, Wyatt slipped past the group and took to running after his limping friend. Mr. Taylor had the sense to go to Herman Fringer's drugstore, which also housed the office of Dr. Thomas McCarty. By the time Wyatt got there, the doctor and the druggist were already dressing Mr. Taylor's wounds. Wyatt admittedly was no doctor, and he thought the two men were doing a good job, but he did say it was a good sign that Willie was conscious and not coughing up any blood. All three of them believed that if there was no internal bleeding into the lungs, Mr. Taylor would survive his ordeal, as the other slug had only graced his right buttock, resulting in a superficial wound.

The only trouble was that Scott, Billy and Petey Hicks, and their drunken followers all showed up ten minutes later and were still worked up into a frenzy. Ignoring the protests of Mr. Fringer and Dr. McCarty, they dragged Mr. Taylor out into the street, and Wyatt went too because he wouldn't let go of the back of his friend's trousers.

"You have gone far enough, gentleman," said Wyatt, still calm and still expecting to reason with them. "You don't have to be familiar with the U.S. Constitution or the

Bible to know that the willing and deliberate killing of a fellow human being is unlawful and subject to . . .”

But Mr. Taylor’s trousers ripped in the back and Wyatt found himself lying in the street grasping a strip of fabric.

“We ain’t killing you, windbag,” said Billy Hicks. “We’re killing the colored coon.”

Someone else pulled Wyatt by his ankles out of the line of fire. My mentor kept talking (but later he couldn’t remember his exact words) as he tried to crawl back to his friend.

“Here you are, you black son of a bitch,” said Scotty Scott. His six-shooter was in his belt, but he raised a heavy rifle and fired. Other shots came from the mob, but Wyatt couldn’t tell who fired them. By then his eyes were closed and so was his mouth, as my mentor (and apparently Willie Taylor’s mentor, too) lay face-down but unharmed in the street.

I heard what must have been the last gunfire of the night while eating crackers as I lay on my bed at the general store. Robert Wright and I had concluded the night work, and he had gone back to his substantial house where the four-handed whist was being played. I was sure the gunshots could have been heard from there, so I could only hope that the game had ended early and Jane

Hankin was back home in her bed sleeping through the commotion. I put on a shirt and my shoes and went outside. I cautiously approached a mob of maybe a dozen men and Lottie, stalwart of the Dodge dance halls. They had circled up around a fallen man (I could only make out the soles of his boots). Most flashed weapons, a few held lit torches. I identified first another fallen man who mostly lay outside the circle. I feared the worst — that some hot-tempered, gun-toting young drinking man had decided to keep the outspoken Wyatt Matters from saying a contrary word ever again.

I couldn't see any blood or movement, not even when I knelt on the street next to my mentor. I was afraid to touch him, let alone turn him over. But then someone from the inner circle shouted: "Clear the street. This is vigilante business. If you aren't one of us, make yourself scarce!" Those words seemed to bring Wyatt to life, because he popped to his feet and unleashed a stream of profanities of the like I had never heard before by any man, drunk or sober. I heard a couple guns cock, and I pulled Wyatt back from the circle of death.

"I will never stop speaking the truth," he said, his voice now nearly composed, though I was shaking all over. "You have shot a good man for no reason at all except the color of his skin. You aren't vigilantes. You are a lynch mob. Of all the senseless killings in Dodge, this is the most senseless . . . so far. I am the voice of reason in this hellhole. Shoot me down in cold blood and you will be the equal of history's most evil men — Vlad the Impaler, Ivan the Terrible, Nero, Genghis Khan, Robespierre, William Quantrill, 'Bloody Bill' Anderson!"

I pushed Wyatt further away from the crowd, since I didn't figure these fellows were interested in getting a late-night history lesson. Several of them marched toward us, their weapons drawn, enough fire in their eyes to match the torches. Wyatt called the red-faced man in the lead the "devil incarnate" and kept talking, unphased by the threat: "This time you'll pay the price, Billy Hicks. He was Colonel Dodge's friend, too. The soldiers will be coming for you."

That temporarily stopped Hicks in his tracks. He then addressed me instead of Wyatt, "Get that nigger-lover back to his tent before we blast him to kingdom come."

A clear path had opened to the dead man, and I could see more than his boots now. I hadn't known William Taylor long, but he was my friend, too. I forgot my fear at that moment and pushed my way past Billy Hicks and then Petey Hicks as if I could still be of assistance to Mr. Taylor. I was ready to lash out at every member of the mob. Maybe only a few of them had done the actual shooting, but all the rest were there to lend their support. "Damn you vigilantes!" I shouted before I felt the butt of somebody's six-shooter on the back of my head. I dropped into stone-cold silence. I don't know if Mr. Matters resumed his verbal assault on Hicks or not, but it wasn't me who took Wyatt back to his tent that night. In fact, nobody did. Nor did I return to my bed until it was time for work in the morning.

Chapter Sixteen

Through the night, the lifeless body of William Taylor remained on the street where the mob of vigilantes had left it. Wyatt Matters stayed awake next to the corpse all the while, as if to protect it from two-legged and four-legged varmints. At some point after midnight, I had awakened but was still in a dazed state when Dr. McCarty came out of the drugstore and took me to his office inside to treat the bump on my head and let me sleep. There was nothing the doctor could do for poor Mr. Taylor, of course, and Mr. Matters insisted the body not be moved until the good citizens of Dodge came out of their houses in the morning and saw the result of the latest foul deed committed by vigilantes gone wild.

Indeed, the founding fathers of Dodge City expressed shock at seeing the bullet-riddled body of the town's most excellent black businessman. For once, Mr. Matters didn't give them a mouthful. The dead body spoke for itself. He did glare at them, as these were the supposed leaders of the Dodge City Vigilance Committee. They had not sanctioned the horrific event, of course, but all had been warned repeatedly about *bad* vigilantes, and none could look Mr. Matters in the eye. I was part of the burial party that transported the remains to Boot Hill. Wyatt came out later with Monique Taylor and a would-be preacher who had founded the town's first church group the previous November. The would-be preacher, who had never met Mr. Taylor, said only a few words over the grave. Mr. Matters spoke far longer — about the foul and cold-blooded murder committed by ruffians operating as self-appointed vigilantes, his friendship with the honorable William Taylor, and the injustice done not only to him but also to his devoted wife, his few true friends in Dodge, and the memory of Abraham Lincoln, the man who had freed the slaves. Monique could of course say nothing. She managed to hold back her tears until Frederick Zimmerman drove up in a two-person buggy. The passenger he brought along was not his wife but Jane Hankin. Monique and Jane then embraced and shed unrestrained tears on each other's shoulders, carrying on so long that they even outlasted Wyatt's verbiage.

I extended my sympathy to the widow and then to Jane, wondering if either woman would hold up under the strain. But after a while, I was the one doing the crying while they removed themselves from the gravesite and, still clutching each other, meandered to the other side of Boot Hill. Robert Wright then showed up with some news. He had sent a telegraph to Colonel Dodge at the fort about the killing, and the enraged colonel had immediately wired Governor Osborn since no civil authorities had yet been elected. The governor had immediately authorized the colonel to arrest and hold "all persons notoriously guilty of a violation of the criminal laws of this State," so the soldiers were coming — just as Wyatt had predicted.

I had to get back to work after the burial, but Wyatt assured me that he would look after the two distressed women before coming to town to give testimony about the murderers. By the time I got back to the general store soldiers had already begun to surround the town. They arrested five vigilante members, including the Hicks brothers and Tom Sherman, who in March had gotten away with filling McGill and Burns with lead.

Rumor had it that Scotty Scott had hid in a large icebox in Peacock's billiard saloon and slipped out of Dodge City unseen.

That afternoon Mr. Matters entered the general store looking haggard and disheveled. Even his bowtie was askew. He removed his top hat and laid it down in front of me on the counter. He then pulled a handkerchief out of his back pocket to mop the sweat off his furrowed brow.

"The women have retired to Taylor Made, and are now in seclusion, sorry and sad but safe and surprisingly strong," he reported, surveying the room instead of looking at me. "Lady Jane is holding up well to the latest unnecessary shooting in town. This is due in part to the fact she is totally focused on comforting Monique, telling the widow that her own beau had also been shot down in Dodge and that they must bear up to tragedy together since they had so much more life to live."

I found it unsettling that Jane still had on her mind the late gambler Matt Sullivan and that she could compare their short-lived relationship to the marriage of Monique and William. But I said nothing. Wyatt walked away from the counter, now muttering, as if lecturing himself. I didn't try hard to make out what he was saying. I was full of my own sad thoughts and had started to wonder when Jane would begin calling me her *beau,* hopefully while I was still alive.

The raised voice of my boss caused me to spin around. I thought he might be annoyed that my mind wasn't on the store. But he had decided to go face-to-face with the already distraught Wyatt. Mr. Wright talked louder but Mr. Matters got more words out. I moved in closer, expecting all hell would break loose, at which point I wasn't sure if I would side with my employer or my mentor.

"Today's Dodge City is a hellhole," said Wyatt. "You know it as well as I do."

"The hell it is," roared Mr. Wright. "We're the buffalo capital of the West."

"The Sodom and Gomorrah of the Plains."

"We became big business fast. The streets of Dodge are lined with wagons, bringing in hides and meat and getting supplies from early morning to late at night. I have never seen any young town the equal of Dodge."

"Not in the number of saloons and dance halls perhaps. Not in the number of young drunken drifters slinging guns, getting into brawls, triggering fear in the respectable ladies, and filling the ground on Boot Hill. Lawlessness prevails. This is *my* town, too, and it is going to hell in a handbasket."

"To hell with you, the carper of the

century! It's not nearly so bad as you make out. With anything new there are naturally growing pains, but the burst into sudden activity all about town is astounding. Call it, in a word, a *boom*."

"The guns in Dodge boom loudest. You must be aware that in ten months, at least fifteen men have been murdered in a town of little more than three hundred residents. In New York City in 1872, with a population of well over one million, there were only sixty-three persons arrested for murder."

"I don't know where you get your figures. I figure you make most of them up. Anyway, I'm sure many men commit murders in New York City and get away with it."

"In Dodge City, *every* murderer has gotten away with it."

"Not so. We have a handful of men under arrest."

"The soldiers do. You did nothing. Never mind the drifters and gamblers who come to town. You vigilantes are the primary murderers!"

"How dare you, sir, tarnish my name and the name of so many other good men. Residing as we do in an unorganized county beyond the reach of civil law, we understood the necessity of forming a vigilance committee.

We were obliged to act or else crime would go unpunished and unpunishable."

"But who will punish the cutthroats you allowed into your organization and gave a free rein to kill whomever they want?"

"I acknowledge there are a few bad apples who fell in amongst us. But they . . ."

"A few? Maybe only a few of your vigilantes shot Willie Taylor to death, but a dozen more came out onto the street last night in support of his brutal execution. And you yourself, Mr. Wright Can Do No Wrong, abetted these unscrupulous men by *not* dispersing the mob or condemning their actions."

"You do me an injustice, sir! You shall leave my store immediately or be removed by force."

I stepped between the two men who were the biggest influences in my life. "Won't the upcoming elections keep such things from happening?" I asked. "We'll have civil law at last."

Mr. Wright cooled down fast. "If the right people are elected," he said.

"Too late for Willie," said Mr. Matters, but he turned away and walked to the door without looking back. He stopped in the doorway long enough to offer an ancient quote. "As Aristotle said, *At his best, man is the noblest of all animals; separated from law and justice he is the worst.*"

Dodge City did get some duly elected officials in June and did have its first murder trial. All the vigilantes except Billy Hicks were released for lack of evidence. Billy Hicks pleaded not guilty. He claimed that William Taylor had been belligerent that night and probably would have been shot even if he were a white man. That argument didn't go over well, so Hicks told the court that the only man who had done any shooting was Scotty Scott, who was conveniently missing, never to be seen again. He made a point of saying he couldn't recognize who else was on the scene, not even his own brother, Petey. It hurt his case, though, when fellow vigilante Tom Sherman, who in March had gotten away with the killings of McGill and Burns, took the stand and testified on behalf of the prosecution, perhaps to escape prosecution himself. Sherman said he saw Billy Hicks pull a trigger more than once. Dr. McCarty and Herman Fringer also fingered Hicks, but the most damning testimony came from Wyatt Matters, even though four times he had to be reprimanded for offering personal commentary about vigilantes and bringing Mr. Taylor's race into the equation ("That bunch killed an unarmed Negro for the fun of it," "Those harbingers of injustice must be condemned," "Murder is the vigilantes' border pastime," and "Hicks and Associates amuse themselves by hunting dark-skinned men instead of bison"). The jury brought in a verdict of second-degree murder, at which point the judge dismissed Wyatt from the courtroom for arguing too strenuously, even if eloquently, that it should have been murder in the first degree.

I missed the entire trial because Robert Wright wanted me to man the general store while he attended the proceedings strictly as an observer. Widow Monique Taylor and her new best friend, Jane Hankin, never showed up either. Jane kept working at the Zimmerman store by day, but every night she was with Monique at the Taylor Made keeping the restaurant business going and even overseeing the Dodge City Express with two new drivers. I was left out of all that, being unable to cook and having seldom driven a wagon. Not that anyone asked me for my help.

During and after the trial Mr. Matters was the only one who spoke out publicly against the Dodge City Vigilance Committee, which seemed to continue to operate secretly despite the June 5 special election of Charles

Bassett as first sheriff of Ford County along with three county commissioners, one of whom was Frederick Zimmerman. Bassett had served in the postwar Regular Army and spent time in various mining towns, but he was still only twenty-seven years old. He was also short (five feet four in his boots) and seemed to have trouble growing a beard. No doubt Bassett had some growing pains too in the new position of sheriff. Even without the self-exiled Scotty Scott and jailed Billy Hicks around, the small colored population of Dodge wasn't safe. In early July, two Negros were shot for no apparent cause except their skin color. One of them, Wallace Dade, was befriended by Wyatt Matters and perhaps had the potential to be another William Taylor. In fact, Wyatt bought him several meals at Taylor Made where Wallace took a shine to the widow and was under consideration by her and spokeswoman Jane Hankin as a Dodge City Express driver. It was not to be. Shot in the head and lungs by an unknown assailant, his wound proved fatal despite the best efforts of Dr. McCarty. There were no white witnesses, at least none who would speak up.

Wyatt Matters was up in arms (not literally, of course) again, and he brought the wounded Negro to tell his tale to Sheriff

Bassett. The victim did not know who had shot him but claimed that more than one man had been involved and that the assailants were some of the same bad vigilantes who had murdered William Taylor. The sheriff responded that Mr. Taylor's convicted killer was behind bars, so he didn't credit the story. That angered Mr. Matters so much that he went about town seeking information about the crimes and any lingering vigilante activity. His behavior brought on the ire of Robert Wright, who insisted the Dodge City Vigilance Committee was now dormant and even if it wasn't there were no longer any "bad apples" in its membership. That the two men never came to blows amazed me.

Mr. Matters spent much of July trying to track down the men who had shot the two Negroes, but he had no luck and became frustrated at *not knowing.* The good news was that nobody tried to shoot another colored man in Dodge and vigilantism didn't raise what Wyatt called "its collective mob head." Both Wyatt and I found it encouraging that Taylor Made welcomed more customers than ever — including some white buffalo hunters tired of eating buffalo parts and pork — thanks to co-owners Monique Taylor and Jane Hankin. I didn't see Jane as much as I wanted, but I was hopeful we still had a romantic future in the cards. It helped my mental state to know that she had no new man in her life and that Mr. Matters was no longer showing signs of overprotectiveness. He was convinced that Jane's devotion to Monique and the restaurant had cured her and that we need not fear a relapse. "Her nervousness and fragility are a thing of the past as long as nobody tries to shoot her or Monique," he declared. "And who pray tell could possibly want to shoot that pair of lovely ladies." They were a pair all right — one light brown skinned, the other still on the pale side; one adjusting to being a widow, the other helping her adjust; one cooking New Orleans style, the other cooking buffalo meat and other Kansas staples; both lithe figures despite all that cooking and food preparation. They were not only working together but also spending their time together after the work was done. But how could I be jealous of Jane's relationship with a mute woman?

On July 21, the two women decided to close Taylor Made for the night so that they could concentrate on what they considered "fun" activity — creating the restaurant's first menu and decorating the walls with paintings of the Mississippi River and of old New Orleans when it was ruled by the French and then the Spanish. Taylor Made was becoming a place to go in Dodge City not only for those who wanted food and atmosphere that didn't remind them they were in Dodge but also for those who wanted hearty meals served by attractive women.

"How does it feel to *not* be needed?" Wyatt asked as we sat in his tent that evening sipping wine and both thinking of Jane Hankin, though I hoped not in the exact same way. "But what do you and I know about menus, son?"

He hadn't called me son in weeks, and it sounded better than it ever had. But I didn't smile. I was in a mood to feel sorry for myself. "Truth is, I haven't felt needed by her since we got back from the Topeka Insane Asylum. I kind of miss those days when she was afraid to leave her room and I brought her food in bed."

"We both brought her food. Now she gets most of her meals and helps prepare them and serve them to others at the restaurant. Lady Jane had you and me in her life but that wasn't enough, nor should it be."

"I thought you were supposed to be encouraging our romance — hers and mine."

"I'm not one to dictate to her, even if it were possible. As I've been saying all along,

Jane Hankin has a mind of her own. Right now, she has found a purpose in life outside of her day work for Zimmerman by befriending and helping a widow woman. We've been over this before, son. Monique was at a total loss after the savage murder of her husband and as needy as Lady Jane once was following the murder of Matt Sullivan."

"I know. I know." I gulped what wine was left in my glass.

"What then is your problem?"

"My problem? No problem. I still can't believe a ne'er-do-well, hard-drinking, gun-carrying transient like Matt Sullivan could mean that much to sweet Jane."

"You forget that Mr. Sullivan gave up his guns, reduced his consumption of whiskey, and planned to settle down in our fair city — all because of Lady Jane."

"I didn't forget. It was all a show. He wasn't right for her. He couldn't have kept it up."

"You should let the dead rest in peace."

"I do, but Matt Sullivan has been resting in peace since last year, and Jane still hasn't turned to me, I mean really and truly turned to me."

"Jealousy! It is like a disease of the mind. I must quote one of the maxims of the French moralist François de La Rochefoucauld: *Jealousy is bred in doubts. When those doubts change into certainties, then the passion either ceases or turns absolute madness.* It is certain she had attached herself fully to Matt Sullivan and that you, a long-time doubter of self, never lost your passion for her and so . . ."

"And so love feels like madness, at least it did until I visited that asylum in Topeka and got my head straight."

"And how do you feel now?"

"The same as I did before but in a more reasonable, mature way. I love her more than ever."

"I do believe you *feel* you do. Whether it is love or not, you largely keep it to yourself."

"What do you mean whether it is or not? It *is* love! I am biding my time. Didn't you once tell me that woman needs man as much as man needs woman as far back as Adam and Eve? Well, there is no more Matt Sullivan. And there does not appear to be any other man, not even you."

That last part slipped off my tongue, and I felt as foolish as if I had tripped over that tongue and fallen flat on my face. I put my glass down, stood up, and turned away. I could not face my mentor, the wise old man, as the late William Taylor called him.

He laughed but quickly explained he wasn't laughing at me. "You still hold way back in your mind doubts about me. Let me say one more time that it is my wish to see the two of you together, living as a couple in harmony but nevertheless including me in both your lives as a guide, a sage, a pundit, a mentor, a compassionate paternal figure."

I didn't turn to look at him, but I began to apologize profusely, as was my habit, not just with him but with practically everyone I knew or had ever known. When he told me to stop, I obeyed and then apologized for carrying on that way. I made two complete circles inside his tent. I was sad to see that not only was my glass empty but so was the only bottle I could spot.

"I don't doubt my love for her," I said, and I was ready to keep repeating that the rest of the night. "Jane made me forget Elizabeth Pepper and every other woman. I only doubt because I don't know how she feels about me. I am biding my time, but sometimes I wonder if I'll be abiding forever."

"Time for another glass of wine, I'd say. But since I'm all out here, I suggest we continue this important conversation over at the Dodge House, where my favorite barkeeper, Dave Burrell, keeps a decent stock for the town's few non-whiskey drinkers."

As we walked to the Dodge House, Mr. Matters spoke of other things, primarily the murders in Dodge during the last year. He repeated a joke that was going around in Kansas newspapers: *A gentleman wishing to go from Wichita to Dodge City applied to a friend for a letter of introduction. He was handed a double-barreled shotgun and a Colt's revolver.*" Even as I chuckled nervously, he reminded me the violence that had taken place in Dodge was no joking matter. He recalled that just over a year earlier, on July 8, 1872, to be exact, a group of enterprising men met at Fort Dodge and formed the Dodge City Town Company with the intent of creating a city on the Plains five miles from the fort. With the coming of the railroad, these men saw themselves as men with vision. Mr. Matters, the only "outsider" present, called these founders "warped visionaries." While he had nothing against a new community emerging on the Plains, he wanted it to emerge as a sunflower rather than a weed. What made it a weed was the greed behind the plan to build the new place on the hides and bones of slaughtered bison.

I had heard that all before, but said nothing, and Mr. Matters' tongue carried on.

"Without law and order or well-thought-out regulations and controls, Dodge did become, as I predicted, a weed," Wyatt shouted. "I am aware of sixteen murders here already, and there could very well have been twice that many in and around town. Not everyone on Boot Hill has a marker. The horror lives on!"

He paused to adjust his *Original* belt and glared at me. The fire in his eyes told me I was still his protégé and I had better say something fast unless I had turned into one of Robert Wright's puppets.

"You're right of course," I mumbled.

"What's that? I didn't hear you, son."

"I said *you are right!* But you say things will get better, right? Why else would you stay here in Dodge?"

"It's simple. Since the Civil War, I have found cause to travel to many places in the West, never staying in one spot too long. I've been called a deserter, a yellow belly, a Jayhawker, a damn Yankee, a slacker, a land-loper, a greenhorn, a tenderfoot, a gump, a gadabout, a flannel mouth, a Mary, a biddy, a bad egg, a revolutionary, an odd stick, a sin-buster, a squatter, a suck egg, a yack, a tarnation, a tumbleweed, a teetotaler, a wino, fish bait, and dead meat — to name a few names meant to insult. Of course, the name callers have mostly been small-minded men and narrow-minded women. But I've had enough. Dodge City is where I stop."

We walked on. I could have added to his long list just from my time with him in Dodge. Robert Wright alone had called him a coffee boiler, a ten-cent man, a wiseacre, a wobblin' jaws, a backstabber, a windbag, an agitator, a repugnant intellectual, and a vagabond. It occurred to me that I hadn't been called many names, mainly because I mostly kept my mouth shut, avoided the local pleasure palaces, and didn't upset too many customers at the general store. "I can understand you wanting to settle down," I said as we approached the usual group of men mingling in front of the Dodge House. "Still, the name calling hasn't really gone away, has it? You haven't spoken of any women besides Jane and Monique to me, but you have pointed out several small-minded men in town."

"For better or worse, inside this tent or whatever abode I hang my hat in the future, I have ensconced myself in Dodge City. It's true that Trader Bob and the rest of the greedy Gang control politics and everything else in town, but that's why men like me are needed here to counterbalance their influence. There is also another factor, son. I have no family elsewhere, and right here I have a couple people who mean more to me than anyone else does anywhere in the world. This is my home and I'll do my best to make it better, not worse."

I knew those couple people must be Jane Hankin and myself, seeing as most other people called him names. I was touched. Also, it was news to me that he had no family elsewhere. He had never talked about the places in the West he had passed through, let alone where he was born and raised, who his parents were, and what had happened to them. There were only a few scattered hints about his past life, such as his mentioning that he had started traveling in the West after the Civil War. Based on how he felt about injustices to black men like William Taylor and to Plains Indians who needed bison to thrive, I assumed he was originally from east of the Mississippi River and north of the Mason-Dixon line, never mind the fact I was from below that line in Bladensburg, Maryland.

"Well, Dodge is getting better," I said as we headed inside the Dodge House and straight toward the bar. "At least we now have a Ford County sheriff on the job."

"Charley Bassett is young and unknown but has the distinction of not being in any way connected with the vigilantes. It's a start. He won't be able to do it alone, though. He'll need to appoint deputies, and it would help immensely to ban the carrying of guns in Dodge. I'll have to start another petition and hope this one isn't ignored. Too bad women's signatures don't count any more than those of children, although I've learned that many demimondes carry hidden derringers on their person."

"I wouldn't know about that. But I know Jane Hankin would be the first woman to sign such a petition."

"Absolutely. And right behind her with pen in hand would be Monique Taylor."

The bar area wasn't overly crowded. Most of the patrons were among the town's more respectable drinkers. Soldiers who came to the town on passes primarily to get crazy drunk felt more welcome in other saloons — that is the barkeepers gladly took their modest U.S. Army pay until the money was gone, at which point the soldiers were either escorted or thrown out into the street. Barkeeper Dave Burrell was more discriminating on orders from Dodge House owner George Cox, who had become probate judge in the June special elections.

When Wyatt stepped up to the bar, Mr. Burrell smiled at him — not the usual response Dodge residents had when the loquacious and judgmental Wyatt approached them. Not even waiting to be asked, the bartender brought out a bottle of wine produced by the Cliff Cave Wine Company, which owned vineyards on the Mississippi River south of St. Louis. The two men talked cordially for the next twenty minutes about viticulture, native hybrid grapes, and a disease called black rot that was ravaging vineyards. For me, who knew nothing about wine except what Wyatt offered me, it was all too much talking, especially since the bottle hadn't been opened yet. I saw no end to the uninteresting chatter, so naturally my mind drifted off to thoughts of Jane and her night of so-called fun with Monique at Taylor Made.

But then I heard Mr. Burrell raise his voice, and I turned to see him pound a fist so hard on the bar top that it shook glasses. I immediately wondered if Wyatt had annoyed the bartender by telling him how the French made their wine or how firearms should be prohibited from all saloons in town, including this one at the Dodge House. But it was another customer he was screaming at — a cowboy named Bill Ellis who lived some miles from Dodge but came into town once a month to buy supplies at the general store and once a week to carouse. With him were two ladies who might not be considered *ladies* in some circles.

"I told you before, Ellis, no drinks for you or these guests," the bartender shouted. "You know we don't allow nymphs du prairie in here, and you look pretty full."

"I admit I've been drinking more or less all day at more hospitable watering troughs but that's within my rights as an American citizen and native son of . . . eh . . . wherever I'm from."

"And as an American bartender I have a right to refuse service to anyone. You want to go standing on your own two feet, if you can manage that, or carried out."

Mr. Ellis gripped the collar of his coat, which he was wearing on the hottest evening of the summer so far. Mr. Burrell suspected the cowboy had a weapon under the coat. So did Mr. Matters, who began a familiar lecture about the deadly insanity of young men — and this cowboy did look about my age — going about town heeled and drinking like an Arkansas River largemouth bass.

"Stay the hell out of this, old man," said Mr. Ellis but he kept his eyes on the bartender, not Mr. Matters. "Nobody gives a hang what is said by a wine-drinking dandy who stands lower than a prairie rattlesnake in a wagon rut and is uglier than a hound with the mange."

"Not bad language for a drunk. Maybe

you have a little something under your hat besides hair."

"Not, Ellis," said Mr. Burrell. "He couldn't hit the ground with his hat in three throws."

"Them is fighting words!" Mr. Ellis started to open his coat.

"None of that," said the skinnier of his two female companions, grabbing Mr. Burrell's right arm. "You look mad enough to spit. I know Dave. He has a shotgun behind the bar."

Violence seemed likely to break out at any second, but I couldn't help looking her over from painted face to close-fitting high button boots and recalling something Robert Wright once said about an underfed sod house dweller who came into the store with her corpulent husband: *She's so thin she could take a bath in a shotgun barrel and he's so fat he wouldn't fit in a buffalo wallow.* Mr. Ellis' other lady companion was fleshier but probably would have fit nicely in any wooden tub. "There's a half-dozen other saloons I'd rather you bought me a beer in," she said, grabbing Mr. Burrell's left arm and tugging much harder than the skinny one. "You don't want to be killed, Bill. The night is young. We best vamoose."

All that tugging did the job. The three of them departed the Dodge House and I was ready to raise my wine glass even before it was filled. "Another example of the wisdom and prudence of women," said Mr. Matters as we found a corner table for two. "Goes to show even sportin' women are more sensible than a young man in his cups."

We started for a corner table, but it was such a warm night, Mr. Matters redirected us to the porch to do our wine drinking in the fresh air. In the next half hour he made a series of toasts — to women, sensible or not, in particular Jane Hankin and Monique Taylor; to law and order on the frontier, with good wishes for the new Ford County sheriff; to men who could get by in the world without sidearms, in particular him and me; free-roaming bison, from their humps to their hoofs; wine, whether made in Missouri or France; and to a better Dodge of the future, where red men, yellow men, black men, and white men would reside harmoniously and never want (or need) to get out of town. He didn't mention his imaginary New Honesty again, but it sure sounded as if he still had utopian principles on his busy mind.

"Come on now, son," he finally said when the bottle was less than a quarter full. "I'm making all the toasts here. Can't you think of even one paltry toast on your own."

"To Elizabeth Pepper of Atchison, the girl I left behind," I said, no doubt tipsy for only the second or third time since coming to Dodge City ten months ago.

"I thought she left you behind for that railroad man."

"God bless her for that. She did me a big favor by not tying me down. Now I have Jane Hankin to have and to hold."

"Perhaps you will . . . in the better future. But I salute your hopefulness and good cheer."

"Cheers," I said, and we clinked glasses. The sound pleased my ears as much as the wine pleased my tongue.

But then came the sound of a raised voice that caused me to drop my glass. It shattered on the floor as I looked out onto the street. Bill Ellis was back, fuller than before and without his two sensible ladies.

"I can whip any damned son of a bitch in that damned hotel," the drunk shouted as he staggered near the porch steps. At first, I thought he was addressing us, but then I noticed Dave Burrell had also come out to the porch, maybe to see if we were ready for another bottle or else to get some fresh air of his own. When Mr. Ellis stopped staggering, he tried to stand his ground, but he began to sway. He grabbed hold of a hitching post to steady himself before continuing. "That includes you, barkeep, so you better keep your bone box shut."

"You're a goddamn liar, Ellis," Mr. Burrell replied. "Whiskey has brought you false courage. But no matter if you're inebriated or just an idiot, you stand before me as helpless as a mouse stuck in molasses."

"I'm a man not a mouse, barkeep, and I'm a-coming for you," said Mr. Ellis, but he didn't let go of the hitching post.

"You're too damned slow," said Mr. Burrell, rolling up his sleeves as he started down the porch steps.

"Don't let this go any further, gentlemen" said Wyatt Matters. "Have a glass of wine. Whiskey makes you bad-tempered; wine makes you mellow."

But it went further. Mr. Burrell reached the last step with two fists formed. Mr. Ellis let go of the post and reached inside his coat.

"Watch it!" Mr. Matters called out. It wasn't clear which of the two adversaries he was addressing. Not that it mattered much. To me it looked as if the barkeeper wanted to settle things with fisticuffs, but he quickly drew his six-shooter when he saw the drunk had something else in mind. I thought Mr. Ellis fired first. I heard three shots in all.

"My God, I am shot!" cried Mr. Burrell

as if surprised that the drunk hadn't missed, even from that short a distance. The barkeeper tumbled off the last step and hit the ground hard.

"Me, too," said Mr. Ellis sinking to his knee and then collapsing onto his side. "Nobody shoots mice."

Those were strange last words, but I suppose he was implying that by being shot, he was a man. I went to him, checking for a pulse, but there was none. Wyatt Matters went to the bartender, who still had signs of life.

"Tell Mr. Cox, I didn't let the son of a bitch back into the Dodge House," he said, gasping horribly for any kind of air.

"Go get Dr. McCarty, son," Wyatt said to me.

"To hell with that," muttered Mr. Burrell. "I'm dead."

Not quite. Dr. McCarty arrived and did what he could before Dave Burrell died from his wound the following afternoon, fittingly inside the Dodge House.

Chapter Seventeen

The deadly Burrell-Ellis confrontation, called "another senseless shootout" by Wyatt Matters, suggested that nothing had changed in Dodge City when it came to violence and that the town's first-year shooting spree would continue unabated. So, it surprised everyone, including Wyatt, that no murders were reported the rest of the summer or that fall or even during the winter. Sheriff Charley Bassett certainly took his job seriously, taking heed of the coroner's report and the jury's conclusion that Mr. Burrell had acted in self-defense and that Mr. Ellis' death was the result of men carrying firearms, "which we emphatically condemn." Among other things, when the district court was in session, Sheriff Bassett disarmed everyone at the door of the courthouse. He didn't go so far as disarming everyone who entered the city limits, something Mr. Matters had long been pushing, but he told Wyatt that when

Dodge offered further gun control, he'd be enforcing it one hundred percent. The town didn't have the money or inclination to build a jail, so the sheriff ordered hard cases out of Dodge and handled unruly drunks by sticking them under a thick buffalo hide staked tight to the ground. That uncomfortable confined space, the sheriff claimed, sobered men up overnight faster than any jail cell could.

Wyatt Matters still insisted the town needed jail cells with iron bars, but when it came to law and order in Dodge City, he had nothing much to complain about and that made him a little grumpy. Sure, he still on occasion expressed his opinion that men shouldn't carry guns in town, but with no recent shootings to cite, his words carried little weight. The town authorities, whom he had so often butted heads with or had aggravated with his unrestrained voice, fully resolved that Dodge City would no longer be disgraced by any more scenes of violence and bloodshed. To me, his protégé still, he sometimes insisted that men were being shot down behind closed doors and their bodies carried off in the middle of the night to be stuck in unmarked shallow graves on Boot Hill. But most of those times were when we had polished off a bottle of wine in his tent.

Yes, we were both drinking more, strictly wine, though. It was partly a matter of taste, but he loved to point out how the majority of both outright bad men and respectable hypocrites indulged in whiskey.

On December 2, 1873, Wyatt worked himself into a frenzy when he heard a rumor that the night before a stranger named Harry Lovett, passing through town on his way to Newton, Kansas, had been shot in the left breast and was not expected to live. Mr. Matters immediately investigated, but Sheriff Bassett hadn't heard of any shooting and neither had the hundred or so other people Wyatt contacted. He even brought me up to Boot Hill, where we surveyed the grounds until dark for any sign of a recent digging. There was none. If the wounded Harry Lovett had indeed been shot, he must have recovered and resumed his ride to Newton. Wyatt, who was fighting a cold, wanted to send me by train to Newton to locate Mr. Lovett, but I convinced him that dead or alive the man belonged to Newton not Dodge and should not be our concern unless he somehow returned to *our* town seeking revenge.

Christmas came and there were no Lovett sightings. That was fine with me. What bothered me was how few Jane Hankin sightings there were. The last confirmed shooting in Dodge City — the double fatality event in July between William Ellis and David Burrell — had not caused her to relapse into her bedbound stupor. Still, even though she hadn't known either man, that episode had been her own final straw, convincing her that she no longer wished to work in a store that sold guns and ammunitions, even if her part in it was to sell only hardware, tinware, and jewelry. In August she had not only quit the Zimmerman store but also moved out of the outbuilding home provided her by Frederick and Matilda Zimmerman. What she did was go to work full time at Taylor Made and take up residence with Monique Taylor. They shared the bedroom behind the restaurant kitchen just as Monique once had with her late husband. I had occasion to look back there a couple times and all the soft colors, lamps, pillows, mirrors, combs, brushes, hats, curtains, and wall hangings suggested this was a young woman's bedroom. But I knew it to be a two women's bedroom, so it surprised me to see that the only bed wasn't much wider than Jane's old sickbed. I was missing the old days more than ever when she had her own bedroom in the little blue house, and I could bring her food in bed knowing she'd always be there alone. Of course, she was dealing with her dreadful nervous sickness in those days, but it became easier to overlook that fact as time rolled along.

Once a week I was going to the restaurant for a meal, sometimes alone, sometimes with Wyatt Matters, but Jane was usually too preoccupied for much conversation and there were no post-meal rendezvous, though I had hinted at them three or four times. I figured I was being too subtle in my approach (actually, Wyatt figured that out for me), and I decided for Christ's birthday, I would really show my true love something — the kind of thoughtful, but confident man I was deep inside. The previous Christmas I had given her the handheld mirror, brush, and comb set, and while she had never properly thanked me for it or my "Gift from Saint Nick" poem, she was still making use of that gift several times a day. I needed to better that this Christmas.

I felt I could afford it, even if it meant missing a few meals. Robert Wright had given me a slight salary increase despite his insistence that business was falling off due to fewer buffalo hides he could buy and ship for profit to the East. "Buffalo must be roaming elsewhere on account of all the shooting," he complained to me, seemingly daily. "Fewer buffalo means fewer buffalo hunters and fewer hides. It's a crying shame, Harry. I reckon the immediate Plains isn't as bountiful as I believed it to be." Mr. Matters had been telling everyone just that ever since Dodge City was conceived by the founding fathers. I didn't much care one way or the other. I had my raise, and I had my renewed determination to have Jane Hankin body and soul.

Ever since Jane had quit the Zimmerman store, I had avoided the place. But two days before Christmas I had a good reason to be there. Matilda Zimmerman was behind the jewelry counter when I arrived. She greeted me like a long lost relative, asking me why I had stayed away so long and what I had been up to all that time. All I could say was "Not much," which wasn't far from the truth. She patted my hand and said: "We miss her, too. She doesn't come around to visit nearly as much as we'd like. I make Mr. Zimmerman all his meals. We rarely go to the colored restaurant."

"They serve good food," I said, but my attention was on the rings, necklaces, and bracelets in the glass case.

"Mr. Zimmerman and I wish Jane would come back to work. Why the poor girl works and lives over there when we treated her so well and gave her everything that . . . Anyway, I just don't understand it."

"I reckon she has a mind of her own, Mrs. Zimmerman."

"Maybe so. We just wish she would change it. She shouldn't live that way."

"I hope one day she won't. Could be I can change her mind."

"Do you really think so?"

"You bet. For starters I aim to buy her a Christmas present she'll hold dear to her heart."

"Something I can help you with, Mr. Hannum?"

"That's why I'm here, Mrs. Zimmerman. You have some nice rings."

"Yes, very nice. You don't happen to be talking about an engagement ring, do you?"

"Why not? My grand plan is to marry Jane Hankin someday."

"How honorable that sounds, Mr. Hannum. And, oh, how that poor girl needs a man to look after her. First, she was so gun-shy and anguished she took to her bed. Mr. Zimmerman and I helped her all we could, giving her food and shelter even though she was incapable of putting in a half day's work. She recovered, of course, with our help, but how did she repay us: She deserted us by quitting her job and moving out of the comfortable home we provided her. And now, gracious me, she is with that colored lady who can't even speak. I must tell you that Mr. Zimmerman and I are bewildered by Jane's behavior. The poor girl can't be of her right mind. She needs a man to straighten her out and support her and save her from herself."

"You bet she does," I said, with perhaps too much enthusiasm, but at that moment I believed Mrs. Zimmerman was showing stunning insight.

While she was showing me every ring in the store, I had to admit, being an honest man, that it was too early for me to ask that Jane consider an engagement. I needed to get her something that would ease me into the next step. Mrs. Zimmerman had just the thing — a silver brooch that at the center had a raised oval with an intricately engraved floral design of a morning glory and forget-me-not. I could recognize sunflowers but not much else. She explained what the flowers were, and she sold the brooch at a discount price because she recognized my employer as a man who pinched pennies when he could get away with it.

"Now you go tell Jane we'll take her back, Mr. Hannum," Mrs. Zimmerman said. "Tell that silly girl she'll have a good, safe home till she marries you."

"Not sure she'll listen to me."

"Give her this brooch and she will listen. If her mind is good, she will listen."

"Thank you. Thank you. Oh, there is one other thing I need. I mean I don't need it, but . . . say, what is this thing over here shaped like a star. That might be it."

"It isn't jewelry. It's a cookie cutter. It is inexpensive."

"Good. I'll take it."

"I never knew Jane to eat cookies or make them."

"I'll tell her to start making them for the customers. Taylor Made is getting more customers these days. I'd better take two cookie cutters."

"Excellent. It's important that a man tells his woman exactly what he wants."

"I'll do my best, Mrs. Zimmerman." I thanked her profusely for her help but wasn't about to tell her that the cookie cutters were a gift for Monique Taylor. I figured that the brooch would accomplish what I wanted with Jane, but it wouldn't hurt to let my true love know that I was not the kind of thoughtless man who would fail to share his Christmas spirit with her present companion.

I had Mrs. Zimmerman wrap the brooch

separately from the two cookie cutters. The store was out of seasonal wrapping paper, so she used plain brown paper.

"What counts is what's inside," she said.

"I hope you're right."

"Good luck to you, Mr. Hannum," she called out as I headed for the door. "Remember to pin the brooch on her good and tight but don't pinch her. She needs to know that you are the right kind of man, gentle but firm."

"She will. And since you offer such wonderful advice, I was wondering if I could ask you something else."

"By all means."

"I know the brooch is great, but would it help my cause to also include a poem I wrote, you know to make my gift extra personal?"

"You wrote a poem?"

"Not yet. I've been hesitant because the poem I attached to my Christmas gift last year didn't go over so well. This time, I'll make it clear who the poem is from, none of that childish Saint Nick business."

"Yes, a poem! How romantic! Sit over there by the stove to write. I imagine it helps a poet to write with a warm heart."

And that's what I did, writing with a pencil and paper provided free of charge by

Mrs. Zimmerman. The words did seem to come straight from my warm heart:

A Gift from Me, Harry Hannum
It is Christmas Day
Please listen to what I say
Forgive my direct approach
But I really must broach
The subject of you and me
Together now,
Tomorrow,
And for all eternity.
I pin this silver brooch
On your tender breast
To let you know for sure
That I love you best

During the next few days, I started to question the whole idea of a poem. I questioned each line I wrote but liked the *for all eternity* part too much to change it. I was especially uncertain about the last four lines. *Tender breast* didn't seem right, and I figured it wouldn't seem right until Jane and I were married. Something also seemed amiss about my *I love you best* finish. Did it mean I loved her more completely than anyone else did, including Wyatt Matters, Monique Taylor, and the late Matt Sullivan, or did it mean I loved her more than I ever loved Elizabeth

Pepper, Alice Wright, and the others who had struck my passing fancy through the years. Yes, I had written those words, but they confused even me. I went back to Mrs. Zimmerman for a clean sheet of paper and wrote the whole thing over again. I changed the ending to this:

I pin this silver brooch
Over your kind heart
To let you know for sure
We shall never part.

On Christmas morning I was reviewing my revised poem again. It wasn't until noon that I folded the page and found a piece of string to secure it to the wrapped gift. I then imagined for some time Jane's reaction, first when she read the verse, second when she did the unwrapping and saw the expensive brooch, third when she kissed me and I kissed her back. Consequently, I arrived at Taylor Made later than I expected, midafternoon. Jane Hankin and Monique Taylor were busy preparing and serving Christmas meals for three loud soldiers from Fort Dodge, a larger and louder group of buffalo hunters, and a dark-skinned, rawboned man sitting alone at a table for two and chewing quietly. Monique was the one who welcomed me. She had me sit on the chair across from the black man after the three of us signaled our approval of the arrangement. He was slowly eating a bowl of gumbo, savoring each bite. When I told him my name and where I worked his ears perked up and he put down his spoon. He said his name was Will Lee Washington, named in honor of the slave who had acted as personal assistant to George Washington and been freed by the president's will. He added that he had hauled lumber for the building of Fort Dodge in '65, helped the blacksmith at the fort, driven on occasion the Fort Dodge Express wagon for Willie Taylor, and tried his hand at skinning buffalo until the stench became too much for him.

"Too bad what happened to Mr. Taylor," I said.

Will Lee Washington turned quiet as if he needed time to digest my words. He wasn't looking at me directly, but I could tell he was sizing me up. Maybe he didn't trust my white face and wasn't sure how to respond. But then he sighed deeply and said: "I reckon you be all right, Mr. Harry Hannum. Willie Taylor was a good man."

"I didn't know him long, but I thought so, too."

"He was my best friend. He was one-word

Willie. I was Will Lee, two words. We were like brothers."

He picked up his spoon and dipped it into his bowl, but then just stirred in lazy circles what was left of his food without taking another bite. I asked Monique to please bring me a bowl of the same.

"I take it you're a gumbo-loving man, Mr. Washington," I said.

"Not particularly. I'll eat anything. That's the way it is when you've been poor and hungry most of your life."

"I suppose you're right, Mr. Washington. But nothing on the menu here is exactly cheap."

"Call me Will Lee. The price doesn't count for me, Mr. Hannum. I'm what you call a preferred customer at Taylor Made."

"Call me Harry. How so?"

"Monique knows what I meant to her Willie and he to me, and she recognizes I'm a Monique-loving man. Now don't go thinking there's anything unpalatable about it, Mr. Hannum. It was that way when Willie was alive, but of course it wasn't mentioned. I still don't say anything now that Willie is dead 'cause I realize Monique isn't liable to forget her husband any time soon. She doesn't say anything because she can't talk, but I can tell how she feels by her eyes.

Never saw eyes that talk so much in all my born days. She was powerfully in love with that man."

"I see. It might interest you to know that I'm a Jane-loving man. Jane Hankin is . . ."

"A fine woman. Monique tells me all the time in her own way how lucky she is to have Jane around. And I'm around, too, but maybe that isn't such a lucky thing for her, more like a burden she must bear."

"I doubt that."

"No, it's true. I'm a dependent who doesn't do dishes."

"I'd do anything for Jane. I brought her a Christmas present."

"That right? Never did celebrate that so-called holiday. But a fellow you know well has been educating me about Christmases past. Did you know George Washington considered Christmas just another cold, snowy day during the Revolutionary War?"

"Do you happen to be talking about Wyatt Matters?"

"He has kind of adopted me, you might say. He's a talker, but he's worth a listen, especially when he shares his wine. Pretty much the same with you, I imagine."

I had no idea that Wyatt knew him, let alone was trying to "educate" him, too. First my mentor had taken William Taylor under his wing and now Will Lee Washington. I must have felt a touch of jealousy because I became silent and didn't let myself think about it. Instead, I thought about getting up from the table and finding Jane, which after all was my reason for being there.

"Sit tight," Mr. Washington said. "Jane will be out of the kitchen with your gumbo soon enough and you can give her your Christmas present."

"Sure," I said. I wondered if Wyatt was teaching his mind-reading skills to Will Lee.

"Mr. Matters tells me you're the bashful type, been pursuing Miss Hankin for better than a year. He quoted this lady writer to me, name of Austen, who says, 'We are all fools in love.' "

"Wyatt might have mentioned her to me. I can't remember everything he tells me. Anyway, Jane Hankin isn't Jane Austen. Maybe I'm a fool, but I'm not going to be bashful tonight."

"Good for you. Right now, Mr. Hannum . . . eh, Harry, we're in the same boat. You're sitting here thinking you'd rather be conversing about Cupid with Miss Jane. And I'm sitting over here thinking I'd rather be making love to Monique. You might get your wish before the day is done. I know I won't. No point even trying. Monique had

Willie Taylor and no other man will ever do."

"Nevertheless, I'm glad to meet you, Will Lee."

"My pleasure, Harry Hannum. Looks like your gumbo has arrived."

Monique brought the dish with a fair-sized smile. Her expressive eyes were telling me to enjoy my meal to the fullest. She didn't once look at Will Lee Washington, who began dishing food to his mouth faster than before. I wondered what Jane was doing back in the kitchen. Maybe she had learned to make gumbo, too. I didn't ask, but Monique seemed to be in the mind-reading business, too. She patted her chest, blew me a kiss, and issued a soft grunt, which called to mind a certain sound Elizabeth Pepper used to make back in Abilene before she ran off with the railroad man.

"That's a good sign," said Mr. Washington. "Miss Jane knows you're here. She must not know you brought her a gift. You want Monique to tell her?"

Monique held out her hand. I shook my head. I was so focused on Jane I didn't remember bringing a little gift for Monique.

"No, now isn't the time. She must be busy."

For the next fifteen minutes I saw just how

busy Jane was as she passed in and out of the dining area carrying food to the soldiers at one table and the buffalo hunters at the other. Only once did she acknowledge my existence by offering me a small smile and a *Merry Christmas* before taking away Mr. Washington's empty bowl. It made me feel awkward because I'd been telling Will Lee how much Jane meant to me, but I made a point of not taking her neglect personally. I concentrated on my gumbo.

It was Monique, not Jane, who came around to take my empty bowl and ask me with hand motions if I wanted seconds. I declined, though I was hardly full. It was just that my mind was too full of worrisome thoughts to think any longer about my stomach. *What if Jane never got free enough to accept my gift? What if this Christmas became just another day, as it was for Will Lee Washington?*

"Hey, wait a minute," I called out to Monique before she could get away. "I got something for you, too. You want it now?"

Monique nodded her head so vigorously that strands of black hair swished back and forth across her eyes and nose. She held out both hands, curled her fingers, and wiggled them. I of course gave in; she looked so adorable. For a few moments I forgot that she wasn't the one about to receive my main gift. As she eagerly unwrapped, I apologized for the brown paper instead of colorful Christmas paper. When she had her hands on the two tin stars, she immediately held them over her heart as if they were brooches.

"No, no!" I shouted too loudly. At least two of the soldiers turned in my direction. "You don't wear them. You cut out dough with them to make cookies. You do make cookies, right?"

She nodded, cackled, pointed to her mouth, and rubbed her slight belly. She leaned over to kiss me on the forehead and then tossed the cookie cutters into the bowl before carrying it away to the kitchen.

"You trying to make me look bad, Harry?" said Mr. Washington.

"Sorry about that, Will Lee," I said. "I was only practicing for my real mission."

It was clear though that I'd have to wait. Mr. Washington waited with me. It was too early to go to bed, and he said he didn't have anywhere else to go. A couple of the buffalo soldiers, neither of whom had cleaned up much for their restaurant visit, came over to our corner table. They didn't fit Wyatt Matters' description of the typical Dodge troublemaker — neither was young, drunk, or armed — but this pair meant trouble and they smelled. They remembered Mr. Washington from his short time on the Plains and without as much as a howdy-do they hovered over the table and began to ridicule him.

"You look fine as cream gravy, boy, sitting all pretty with this gentleman of the first water," said the smaller of the two who still must have been twice the weight of Mr. Washington or me for that matter. "When you was skinning for us you looked like a dime's worth of dog meat."

"The way you threw up the sponge and skedaddled, we thought you was a goner, but here you be," said the other, who in his oversized buffalo coat looked big enough to be a buffalo. "We should of known better than to tie to a mudsill like you."

"Carving up carcasses just wasn't my calling," said Mr. Washington.

"You was so shoddy with your skinner knife, boy, it's a wonder they give you a knife to cut your own meat," said the first, pounding a fist on the table, making it rattle. "This scamp do all your cutting for you, boy?"

"We had gumbo," I said. "No cutting necessary."

Both buffalo hunters laughed as if I had made a joke and the big one slapped me on the back so firmly I fell forward and my chest struck the table, rattling it again. The second hunter stopped laughing first and continued prodding Mr. Washington by saying how where he came from they would make cottonwood blossoms out of his kind. I didn't catch the meaning of his reference (later Mr. Matters told me he was referring to men lynched from the limbs of a tree), but I knew it wasn't anything said in polite conversation. It did cause Mr. Washington to push back from the table — which caused the edge of the table to jab me in the belly — and stand as tall as he could. I felt obliged to get out of my chair as well. I checked the room. I figured I could beat these two clodhoppers to the door, but the other three buffalo hunters had also stood up and were blocking the exit. The odds were five to two against Will Lee and me, to say the least, because not one of them was shorter or skinnier than us. The only good thing was they didn't have their buffalo rifles or other firearms handy, so at least it wouldn't be another Willie Taylor situation. Still, I would have done most anything to avoid a thrashing. I tried to put myself in Wyatt Matters' shoes. How would he talk his way out of this dire situation? And just like that, words began to flow as if some invisible being had taken control of my tongue.

"You are delightful fellows with wonderful senses of humor," I told them. "I bet you have a riotous time while felling the great woolly beasts of the Plains and can even chuckle over your prowess when you have retired from a hard day in the killing field and are fast asleep in your bedrolls. Your laughter-loving ways give evidence of health and hearty dinners. In short, you are men of unabated appetites and vigor while we are but two tiny, insignificant human beings who hate nobody and profess no readiness to do combat with anyone. We are unskilled in fighting matters and are ignorant of the accomplishments of weighty, forceful, dutiful, and highly energetic men like yourselves, the epitome of manhood. Surely, men such as yourselves can see the humor in our predicament."

That I was capable of such a speech amazed me, as it did everyone else in the room, for now even the soldiers had become part of my audience. The two buffalo hunters — one with arms crossed, one with hands on hips — listened to my every word. They weren't laughing, but neither were they raising their fists or telling me to shut the hell up. If Mr. Matters had been there, he might have patted me on the back or possibly himself on the back for teaching me so well. But, of course, if he had been there, I wouldn't have been able to get in a word edgeways.

"He can talk," the big one simply said, uncrossing his arms to scratch both his temples at the same time.

"That's all he is — all talk," said the other. "He didn't sound particularly funny, though."

Mr. Washington wasn't trying to look amiable. He was pressing two fists together at chest level and scowling, more at me than the two brutes. I decided I best keep talking.

"Look," I said. "No reason for any of us to kick about anything. Will Lee and I are finished eating. If you'd like us to leave so you boys can finish your meals in peace, we'd be happy to oblige. Last thing either of us would want to do is disturb your digestion." I bent down low as if to bow to them but then reached under the table to secure my gift for Jane. If I got out of this in one piece, I could always come back later and make it a late-night Christmas present.

"I am capable of speaking for myself, Harry," said Mr. Washington. "I'm a regular customer here and they aren't. If anyone should leave, it's them."

The faces of the two buffalo hunters reddened, and one of them snorted, more like a buffalo than a man. I grimaced, wondering why my new friend was acting so brave, which under the circumstances seemed plain foolish. All those words I spouted — some of which I had heard before from my mentor — seemed wasted; I expected our thrashing to commence at any second. When the intimidating hunters looked at each other, however, something burst inside them, and they carried on as if they truly were laughter-loving fellows. All I could do was clutch my gift and wait to see what happened when their laughter petered out.

Before it did, Monique Taylor stepped out of the kitchen doorway and marched to our table without the slightest hesitation. It was just the right moment to assure the safety of Will Lee Washington and probably me as well.

She rubbed large circles on her stomach and made noises as if she were swishing saliva around inside her mouth. I wouldn't have blamed her if she had spit in the faces of those buffalo hunters, but she was employing a different, far wiser tact. She next produced a sound that was a cross between a baby cooing and a polite lady suppressing a cough.

"What the hell is that lady saying?" shouted the big hunter.

I made an educated guess. "Cookies!"

Monique smiled and pretended to be stuffing them into her delicate mouth.

"What's them?" the second hunter asked.

"Dessert," I said. "Cookies straight out of the oven. Shaped like stars, I'm guessing."

"Like cake?"

"Something like that. A sweet treat."

Monique directed the two buffalo hunters back to their own table. They went like lambs. She motioned for them to stay seated and then scurried into the kitchen. When she didn't return right away, the buffalo hunters started to grumble, and Mr. Washington suggested I go over and try to "sweet talk the bastards again." I was apologizing to him even while denying I had been groveling to them when both Monique and Jane emerged, each carrying two plates of star-shaped cookies — enough to please not only the buffalo soldiers but also the trio from Fort Dodge. By the time the two women made it over to our table, they were holding plates, empty even of crumbs.

"That's a fine way to treat a preferred customer," Mr. Washington said.

I thought he was serious, and I was ready to scold him for failing to realize that Monique's cookies had probably saved our bacon, but then like a protective mother she took his hand and led him back to the safety of the kitchen. With everyone else occupied with dessert, I bowed to Jane, who stood within my reach, her loveliness presenting itself even behind the bare plates, the dirty apron, and the specks of food substances on her nose, cheeks, and chin. Words, which had flowed out of desperation minutes ago, now escaped me. I thrust forward my wrapped brown package with card attached to it with string.

"Merry . . . eh . . . Christmas," I said.

"For me?" she asked with arms straight down at her sides.

"Who else?" I said, thinking it wasn't really a stupid question, just a young woman behaving like a young woman.

"More cookie cutters?"

"Certainly not. This is a special gift just for you."

"Why?"

"Because . . . you know."

"What is it?"

"Open it. But read the attached poem first."

"Right here in the dining room, in front of everybody?"

"Oh." I glanced over at the other tables. The cookies were all gone, but the five buffalo hunters were now conversing with the three soldiers. None of them were paying any attention to Jane, so I knew they weren't talking about women.

"Just listen to them," Jane said, peeking back over her shoulder as if afraid to look directly at those eight rugged men.

And so we listened, both transfixed. I heard mention of dwindling buffalo herds, unscrupulous traders, Army deserters, foolish emigrants on the Santa Fe Trail, untrustworthy Comanches and Kiowas, and the drinking habits of officers. It wasn't heated talk, just loud. And it got louder when they began to debate whether General Philip Sherman had really said, *The Only Good Indian Is a Dead Indian.*

"Would you rather . . . you know, go someplace to open them?" The only place in my mind was under a cottonwood tree in the moonlight.

"I'm working," she said.

My arm was getting tired holding out the gift toward her, but I was determined not to lower it.

"But it's Christmas, Jane. You really need to open it before Christmas is over."

"I have to go back to the kitchen."

She started to walk away without the present, and I must say I felt hurt or angry or maybe both. The two always seemed to go together like two black peas in a pod. "What about me?" I called out.

"Come along," she said, still walking away from me but now waving her arm to get me moving. "You do do dishes, don't you?"

Chapter Eighteen

While I was washing dishes in the kitchen, all hell broke loose in the dining area. The talk there had gotten so heated between the soldiers and buffalo hunters that it spiraled into pushing, shoving, and throwing of silverware, mostly knives. Three glasses and two plates were shattered over heads and one of the soldiers had to pull a fork out of his blue belly. The largest of the hunters, the one who had earlier compared Will Lee Washington to dog meat, lifted one of the tables and pinned two soldiers with it against a wall. Monique Taylor crossed her arms in front of the kitchen door so that neither Mr. Washington nor I would go out there and get mixed up in a fight that didn't concern us. That was kind of funny because I never stopped doing the dishes that weren't broken, and Mr. Washington, who had consented to drying, started laughing so hard he dropped a plate himself. Jane Hankin, who showed plenty of pluck by picking up a broom to use as a weapon in case any of the rowdy customers showed his face in the kitchen, demanded to know why Will Lee was laughing his fool head off.

"I tell you, Miss Jane, it's like this," Mr. Washington said after he caught his breath. "I feel toward those white men out there the way the Comanche Indians felt about white men during the Civil War. In Texas the Comanches raided the settlements of Confederates. Here in Kansas other Comanches engaged in depredations upon the lives of Union men and women. As far as the whole tribe was concerned, all white men were their enemies. Kiowas felt the same way, the Cherokees, too. They thought white men fighting white men was reason for exultation. All roused up, they went on the warpath themselves. Western Kansas saw a general Indian outbreak."

Monique began stamping both her feet. If she had been able to speak, she no doubt would have lashed out at Will Lee for that kind of talk. Jane picked up on that and swatted Will Lee on the backside with her broom. "You better not go on the warpath," she said. "Monique wants you to stay in here. You're no redskin."

"That's for certain, Miss Jane. And my

skin ain't white either. If those fellows out there want to kill each other, it's no skin off my nose." He picked up the broken plate and began wiping both halves with the drying towel.

"What one of you men might do is crawl out the bedroom window and go for help," Jane said. "We do have a sheriff in town now. Isn't he supposed to break up brawls like the one going on in our dining room?"

"He'd probably blame me for starting it," said Mr. Washington. "Harry had better go for Sheriff Bassett."

All I wanted to do was finish the dishes and have Jane read my verse and open my Christmas present like she promised.

"I'm working," I said and immediately regretted it. Jane was giving me a half-puzzled, half-scornful look. She didn't like men using their fists let alone their guns, but she apparently wasn't too fond either of men who behaved in cowardly fashion. "I'll go," I said. "I'll be back with the sheriff."

It wasn't necessary. The noise coming from the dining area suddenly stopped. Monique was the first to peek out the kitchen door; the rest of us followed. It seemed the buffalo hunters and Fort Dodge soldiers had all cleared out on their own — maybe to take their fight outside or to break things off because they weren't drunk enough to want to kill each other. It turned out there was someone else in the room, a short figure standing in the corner straightening one of the framed New Orleans paintings on the wall. Jane was the first to spot him.

"Why Wyatt Matters," she called out. "When in heaven's name did you get here?"

"I was in the neighborhood," said Mr. Matters. "I was expecting Harry to stop by for some good cheer after he gave you his Christmas present. I wondered what had happened to him."

I hadn't even told my mentor about the brooch, let alone the verse, because I had something to prove to him and myself — that I could court my true love without any assistance from him. "She hasn't opened it yet," I muttered.

"How'd you get everyone to leave, Wyatt?" asked Jane, as if she hadn't heard me or else was ignoring me. "One minute they were fighting and the next minute they were all gone."

"All I did was walk in and announce that Marley was dead. That immediately caused everyone to pause in their fighting and shouting. The soldiers wondered if the dead man was a Private Marley, a hotheaded soldier who deserted from Fort Dodge last week.

The three bison hunters knew a Canadian named Frank Marley who came down from Wichita last year to hunt on the Great Plains with the Masterson brothers. The hunters all seemed to like this Marley fellow but also believed he was foolhardy and would one day be caught in a bison stampede or scalped by Comanche raiders."

"How horrible!" cried Jane. "Which Marley is it who died?"

"Not one that those cretins know. It being Christmas, I naturally was talking about Jacob Marley from *A Christmas Carol,* by Charles Dickens."

"Naturally," I said, though at the time I was unfamiliar with any of Dickens' work.

"While I had everybody's attention, I decided to recite the opening lines of that outstanding seasonal work from memory." And he proceeded to recite them again for us:

Marley was dead to begin with. There is no doubt whatever about that. The register of his burial was signed by the clergyman, the clerk, the undertaker, and the chief mourner. Scrooge signed it. And Scrooge's name was good upon 'change, for anything he chose to put his hand to. Old Marley was as dead as a door-nail.

"So, the dead Marley is only a fictional

character," said Jane, and her sigh of relief was loud enough to startle Monique.

"Exactly, Lady Jane. Neither the hunters nor the soldiers gave me the chance to explain. I do believe they were all Scrooges, lacking in any Christmas spirit and having no literary bent. Every last one of them rudely walked out in the middle of my reciting. That's bad enough, but they left without paying for their meals, didn't they?"

Nodding her head vigorously, Monique Taylor stepped up to Mr. Matters and made assorted sounds of displeasure. She waved Will Lee Washington over and together they righted an overturned table before Monique made a series of hand gestures that included two sharp points at Mr. Matters.

"Monique feels you should have kept Mr. Dickens to yourself, at least until they'd paid up, Mr. Matters," Will Lee said. "Oh, and merry, merry to you, sir."

"And to you too, Mr. Washington, and to dear Monique. She need not fear. After I leave your good company, I'll pay Sheriff Bassett a visit. I'll wish him a Merry Christmas and tell him what happened. I have full confidence that the sheriff will collect what's due for the meals and for the damages."

"We don't even know their names," said Jane.

"No problem. The sheriff and I will get them. If necessary, I'll even go out to Fort Dodge or the bison grounds to see that justice is served."

"You are too kind, Wyatt. I'm glad you stopped by on Christmas. Monique and I should have invited you for a holiday meal."

"Don't give it another thought. Oh, that reminds me. I have something for you, Lady Jane."

"For me?" she said moving closer to him.

From behind his back, he produced a hat-sized box neatly wrapped in green and red striped paper. Jane reached out and accepted her gift. With both hands she held it to her ear and gave it a good shake.

"It's too heavy to be a hat," she said. "How many guesses do I get?"

"Too late for guessing, Lady Jane. Just open it up and enjoy."

She did, and then she gasped — twice. What she revealed was a foot-high case containing about ten times as much silver as my unopened brooch contained. The case had a ram's head handle on each side and cut-out panels that revealed what was inside — three crystal bottles. In front was a lock. I was befuddled. I couldn't think of any liquid that needed to be under lock and key except for nitroglycerine, which miners used to blast rock. But I didn't have to ask for clarification. Wyatt had Jane put the silver case on the table, presented her with a key, and offered an explanation.

"The most exquisite wine decanter box I've seen west of the Mississippi," he said. "Decanting wine, that is the act of pouring the wine from a bottle into the decanter, allows the wine to breathe and wake up. You see the wine needs to interact with the oxygen in the air for at least a few minutes — as much as a half hour for the older, finer vintages — so that the tannins mellow out and the flavors and aromas of the wine become more apparent. Notice that the top of the lid has a magnificent cast grapevine finial, and the regal engraved monogram in front. It's a family heirloom."

I got close enough to read the two interlaced decorative letters — *AD*. "Whose family?" I asked.

"Just trust me on that," he said, no more ready on Christmas night to discuss family matters than he had ever been. "All that matters is that this three-decanter box is something special that I have kept in my trunk to give at just the right moment to the most special person."

"Oh my," Jane said upon trying out the key and finding that it really worked. "It is so

. . . so . . . exquisite. With beautiful decanters like these, I'll really have to develop my appreciation of wine."

"And so you shall, my dear girl. I have none to offer tonight. But just you wait until New Year's Eve."

"I can't say I've ever seen a decanter before," said Will Lee Washington. "To *decanter* sounds like what you do when you slow a horse's gait from a canter to a trot."

Only Monique Taylor laughed. Wyatt and Jane embraced. The latter appeared to be crying for joy. Wyatt's eyes were clear. It occurred to me I had never seen him shed a tear. I felt like crying myself. I slipped back into the kitchen and had a devil of a time trying to locate my wrapped gift for Jane. By the time I had found it next to a bar of soap above the sink and brought it back to the dining area, Wyatt had left to see Sheriff Bassett. But that was just as well. He didn't *need* to see what I was giving Jane.

"This isn't so grand as what Wyatt gave you, Jane," I said. "But it is something for you to wear, straight from my heart."

I wasn't sure whether it was preferable for her to read my personal verse before she did the opening. While debating that in my mind, she tore off the unseasonal brown paper without even noticing the page of rhyme. The brooch left her speechless. She was good for one gasp. She held the brooch against her bosom and looked as if she might start crying again. Monique came over to her for a closer look. She made a gurgling sound and patted Jane on the back. The two women then turned their heads at the same to look me in the eye.

What is the meaning of this? was what Monique's eyes seemed to be saying.

"It . . . it is too much," said Jane.

"But do you like it?" I asked.

"Yes. Yes, of course. I see a forget-me-not." She ran a finger over the engraved flora design, and I couldn't have been more thrilled had that finger been running over my lips.

"There's a little poem that goes with it," I said. "It's there on the floor."

Monique picked up the piece of paper, more than glanced it over, and then handed it to her friend and partner in Taylor Made. As she read quickly, Jane mouthed the words, only some of which I heard. The page slipped out of her fingers and took its time floating back to the floor.

"You want to broach the subject of you and me?" she asked.

"Well, yes. It doesn't have to be this instant, but . . ."

"It can never be." Jane handed the brooch

to Monique. "For you see, I am not free. I have a history."

I was thinking of her own rhymes, probably unintentional, not the meaning when she ran to me, kissed me on the forehead, and ran again, into and through the kitchen to the bedroom beyond. I couldn't grasp what was going on. I wondered if I should follow. And then I heard the bedroom door slam shut.

Sheriff Bassett arrived with a hand on the butt of his holstered six-shooter. He looked ready and eager to stop a brawl or disarm a drunken rowdy. Instead, he found a quiet dining area. All the tables and chairs were in the right places and largely intact, all the broken glass swept away, and the floor mopped, though no blood had been spilled. Monique had retired to the bedroom to see about Jane. Will Lee Washington and I were on the way out. The sheriff looked at us with suspicion, but seeing that we were unharmed, he didn't draw his weapon.

"Were you two fighting?" the sheriff asked. "Mr. Matters didn't say a colored man was involved."

"Does it look like we were fighting, Sheriff?" said Will Lee. "We're comrades without arms. It was whites against whites."

"Mr. Matters led me to believe I better do something about the dangerous situation, but everything looks fine here now."

"Fight ended some time ago. Except the fighting customers didn't pay."

"So, I heard. But I can't arrest anyone if you're the only two here. Who owns this restaurant anyway?"

"Two women," I said. "They went to bed."

"Is that right? Hell, that's where I'm going — back to bed. I suggest you two comrades do the same. I'll come see the owners tomorrow."

The three of us walked out together and went our separate ways. It was late, maybe close to not being Christmas anymore, but I went over to Wyatt Matters' tent anyway. It wasn't wine, whether poured from decanters or not, I was after, but I was hoping my mentor could shed some light on Jane Hankin's latest peculiar behavior.

I found him reading by candlelight. He was on page 101 — and not for the first time — of the 120-page first edition of *The World Almanac,* which came out in 1868. He immediately began to read aloud about the assassination of President Abraham Lincoln, Reconstruction, and the impeachment of President Andrew Johnson. Occasionally he interrupted himself to make comments such as "They got this right," "That's not the whole picture, of course," and "I don't believe they asked the opinion of any Negroes on this matter."

My attempts at interrupting him went for naught until I finally shouted, "I can't believe you're reading this stuff on Christmas night!"

"Educating oneself is an activity that must be pursued 365 days a year, 366 days on leap years," he said. "Men like you and me owe it to ourselves. How else can we avoid the pitfalls of the past and make the world a better place? As curious male children we are encouraged to learn something new every day, but when we — and I put this in quotes — 'grow up,' most of us fall into the routine of unrewarding daily work and pathetic nighty escapes into carousing and abusing our wives and children."

He paused to let his words sink into my tired head. Neither of my parents had ever encouraged me to learn a new thing any day at all that I could recall. They had just wanted me to do as I was told, which meant not questioning their lives or my life and not acquiring fancy ideas through too much schooling. I knew all about beatings and carousing from my ne'er-do-well father and all about dull, unrewarding routine from my suicidal mother. While in school, I wanted to escape not learn. Often my mind had wondered to remote places in the West where I could live free of parents and teachers. Of course, those dreams featured many more mountains and trees than could be found in Kansas. Still, I told myself, the Dodge City, Kansas, present was far superior to the Bladensburg, Maryland, past even if on this Christmas night I felt as discarded as a buffalo chip.

I knew I should be more grateful to Wyatt than I was showing. He clearly saw it as his mission to do what my parents had failed to do — encourage my curiosity and belief in the value of continual education and discourage my acceptance of unrewarding daily work and harmful escapes. Somehow, he had the means to avoid having a paying job (yet still be able to live comfortably, albeit in a tent); to buy the food, wine, and books he wanted; and to give away family heirlooms. He also had the good sense to avoid carousing (occasionally overindulging in wine didn't count). I certainly couldn't see him ever beating a wife or children. He was a man of peace and goodwill and furthermore he never admitted to having been married.

"I like to learn things with your help," I said. "But I'm curious about things you never tell me about — namely your own past. Is it full of pitfalls? Shouldn't I know those pitfalls so I can avoid them?"

"No. All you need to know about me is I am a man with a wealth of experience who has traveled the West and the world and now has settled right here in Dodge to make it my permanent home. How I came to be such a man is due to my own diligent study and perseverance. My personal bygone days are of no consequence to you in developing yourself into a modern-day Renaissance man like myself."

"If you say so. I am confident you never once were a drunken young man who fired pistols indiscriminately and shot down a mayor or the son of a preacher man. I only wonder about whether both your mother and father encouraged you to learn something new every day."

"No point in wondering. Such details don't matter now or ever."

"But in all other areas outside yourself, you want me to wonder, to be curious, to think, to seek knowledge."

He shut his almanac with a bang. It occurred to me I might be annoying him the way he annoyed so many other people in town. Still, I persisted. "What struck my curiosity tonight — well, one of the things

— was that gift you gave Jane. You called it a family heirloom, and since your last name is Matters, I wondered why there is an *AD* on the silver case. What does the *D* stand for?"

"Make it *Denouement.*"

"That's a family name?"

"That's my idea of a joke, son. A denouement is the final part of a play or narrative in which the strands of the plot are drawn together, and matters are explained or resolved."

That had me scratching my head, which made him laugh. "Stop wondering and start reading," he said, handing me the almanac. "Consider this my Christmas gift to you. No, don't thank me. I've been through it at least ten times and the impeached Andrew Johnson never looks any better. Besides, I have the 1872 *World Almanac* on order."

"Wonderful. I'm afraid I have no Christmas present for you. It was an oversight, considering all you've done for me. It's just that I . . ."

"I know. You had Lady Jane on your mind and your total focus was on giving her that brooch."

"But how did you know? You weren't there when she opened it."

"My source, if you must know, was Matilda

Zimmerman. She thought it was a fine, meaningful gift for the lady you love, and so do I, if I don't say so myself."

"Too bad Jane didn't think it was fine and meaningful. It must have been a big letdown for her after that silver, three-decanter case from you."

My words triggered more laughter, and I started to get offended.

"It was no letdown, son. I'm certain she was simply overwhelmed. We can both love her, you know, in our own ways. Me as a father's love for a daughter. You as a young man's love for a young woman who has captivated him with her winsomeness."

I didn't ask him what *winsomeness* meant, but it sounded right. Trouble was I hadn't *won* anything from Jane. She had disappeared into the back bedroom at Taylor Made. Her last words haunted me: *It can never be. For you see, I am not free. I have a history.* I repeated those words for Wyatt or rather so Wyatt could give me his wise interpretation.

"Hell, it's something neither of us can control," he said.

I felt as if he had socked me in the gut. I squeezed the almanac to my chest as if that would help hold myself together. But he must have read my face — no Christmas gleam on it, only the gloom of what must have been by now the morning after Christmas.

"Don't worry about it," he said, giving my neck a squeeze. "This isn't the end, son. We all have histories, secret or not. Our lives shall continue into the New Year and beyond. I wouldn't take those words of Lady Jane as some sort of denouement."

I took to reading the *World Almanac* every night after work for a week in a futile attempt to keep my mind off Jane. Mr. Matters told me the key with her at this juncture was to show patience, and if I did, I would ultimately be able to win her over. He added that he wanted that to happen as much as I did, but he wouldn't say if he knew why Jane said those disturbing words — *I am not free*. If it wasn't Wyatt curtailing her freedom, who else could it be? The only name I came up with was Monique Taylor, for the Zimmermans had not interfered with her leaving them, Matt Sullivan was long dead, and no other man occupied her time. When Wyatt invited her and me over to bring in the New Year in his tent, I thought I might be able to pry some answers out of them. That didn't seem possible, though, because along with the three decanters Wyatt had asked her to bring, Jane also brought along the uninvited

Monique. The two women had been spending all that time together running Taylor Made and sharing a bed in back, yet that wasn't enough for them. They had become inseparable. If I had known about Monique being there, I would have invited my new friend Will Lee Washington, who wasn't having any more luck with Monique than I was having with Jane. Worse, though, for me, was what Jane didn't bring — the brooch. I kept looking at the spot on the front of her dress where the brooch should have been attached.

As we sat around the inside-the-tent fire pit, the wine flowed and two of the decanters were put to immediate use. I fixed my eyes on Jane, whose face stayed flushed and who wore the red dress she used to dance in so many months ago. Surprisingly the two women were both consuming more wine than the host, but none could match me. Jane showed more inclination to talk to Monique, who could only talk back with her eyes and hands, than to me. Meanwhile Wyatt was his usual self. First, he went on endlessly about New Year's resolutions just as he had done the previous year. When I told him I already knew about ancient Babylonians making resolutions, he said that was fine but that he was enlightening the two women.

Finally, he changed the subject and began congratulating the work Charley Bassett was doing. The sheriff had gone out to Fort Dodge and not only learned the identities of the three soldiers who had eaten at Taylor Made Christmas night but also convinced them to pay up for the food, a cracked table-top, and three broken glasses. As for the five buffalo hunters who had fought with them, Sheriff Bassett could locate only one on the prairie south of town, but that one did pay for his meal. The other four had migrated to the southern Plains in search of a more substantial buffalo herd. Because of the way the other three in the tent seemed to be leaving me out of every conversation, I began to sulk. The more I sulked the more I drank — or maybe it was the other way around. In any case by the time Wyatt had directed the conversation back to resolutions, I was beginning to tip over, twice nearly falling into the fire at the center of the tent. The second near fall did attract Wyatt's attention.

"I never saw you that drunk before, son," he said.

"Neither have I," I said. "At least it's on your precious wine. Hand me the bottle, would you, old man. I don't much care whether the stuff is decanted or not!" It occurred to me that I just might be a *mean* drunk, but right then it didn't bother me in the least.

Monique went through some hand gestures, including a few imitations of a drinker raising a glass. Her every movement irritated me. I didn't know what she was trying to say, but Jane picked right up on it.

"Moni suggests you resolve *not* to drink so much in 1874," said Jane.

"Does she now? Moni, Moni, Moni. The hand talker should mind her own goddamned business.!"

"That's not nice."

"What is nice? Is she nice? Are you nice? Is Dodge City nice now that nobody is getting shot regular anymore?"

"You aren't making sense. Moni is right about you drinking too much."

"What do you say, Lady Joan of Arc? By the way, are you a legitimate saint?"

"My name is Jane. You're not yourself, Harry. And, yes, I think you should make that resolution. As Wyatt says: *Men who are drunk tend to act like skunks.*"

"And he says whiskey and guns don't mix. But I'm no carrier and this is wine, so it's jim-dandy."

"You don't look jim-dandy."

"I'm harry-dandy."

"I don't think so."

"No? How did Matt Sullivan look when he was drunk — you know before he was dead?"

Jane shook her head and backed away from me on the seat of her red dress.

"I think, Monique and I had better leave. We don't need to wait for 1874."

"You are free to go and free not to go. Who says you're *not* free?"

"I said it to you, Harry, because you want so much more than I can give you."

"All I want is for you to leave the bedroom behind the restaurant and me to leave my storeroom bed at the general store and for us to move . . ."

"To move into Wyatt's tent?"

"Saints must make sacrifices for a worthy cause."

"Stop calling me a saint. I'm not one and never said I was."

"Wyatt won't mind us moving in for a while. I am his protégé and you are his . . . whatever. Oh, I get it, Juliette. We'll get married before we move in."

"Come on, Monique. Let's go."

"And she can marry good old Will Lee. We'll have a double ceremony. And you can be best man, Wyatt. No guns will be allowed at the ceremony. You can count on that, Wyatt."

"Five minutes to midnight, youngins,"

said Wyatt, who was seemingly content to just listen to others for a change. "Shall we continue with our resolutions?"

"All right," I said. "I'll resolve to stay sober every day in 1874 right after you, Josie, resolve to wear the brooch I gave you every other day."

"Impossible. And I am Jane."

"All right, once a week then."

"I can't do that either."

"Then twice a month, Jocelyn."

"Why should I? You can't even remember my correct name."

"Jane. Jane. Jane. Jane. I say your name in vain. I'm a natural born rhymer, Lady Jane."

"What time is it, Wyatt?"

He consulted his pocket watch, waited a few seconds, and then announced, "Three minutes to go."

"I bet you'd wear the brooch every single day if Matt Sullivan gave it to you."

"I would not. Leave him out of this. I . . ."

"You'd wear it all day and all night and to bed, too, if Monique gave it to you."

"You're talking crazy. Time?"

"Two minutes," said Wyatt.

"I resolve to avoid all drunk men," Jane said.

Monique nodded her head, gestured wildly, and then pointed at me.

"Monique resolves the same, unless they happen to be paying customers who don't fight or throw chairs."

"Less than a minute now," said Wyatt. "I resolve to kiss all three of you when the clock strikes twelve."

"Well, I'm not waiting," I shouted. I didn't feel well enough to stand, but I scrambled onto my knees, accidentally knocking over my empty glass with the left one. I tried to set the glass upright but instead shattered it with my hand. My cut hand began to bleed. The blood was the same color as the wine. I licked the red running along the lines of my palm. "You can't forget Harry Hannum ever again," I announced. "Here I come!" I advanced on all fours like a bull chasing a matador's red cape. No, I didn't try to kiss my mentor or Monique. But I pounced on top of Jane Hankin, knocking her onto her back and then smothering her with kisses — first her face, then her neck, and finally the place on her red dress where the brooch should have been pinned.

Chapter Nineteen

That winter Sheriff Basset took on the added role of Dodge township constable, and in early 1874 the county commissioners gave him a deputy sheriff to help keep the peace in Ford County. The saloons and dance halls could at times be as still as the night. In its first issue on February 26, 1874, the *Dodge City Messenger* noted that the shops in town were all doing good business, adding, "The saloons are kept in good shape, and very orderly, by gentlemen who fully understand their business." Buffalo hunters rarely showed up in Dodge City; most had fled the area in search of greener pastures. Hard cases, if not outright desperadoes, found little reason to stay either, even if the sheriff didn't tell them to get out of Dodge. The town had gained an appalling reputation across Kansas and beyond as a place where Negroes were hunted like buffalo and well-developed murderers walked the streets doing whatever dirty deed pleased them. The *Messenger* called for a total reassessment. "Now," the newspaper claimed, "instead of those terrible scenes that we read of being re-enacted, quietude reigns supreme. The desperadoes have all taken their departure, leaving the peace-loving citizens in possession."

The *Messenger* had it right. Wyatt Matters was of course delighted that law and order had come to Dodge. Not that this development totally quieted him. He kept pushing for the passage of gun-control ordinances, reminding the likes of Robert Wright, George Hoover, and Frederick Zimmerman, "Gun violence is always lurking in the shadows of our saloons and dance halls."

He was not shy about taking credit for two resolutions made by Ford County's commissioners — the banning in March of concealed weapons in Dodge and the banning in May of carrying pistols in Dodge by everyone except those involved in "legitimate business." After that success, he took up a new cause, the hiring of a town marshal. "The sheriff and his deputy must be concerned about the entire Ford County," he reminded everyone he met. "What we need is a dedicated lawman who makes Dodge itself his sole priority." He would have to wait on that, but at least it gave him something to grumble about.

It took me until late spring to get over most of the shame I felt for my drunken, ungentlemanly New Year's Eve behavior toward the woman I loved. I had been avoiding not only Jane and Taylor Made but also wine and Mr. Matters' tent. By day, more than ever, I was living the kind of life Wyatt frowned about: following a dull, unrewarding routine six days a week at the general store. At night, at least, I didn't resort to whiskey, gambling, or hurdy-gurdy girls, even if the new gun controls had apparently made things safer in the saloons and dance halls. I did plenty of reading, starting with the 1868 *World Almanac* given to me by Mr. Matters. After that I raced through an 1862 copy of *Uncle Tom's Cabin,* loaned to me by Will Lee, who had inherited the book from a great uncle. I felt I must finally read it, since several times Mr. Matters had quoted President Lincoln as saying upon meeting author Harriet Beecher Stowe, "So this is the little lady who started the Great War." I also read the *Messenger,* which came out irregularly and was "so neutral and inoffensive to be excessively humdrum," according to Wyatt.

Will Lee Washington, who had started to call me *brother,* continued to drive the

Dodge City Express wagon, but it didn't run regularly and sometimes he took the wagon out on the prairie to gather buffalo bones, which could be sold for six to eight dollars a ton. He talked me into helping him. I developed a certain morbid fascination with the activity, and it was a good change of pace from all my time indoors. He explained that the bones were high in phosphorous content, and were ground by machines and sold as bonemeal, which was tilled into poor soils as a fertilizer.

"You sound like Wyatt Matters," I told him.

"Who do you think told me about this? Of course, Mr. Matters has no interest in hunting bones with me — too much hard work under the sun. I thank you for volunteering."

That was an exaggeration, but since I was generally glad to be out there with him, I loaded the wagon for free. "No need to thank me. I enjoy it. No place I'd rather be than out here helping you and the fertilizer industry."

"Shit, Harry! You're one crazy white man, working away for nothing and whistling while you work."

On our third trip out together in June, he led me to a spot where earlier he had erected several cairns of buffalo chips to serve as a landmark. After we cleared the bones from a particular flat area, he declared this was the place to play instead of work. Naturally, I was confused.

"Long before I got into buffalo bones, I was using buffalo chips for heat and cooking in the absence of suitable wood," he said. "But they also make good bases, brother."

"Bases for what?"

"For baseball, of course."

He laid out a diamond in the rough with four buffalo chips. From the back of the wagon, he pulled out a piece of three-foot rounded lumber he called a bat and then tossed me a nearly round, dark ball. I tried to catch it with one hand and dropped it.

"Two hands for beginners," he said, picking up the ball and rubbing it between his palms as if it were a smooth gem. Again, in a Matters-like manner, he told me the ball was made from the rubber remnants of old shoes with the rubber core wrapped in a single piece of leather tied off with four distinct lines of stitching. He called it a "lemon peel" and said it was an old-fashioned ball given to him by the same uncle who owned the copy of *Uncle Tom's Cabin*. When I confessed that I'd never heard of baseball or peeled a lemon, he explained the game as we engaged in a game of catch. I got the hang of that, but when he tossed the ball to me to strike with the bat, I missed every time, so we changed places. Most of my underhand deliveries, he hit right back at me and on occasion I had to dodge out of the way. Those balls he knocked far into the prairie, well beyond the second buffalo chip, he made me retrieve while he stayed put, pointing the bat in the general direction of the spot where the ball stopped rolling. I told him the game didn't seem like much fun, but he said it was much better when you had nine players on each side and were trying to score more runs than the other team.

"Where in the world you going to find players?" I asked him.

"No problem," he said. "Ballplayers are out there at Fort Dodge already and all over in eastern Kansas. There are ball teams in Leavenworth, Topeka, Lawrence, and . . ."

"Lawrence, huh? Site of Quantrill's raid."

"I guess everyone has heard of the Lawrence Massacre in August 1863."

"Sure," I said. I didn't want to admit I had only learned about the tragic event recently from Mr. Matters, despite having been a swamper in a Lawrence saloon seven years after the massacre. In 1863 I had been in Bladensburg, Maryland, paying attention to horrible events closer to home, some related to the Civil War, some to life in the Hannum home. But now it seemed like not knowing what had happened in Lawrence that year was akin to not knowing what happened the previous month in Gettysburg. Jane Hankin saw it, saw Bloody Bill and company murder her father and three brothers.

"I did know that. Miss Hankin told Monique and Monique told me. Miss Hankin still has nightmares about the massacre."

"I know. I . . ." I abruptly closed my mouth. I was attacking the baseball with my fingers as if trying to unravel it. Mr. Matters also had told me about Jane's awful dream, the one that not only involved Bloody Bill Anderson in the act of killing but also Harry Hannum, wearing a Union cavalry uniform, in the act of violating her. I could only hope that Jane had not chosen to reveal that dream to Monique. "Anyway, when I was in Lawrence, I didn't know any ballplayers."

"That doesn't mean they weren't there playing ball, maybe as early as the Civil War."

I pictured William Quantrill and Bloody Bill playing catch with the severed head of a staunch abolitionist while Jane Hankin watched in horror and the town burned behind them.

"Kansas and Missouri ball teams were battling soon after the slave states were vanquished," Will Lee continued. "It's a known fact that in 1866 the Atchison Pomeroys played the Kansas City Antelopes in a best of three series. The teams split the two games but a third seemed unlikely because play was marred by wrangling, disputing, and coarse epithets, and the umpires were pelted with vegetables and fruits, perhaps even some lemons. The headline in the *Kansas City Daily Times* the next day read, 'The Town Disgraced.' After the Pomeroys apologized for their peppery behavior, a decisive third contest was played in Kansas City. To keep peace and order, the Antelopes brought in gunfighter Wild Bill Hickok as umpire. It worked. Nobody was shot, or otherwise harmed, during a lopsided 48-28 Antelope victory. By the way, none of this comes from Mr. Matters. When it comes to baseball, I know far more than the wise old man does."

"I also lived in Atchison before coming to Dodge, but I never even heard of the Pomeroys, let alone any baseball games being played," I confessed. "Of course, the only thing on my mind and my body at that time was a young woman named Elizabeth Pepper who was no painted lady but even without the paint was . . . eh, enticing."

"I see. Sort of like Jane Hankin, except of course Jane is *only on your mind.*"

"No need to remind me. But there's another big difference. Elizabeth was a wild blond lady who deserted me to run off from Atchison with a railroad man. Jane, with her auburn hair and mild manners, is staying right here in Dodge and doesn't have a man."

"Right, but she does have a woman — Monique Taylor."

I thought I saw Will Lee wink, but I might have been mistaken. I kicked the buffalo chip that he labeled "home base." I figured it might be best to drop the subject, but it seemed like a much more important topic than baseball.

"What made you pass a remark like that?" I asked, stepping on home base.

"Just stating the facts. Monique once had my best compadre Willie Taylor, but he died. Jane once had the gambler Matt Sullivan, but he died. In other words, they both became free women, so to speak. But what happened? Monique has kept me at arm's distance, and Jane doesn't even let your silver brooch touch her breast. Let's face it, brother, the woman of your current fascination and the only woman I've been totally taken with in the last ten years are, in fact, in love with each other."

Then it really is Monique who has kept my Jane from being free to return my affection, I declared to myself as I dug my fingernails into the baseball hide. Will Lee didn't like what he saw and took the baseball away from me.

"Don't tell me, Harry, you haven't noticed their fervent relationship."

"There's all kinds of love in the world," I said more calmly than I imaged I could, what with me all stirred up inside. "Why shouldn't one form be a woman's love for another woman?" Just saying those words agitated my brain. How many times had I wondered what went on between Monique and Jane in the bedroom they shared at Taylor Made? Jane sure hadn't needed me all these months, and Monique hadn't needed Will Lee. "I'm just saying . . . I don't know what I'm saying. What are you saying?"

"I'm saying, amen, brother. Women can love other women most. It's just hard to identify the kind of woman who wants that and nothing more."

"But you told me how much Monique loved her husband."

"No doubt about that. But Willie is gone and not me or any man shall be allowed to fill his shoes. Jane Hankin is no man."

"For land's sake, Will Lee. Tell me something I don't know."

We strolled in silence around the buffalo chip bases and then out to left field, where there were five or six circular depressions that showed far more dirt than grass. "Buffalo wallows," said Will Lee. "Places where buffalo trampled, rolled around, and took dust baths." We moved over to deep center field to get a closer look at the enormous skull of what Will Lee remarked must have belonged to a fully mature buffalo bull. "I may have skinned this big boy with tears in my eyes."

"No doubt the buffalo hunters didn't understand why you were crying."

"No love lost between the curly wolves and me. I soon enough broke free of those brutes, and I mean the two-legged ones, not the four-legged. I wasn't cut out for skinning. They weren't cut out for sympathy. Maybe only a buffalo hunter could love another buffalo hunter. They are a dying breed, just like the beasts they hunt. Mr. Matters has convinced me of that. This place is played out for hunting; now a place to play ball. We'll leave the skull here. If anybody ever hits a baseball this far, we'll declare him King of the Prairie."

We walked from the outfield to home base,

the largest of the buffalo chips. I sat down on it and shaded my eyes from the sun. Our little walk hadn't exhausted me, but our talk of Jane and Monique had. I didn't want to return to the subject of unrequited love or for that matter to the unpleasant world of the doomed buffalo. "Tell me, Will Lee," I said. "I know all the ballplayers want to score runs but how does one side stop the opposite side from scoring?"

"A team stops scoring runs when it makes out — three outs per side up. In other words, the team that's up tries to score as many runs as it can each inning, that is, each turn batting. And the team in the field — positioned out there on the diamond and beyond — tries to get three outs."

"I think I got it. But how are outs even made?"

"Various ways. Three strikes and you're out. Pop up a ball that is caught in the air by a fielder and you're out. Hit a ball on the ground and the fielder's throw to the first baseman beats you, you're out. Be on first and someone steps on second with the ball before you get there and you're out. Oh, and there's another way, although it has been outlawed in some places."

"Outlawed? You mean by umpires like Wild Bill Hickok?"

"No, the umpires don't make the rules. Their job is to enforce the rules agreed upon by the two sides — the home team and the visiting squad. Now, allow me to demonstrate this alternative way of putting someone out. Pretend you have just batted the ball — which I know takes a lot of imagination — and now you are off and running to first. Go on. Run, Harry, run."

"Where to?"

"I just told you. You run to first base first. That's the first buffalo chip to your immediate right."

"If you insist." I took off for the designated buffalo chip and moved faster when Will Lee told me to go faster. I was three-quarters of the way there when something struck me between the shoulder blades. I knew it wasn't a bullet, but it could have been a rock. I stopped dead in my tracks, reaching behind me as I arched my back. "What the heck was that?"

"I put you out, brother."

"No, I'm not out yet." I continued boldly on in a half-run, half limp the rest of the way to the first base, which I jumped on emphatically with both feet. "I made it," I announced. "Does that count as a run?"

"Not by a long shot. You need to circle the bases and get back home to score a run. But you didn't even make a hit since you didn't reach first base safely."

"But I did. I'm here, aren't I?"

"Not before I hit you directly with the baseball. That's what's called getting plugged or getting soaked. No matter what you call it, friend, you are O-U-T out. Two more of those and your team is done for the inning and must take the field."

"Those outs hurt. No wonder there was all that wrangling and hard feeling between the Pomeroys and the Antelopes and they needed an umpire like Wild Bill."

"True enough. In two or so weeks, I'll try to recruit Sheriff Charley Bassett to be the ump when we play our first real game here."

"Who is we?"

"The opposition will be the Fort Dodge Ballers, who are already formed. The boys in blue will be taking on the newcomers, my team, the Dodge City Desperadoes. It'll be an official nine-inning game of baseball for Ford County, Kansas, bragging rights."

"Huh? Did you say desperadoes? I thought the sheriff ran all those types out of Dodge."

"Ball-playing desperadoes are *not* real desperadoes. The Dodge City players can be from any walk of life just as long as they are able and willing. You, too, can be a ballplayer, Harry. You'll need to be educated on the game, of course. And it will take plenty of practice. Developing skills won't be easy, but if you can develop the right attitude . . ."

"What do you mean, attitude?"

"That's what I mean. You need to alter your attitude, brother, if you want to be part of the Desperadoes. I'll help you all I can. No more sulking."

"I want to go home."

"Bad, bad attitude. You got to feel at home at home base, the one you are sitting on. Grab the lumber, Harry, and try taking a few more cuts."

"What?"

"Stand up at-bat. I'll pitch you a few more till you get the hang of batting."

"Look, picking up buffalo bones is one thing, but picking up a baseball bat is another. Never in my life have I wanted to be a soldier or to even play soldiers."

"I get you. But what we want to do is *beat* the soldiers. They're too full of themselves. It's a tall order. Some of those Fort Dodge Ballers are veterans of the game. Baseball might be new to you and others in Dodge City, but not to the Ballers."

"I never wanted to be a desperado either except maybe at times when I was a boy."

"We'll need nine players to represent the Desperadoes. We can't count on Mr.

Matters. He's willing to learn about the game and watch it but *not* play it. Anyway, he's on the small side and the old side, and all the talk in the world won't help a fellow field, hit, or throw. Not sure either if we can recruit respectable Dodge citizens. They all want to work, not play. Can't see Robert Wright soaking a soldier, Frederick Zimmerman swinging a bat, or George Hoover trying to run down a fly ball in the outfield. Some of the buffalo hunters could have an interest, but most of them have scattered to the four winds and who wants them anyway? Those stinkpots don't play fair, and I'm not about to ask any of them to join my team."

"Sounds hopeless to me. How you going to find nine men to take the field?"

"Not all nine need to be men. I'll get Monique. I know she's a fast runner and is good with her hands — never drops a plate at the restaurant. I'm sure she can break away from Taylor Made and Jane Hankin long enough to play nine innings. Maybe even Jane would consent to come out here and . . . never mind. She'd never wanted to be a Desperado. And she seems a little too fragile for this kind of thing anyway. Even if we convince Sheriff Bassett to umpire and we ban all firearms from the playing field, I'm afraid things could get rough."

"Stop with the *we* please. It's not my game."

"You need the game, brother. Life can't be all work, reading, and longing for Jane. For a change, toss aside your book, your newspaper, your broom, your mop, your insincere store-bought smile, and experience the joy of swinging a bat and making contact."

"All right, all right. For your sake, brother, I'll give it one more shot." I got up from home plate, took bat in hand, and struck at the air so hard that I spun around in a circle.

"That's the right attitude anyway," said Will Lee as he headed out to the dirt mound that he called the pitcher's place. It must have been fifty feet away, but when he got there, it looked closer — too close. "Now step up to the plate, Harry. That's it. Yes, the plate is the home base. Not too close now. You don't want me to hit you. Get in the proper stance I taught you. Feet apart. Bend your knees slightly. Raise the bat any time now. No, not like that. You must be still but not a statue."

I nervously tapped the bat several times against the buffalo chip and then a few times against the heels of my shoes to knock off small clumps of dirt. I couldn't make myself comfortable. Maybe it wasn't as bad as facing a gunman about to pull the trigger. But it was worse than facing my father about to strike me with a closed fist. By the time I finally lifted the bat to my shoulders, Will Lee had thrown the ball across the so-called plate and well past me.

"You got caught looking, but don't fret," he said. "Get the ball and throw it back to me. We'll try again."

"What you're saying is I have to fetch the ball when you hit it way out into the field and I also have to fetch the ball when you pitch it past me, even if I don't swing?"

"Quit bleating like a sheep. Make haste, Harry."

I got him back the ball and had the bat on my shoulder in time, but I swung late at his next offering. The ball flew past like a peregrine falcon.

"Got to get the bat off your shoulder before you start your swing, Harry."

He was making me mad. I crouched at the home base and raised the bat higher. He pitched me a fast one, but I kept one eye open as I swung the bat with all my might and sent the ball back at him twice as fast as it came in. He didn't duck in time. The batted ball conked him in the middle of his forehead. He screamed like he'd been shot and dropped to his knees. I dropped the bat in horror, for it now seemed more like a weapon. I rushed out to him and crouched beside him, offering my apologies. I wanted to help him to his feet, but he wasn't ready. He was dizzy. But surprisingly enough, he wasn't angry.

"By gum, you're getting the hang of it, brother," he declared. "You'll be a hitter before you know it. It's always been in you to show some fight, and I'm proud to bring it out into the open here on the playing field. I know you'll have the same fighting spirit when us Desperadoes take on those brassy Ballers from Fort Dodge."

"Even if I do decide to play and you get Monique to engage, where are the other players coming from if you can't get the good citizens and don't want the buffalo hunters?"

"All right, I'll tell you, but keep it under your hat. I got a brother who's a herder."

"Of sheep?"

"Of course not. Cows. He's a cowboy from Pleasanton, Texas."

"That's a long way away."

"He was with an outfit working for Shanghai Pierce that recently trailed a large herd of longhorns up to the stock pens in Ellsworth for shipment east on the Kansas Pacific Railroad."

"A colored cowboy, huh?"

"That's right. Black as a storm cloud. Goes

by the name of Maverick. Great with horses and steers. But of more significance here, he's also an outstanding center fielder when in Kansas, and he is headed this way with five other cowboys — two white, two black, one Mexican — all of whom have playing experience on town clubs. The best of the bunch, a whiskerless vaquero name of Babe Herrera, pitched the ball so fast for the Topeka Shawnees in last season's city championship game that he struck out twenty-two of twenty-seven stupefied Topeka Capitals' batsmen, earning him the nickname 'The Express Train.' He's our secret weapon, brother. The Fort Dodge Ballers ain't never seen the likes of the Express."

Will Lee Washington set the Fort vs. City clash for the Fourth of July, and I practiced my tail off before and after his actual brother and the other cowboys arrived from Ellsworth in mid-June. Trouble was the cowboys preferred racing their horses through town and spending the last of their pocket money in the Dodge City saloons. Sheriff Bassett found cause to repeatedly lower drunk cowboys into the "cooler," an old well fifteen feet deep where they stayed until they were sober enough to climb out of the well without any help. All the cowboys did cooler time except Babe Herrera, who didn't drink or smoke or do much of anything besides throw rocks into the Arkansas River and occasionally dip his precious left arm into the water to cool it off.

On the eve of the Fourth, Maverick Washington and two of the other players ended up in the cooler for celebrating the national holiday a day early. Bassett had already agreed to be an impartial umpire, but he also said that he was a fair-minded sheriff and wasn't going to pull the cowboys out of the well just because they had a game to play. That left the Dodge City Desperadoes with just six players: the three cowboys who had limited their whiskey intake; player-manager Will Lee Washington; me, who proved that practice didn't make nearly perfect; and Monique Taylor, who could already hit better than me after spending time using a broomstick to connect with pebbles tossed by Jane Hankin in the empty lot behind Taylor Made.

Jane didn't want to play for real with all those strange men, even with Monique shining at the plate and in the field. Mr. Matters couldn't be talked into playing. In lengthy fashion, he told everyone how he had injured a leg while trying to break up a street fight between one of the cowboy players and a boastful sergeant from the fort. The Dodge

City citizens — strapping or not, big bugs or not — all turned down invitations to learn baseball, let alone play in the Dodge showdown, mainly because their lives were focused on making money, not games for boys. Several of them also suggested they would never be managed by a Negro or accept three colored teammates. The Fort Dodge Army officers considered their Ballers the winners by forfeit, and they held their own July Fourth celebration, which included a social, all-military ball game before the evening fireworks.

Will Lee Washington virtually lost all hope. "Looks like it's back to bone gathering for me, Harry," he told me. "Or I could borrow some train fare and head over to Topeka or Leavenworth and catch on with a town team, if any of them will have a colored catcher. Then again, I might wait for my brother to climb out of the cooler and head with him down to Pleasanton, Texas, to become a cowboy. It doesn't appear the cattlemen care what color you are if you know your way around the steers. 'Course it will take some learning. It wasn't so long ago that I didn't even know the difference between a bull and a steer."

"I find that hard to believe."

"No fooling, Harry. I've spent my life so

far around milk cows and an occasional heifer."

"Too bad about the ball game. I was starting to get used to those buffalo wallows out in left field. I sure do hope you stick around in Dodge City, Will Lee. Friends are hard to come by. Maybe we can get a game up later in the summer."

"Nope. Maverick and the other cowboys have run out of drinking money. They'll be heading south again to hire on with another drive or drift back to Ellsworth or to Wichita. Those are the real cow towns, not like Dodge. For that matter, I'm a bit short of funds myself and counting on the charity of Monique has started making me feel less like a man. She won't be my second baseman now, and Lord knows I'm tired of waiting for her to let me be *her* man."

"Hold your horses. Don't rule out baseball."

"No offense, brother. But what the hell can you do about it?"

"Not me. Let's go see Mr. Matters."

"He doesn't know third base from first base, a hit from an error, a shortstop from a second baseman."

"Maybe not. But he knows talking."

Wyatt Matters came through for Will Lee and me in a big way. He went out to the fort as a representative of the Dodge City Desperadoes Baseball Club and apologized on behalf of the manager for the no-show on July Fourth. He told the fort commander and anyone else who wore stars or stripes that baseball had a rich tradition in western Kansas just as it did in eastern Kansas. He cited a game played as early as May 1867 in which a half-dozen visiting officers from Fort Dodge joined with the officers on the field behind Fort Hays. "Besides," he said, "a ball game between your soldiers and the people of Dodge City will help strengthen your frontier bond and ensure cooperation between military and civilian authorities in future endeavors."

No doubt Mr. Matters had uttered a thousand other words, too, and he achieved success, getting the Fort vs. City clash rescheduled for the end of July. After making a few suggestions about how colored civilians should be treated with the same respect and consideration of colored troops, Wyatt shook a hundred soldier hands before catching the Fort Dodge Express back to Dodge. Maverick, filling in for brother Will Lee as the wagon driver, got a good taste of Wyatt's golden tongue. By the time the wagon reached Taylor Made, Maverick had agreed to stay on with the other cowboys in Dodge and to stay sober at least until the big game was played. It took more than talk, though. Wyatt agreed to let the cowboys make camp in and around his tent and to provide them with a couple of meals a day along with plenty of reading material and historical lectures. The one lecture I heard centered around a Scot named George Grant who in 1873 brought four Angus bulls to the Kansas prairie and crossed them with Texas longhorns to produce many hornless black cows that wintered better and weighed more the next spring than either longhorns or shorthorns.

"We're itching to hit the field," said Maverick one evening after practice when I was standing outside the tent with Will Lee but we both had our ears to the tent flap. "You got a fine tent here, Mr. Matters. And Dodge is a fine open town. Mind if I have another taste of your fine wine? Thank you, kindly. Yes, sir, it's a mighty fine wine. Not sure why Will Lee would consider leaving this town. I know his friend William Taylor was killed by some Negro haters and none of the townsfolk seem to want to play ball with us dusky types. Still, my brother can wander freely on the streets and eat as much as he likes at Taylor Made, where me and the boys were welcomed like we were bigwigs. I got to tell you those two lovely ladies serve up the best food this side of New Orleans. On top of that my brother has two small but grand friends in you, who even sounds good talking with his mouth full of vittles, and that plucky left fielder we call HH, or Double H."

"You mean Harry Hannum?"

"Right. But to us ball-playing cowboys the HH stands for *hardly hits.*"

"Whatever you say, Maverick. I haven't found him to hit much, even off the field. You see, I taught him to be a peacemaker not a troublemaker and he listens, well, like a jackrabbit."

"Harry is all right. I'm not bothered by the fact that Will Lee calls him *brother.* He listens well but no amount of advice the boys give him leads to improved batsmanship."

"I'd say Harry is better with his brain than his body, better with his mouth than his hands. I'm teaching him about the ways of the world, past and present. He's rather naïve, but he usually demonstrates a willingness to learn. He's my protégé, you know, like your brother."

"That right? Will Lee is one of those, too? What's that word you called them."

"Protégé."

"If they got any of them in Texas, I ain't heard about it."

“I’m sure they must. A protégé is like a gawky colt you help to become a stalwart stallion.”

“I’ve seen some good horseflesh in Dodge and as many hogs as people. What’s missing from your town is Texas cattle. Hell, I’d be all-fire ready to move in with Will Lee if Dodge were a cow town.”

Chapter Twenty

The cowboys took full advantage of the food and wine, if not the educational talks, provided by Wyatt Matters, but they got restless and started to backslide to the barrooms and dance halls and on occasion Sheriff Bassett's coolers. They began missing practices, but Maverick Washington, for one, was unconcerned. "Once you learn to ride a horse, you never forget," he said. "Same with throwing, catching, and hitting a baseball. We need more practice like cattle need anthrax. We need to play ball. And if we don't play soon, we hit the trail." Most of Dodge City's respectable citizens would have gladly waved them goodbye because cowboy conduct was proving as disorderly as that previously displayed by buffalo hunters and their skinners.

"The last thing we need in Dodge is a bunch of rowdy Texans who'd rather play games than do a good day's work," Robert Wright told me one day at the general store.

"They don't ever come in here and buy anything. Wyatt Matters seems to provide them with everything they need except saloon gals, and they find them easily enough on their own. Where in the Good Lord's name does that grand loafer get all that money to spend on visiting loafers and vagrants?"

"I still haven't figured that out, Mr. Wright," I said. "But I don't believe Mr. Matters loafs. He's always educating himself and others. And he supports others, too . . . like those cowboys. They aren't really loafers or vagrants themselves. They've made themselves at home in and around Mr. Matters' tent while they get ready to face the Fort Dodge Ballers. Will Lee Washington tells me they all work hard while on the trail pushing the longhorns."

"Then I say to them, *Git on the trail and start pushing!*"

Truth be known, I agreed with my boss but for a different reason. I truly wanted the big game to finally be played so the cowboys could head back to Texas or at least to other places in Kansas where the feeding and shipping cattle east was happening. It wasn't that I didn't like taking my designated practice position in left field or even stepping up to the plate for another futile try at making contact. In theory, I should have liked those practices because they gave me many opportunities to see my true love. Jane Hankin missed fewer practices than most of the players. She had stunned me, and Mr. Matters, too, by regularly asking him to accompany her to the diamond on the prairie. No, she wasn't playing the game (she was afraid of the ball, for one thing), nor was she there to watch her restaurant-partner-turned-second-baseman scoop up grounders and range far for pop flies. It was all about the young, handsome, long-limbed fast-balling vaquero, Babe Herrera. To put it bluntly she had become fascinated by him and not only because every batter who faced him — me especially — might as well have gone to the plate with a quill pen instead of a bat.

At first, I almost welcomed this development since I had gotten it in my head, with plenty of input from Will Lee, that Jane was so enamored of Monique Taylor she might never turn again to a living man. But then it became clear the man she was turning to was about as far a cry from me as could be imagined — a dashing vaquero with a golden arm, not a dull store clerk with a sunburned nose. Without saying a word in English, he had caused her to transform from a quiet-as-a-mouse lady into a shrieking vixen. At practices, the new vocal Jane unleashed from the sideline streams of encouragement to the cocksure pitcher, as if he really needed any. In the beginning she called out things like "That's it, Mr. Herrera, give him another fast one" and "He couldn't hit you with a broom, Mr. Herrera," but it progressed to "Looking good as gold, Babe" and "Don't strain yourself out there, Babe; he can't touch you." Even from my position deep in left field, I could hear her. What's more, Babe Herrera could hit, too, often blasting the ball over my head even though I always moved back whenever the handsome vaquero sauntered up to the plate.

One time I twisted an ankle on a prairie dog hole and came limping in from left field. I plopped down on the ground right behind the blanket Jane and Wyatt were sitting on, but they paid me no mind. They were talking about the Babe. What else could I do but listen and grimace.

"Isn't he the most beautiful man you've ever seen," Jane said to Wyatt.

"He has a certain charm, but hardly the Classical Greek ideal of the male body — too skinny, too angular, chest too small, shoulders not broad enough, buttocks too . . ."

"Wyatt! Don't tease me with your knowledge of sculpted Greek men and gods."

"Being an ugly, plump little old man, I can't help but point out physical imperfections in others."

"Nonsense. You are normal looking. But Babe Herrera is so . . . so eye-catching. He has this baby face and charming innocence about him, yet he overpowers all the other men on the field."

"How innocent is he? You did join him in the Arkansas River several times when he was cooling off his arm."

"Stop that, Wyatt. Everything was perfectly respectable. I kept clothing on when I swam."

"How uncomfortable for you."

"Oh, I don't mind you teasing. I adore him. He doesn't talk in a condescending manner."

"How can you tell? You don't know Spanish."

"His voice is soft in any language. He is strong yet gentle, doesn't drink or carry a weapon, has an easy walking gait but is the fastest rider of all the cowboys. Remember yesterday how he raced the others back to town and left them all in the dust."

"It's quite the infatuation you have, Lady Jane."

"He plays such a beautiful game. You've seen that for yourself."

"Are you an admirer of baseball or just Babe Herrera?"

"The Babe shines on the baseball like the moon shines on the Earth. He stands out on the ball field like the Big Dipper in the evening sky."

"That sounds downright poetic, Lady Jane."

"He is my inspiration."

"Astounding. I never heard you carry on this way before about any man, Lady Jane — not even Matt Sullivan, who you were engaged to marry."

"I wasn't really. It never went that far. Let him rest in peace."

"What about Harry Hannum, who is mad about you?"

"Oh, Wyatt. Don't start that again. HH is my good friend, our good friend, but . . ."

Mr. Matters nudged her on the shoulder and pointed back at me. She finally turned away from the playing field and looked at me as I gripped my sore ankle. She now showed sympathy, as if I were a lame horse.

"Oh, Harry, I didn't mean to carry on so," she said. "You've hurt yourself."

Yes, yes. I am badly hurt but not as badly as you've hurt me! I was shouting that inside my brain, but no words came out. Perhaps I was too busy pouting. When she touched my ankle in different places to see where it hurt, I groaned and grimaced but hoped she would never stop.

Game day didn't happen until August 2. The Fort Dodge command wanted no part of the field that Will Lee Washington had fashioned on the buffalo grounds near Dodge City and that the Desperadoes had been practicing on all summer. The only acceptable site for the Army brass was the field behind the fort where the little bluestem grass was greener, the infield had flour sack bases instead of buffalo chips, the outfield had a partial cottonwood home-run fence and no prairie dog holes, and the home team's sideline had chairs for the spectators. Mr. Washington, the Desperado player-manager, complained mildly about losing the home field advantage, but he decided the big game had been delayed long enough and was assured the Fort Dodge Ballers would visit the Desperado diamond in the rough in September if possible. The entire nine-person Desperado squad — six cowboys, buffalo bone gatherer Will Lee, restaurant owner Monique Taylor, and general store worker me — squeezed into the Fort Dodge Express so we could arrive together at the fort.

The only two Desperado fans, Jane Hankin

and Wyatt Matters, followed in a buggy that Mr. Matters rented from Frederick Zimmerman and that Jane decorated with purple coneflowers since the sunflowers were yet to bloom. The *Dodge City Messenger* elected not to cover the game as the team was not representative of the town, what with six non-resident players alongside three less than stellar citizens — a black man without steady employment, a black woman who dared play with men, and a white man whose participation was even discouraged by his boss, the honorable and influential Robert Wright. Mr. Wright and most of the other town founders frowned upon soldiers frivolously playing ball when Indians were acting up in the region. In June warriors led by Comanche Chief Quanah Parker had attacked a small outpost of buffalo hunters at Adobe Walls in the Texas Panhandle, and in July warriors led by Kiowa Chief Lone Wolf had attacked a patrol of Texas Rangers. Even worse, Kiowas and their Cheyenne and Arapaho allies were raiding right in the state of Kansas, murdering four people near Medicine Lodge and three times attacking the new white settlements of the Gypsum Hills. Even the Osages were acting warlike, according to Governor Thomas A. Osborn, who had created a public panic by warning of an impending Indian invasion. "We're ready!" declared one captain at Fort Dodge, but it wasn't clear if he was referring to facing hostile Indians or the Dodge City Desperadoes baseball team.

Sheriff Bassett decided he couldn't back out as umpire for the game since Fort Dodge was as much a part of Ford County as Dodge City. Besides, Wyatt Matters gave him twenty dollars in advance and promised him another twenty dollars after the nine innings were played. The sheriff rode out to the field on a fine sorrel and wondered if he could do the umpiring on horseback. He was discouraged from that notion by everyone who knew anything about baseball and how long it took to play nine innings. He also received a quick lesson in the rules of the game from Mr. Matters (who was still pretty shaky on them himself) and me since he didn't want a Negro, Will Lee Washington or brother Maverick, telling him how to do his job. The Army captain who was also the captain of the Dodge City Ballers made Sheriff Bassett swear that he would make his field judgments impartially and not be prejudiced against the soldiers just because they were playing this game on their home field instead of taking to the much larger field to skirmish with hostile Indians.

The game itself is of little consequence, but the aftermath broke my heart and didn't do Mr. Matters' heart much good either. As the visitors, the Dodge City Desperadoes batted first, facing Fort Dodge Baller lefty Lieutenant Sharp, who wasn't too sharp. He walked lead-off man Maverick and another cowboy. That brought up number three hitter Babe Herrera. Though he was my teammate, I was silently wishing he would strike out. Instead, he blasted a towering drive that had Jane screaming her lungs out. The ball did tail off just before the outfield fence to become a loud foul instead of a home run, at which point Sharp was content to walk the Babe, even though it meant loading the bases. The soldiers, those in the field and those watching, questioned the eyesight of sheriff-turned-umpire Charley Bassett. Lieutenant Sharp began to curse, but when he caught sight of Jane on the sidelines, he apologized for his bad language. One sergeant threatened to shoot the sheriff, and then a second lieutenant said that throwing him in the stockade for a week should suffice.

Bassett kept his cool while pointing to his badge. He wasn't outwardly armed, but a bulge inside his vest near where the badge was pinned suggested a hidden derringer or other small pistol. "I call 'em as I see 'em," he said when the complaints didn't die down. "Play ball!" His strike zone expanded, and the next two batters — the largest of the cowboys and Will Lee Washington — both struck out looking. Sharp quickly got two questionable strikes on the next batsman, who was in fact a batswoman. One more strike, which seemed a certainty, and the half inning would have ended without a run scoring. But the lieutenant's third delivery struck Monique Taylor, who was fearlessly crowding the plate, in the small of the back. She hunched her shoulders and grimaced and no doubt would have screamed if capable of doing so. It did entitle her to first base and sent Maverick from third to home with the game's first run. Nevertheless, Will Lee was unhappy. He checked on Monique's condition, and though she indicated she was fine, he charged the pitcher like a Cheyenne eager to count coup. Lieutenant Sharp stepped back off the mound as he reached to his side where on other occasions his service revolver would have been holstered. If Will Lee had kept going it would have been trouble for the lieutenant but bigger trouble for him. Fortunately, the sheriff/umpire stepped between them and stated: "They'll be none of that. I stand for law and order no matter where I'm standing. I treat colored men just the same as I do lieutenants when it comes to fair play. You, Will Lee, best take a seat and cool your heels. You, Lieutenant, best get back on the mound. And batter up!"

That batter was me. My knees were shaking, and I gripped the bat so hard that my hands ached as if I'd been working a plow all day. I struck out on three straight pitches, not swinging once. Our side was retired, but we did lead 1-0. I apologized to my teammates for standing at the plate like a statue, and on the way to my defensive position in left field I complimented Sheriff Bassett on his good eye. He told me not to say one more word or he'd boot me out of the ball game. He must have thought I was being sarcastic, but I wasn't.

Out in left field, I wished for the Babe to disappoint Jane by issuing a few bases on balls and even more hard-hit balls (but none in my direction, of course). Instead, Babe struck out the side in the bottom of the first, and he repeated that feat in five of the next eight innings. The only base hit he allowed was a pop-up that fell in front of me like a dying quail. The Babe was like a silent assassin. But his biggest fan was louder than George Hoover's saloon on a Saturday night. She clapped and cheered and danced around, sometimes jarring Mr. Matters with a hip or elbow. She called out the name "Babe" so often that I wished he or me was never born.

And things got worse. In the top of the eighth inning, I swung from the heels and struck out for the third time in the game. In the top of the ninth, with Maverick hugging third after a three-bagger, Babe Herrera took the same kind of wild swing, but he connected, sending a rising high line drive that frightened a black-billed magpie off the center-field fence before finally landing in the fort's corral, startling four Army mounts. That "prodigious gravity-defying shot," as Mr. Matters described it, boosted the Desperado advantage to 3-0, not that the extra two runs were needed. Babe Herrera, the hero in the game and in Jane's heart, set the Ballers down in fast order in the bottom of the ninth.

Unknown to Wyatt Matters or me, Will Lee and Maverick had made a bet with the Fort Dodge commander over the outcome of the baseball game. A Baller win would have resulted in the brothers spending a year of civilian service with the Army, requisitioning and training horses for the cavalry. The brothers considered it a safe bet because they had Babe Herrera on their side. Indeed, the Babe's skunking of the Ballers meant the soldiers must provide materials to build a new Dodge City saloon that catered to cowboys, black and white. This news temporarily stunned Wyatt, who thought the last thing his chosen town needed was another drinking establishment and took the Babe by surprise since the tall young vaquero didn't even drink tequila.

All six cowboys decided to prolong their stay in Dodge — specifically, in and around Wyatt's welcoming tent — because they could play more ball when they so desired and still hunt mustangs for military use while waiting for the new saloon to rise on Front Street. Wyatt came to support the project, financially and otherwise, once he was assured the new establishment would serve not only whiskey and beer but also wine, champagne, milk, tea, lemonade, and sarsaparilla while prohibiting the carrying of guns inside the batwing doors. Will Lee Washington, Mr. Matters' second protégé (after me), surprised everyone by becoming the chief builder, following plans he developed by consulting with Wyatt as well as most of the original founders of Dodge City.

"To think," Will Lee Washington said to me at the building site, "just a week ago I was a desperate buffalo bone gatherer, periodic Fort Dodge Express driver, sponger at the Taylor Made restaurant, ignorant catcher, and low-life Negro barely allowed to breathe the same rarefied air as the town fathers. But just look at me now, brother. I'm an upstanding not particularly dark man who is contributing to the growth of Dodge as the founding father — along with Mr. Matters, of course — of a *refreshment* palace where every man, woman, and child shall be welcome."

"Children, too? Really?"

"That's who'll drink the milk and lemonade with their mamas and daddies."

"What about tequila?" I asked since Babe Herrera was still in town and still very much in Jane's heart.

"Not for children, of course, but tequila — why the hell not? And we'll offer Sazerac and other New Orleans concoctions in honor of Monique."

"And what will you call *your* watering hole?"

"Several names have come to mind, such as the Desperado, which was a fine jocular name for a baseball player but triggers an association with the kind of people Mr. Matters and I wouldn't like to see frequenting our new establishment; the Diamond, since a baseball game made it all possible and otherwise suggests glitter to more refined folks; Worldly Matters, in honor of Wyatt Matters and his desire for Dodge to become a sophisticated and well-rounded community rather than a wild and woolly frontier town; and the Great White Buffalo, not only because that describes a rare and wonderful beast of nature but also because we don't want potential white customers to get the false impression we're a totally black enterprise. If truth be known, though, I am leaning toward calling it — and you are the first to hear this, Harry — the Longhorn to honor my brother Maverick and the other cowboys who won that big bet. What do you think?"

I was surprised that this up-and-coming black entrepreneur, though still my friend, would ask the opinion of a lowly store clerk like me, so I needed time to think. "Longhorn doesn't sound right, not for a saloon in Dodge," I finally said. "We aren't in Texas, and we aren't a Kansas cow town. In fact, we don't have many real cowboys around here except for those ball-playing half-dozen, and they *must* go back to Texas eventually." I was thinking of Babe Herrera again.

"Point well taken, Harry. But Mr. Matters, who we both know knows more than the rest of us combined, says flat out that one day soon the cowboy will be coming to Dodge. He means lots and lots of cowboys and even more longhorn cattle will arrive. The vanishing buffalo — the bison — will be replaced by cows and the hunters of bison by the herders of cows. It's only natural that Texas cowboys will want to flock to a saloon called the Longhorn."

"I'm not usually one to question Wyatt, but it doesn't figure that the drovers would bring their cattle to Dodge instead of to Ellsworth or Wichita."

"Mr. Matters says he has been educating himself on the matter and predicts Dodge is bound to be the next big Kansas cow town."

"Oh. How will that happen if you don't mind telling someone who is uneducated on the matter?"

"First, Harry, it is only a matter of time before those communities to the east won't be welcoming often-diseased Texas longhorns and the quarantine line will move west. Second, once the Army subdues the hostile Indians here and in west Texas, large-scale ranching will start up in the Texas Panhandle, and Dodge will be the safest and most convenient place to drive the cattle for shipment to the eastern packing houses. Third, Dodge City saloon owners and other businessmen will consider cowboys, no matter how rowdy they get, good for business. Hell, the Longhorn saloon could have this little old colored man rolling in money. Imagine that!"

"Money isn't everything," I said, trying not to sound jealous of not only his potential success but also all the support he was getting from Wyatt Matters. In the past, Wyatt had always looked down on the money-hungry crowd, especially the ones who had an education and should have realized there was more to life than making a personal fortune.

"Maybe that's true elsewhere. But not in Dodge City. Look no further than your own boss. I'd say Robert Wright is the richest man in town and wants more."

"Right," I said, but I sure wasn't becoming rich working for him. I began to contemplate quitting the general store and getting involved in the new saloon. After all, builder Will Lee and financial backer Wyatt were my best friends, in fact my only true friends in town now that Jane Hankin had thrown me over for a vaquero with a fastball. They should have at least asked me to be a part of their visionary endeavor, even if I intended to say no, since I didn't want any part of Texas cowboys or their business, not to mention their competition in matters of romance.

■ ■ ■ ■

I knew I would never excel on a baseball field but was still disappointed that a second game was not played that summer. Baseball, though frustrating for those of us who weren't naturals, was at least something to do besides my daily labor at the general store. The Fort Dodge Ballers had no interest in seeking revenge. The fort commander claimed the soldiers were all too busy patrolling for and skirmishing with hostiles. Maybe so, but I suspected he knew that batting against the flame-throwing Babe Herrera was like trying to use a flyswatter to subdue a Comanche warrior. The Dodge City Desperadoes essentially disbanded.

Monique Taylor had enjoyed being a second baseman, but she now devoted herself more than ever to Taylor Made, which was necessary because Jane, due to her new romantic life, was slacking off on her restaurant duties. Will Lee Washington was busy with building the Longhorn; two cowboys labored for him for small wages provided by Mr. Matters, and the other three worked as mustangers for the Army. One of the latter was Babe Herrera. He handled horses as well as he handled baseballs, and though he reportedly wasn't used to handling women, the young vaquero was getting better and better each day with Jane. The Babe rode into town from the fort practically every other night to engage Jane in moonlit walks, intimate talks, sunset sitting, star gazing, slow dances, and adoring glances. While I was taking the measure of the Babe, all of Dodge took notice of the young couple. I kept overhearing comments about their attractiveness together (he with the sombrero and dark but not too dark looks of a Mexican matador, she with the piles of shiny auburn hair and the gleaming dresses of a stage performer).

Wyatt was a busy man, what with entertaining and educating his cowboy tent guests, ordering wine from who knows where, seeking funds from a mysterious out-of-town source, mentoring Will Lee, pushing for gun control despite the tremendous drop-off in Dodge City criminal activity, and trying to keep an eye on lovesick Lady Jane. I mostly stayed away from his tent, just as I mostly stayed away from Taylor Made. I didn't want to run into Babe Herrera and Jane Hankin, together or separately. Rumor had it that she was often seen in his company wearing a fine silver brooch on her red dress — yes, my brooch over what had become Babe's bosom!

What I spent most of my nights doing was bemoaning my lot in life, in particular the absence of a two-sided love life with my true love. Sure, there had been Elizabeth Pepper of Atchison who went off with the railroad man, but nobody else (OK, the very married Alice Wright, but she put me in my proper place soon enough). I had come to believe that there could be no substitute for Jane Hankin of Dodge City. I can't say I never gave a second look at some of the town's very available sporting girls for they did come out onto the street in daylight on occasion. Any man who entered the general store when Mrs. Wright was present would be expected to run his eyes across her fine motherly form — and I was there most of every day and every night, since Robert Wright never had cause to dismiss me or to bar me from the bed he provided me in his storeroom. Looking wasn't touching. Lusting wasn't loving. Over and over, I told myself *Jane is the only one!* It made me feel noble sometimes, miserable most of the time.

The hot summer days on the Kansas prairie were fading fast when I finally convinced myself I must let my heart, rather than my defeatist mind, rule. No more bemoaning. No more inaction. Somehow, I must act. I wrote Jane a poem. I jotted it down straight from my heart onto an old copy of the *Dodge City Messenger*. That wouldn't do, so I copied it in my best penmanship on a sheet of fancy stationery I borrowed from Mrs. Wright. The slightly scented page had floral embellishments and edges lined in gold. I decided not to sign the page because it could clearly not have been written by anyone else but me, certainly not by Babe Herrera, even if he could make up verse in English and knew how to write. I read it over three times with much pride, and on the fourth read I felt more like tearing it up and burying the pieces either on Boot Hill or somewhere out on the prairie where Babe Herrera first struck me out. I didn't want to show it to Mr. Matters with all those cowboys present, so in desperation, while her husband was occupied with customers, I presented it for inspection to Alice Wright.

"It's a poem, isn't it?" she asked.

"Sort of. I mean, yes. Yes, it is."

"A love poem?"

"A vow-of-love poem, I'd say. Don't worry, it's not for you. I mean I want you, a married lady, to look it over."

"And the intended recipient is whom?"

"You know, Jane Hankin. I haven't hidden how I feel about her. But, you see, this cowboy has been occupying her time of late and . . . anyway, please tell me what you think."

"I know about her cowboy. I believe it is a mistake."

"I do, too. I'm the one who should be spending time with Jane, not him."

"I understand, but what I mean is that writing this for her won't do any good."

"How can you say that? You haven't even read it yet. I want to know if you think Jane will like it. I know I'm no John Keats; Mr. Matters has told me that more than once. But it might not be as bad as you think. Please read it, Mrs. Wright."

"I shall, Harry." She held the page close to her face and read it over in silence while I stood looking over her shoulder. Then she had me sit down on a stool and pulled up another stool for herself. "And now aloud," she said.

I thought she wanted to hear it from me, but she sniffed the page and proceeded to do the reading in a soft whisper that embarrassed me, in part because her voice was alluring but more so because her reading couldn't disguise the silliness of my rhymes.

There is a Tex I know
With ties to Mexico
How he loves to tip his sombrero

This fast-moving vaquero
To the fairest maiden of Dodge,
Where I happen to lodge
And where my love has long been true
To the fairest maiden — that's you.
How much longer will he stay?
For I would marry you today
You love me more than anyone . . . maybe
Forget the Babe, have my baby!

When she was done, Alice dropped the page on her lap and shook her head. "Oh, you poor dear," she said, still whispering.

"That bad, huh?"

"Well, it's not so much that. Your last line stands out. You really want to have children?"

"Sure. I like kids, your kids — yours and Mr. Wright's. But I want it with her, you know, for her to have my baby. I first thought to say *Forget the Babe, be my baby.* But to say *have my baby* seemed more serious, more mature, more committed to the marriage. Am I wrong?"

"Not about that, Harry." She stopped whispering. "As you must know from observing Mr. Wright and myself, I firmly believe that marriage and children give meaning to life. And for a man your age to be serious is fine in principle and would be welcomed by many a woman wanting to settle down, even in a wild frontier town like Dodge, not that we are so wild anymore thanks to our growing up and the real possibility that next year we can be recognized as a city of the third class and not a small, lawless . . ." She cut off her nervous speech. Her voice now sounded raspy and distressed as if she had just swallowed a mouthful of too-hot beans. She handed me the page, stood up, and patted my head as if I were one of her children who didn't understand an arithmetic lesson.

"You don't like my poem?" I said, dropping the page on my lap and crossing my arms.

"I do, Harry."

"But you don't think Jane will like it, is that it?"

"The truth is, Harry, I don't think Miss Hankin will ever see it."

"Sure, she will. I'm not going to back off. I love her and I'm going to find her this minute."

"That won't be easy, Harry. Mrs. Zimmerman told me something last night and it has been confirmed this morning by reliable observers. Jane Hankin is gone."

"Gone? Gone where?"

"Gone to Texas. With her vaquero."

Chapter Twenty-One

The news of Jane's departure from Dodge left me alternately angry and forlorn. History was repeating itself. Elizabeth Pepper had done me wrong by hopping on the Atchison, Topeka & Santa Fe with a railroad man. Now Jane Hankin, who I viewed as superior to Elizabeth in every way, had saddled up with a cowboy and gone south, whether to a Texas ranch or a Mexico hacienda I didn't know. Neither had said goodbye. But with Elizabeth there at least had been a note, though it didn't adequately explain her abrupt jilting. She had been gone three days before I found it tucked into the sleeve of a shirt that she used to launder for me. I destroyed the note but only after memorizing it: "You'll have to wash this yourself, H. The conductor bought me my ticket to a brighter future. Never mind where I'm going. One of us had to go, and you aren't going anywhere. In case you haven't used the washbasin yet, look for your ring inside. All ties now broken. Don't try to find me. Find yourself. — Yours Sincerely, Miss Pepper."

For three days I looked unsuccessfully for a note left behind by Jane. I searched my shirts, my shoes, my long johns, every corner of the general store, the Zimmerman store (where Jane had once worked), the Zimmerman outbuilding (Jane's old residence in Dodge), and the Taylor Made. When I arrived at the restaurant, Monique was sitting at a corner table with her head in her hands. Since she couldn't speak and wasn't in a mood to explain herself with hand gestures, she didn't prove helpful, too busy concerned for herself than to sympathize with me. I suspected she felt jilted herself, for there could be no doubt now in anybody's mind that Jane had not rejected *all men* as romantic partners. It was Will Lee Washington who told me Monique hadn't received a note either and that he was filling in for Jane as much as he could while still devoting his daytime to erecting the Longhorn saloon. His brother Maverick had gone to Texas, too, but two cowboys were still helping Will Lee, and, by putting more of Wyatt Matters' money to work, he had hired several part-time laborers from out of Dodge's existing saloons. Besides Jane's young lover, the other two cowboys who had been breaking horses for the soldiers had departed for Texas. They had promised to be back to Kansas once they caught on with another cattle drive. Babe Herrera, on the other hand, made no such promise.

"I don't care to hear that bastard's name ever again," I told Will Lee.

"It takes two to make a romance, my friend. The ladies go for the Babe like thirsty cattle for water. Miss Hankin was smitten."

"She told you that?"

"Me and Monique. You thought the Babe took her against her will?"

"No. Just against her right mind. What if she has another nervous attack that again leaves her utterly prostrate for days, weeks, months? This vaquero won't know what the hell to do. Most likely he would ride off into the Lone Star night with some other smitten lady."

"Oh, no, Harry, the Babe ain't like that."

"You defending him? You know how I feel about Jane. He ruined things between us."

"I understand. It hurts, but if it's any consolation to you, her departure has helped me. I've grown ever so much closer to Monique. It's like she needs me now."

"All right, I'm happy for you. Doesn't help me one lick. How could she just up and leave like that without a word about it to me."

"Oh, hold on. I almost forgot. She did leave you something."

Will Lee walked away, but I followed him into the Taylor Made kitchen. He opened the silverware drawer, fished around in it, and produced something rounder and more lustrous than the rest — the brooch I had given Jane last Christmas.

I gasped but did not grasp the brooch when Will Lee tried to hand it to me. I backed away until I was in the dining area again. Monique seemed to be weeping. Will Lee came out of the kitchen waving the brooch at me, but when I kept moving toward the front door, he slid over to the corner table and put a comforting hand on Monique's back.

"Give it to her," I said.

I staggered out the door like a drunk. Too much dismal sobriety can have the same effect as one who has imbibed too much whiskey. I cursed myself for even thinking of Jane Hankin, not because she had left me in the lurch but because I was questioning my own worth as a man and whether I had the right to let Jane stay lodged in my mind. Addled and muddled, I finally made my way to Mr. Matters' tent, which I had been avoiding not only because of the cowboys staying there but also because I had failed him as his protégé by not winning over my true love as he had wished, not working hard enough at developing my mind, and not doing anything but wallow in self-pity during what had become, since the end of baseball, a stagnant summer.

If I was looking for sympathy that evening, I didn't get it from my mentor. He spoke of unrequited love and then gave me three examples from his vast knowledge of literature. First, he cited *Great Expectations,* by Charles Dickens. Pip has long loved and devoted himself to the cold-hearted beauty Estella, a thankless task since she never returns his affection. In other words, Pip loves without hope, and in so doing misses out on the love of the kinder, more understanding Biddy. I had to admit that my one-sided relationship with Jane did seem hopeless now that she had ridden off with the vaquero, but I couldn't help how I felt and, in any case, there was no Biddy waiting in the wings.

Next, from Victor Hugo's *Notre-Dame de Paris,* Wyatt mentioned the deformed bell-ringer Quasimodo (and, yes, I took some offense at being compared to a hunchback) who falls deeply in love with the gorgeous Esmeralda because she has been kind to him. But he is too ugly for her, and she sees him as only a nice loyal friend. Esmeralda eventually hangs, but instead of moving on with his life, Quasimodo lies with her corpse until he dies of starvation. I told Wyatt I would never do anything that absurd even while thinking it might not be a bad idea should Jane die before me and I was able to locate her grave.

Wyatt was on a roll. He turned to Johann Wolfgang von Goethe's *The Sorrows of Young Werther.* The title character is besotted with the beautiful (what else!) Charlotte, but she marries another man. Young Werther's passionate feelings for his true love run wild, but the tortured soul is unable to harm Charlotte or her husband, so he shoots himself in the head. I told Wyatt that suicide was ludicrous, but I had second thoughts when Wyatt suggested Charlotte felt such grief, even if Goethe didn't spell it out, that she might die of a broken heart.

"It might be worth it," I said. "Of course, I would have to borrow a gun from somebody like Sheriff Bassett or else steal one from Zimmerman's store."

"You can't be serious. You shun guns the way I do."

"Well, there are other ways. I could drown myself in the Arkansas River — you know my mother did that kind of thing — or step in front of a herd of stampeding buffalo, if I can find any."

"Or go out on the lonesome prairie, maybe the old left field, and starve yourself to death like Quasimodo. I think that more suits you."

"Tease me all you want, but I could do it."

"There's nothing a man thinks he can't do, especially when he isn't in his right mind."

"What do you mean? My mind has a perfect right to be tortured right now." I lowered my head into my chest and squeezed my eyes tight until a tear surfaced but wouldn't quite fall.

"And so, self-pity swept over him like a plague of locusts across the Great Plains."

"What are you talking about?" I muttered with chin still pressed over my heart. Yes, I knew what he was talking about, but couldn't he let me wallow in it just a little bit longer?

"I'm talking about a curse, a perilous state of mind. You see the loss of the only woman you think you could ever want and need as the greatest catastrophe imaginable, for what could possibly be worse than the destruction of your little dream world of idealized romantic love."

"What do you want me to do, apologize for feeling the way I do? I can't help that I love her. Who can control such things? There was a time you thought I was right for her, too. Have you forgotten?"

"I haven't forgotten. Let's go for a little walk, son."

He put an arm around my shoulder, and we headed out of the tent. We moved slowly but sometimes got out of step and once or twice I staggered. Anyone observing us must have thought we were two drunks helping each other home. He took me up to Boot Hill, and we came to a halt by the grave of Matt Sullivan, the former lover of Jane Hankin.

"You took a shot to the heart when Lady Jane left," Wyatt said. "But it's nothing like the fatal short *our* Mr. Sullivan took."

I took a deep breath. It was a warm night, but a slight breeze made the air refreshing. The whole town smelled better now that buffalo hides were no longer piling up. I confessed that I was glad to still be alive and apologized for not being myself lately and even hinting that I might prefer the alternative. "But I ask you, Wyatt, why'd she do it? I also apologize for being too dumb to figure out what made her get out of Dodge with that Herrera fellow."

"Could be she loves the Babe. He is a likeable fellow, tall and strong yet gentle as a lamb and surprisingly well educated. I heard him recite to her a short poem by the Spanish poet Gustavo Adolfo Bécquer."

"Never heard of him. In Spanish?"

"First in Spanish, then in English. He's a fast learner."

"Really? I didn't think she even liked poetry. She certainly wasn't impressed with mine."

"Oh, she likes the poetic work of the masters, all right. She learned about them from me. But with him, she pretended she didn't know anything. She asked the Babe what poetry was and that's when he brought forth the poem that Bécquer apparently wrote in response to a lover who asked that very same question — *What is poetry?*"

"Good question. I reckon I don't know the answer to that. I thought it was a bunch of rhymes put together."

"The Babe recited it to her in fine voice, no Texas drawl. I'm afraid I only remember how it sounded in English." Wyatt proceeded to speak in a booming voice that might have awakened some of the dead.

What is poetry? you ask, while fixing
your blue pupil on mine.
What is poetry! And you are asking me?
Poetry . . . is you.

"Damn," I said. "He got it right. I mean Bécquer did. I don't know why I didn't think of that. Poetry *is* Jane Hankin."

Wyatt sat down on Matt Sullivan's stone marker and issued a plaintive sigh. "There's something else you should know, son. Lady Jane's leaving with the Babe that way will hurt me more in the long run than it hurts you, not that anyone can truly compare degrees of hurt. I lectured you about self-pity, but I can't put into words my own unhappiness at what's happened."

That was hard for me to believe for two reasons. For one, Wyatt never seemed at a loss for words about anything. For another, he couldn't possibly have loved her the way I did. He had liked Jane very much, of course, but it hadn't been like he wanted the young woman to be his wife and the mother of his children. I didn't doubt anymore that he had wanted Jane and me to have a flourishing romance. I took a five-minute stroll to read some of the other markers that had names and when I came back, Wyatt had slid to the ground, his back against Matt Sullivan's gravestone. He was displaying his most hidden emotion — crying without restraint.

"What's the matter, Mr. Matters?" I asked. "You hurt yourself?"

"No, son. It's only my own self-pity. I am not above such ineffectual behavior."

"Oh. Does this have to do with Jane leaving?"

"I told you more than once that she was like a daughter to me."

"I remember. And you've said I'm like a son to you."

"Right, But, you see, the difference is I have no birth son, but Lady Jane is my undeniable genuine daughter."

This shocking news drove me to the ground next to Wyatt Matters. I began to cry, too, but for his sake not mine. While my father never had exhibited much need of me, I had never left him. Of course, I would have done so with little remorse except that the speeding train ran him over first. Still, I was able to step out of my own shoes and see where an old man losing his daughter was at least the equal of a young man losing his true love. While trying to comfort my mentor there on Boot Hill, he revealed to me that Jane hadn't known she was his daughter until two days before she left with Babe Herrera. She hadn't planned to leave Dodge at all until Wyatt revealed his identity. "I thought the news would keep her in Dodge," he said, "but it had the opposite effect." I was confused, naturally.

"How'd it happen? . . . I mean you being her father?" I asked once we had both dried our tears.

"The usual way. Susannah Hankin was the loveliest lady I ever came across during my travels across Missouri. In Jasper County it was. 1852."

"Two years after I was born. So, it was in Missouri?"

"Kansas Territory wasn't even created until four years later."

"You lived in Jasper County, too?"

"Hell no. Just passing through."

"From where to where?"

"From Jefferson City to anywhere I wanted to go. I was a traveling salesman who didn't need the work, but I liked moving around and meeting people — rich or poor, male or female, black or white. I happened by the Hankin dirt farm where Susannah lived with her husband, Miles, and three sons. My wagon was loaded with pots and pans but mostly books. Even then I was a reader. Miles was out in the fields with his three young sons. Susannah and I got to talking. Times were hard and Miles was taking the hard times harder than he should. He had stopped talking to Susannah, stopped loving her, stopped being a husband. You get the picture?"

I could picture Wyatt talking. I imagined Susannah must have looked something like Jane. "You seduced her with words?"

"I reckon so. It didn't take much. She was about ready to leave the farm and family behind. In fact, she left in the wagon with me that very afternoon. She overlooked my appearance. Even in my younger days I was unprepossessing. I told her I had money, but that wasn't the only reason she went with me. I believe it was the books I gave her for free — Emily Brontë's *Wuthering Heights* and Charlotte Brontë's *Jane Eyre.* We were on the road for no more than three days together before I talked her into going back to the farm. It wasn't like I came to my senses and turned noble. She didn't realize how much she missed her boys, and I didn't realize how much I liked my freedom. I was used to going off anywhere any time I pleased."

"What happened after that?"

"I stayed free, but I never stopped thinking of Susannah. I passed by again about a year later. She'd given birth to a baby, my baby, calling her Jane after Jane Eyre. But things were different on the farm. She was happy. The new baby girl gave her life new meaning. Miles and the boys were happy. The crops were growing, and everyone found reason to laugh. Susannah said she'd never forget me, but every night she thanked the stars that I talked her into returning home. I left but vowed to support Jane through good and bad times. I could afford it."

"As a traveling salesman?"

"I only did that for fun. I was from a well-to-do family, you might say, one whose wealth kept on growing. Next time I brought my wares to Jasper County was three years later. The farm was still there and doing well but the Hankins were gone. I tracked them to Lawrence in the new Kansas Territory. Miles Hankin had sold the farm and bought a business — you'll love this, Harry — a general store, which he called simply enough Hankin's Store. He was selling pots and pans and most of the other things I carried in my wagon, including books. That was Susannah's idea. And today it's you, Harry, who works in a general store. Of course, Mr. Wright Can Do No Wrong carries no books, being small-minded when it comes to improving the minds of the customers."

"Did you then start taking your wagon to Lawrence?"

"Sure, sometimes, but only to observe Jane from a distance. Hankin's Store was doing well, and Susannah wouldn't take any of my money. I did leave her with books sometimes. It might interest you to know that

I gave her the 1840 edition of *The Poetical Works of John Keats*. I remember how much she enjoyed his "Hither, Hither, Love," four lines of which I still recall:

Though one moment's pleasure
In one moment flies
Though the passion's treasure
In one moment dies;

"I should have brought Jane John Keats instead of Harry Hannum," I muttered.

"No good comes from saying *should have.* Always too negative. It's all things in the past that can't be changed."

"Like you pirooting with that married lady in Jasper County?"

"Not exactly. Wouldn't want to change that because beautiful Jane came out of it. Thank the good lord she came out of it looking like her mother and not me. I'm sure Miles Hankin must have known he wasn't Jane's real daddy, but he never said anything about it to Susannah, let alone Jane. He might have suspected me since I was giving his wife all those books, but he figured I was far too ugly to have fathered a girl as stunning as Jane." Wyatt almost laughed but then took off his top hat and banged it against his knee. "I should have never told

Jane I was her father the other day. She couldn't stand being deceived. There I go with my own *should have.* Can't even follow my own advice. What kind of mentor am I?"

"You're a good mentor, Wyatt. And now that I think about it, a good father, too, here in Dodge that is."

"It's been a long journey getting to Dodge from Jasper County."

"How long did you keep bringing books to Jane's mother?"

"Right before the war I brought *Uncle Tom's Cabin* to the Hankin house in Lawrence. By then my wagon had no more pots and pans, only copies of that book and anti-slavery pamphlets. There was no stronger abolitionist in Missouri than me. For the next couple years I was helping the Kansas abolitionists entice Missouri slaves to flee across the border, hundreds of them to Lawrence. I didn't get back there myself until several months after Quantrill's raid. Miles and the three boys were dead. Susannah was alone with twelve-year-old Jane, or so I thought. But when I got there, I discovered Susannah and Jane had already found a new home in Lawrence belonging to a one-armed former Union soldier named Calvin Perkins and his demented son, Luther."

I was having trouble digesting all this

information. Jane had never told me much about her past and Wyatt had never told me much about his past. Now, with Wyatt finally revealing so much to me on account of our mutual misery over Jane's departure, I was finding out just how connected their two pasts were. Unlike Jane, I didn't feel deceived to learn Wyatt was her birth father. I felt relieved because it explained why he had shown her so much attention in Dodge. Of course, what relief could there truly be with Jane gone to Texas with the Babe. I wanted to ask Wyatt about his rich family and why that silver decanter case he gave Jane had the initials *AD* on it, but that word *demented* kept circulating inside my head.

"What about that Perkins and his son?" I asked. "The widow Hankin and Jane went to live with them?"

"Calvin had been a captain on the right side during the war. While he was losing his arm in the Battle of Independence, Missouri, in August 1862 his wife was home in St. Louis dying of dysentery while thirteen-year-old Luther was torturing cats, small dogs, and mourning doves. Not long after the Army sent Calvin home, the widower took his son to Kansas City, where he became a banker, and his son was kicked out of two schools and only stayed out of jail because of his father's influence. After Quantrill's raid in Lawrence, Calvin saw opportunity and opened a bank there and took an immediate shine to Susannah. He had money and the pretty widow needed a man. They married pronto, and Luther proved to be the stepbrother from hell. Poor Jane. Nothing I could do. The Perkins household was off limits to me. And then Susannah gave birth once more, but mother and baby didn't survive it. That left Jane alone with a cold stepfather and a hot-blooded stepbrother but not me. Instead of trying to keep an eye on her I stepped out of her life completely thinking she didn't need me, what with Calvin Perkins being a well-to-do banker and all. I should have known . . . there I go again. That's it. I'm done for tonight."

"But you got back in Jane's life."

"Yes. I did that later, a little late."

"Explain. I never thought I would need to say this to you: Keep talking."

"I suppose I do owe you that. Like Chaucer said in the fourteenth century, better late than never. She was my daughter, and she needed my protection. After things became unmanageable for her in the Perkins household, Jane left town. I followed her secretly east from Lawrence to St. Louis, then west again to several places in Kansas, including Fort Dodge, where she knew this sergeant and was hired as a laundress. The sergeant deserted, but Jane stayed for a while. I kept my eye on her, of course, because lonely privates and such saw an opening there, and that can be dangerous for women, especially young ones who look like Jane. From the fort, she moved — escaped, you might say — to newborn Dodge City, and that's why I came here, too. I was hoping Dodge was where we'd both stay, at least to the end of my days. But now . . . Damn!"

"Damn," I echoed. "I ask again, why'd she have to leave? You'd think she'd like knowing you were her father. You were so good to her here in Dodge."

"I already told you she didn't like me keeping that secret from her for so long, even after the man she thought was her father was long dead. But it was more than that. After I told her the facts of life about her father — me — I didn't stop there. I talked of the future, and it included you, Harry. I told her it was my wish that the three of us not only stick together but also live together, not in the tent but in a solid brick house, and to go forth fearlessly and peacefully as proud citizens of a better Dodge. We would work together to eliminate our burdensome thoughts about the past with all its *should haves.*"

"Really? She didn't like that idea?"

"She said it was impossible, and, you know something, Harry, she's right."

"Why, why? I'd marry her in a second. You know that."

"Yes, I know that but there are at least five complications. First, she told me she was madly in love with Babe Herrera. Second, she told me she wasn't in love with you. Third, she told me that even if I were her father, I had no business trying to control her life. Fourth, she told me that she would never fall under the thumb of any man ever again and that one of the joys of the Babe was that he wanted nothing under his thumbs except baseballs and wild horses. Fifth, she told me . . . and this is something I have avoided telling you until this very second . . ."

"Yes, yes. Don't hold me in suspense a second longer, Wyatt."

"Jane wanted me to keep this a secret, too. But now that she has left us, I suppose it can be told."

"Tell. Tell."

"Jane is technically a married lady."

"What? Impossible!"

"I don't lie to you, Harry. I don't tell you everything, but I don't lie."

"Then who is it? Who is her husband? That sergeant she knew at Fort Dodge?"

"No. She was infatuated with him because he told her he didn't like weapons any more than she did and was going to leave the Army as soon as possible. Then, as I've mentioned, he deserted with his weapons without saying so long or see you later."

"I don't understand. You mean she married someone after the sergeant left? That would mean someone in Dodge City. How can that be? There's Monique. But a woman can't marry a woman."

"Of course not. But this person, thank God, is not in Dodge. The marriage happened long ago, back in Lawrence after her mother died. In fact, the ceremony happened in the very house where she was living. The owner of the house, her stepfather Calvin Perkins, sanctioned the ugly, unholy union. She was only sixteen."

"What in God's name are you saying?"

"I'm telling you the god-awful truth, Harry. The demented Luther Perkins is Lady Jane's husband."

Wyatt Matters dismissed me and spent the night lying out in the open on Boot Hill next to Matt Sullivan's grave, which for all intents and purposes he may have viewed as

Jane Hankin's grave, too. I returned to the general store for a sleepless night in my own bed. I had too much to think about for just one night of lying awake. I went through the same the next night. And after that, in the middle of the day while behind the counter and in front of a customer, I fell asleep standing up for the first time in my life. Jane's leaving was a catastrophe, as much for Mr. Matters as me, but I avoided him because a protégé can't overcome his sorrow when his mentor is equally sorrowful.

Next time I saw Wyatt he was standing in the middle of the train tracks, but he assured me he wasn't waiting for a train to run him over and reminded me if Jane ever returned from Texas, it wouldn't be by train. He said his thoughts were suffocating him in his tent, so he had come outside for fresh thinking. I decided to stand with him on a tie between the rails.

"A penny for your thoughts," I said. "No offense. I'm sure they're worth a Liberty Head double eagle."

"You'd be better off not considering me the *beau idéal* of thinking. I thought I could hold on to Jane, but she let me go."

"Us go. As far as I'm concerned, you *are* the Thinker. Don't start going modest on me. It doesn't become you."

"You'd get an argument about that from Trader Bob and most of the citizens of Dodge, good and bad. The other day when I was talking history with my friend Will Lee Washington, I brought up the evils of slavery, as if America hadn't yet cast aside that peculiar institution. Will Lee complained that I sounded like President Abraham Lincoln issuing the Emancipation Proclamation."

"Interesting for him to say that, since you are hardly a Lincoln lookalike. His stovepipe hat was far taller than your top hat, and the lanky president looked about twice your height. So how is Will Lee doing? I've meant to go to Taylor Made to see Monique and him, but the place makes me think of Jane too much."

"That also why you've been avoiding the tent?"

"You've been staying away from the general store."

"Touché. But here we are, out in the open. I suspect you have more questions for me."

"Let's see. I was mostly wondering some more about the guy who married Jane."

"Luther Perkins. A horrible human being. Now Calvin was an avaricious ass who thought he could control everything by waving his one arm, but even he had a hell of a time trying to keep the boy in line. Widower

Calvin thought a feminine touch would help, but he couldn't find a perspective wife who would handle the job. That's when he decided sixteen-year-old Jane would help the family situation more as a daughter-in-law than a stepdaughter and arranged the coerced marriage. Luther was eighteen, eager and ready, and already making Jane uncomfortable. Of course, I learned all this later. Remember, I had stepped out of Jane's life."

"Poor Jane."

"You bet. Luther had advanced from torturing and killing small animals to mistreating people, including Jane, even more so when she went from being stepsister to wife. He didn't even have to be drunk to do that, came naturally to him. His favorite pastime was shooting off his guns at any kind of target, once missing a bull's-eye by a foot and the top of Jane's head by two inches."

"First William Quantrill and Bloody Bill Anderson, then Calvin Perkins and Luther Perkins. It's all so horrible. Jane ran away, didn't she?"

"Not till later. She hated where she was, of course, but the outside world seemed no less frightening to her than the Perkins duo — the one-armed controlling old man and his demented son. In 1867, a few months into the so-called marriage, Jane saw Luther kill two transient Negroes who were trespassing in the Perkins apple orchard because they were hungry. It caused a buzz in Lawrence, where there hadn't been many killings after Quantrill came to town. Luther stood trial; after all, it was an old abolitionist town. Old man Perkins got his son the best lawyers that money could buy, and the three-man defense team got Luther off on a self-defense plea. Jane saw it differently, but she wasn't allowed to testify against her husband. Luther was a free man, so what did he do?"

"Don't tell me he did something awful to Jane. I can't stand it."

"Nope. In 1868 he did something he couldn't get away with. Showing no gratitude toward his father, Luther helped two would-be bank robbers gain access to the safe in daddy's bank. Having a son who murdered two innocent Negroes was one thing, but having his son steal from him was something Calvin could not tolerate. Luther and the other two robbers botched the robbery, were all caught with the help of Calvin, and sent to the Kansas State Penitentiary at Lansing, Leavenworth County. Not long after that, while Calvin was at his bank counting other people's money, Jane stole some money from her father-in-law — who oddly enough kept some of his riches at home — and hit the road for St. Louis. I read about Luther Perkins' conviction in the papers. That's when I stepped back into my daughter's life, tracking her down easily enough in St. Louis where I proceeded to help her without asserting any paternal authority. She'd had enough of that with Calvin Perkins."

"And then she headed back to Kansas?"

"Correct, but not back to Lawrence. And not with me. But I did follow her everywhere she went. That must have struck her as odd, but she saw that I was harmless, even helpful, and befriended me. She never suspected I was Papa. She would soon meet that handsome, deceitful sergeant from Fort Dodge somewhere out on the Plains and become an infatuated laundress at the fort. You know the rest."

"Thank you. You've given me a lot to think about." I mostly thought of Jane being married to a convict.

"Don't overdo it, son. That's all in the past, and it keeps getting more distant. Right now, Lady Jane is infatuated with a vaquero somewhere down Texas way and my days of tailing after her are over."

"It would be hard to find her, I suppose. Texas is a big place."

"What good would it do to find her? In

any case, I'm putting down roots in Dodge City. I'm not going anywhere. This time she'll have to come back to me on her own free will."

"But you have been standing here on these tracks thinking about her."

"Some. Mostly I've been thinking about trains."

"You mean the Atchison, Topeka & Santa Fe Railroad?"

"That's the one. I have another secret to disclose if you can keep it to yourself, and I know you can do that. It involves something you, Trader Bob, and so many others in Dodge have been wondering about: How does Wyatt Matters get all his money?"

"By railroad?"

"More truth to that than you think. My father is the late railroad executive Grover Sheridan, a distant cousin of 'Fighting Phil' Sheridan. Grover had been the largely silent partner of Cyrus Holliday, founder of the AT&S. I inherited a fortune, which is maintained for me by my father's trusty accountant-turned-executor in St. Louis, Samuel Friese. You look more bewildered than impressed."

"Oh, it's impressive all right. I mean even I have heard of Cyrus Holliday. But it made me wonder about those initials *AD* that appear on the decanter case you gave Jane."

"*AD* for Adelaide Dimock, my mother, a woman from Virginia who had a beautiful soul and a compassionate face. She married my father in the nation's capital in 1830, the year I was born. Like you, I was an only child, as far as I know. Adelaide Sheridan died of consumption in 1867. Grover wasn't as devastated as he might have been. He died in 1869 from a flesh-eating gangrene of the genitals. But he was a generous man to his only son. And understanding. He didn't hold it against me that all the while I was attending classes at the Indianapolis Business University, graduating with honors, I was educating myself by reading the great histories and literary classics, nor did he make a fuss when I decided not to use the name Sheridan and to become a traveling salesman instead of the son of a railroad tycoon."

"You used a made-up name?"

"Not the first name. I was born Wyatt Samuel Sheridan, Wyatt being an old English name meaning *brave at war.* My mother's father was Samuel; she got to pick my middle name. The last name *Matters* is all mine. I first thought of being Wyatt Dimock, but the connection between Dimock and Sheridan was too well known."

"How did you come up with Matters?"

"I determined that though I was fortunate to never *need* to work, what mattered most in my life were never-ending learning and responsible philanthropy, not railroad building and money making. At times I've felt I must atone for the avarice and immorality of my late father and my own turn as a Lothario when traveling Missouri and Kansas in my wagon. I, of course, chose not to reject my father's accumulated wealth, but I live in my humble tent because I have no wish to flaunt my inheritance. I have avoided common labor but by no means am I a selfish gentleman of leisure. My purpose in life is to acquire and dispense knowledge for the betterment of the world, and more particularly in the last couple years the betterment of all of Dodge."

"Dodge is getting better, some law and order and safer and . . . But without Jane, how can it be better for me . . . I mean for us?"

"We must live well every day, son, and hope for my daughter to come to her senses."

By fall 1874, as Wyatt Matters predicted, a few adventurous cattlemen had slowly begun to drive their longhorns to Dodge City over what became known as the Great Western

Cattle Trail. Although it was too much to hope for (though I naturally shared the same hope), he was still disappointed that Jane Hankin had not come to her senses and returned to Dodge.

The drovers who showed up made a point of testing the waters and the whiskey in the newly opened saloon that had come into being because of the Washington brothers' winning baseball bet with the Fort Dodge soldiers, the planning and labor of Will Lee Washington, and the financial support of Mr. Matters. It now had a group of owners, including Sheriff Bassett, which Wyatt saw as improper for a man in his position. Nobody else in town seemed to see it that way; even a dedicated lawman had a right to make good money. The new owners had changed the name from the Longhorn to the Long Branch because they wanted more than just Texas cowboys patronizing the place and because the hometown of one of the owners was Long Branch, New Jersey.

On October 23, Wyatt and I went to the Long Branch to taste its wine but more importantly to question the cowboys. It turned out the first order of wine hadn't arrived yet and not one of the boys from Texas had any information about the Babe or Jane. Wyatt had mixed feelings that none of the drovers to appear was named Babe Herrera because he had the same burning question for the vaquero that I did: *What the hell have you done to Jane?*

"I'm sorry about the delay in the wine, something to do with lower yields and lost grapes in droughty Kansas," said Will Lee after he found a place for Wyatt and me to sit in the crowded saloon. "May I offer you gentlemen our finest rye whiskey?"

"No," said Wyatt.

"Hope you fellows are doing well. The place is hopping. I can afford to buy my meals at Taylor Made every night, if I can find the time."

"How's Monique doing?" I asked.

"Busy like me. Still missing Jane. And no, Harry, she hasn't heard from her either. Taylor Made isn't so crowded she couldn't find room there for you two gents."

"I've been meaning to take a meal there again. Maybe when the cold weather comes."

"Well, at least you're both here. I see a bright future for the Long Branch, and the new owners want me to be a part of it."

Wyatt wasn't listening. He was leaning half off his chair and pointing across the room to where three men were emptying a bottle fast. "Why does that cowboy in the black hat and black shirt have a gun in his belt?"

"Must not have read the sign," said Will Lee. "I suspect he can't read."

"Then maybe you should read it for him since you have a stake in this place. You know how I feel about young men partaking in whiskey with guns on their person."

"Guns aren't banned in most saloons in town, and Dodge hasn't had a shooting in ages."

"I didn't come here to argue with you, Will Lee."

"I know. You came for the wine. Like I said, so sorry to disappoint. Maybe you'd enjoy a pitcher of lemonade."

"No. Never liked it as a kid. He really shouldn't have that gun in here."

"Some of these boys don't take kindly to being corrected by a Kansas Negro. If he causes any trouble, I'll send for Sheriff Bassett, who, as you know, is one of the owners of our establishment but at the moment is out taking care of some of his lawing. He handles them fine."

"What do you hear from brother Maverick in Texas?" I asked.

"He busted a leg busting a bronc in Bandera. That's all I know. And he doesn't know a thing about what happened to the Babe and his girl."

"His girl? It won't be forever. Is Texas so big that they can't be located?"

"Maverick is laid up in bed. He isn't locating anybody right now. Could be the Babe and you know who crossed the border. Could be nobody's looking for them. The Babe's not wanted for anything, not like the time the Texas Rangers accused him of being part of a horse-thieving gang out of Round Rock. Of course, he was innocent."

"I bet," I said. I didn't want to hear more about it. I didn't care about anybody's horses. I just cared that the Babe had stolen my girl. The hurt wasn't ever going away, and I was sorry I had stepped into the Long Branch saloon. "Jane is wanted!"

"If you had a mind to, you could go to Texas yourselves and look for her," suggested Will Lee.

"I've thought about it," I said. "But she didn't go down there against her will. What chance do I have down there of stealing her back?"

"None," said Wyatt. "Dodge City is my town for life, and I got to keep watch on it, what with all these ill-bred cowboys starting to invade Ford County. Lady Jane knows where I am and who I am. Like I've been saying all along, she'll have to come back on her own free will."

"That's right," I said. "And it won't be on some cattle drive with a bunch of rowdy . . ." My voice trailed off. I was about ready for a whiskey, but it was up to Wyatt to ask for a bottle, and he showed no inclination to celebrate the rise of the Long Branch or to drown our sorrows over the fall of Jane.

Will Lee had shown no signs of drinking himself, but he pounded his fist on the table. It was a daring display, for he was not one to talk back or express anything but gratitude for the sometime generous Mr. Matters. "You fellows shouldn't disrespect the cowboys. This town was practically built on the backs of the buffalo hunters, but they're practically all gone. Dodge, and not just the Long Branch, needs cowboys. Cowboys are good for . . ."

"Nothing," said Wyatt, who of course didn't mean it, but he was in a mood at least as foul as mine. "I don't need a history lesson from you or anyone else. I was here from the beginning. Now are you going to tell that cowboy to either leave the Long Branch or leave his gun at the bar?"

"Why start something when nothing is likely to happen. We want cowboys to feel welcome at the Long Branch."

"You make me sorry I put any money into this place."

"Don't say that. We got the place built thanks to you, and the managerial partners say they will pay you back. How much do they owe you?"

"I don't want their whiskey money."

"Look, it's my job to make sure everybody is happy and spending money, whether they are drinkers, gamblers, or talkers like you. If I say something to that cowboy in the black hat, he would not be happy and would stop buying whiskey. I'll go talk to the owners about the wine situation. They're in the office still counting last night's take. Excuse me, fellows."

Wyatt frowned until Will Lee was out of sight. "And excuse me," he said. He stood up, adjusted his bowtie, and walked straight toward the table with the cowboy in the black hat.

"You want me to come along?" I called out to him.

"Sit tight, son. I can handle this."

I tried to stay seated, but I soon was hearing the unpleasant voices from across the room, and I saw the cowboy in the black hat take out his six-shooter. He looked as if he might be trying to hand it to Wyatt, but then he twirled it several times in rapid fashion and pressed the barrel against Wyatt's large nose. That was too much for me. I jumped up and advanced, unarmed but full of surprising courage. I closed in fast, but not fast enough.

"You want it, old man," the cowboy said. "I'll give it to you."

He didn't mean the Smith & Wesson itself, only several of the .38-caliber bullets in the chamber. Wyatt was still talking as he backed away, and he even kept up his chatter as he stumbled over a shiny new brass spittoon and stumbled back further. Wyatt's lack of height worked in his favor. The cowboy fired his first two shots high, and both slugs passed through Wyatt's top hat. The third clipped Wyatt's purple bowtie before it struck his left shoulder. He went down, but the cowboy was ready to fire a fourth shot anyway. He never got it off. I grabbed from the table an almost empty whiskey bottle and brought it down on his head, causing him to drop his weapon before he himself dropped to the floor of the Long Branch. *Whiskey can kill without a gun,* I thought before I passed out from the shock of it all.

Chapter Twenty-Two

The cowboy in black, whose name I never learned, did not die. He lay in bed unconscious for two days. Sheriff Bassett wanted to question him about the shooting, but on the third day, the cowboy's pals ushered him out of Dodge and the lawman never got the chance. I was glad not to have killed a man, though I had reason to hate him. He had shot my mentor. No, the bullet did not kill Wyatt, but we all had to live with the damage done. I thought about the tragedy in the Long Branch both day and night and at my worst moments I thought suffering Wyatt would have been better off dead. But the rest of the time I patted myself on the back for saving my mentor's life, even if it was by using violence in the form of a whiskey bottle.

Dr. Thomas L. McCarty said the bowtie, though hardly a hard object, had deflected the third bullet just enough to keep it from piercing a vital organ or major blood vessel. The slug had missed Mr. Matters' heart by less than an inch. It fractured Wyatt's collarbone and stayed lodged in his shoulder but came close to passing all the way through his body. Dr. McCarty removed the bullet with relative ease and then, with somewhat more difficulty, removed pieces of shattered bone and stopped the bleeding. The wound paralyzed the muscles of Wyatt's left shoulder and upper arm. But all that was expected. What came as a complete surprise to me and no doubt to everyone else in Dodge who had ever encountered him was that Wyatt Matters stopped talking.

He hadn't gone into shock, and there was no physical reason he couldn't speak. I noticed some of the symptoms that Jane had displayed after Matt Sullivan was shot — anxiety, irritability, no energy, little appetite, sadness, withdrawal, and unwillingness to talk about the tragic event. In trying to deal with the armed cowboy in the Long Branch he had used words as usual, but the words had failed him. He chose to communicate with me using scratch pads and pencils. His first note said it all: *I talk, nobody listens. I talk, my daughter leaves. I talk, I get shot. I talk no more. This is my vow of silence, son. I speak with my silence. My message is loud and clear. When the people of Dodge listen and the shooting and killing stops, I shall speak once more.* I protested at first, telling him that I had listened most of the time to his lectures on everything from the evil of mixing whiskey with guns and the dire need for law and order on the frontier to the nature of Zeus' dalliances on Mount Olympus and how the greatest of all Renaissance men, Leonardo da Vinci, was largely self-educated, having received no formal education beyond basic reading, writing and mathematics.

"How can I self-educate without your help?" I asked him.

He wrote on his scratch pad: *Read. Read. Read. You have access to all my books and any educational material you find in my trunks. Listen to your own voice.*

"Sure," I said, tapping my Adam's apple with two fingers. Looking after Wyatt and reading his books, along with scribbling simple but mean verses for my eyes only, was in fact about all I was doing before and after my work hours at the general store.

The week after the shooting, I moved out of the storage room and into Wyatt's tent to better care for him. Robert Wright didn't mind because I kept up my work and he could always use the extra space. Dr. McCarty, though, insisted that for Wyatt to recover he needed a regular bed in a regular house, especially with colder weather coming on and me having trouble maintaining the right level of heat in the fire pit without smoking Wyatt out. I came up with the idea of moving with Wyatt into the little blue house once occupied by Jane. I thought Wyatt would put up a huge fuss, but when I brought the subject up, he answered me with a note that read: *Doc is a crock. But life in tent is spent. Let us go blue. Me and you.* I wasn't sure why he put those words in rhyme. I suspected he knew I was still writing verse. I had no reason to complain, though. He was willing to go, and while I didn't mind his tent, I had always wanted to live in that blue house, albeit with Jane, not Wyatt. While the Zimmermans had no love for Mr. Matters and didn't give me much thought, they were delighted to have us in their old outbuilding because it had remained empty since Jane left to move in with Monique and because Wyatt, through his man in St. Louis, had agreed to pay them a generous rent.

Robert Wright sold me at what he called a generous price (he took it out of my salary) the old bed in the storage room. I borrowed the old Fort Dodge Express wagon to move Wyatt's belongings from the tent. Will Lee, maybe feeling a little guilty about how things had transpired at the Long Branch on October 23, helped me with the trunks. Wyatt told me in a note that the empty tent must remain standing in case the deal with Mr. Zimmerman ever collapsed, but he did have me put up a sign at the tent entrance saying USE AT YOUR OWN RISK — THE OWNER. Wyatt slept in the blue house bedroom on Jane's old narrow bed while I set up my even narrower bed in the kitchen. The door between the rooms was always kept open, though, in case Wyatt woke up in the night and growled for a cup of water, for help with the chamber pot, or for whatever comfort his old protégé could provide. So it went through the rest of 1874, with fewer and fewer spoken words from me, sporadic written notes from him, and long stretches of silence. Wyatt did slowly recover from his gunshot wound, though it didn't look likely he'd ever be able to raise his left hand to make a point ever again. And still he said nothing to me, nor to anyone else who showed up: Dr. McCarty when he appeared in his professional capacity, Monique Taylor or Matilda Zimmerman on those rare occasions they brought nourishment, Will Lee on those even rarer occasions when he showed up to ask a question or two (only to receive short answers in hastily written notes; Matilda complained about Wyatt's penmanship), or Frederick Zimmerman on his monthly visits to collect rent money.

By New Year's Eve Wyatt could walk around almost comfortably, though he still preferred to stay in bed, as if he wished to duplicate those bedridden days of Jane. Whether in the blue house, at the general store, or on the street, I came to hate the sound of my own voice. The only exception was at the Wright home when I was looking after the children and could talk gibberish to entertain the giggle-prone Clara Belle Wright and her younger brothers. I didn't much like listening to the voices of other people either. I found no pleasure in idle conversation about the weather and other unimportant subjects that I was forced to engage in by general store customers and the few residents who stopped me on the street. I had to talk to my boss when he was so inclined to give me the time of day, but even talking to his wife brought no joy for me anymore as she treated me like an employee, too, albeit one who worked with children instead of canned goods. I avoided talking to Will Lee Washington because I associated him with not only the loss of Jane but also the wounding of Wyatt. If only Will Lee had done his job and gone over to disarm that cruel cowboy, Wyatt wouldn't have had to do it and wouldn't have taken that bullet. In any case, Will Lee was always busy with his Long Branch work or his voluntary duties at Taylor Made. The few times I went to the restaurant to bring back food to Wyatt, I hardly said a word to Monique. Yes, she still also reminded me of the loss of Jane, plus it was frustrating trying to interpret her facial gestures and hand signals. Unlike the self-imposed silent man, the mute female restaurateur never communicated with handwritten notes.

As midnight approached on the last day of 1874, I asked Wyatt about New Year's resolutions since he had shown interest in them the previous two years. His return note was only two short sentences: *To hell with the New Year — I resolve not to talk about it.* Yes, it was a blunt statement, but I also sensed a little tongue in cheek since when a person wasn't talking about anything at all, how could he resolve not to talk about something? I tried to encourage his playful side to no avail. Since the shooting, I could count his smiles and half-smiles on one hand. I came up with my own resolution — to get Mr. Matters to break his vow of silence, not for a day or a month but for all of 1875. I whispered this to him, perhaps too softly, for he made me repeat it. Then he took out pencil and scratch pad and scribbled an even shorter note, which read: *To hell with resolutions — need to piss!*

I spent a restless night thinking how, resolution or not, I could convince him to speak to me again. In the morning, when he finally awakened from a long noisy sleep (full of moans and groans as usual yet managing *not* to talk in his sleep), I made him flapjacks for the first time, as if that might soften him up. After serving a tall stack to him in bed, I made my little prepared speech, which I had written down before dawn and had since memorized: "Is it possible your vow of silence isn't indeed necessary? I know you have suffered, Wyatt, and are in pain from your gunshot wound, but you aren't going to die. And that bad cowboy who I bashed over the skull with that whiskey bottle recovered and skedaddled. So as far as you and me and Sheriff Bassett know, there haven't been any killings in Dodge since Dave Burrell and Bill Ellis shot each other down outside the Dodge House on the night of July 20, 1873. That was nearly a year and a half ago."

A long silence followed. Wyatt sat up straight and looked me straight in the eye. I felt my blue eyes drowning in his brighter, more powerful blue eyes. His mouth opened several times out of old habit, but no words came out. Finally, he ripped out a page from his scratch pad and began to write. He wrote in such large letters that it required three pages to get his message across: *Listen to me, my son. There is but a temporary lull. I was shot and left for dead. More wounding and killing will follow. The bison hunters will fade away. But the cowboys will come and keep coming. Like the hunters, they are crude, uneducated figures. The Long Branch and every saloon in town will be overrun by young whiskey-drinking cowboys with guns. Firearms, if not whiskey, must be prohibited. More lawmen must come and enforce the ban on weapons. Nonaction by men like Will Lee Washington can no longer be tolerated. Innocent women like Jane Hankin should never again need to suffer from wanton gunmanship. Do what you can to ensure peace in Dodge. You are not made to be a lawman. You may never achieve the goal of becoming a Renaissance man. But, my son, there can be no excuses. You must be a MAN!*

Clearly, Wyatt Matters was not ready to break his vow of silence. I wasn't sure what he wanted me to do to be the kind of man he wanted me to be. My mentor was being more realistic about the prospects of me ever becoming a Renaissance man.

Knowing my limitations I was glad for that. But I considered myself a peaceful commonplace man right now. What else could I do? Start a petition against the drinking of all alcoholic beverages except wine? Go to town officials and push for ordinances that banned guns everywhere? Run for mayor? Be adventuresome and take up with lively saloon gals and soiled doves? Tell Robert Wright that I would quit unless he started treating me with more respect and working me less hours? Locate an innocent farmer's daughter somewhere in Ford County to replace Jane Hankin? Go to Texas and drag Jane back by her auburn hair? As far as him wanting me to do what I could to ensure the peace in Dodge, I wasn't visiting the saloons and dance halls but the town didn't seem so bad lately. Anyway, hadn't I already not only ensured a little peace but also saved Wyatt's life by breaking that whiskey bottle over the head of the cowboy in the black hat? I had never gone around boasting about my feat, but he could have at least acknowledged what I'd done, if not thank me. Of course, at times while seeing him lying there in bed with his sadness, discomfort, irritability, and pessimism, I wondered if he was even glad to be alive.

"I'll do my best," I said, and that was all.

■ ■ ■ ■

As Wyatt Matters predicted, the bison were virtually gone from the Dodge area by 1875. General William Sherman had reportedly ordered the slaughter of the buffalo to drive the Plains Indians onto reservations, which most of them preferred over starvation. In any case, hundreds of buffalo hunters were going out of business, and only the occasional bone gatherer remained on the scene of what Wyatt, on paper, called "the unsightly aftermath of the dastardliest crime of the century." But he wasn't right about everything. More cowboys were indeed coming to Dodge City but not in such great numbers in '75, when most of the cattle drives north were still landing in Wichita. Furthermore, month after month passed by without any reported deaths by shooting or other violent means. Wyatt argued, still on paper, that not everything got reported and that there must be at least some non-fatal shootings such as the one that hit him hard the previous year. Throughout the year Robert Wright and the other civil leaders boasted how peaceful Dodge had become, and when my boss (no, I didn't quit) declared around Thanksgiving that there hadn't been a single killing from the summer of 1873 until now, neither

Wyatt nor I had found any evidence to say otherwise. Still, Wyatt let his displeasure be known in his notes to me and letters to editors of various newspapers. He stressed the "indisputable fact" that even if there were no murderers currently running loose (which he doubted), Dodge was still infested with six-gun carriers, crooked gamblers, burglars, horse thieves, prostitutes, saloon brawlers, and other disturbers of the peace.

In November 1875 Dodge City, now with a population over eight hundred, had taken another step in its development by becoming a formal municipality (a so-called city of the third class). With Dodge's new upgraded status, the city council decided, even with no recent shootings, that banning concealed weapons would continue unless you were a federal, state, or local law enforcement officer. Violators were subject to fines up to $25. Wyatt Matters naturally wanted more, that carrying any firearm, concealed or out in the open, be strictly prohibited and that repeat violators be banned from Dodge for at least a year. He bombarded Robert Wright and other civil leaders with letters calling for "complete gun control" but sustained his no-talking stance because he believed that walking about town (yes, he had healed enough in body and mind to do that) in silent protest packed a greater punch than shooting his mouth off — his old, ineffective method of trying to bring about change for the better.

Robert Wright and the other business leaders, whom Wyatt increasingly referred to as "the Gang" rather than "the town founders," decided in December to set the municipal election for the following April. In the meantime, they chose Peter L. Beatty, who ran the Alhambra Saloon with James "Dog" Kelley, the acting mayor. Wyatt found fault in that, writing to me and to the *Wichita City Eagle* (since the *Dodge City Messenger* had suspended publication that year): *Typical. Putting another saloon owner in charge.*

With Wyatt up and about, I had more free time, but I did not break out of my sedentary lifestyle of working in the store by day, reading in the blue house by night (Wyatt's collection of books, some of which I read more than once, as well as his scratch pad offerings). We shared in the cooking and house cleaning. Our talking/writing conversations only occasionally called up Jane's name, but there were indications that Wyatt was still missing her as much as me. Since he wasn't speaking and didn't want to chance somehow offending an armed cowboy, he gave me a note requesting that I keep asking

Texas drovers I encountered on the street whether they had heard of either Jane Hankin or Babe Herrera. I had no luck.

But then another New Year's Eve came around and Wyatt and I decided to take a rare meal at Taylor Made. Wyatt brought along his scratch pad and two pencils. Will Lee Washington happened to be there helping Monique because she had crammed three more tables into the dining area and the place was packed. There was no place for Wyatt and me to sit but Monique Taylor directed us to a table with two chairs in the kitchen. She even lit a candle in the center of the table and brought out a couple of embroidered napkins, initials *M.T. & W.T.,* for her and her late husband, William.

The jambalaya was as excellent as I remembered it, but the conversation was spotty what with Will Lee and Monique running back and forth, Wyatt communicating with words on paper, and Monique communicating with well-practiced but still confusing hand and head gestures and eye movements. Wyatt and I, each in our own way, made resolutions to come to the restaurant at least twice a month in 1876. Will Lee was clearing our plates when he remembered something. He tore a page from Wyatt's pad and wrote it out, as if he had forgotten that Wyatt was as capable of hearing as Monique. He wrote: *Maverick Washington ramrodding early cattle drive in June, bringing the Babe.* He then ran out of the kitchen to bring two orders to customers, but as soon as he returned, I began peppering him with questions and Wyatt passed him a note with only three words on it: *What about Jane?* Will Lee had to admit he didn't know. He only knew about his brother coming in June because one of the dining cowboys knew Mr. Herrera and had delivered the message. Wyatt sent me to the dining area to question this cowboy, who had red hair to match his red bandana and a face that looked as tough and hard as dusty leather. At least he wasn't armed.

"Excuse me, sir," I said. "But I was told you know Babe Herrera."

"You bet. What's it to you, mister?"

"I played ball with him. He's one hell of a pitcher."

"He sure has been. A bad hoss he was trying to break stomped him. Pitching arm got mangled. Would have been in Dodge this fall if not for getting throwed and stomped. He swears he'll be coming your way in June."

"Alone?"

"With a herd, mister. He sticks with whatever outfit Maverick Washington signs up with. You know Maverick, I assume."

"Yes, Will Lee's brother. They were both on the ball team with me and the Babe. Tell me, how's the Babe doing, other than his broken arm?"

"What you driving at, mister?"

"Just wondering. He left Dodge with a girl. They didn't happen to marry or anything like that, did they?"

"The Babe married? That'll be the day. I never knew him to have just one lady on his arm. Right now, of course, his best arm is broke."

"Yes, too bad. The girl I'm talking about has auburn hair. Her name is Jane."

"I tell you, mister, I can't keep track of my own gals, let alone the Babe's. Now, ask me the name of our favorite riding horses and I can tell you those in a second."

"No," I said, suddenly tired of being polite. "When you get back to Texas, tell the Babe, he's horse manure."

The redheaded cowboy looked stunned, as did the other three cowboys at his table. The party was unarmed, so I knew I wouldn't be shot. But I expected to be attacked or challenged at any second. I spoke again anyway. "Listen up, cowboy. You tell him to either marry Jane and be true to her or else send her back home to the ones who truly love her in Dodge. If he hurts her in any way, there will be hell to pay. That's my message to Babe Herrera. Deliver it, you hear."

"Yeah, I hear you all right. You must be loco. You looking to step outside?"

"No. You go ahead. I ain't yet et my dessert."

I hitched up my pants, turned my back on the table, and took my sweet time walking back to the kitchen. I was surprised that nobody followed me. Wyatt Matters quickly ripped a page from his scratch pad and wrote those same three words again: *What about Jane?*

"The way I figure it," I said. "we're liable to be seeing her soon."

On January 14, 1876, Dodge City had another killing. Black barber John Tyler, owner of the Tonsorial Parlor on Front Street, was out to kill his wife's suspected lover but instead shot the wrong man, a German immigrant who was passing by too close to Tyler's home. Wyatt, who had long supported the cause of Negroes even before coming to Dodge, hated that blood was spilled again in his hometown, but he called the shooting a "tragic mistake." Tyler also had the support of George Hoover, a liquor dealer, yes, but one who wasn't part of the Gang. Because Hoover believed in justice and law and order, Wyatt Matters considered him a vast improvement over Beatty and gave him his vote in the April mayoral election. Hoover won, which didn't please Robert Wright, who often didn't see eye to eye with Hoover. Still, my boss took it well, telling me: "Let George have his turn. I'll be mayor one day when the time is right and I hear the call of the people." Wyatt wasn't as approving of the man Hoover appointed first marshal of Dodge, Larry Deger. While Deger was an imposing figure at over three hundred pounds, Wyatt considered him a questionable character and didn't like the fact the marshal was allowed to remain a partner in a saloon. Dodge might have divided into two factions, the Gang vs. the Hoover men, but "whiskey merchants" were prominent on both sides. Wyatt did some investigating and figuring and concluded that Dodge, now with a population of 1,200, had ten licensed whiskey-selling establishments and that customers, residents, and visitors consumed some three hundred barrels of whiskey a year.

Despite his size, Deger didn't prove to be a man willing to challenge lawbreakers, especially when they were armed. Hoover's answer in May was to appoint an assistant marshal, a fellow to serve as Deger's right-hand man during Dodge's first big cattle-drive season. Interestingly enough, the new lawman was named Wyatt Earp, the second notable "Wyatt" to come to town. Not that anyone would confuse the two Wyatts. For one thing, while forty-five-year-old Wyatt Matters was short and pudgy, twenty-eight-year-old Wyatt Earp was tall and sinewy. Mr. Matters had faced would-be troublemakers with nothing more than words, and it had largely worked until that cowboy in the Long Branch refused to listen. Deputy Marshal Earp, in contrast, was a man of few words who strapped on a gun when he fearlessly faced out-of-line cowboys. He didn't shoot anyone, though, preferring to use his fists or the butt of his six-shooter to settle matters. My mentor, no doubt remembering that time words had failed him, wholeheartedly approved. He also commended Mr. Earp's idea to create a "Dead Line" at the railroad tracks. South of the tracks, where Mr. Matters' unoccupied tent still stood, rowdy cowboys were nearly given a free gun hand, but north of the tracks, where Front Street and the blue house were located, misbehaving drovers faced arrest and heavy fines if not a severe beating. The crowning development was that Dodge also added several other peace officers to its police force, including

Jim Masterson, the brother of Mr. Earp's friend Bat Masterson, and later Bat himself.

As May wound down, Mr. Matters delivered a scratch pad note to Deputy Marshal Earp with a positive message: *Deger is a desk sitter. But you and the Masterson brothers are town tamers without shooting anyone. I salute you for preventing Dodge from spinning out of control and becoming a killing hotbed again. I met the Mastersons way back when they were fed up with skinning bison and, to their credit, got out of that vile business. I am proud to have the same first name as you, Mr. Wyatt Earp — Yours in the best interest of Dodge City, Wyatt Matters.*

Wyatt Earp nodded but stared down at Wyatt Matters as if he were a sheep herder in a cow town. Mr. Earp no doubt wasn't used to small, sober, unarmed men who kept their mouths shut and knew how to write well. I stepped in to end the assistant marshal's confusion, explaining why my law-abiding, peace-loving mentor no longer spoke, and adding that his hearing was above average and his comprehension exceptional.

"That's a helluva note," Mr. Earp said. "How much more peace do you need north of the Dead Line to get to talking again?"

Mr. Matters wrote another note: *Silence has been good to me. It's about more than law and order now. My daughter went to Texas with a cowboy in the summer of '74. Haven't seen or heard from her since. The day Jane returns to me in Dodge is the day I break my vow of silence.*

"Can't help you there, Mr. Matters. But I wish you luck in getting her back. I'm proud to meet a good citizen like yourself. I'd like to shake your hand, Wyatt."

The two men grasped each other's hands and shook as if in mutual respect. I felt like a third wheel or maybe a fifth wheel — in any case, no longer necessary.

Mr. Matters' next note read: *Dodge needs you, Wyatt. Keep up the good work.*

"If people were all like you, Wyatt, they wouldn't need me in Dodge or any place else."

Mr. Matters wrote: *In June when the Texas herds arrive, if you come across a cowboy named Babe Herrera, I'd appreciate you letting me know, Wyatt.*

"Babe Herrera? Got it. You figure he's a lawbreaker, Wyatt?"

Mr. Matters' last note read: *Might be that, Wyatt. But he for damn sure is a breaker of hearts.*

Wyatt Matters, if not Wyatt Earp, got more than he bargained for in June 1876. So did I.

During the first week, the first Texas herds arrived, including one ramrodded by Maverick Washington, who was recovered from his bucking bronc accident but still had a limp. He celebrated with brother Will Lee Washington north of the Dead Line at Taylor Made, and even more so with his fellow drovers in the saloons, gambling parlors, and dance halls south of the Dead Line. Of far more interest to Wyatt and me was the presence of Babe Herrera, who had become a whiskey-drinking man in the aftermath of his own fall from a bad hoss. His left arm was permanently bent, and he couldn't raise it over his shoulder. That arm was as limited as Wyatt Matters' left arm had become since he took the bullet to his shoulder. The Babe would never pitch again unless he learned to do so right-handed.

Because neither Wyatt nor I wanted to confront Mr. Herrera amid all his rowdy cowboy friends south of the Dead Line, we had the Washington brothers arrange a meeting at Taylor Made. We caught him in the middle of a meal. He hadn't lost his looks, but he had more lines on his brow and his bronzed skin seemed too leathery. His hair was slicked down and he looked and smelled as if had just gotten his first shave. Although a lefty all the way, he was manipulating his eating utensils with his right hand and only using his left hand to rub a mustache he was still growing. His eyes flashed recognition and he remembered both our names, but none of us extended a hand. I told the Babe I was sorry to hear about his horse taming accident. He replied in Spanish, *"No hay problema."* Wyatt was busy scribbling a familiar question on paper: *What about Jane?* But I asked the same thing out loud first.

We got our answer in bits and pieces, mostly English but a little Spanish thrown in. He said he had experienced *"muchos momentos felices"* with Janey, as he called her, but that they had departed company last September in Fort Worth, Texas. Wyatt said in an angry note that if Mr. Herrera had harmed even a single auburn hair on Jane's head he would exact revenge, which was as close as I'd ever heard Wyatt come to threatening violence against anyone. "No, no, not me, *señor,*" Mr. Herrera replied, tapping his bib shirt at heart level. I followed my own line of questioning, wanting to know if the separation was due to the presence of another woman; in other words, was there another *señorita* in the Babe's life as a dashing bachelor?

"No, no, *mi amigo*. It was an *hombre, a mal hombre*."

"That means 'bad man,' right? But what do you mean?"

"He came to Texas after spending seven years in prison. He wanted Janey."

"What do you mean by 'wanted'? To have her or to hurt her?"

"*Have again,* I think."

"You think? Who was it?"

"Hankin, I think."

"Hankin is Jane's name."

"That's not right. His name not Hankin. Her name not Hankin."

"What the hell are you saying? You let this man take Janey . . . I mean Jane . . .
Just like that? How could you?"

"He is *el esposo* . . . you know, husband."

"My God!" shouted Wyatt, breaking his vow of silence. "Demented Luther!"

Chapter Twenty-Three

Babe Herrera didn't have much to add, and I filled him in on a few basics about Luther Perkins and his father, Calvin. He said "*lo siento mucho*" many times, apologizing for everything from letting the loco husband take Jane away and not knowing where they had gone to having had no previous understanding of how we felt about Jane and not waiting for us before enjoying Monique's *deliciosa* gumbo. He explained that the cattle drive had made him *tengo mucha hambre* because Cookie caught a fever and had to be replaced at the chuck wagon by Maverick Washington, a good ramrod but a lousy cook. None of that interested Wyatt, who got up abruptly and left without saying another word. I stayed on a little longer and did my own apologizing for assuming he had done Jane wrong and for having no appetite for gumbo or anything else. I also apologized to Monique Taylor for failing to order a meal, but she waved me away and rushed back to the kitchen with tears in her eyes. I started to follow her, but Will Lee Washington cut me off at the kitchen door. He had taken the night off from his duties at the Long Branch to help Monique once again on a busy night. He explained that she was upset for having learned for the first time that very night about Jane's appalling eight-year marriage and the return of an unsparing husband.

"What are you going to do now, Harry?" Will Lee asked after pulling me into the Taylor Made kitchen.

"What do you mean?"

"Luther sounds like big trouble."

"He happens to be her husband."

"Who has spent almost all of their marriage locked away behind bars, right?"

"Yes, but it was for bank robbery, his father's bank. It's not like he murdered anyone." But then I remembered Wyatt telling me how Luther had earlier killed two hungry Negroes and gotten away with it. "I'm sure, he wouldn't do anything to Jane. Why would anyone hurt . . ." But Wyatt had also told me that as her stepbrother at first and then as her husband, Luther had mistreated her. "He was a bad kid all right with a bad father. Luther is much older now."

"And you think because he served seven years in the pen he has reformed?"

"I don't know."

"The way Babe told it, Luther tracked down Jane not because of any genuine love for her but because he considered her his property. I'd hate to think his intent for going to all that trouble was to punish her."

"Poor Jane," was all I could say.

"Have you thought of going down to Texas to save her from the bastard?"

"I haven't had time to think it all out yet. They likely aren't even down there anymore. Before Luther went to prison, he was living with his father in Lawrence. Maybe he took her there, although he might have had a falling out with Calvin since the old man testified against his son in the robbery trial."

"Lawrence is a hell of a lot closer than Fort Worth. Seems like you could start your search there. After all, if Luther found her, so can you."

I had a sudden vision of Luther beating his wife in the Perkins home and me rushing in and busting a whiskey bottle over the bastard's head. Heck, I'd saved someone that way before.

"It's something to think about, Will Lee," I said as I started out of the kitchen. "I'll go find out what Wyatt thinks."

I went home to the blue house, but Wyatt Matters wasn't there. He had no wish to mingle among the boisterous cowboys socializing and celebrating south of the Dead Line or even to visit the more respectable night spots on the north side. Lately, he hadn't been making the rounds in town to push for law-and-order measures, because even he had to admit that Wyatt Earp and his fellow peace officers had things under control in Dodge. There was only one place he'd go. And, indeed, I found him there, sitting in the dark among the gravestones and fanning himself with his top hat on what already felt like a hot summer night. Boot Hill was a nice quiet place to think, and not necessarily about death.

"Mind if I join you, Wyatt?" I asked.

He patted the dirt next to him. I strained to read the marker beside me as I sat. I figured out I was on Matt Sullivan's grave and wondered if maybe my mentor was thinking about death tonight. I knew for sure that Jane was on his mind, too.

"Did you figure on Luther looking for Jane once he did his time in prison?" I asked.

He nodded.

"What do you think his intentions are? You think he'll take Jane back to Lawrence?"

He nodded again.

"I'm trying to figure out what to do? I know he's her husband but him being *demented* like you say, you think I should go there anyway, maybe bring Jane back to Dodge?"

Wyatt now shook his head.

"Then what should I do? What should we do?"

He didn't nod or shrug. He scratched out something on the notepad, but it was too dark to read the three words. Now it was my turn to shrug. We spent another half hour on Boot Hill, the silence only broken by the periodic hoots of an owl who I figured wanted to keep reminding us that we were in its territory. Finally, we went back to town and in the light of the Long Branch saloon, he took out the note he'd written on Boot Hill. The three words surprised me — *They are coming.*

"You mean more cowboys are coming?" I asked. "I know that. Dodge has become a cattle town."

He wrote out his response: *What have we been talking about tonight? Not cowboys! The Perkins couple – Jane and Luther!*

"You mean to Dodge City? Why would you think that?"

Wyatt reached in his vest pocket and pulled out a folded sheet of paper, opened it, and held it to the light. There were a lot of words already on it, and they were written in verse.

BOOT HILL DREAM
DODGE CITY WAS A WICKED PLACE
STINKING OF HIDES, WHISKEY
AND GUN SMOKE
KILLING A MAN WAS COMMONPLACE
AND LAW AND ORDER WAS A JOKE.
BUT TO ME IT WAS MY CHOSEN HOME
ONE THAT BAD MEN TRIED TO USURP
UNTIL WE GOT SOME LAW AND ORDER
WITH THE LIKES OF WYATT EARP.
STILL ONE GREAT THING WAS MISSING
MY BEAUTIFUL MARRIED DAUGHTER
UNTIL I SAW HER ARRIVING
IN A DREAM
HER DEMENTED HUSBAND
BROUGHT HER.
I KNEW NOT THEIR INTENTIONS
SHE WAS MY CHILD BUT
LUTHER'S WIFE
THERE WAS A RECURRENCE
OF GUNFIRE
MORE THAN ONE MAN LOST HIS LIFE.

It must have been something Wyatt wrote on Boot Hill when there was still enough light to see. I read it over a second time.

Compared to the short verse he had written in my name for Jane back in fall 1972, it was positively brilliant. But as much as I wanted to see my true love again, I didn't want Luther Perkins to come to Dodge with her, and naturally I was disturbed by the ending.

"You really had this dream?" I asked.

He nodded.

"But it's *just* a dream," I continued. "You truly believe they will be coming here just 'cause you dreamed it?"

He put pencil to paper: *American Indians believe the dream world is as real as the solid world. They use dreams for spiritual guidance and to foresee future events. In my dream, the Indians and the bison watch them come on the steam-belching iron horse. One of the chiefs who watches wears a belt buckle that says "Original," a top hat, and a purple bowtie. It is I!*

"And you actually saw — in your dream, that is — Jane and Luther on the train?"

Wyatt wrote: *Absolutely. She wears a red dress and silver earrings. He is dressed in black with two six-shooters shoved into the silk red sash around his waist . . . just like Wild Bill Hickok.*

"That's not good. They come to Dodge. What then?"

He wrote: *They say Shawnee Chief Tecumseh foresaw his own death.*

"I can't stand this. Who dies in your dream? Not you, I hope."

He shrugged.

"What does that mean? No, don't put it down on your sketch pad. Speak to me, Wyatt. Who is going to die? Not that I believe dreams can foretell death or anything else. I don't even believe Jane will be coming here with him. I mean, I want her to come here without him. It's been so long since she departed with the vaquero. But how could she get away from Luther? He's nothing like the vaquero, right? He's . . . he's *demented.* Jesus Christ, Wyatt. It was just a damned dream!"

Wyatt said nothing nor did he try to write another note. The other Wyatt, lawman Earp, came up Front Street in long strides and grasped Mr. Matters' hand.

"Howdy, Wyatt," said Deputy Marshal Earp.

"Howdy, Wyatt," Mr. Matters replied, almost too softly for me to hear. For the moment he must have forgotten his vow not to speak.

"I remembered what you said about that Mexican cowboy, how you wanted me to watch out for him. Who could forget a name like *Babe*? A little while ago I was called over to the Taylor Made restaurant. Widow

Taylor, the owner, was complaining about a customer she claimed was acting drunk and disorderly. When I got there the fellow had some whiskey on his breath, but he was quiet and polite. Mrs. Taylor doesn't speak, not the way you can't speak, mind you; she isn't capable of it while you choose not to. Anyway, it seemed to me she didn't want to press charges, just wanted the fellow to leave her place. I led him away, and we chatted some. He said he hadn't done anything wrong except leave some gal behind in Texas, and that Mrs. Taylor knew the gal. He promised not to go back to Taylor Made while he was in Dodge. We shook hands and he headed off south of the Dead Line. Nothing I could charge him with, but I did get his name — Babe Herrera."

Wyatt Matters patted the other Wyatt on the back and mouthed five words, "You did good, Wyatt Earp." For a minute I thought Mr. Matters would show his poem to Deputy Marshal Earp, but instead he folded up the page and put it back in his vest pocket.

"We saw him earlier," I said. "He's no longer of any concern to us. He probably isn't what you'd call a hard case. Not that I don't sympathize with Mrs. Taylor. I'm thinking I pretty much feel the way she does when it comes to Babe Herrera"

"Say no more, eh . . . Mr. Harrington, is it?"

"Hannum, Harry Hannum."

"Right you are. What anybody did in Texas is no concern of mine. My job is to stop people from disturbing the peace in Dodge City. I fine the lawbreakers and escort them to the calaboose south of the tracks. People are allowed to have all the disturbing thoughts in the world until they act and break the law."

"Yes, forget Babe Herrera, Wyatt," Mr. Matters said, not bothering to go back to his scratch pad. "I have another name for you and the other law enforcers to watch out for, a much worse hombre."

"You don't say. Another cowboy?"

"Nope. He's a mean-Missourian-turned-mean-Kansan. He's done prison time. That was for bank robbery, but he has killed before and I believe can kill again. He's one bad hombre. And not right in the head. Luther Perkins is his name."

"You've seen this fellow? North or South of the Dead Line?"

"Neither yet, Wyatt. But he's on his way."

I found it hard to believe that an extremely intelligent man like Wyatt Matters put such faith in his Boot Hill dream. It was true that back when Jane Hankin was in bed with her nervous sickness he told me he was interpreting her dreams, including that awful one she had about Bloody Bill Anderson raiding Lawrence (based on fact, of course) and then a Union soldier who supposedly looked like me coming around to molest her (purely errant fantasy). At the time he had told me things like *dreams aren't always logical* and *dreams are figments of the imagination.* Why now then was he acting like an Indian shaman whose uncommon abilities included predicting the future?

His answer was simple enough and given vocally, since he was so confident Jane was coming that he was breaking his vow of silence ahead of time: "It's all part of my continual self-education, which includes spiritual growth. Meeting and conferring with Indians is not something I have been able to do in Dodge City, but the literature strongly suggests that many native visions and dreams have indeed come true. Such a gift is not limited to American Indians. Aristotle admitted that some dreams are tokens of future events. The Indians from India believe dreams have information about the future. Buddhists recognize dreams that warn us of impending danger. Why should such dreams be limited to men of a certain time, age, religion, or race? I pay attention to my dreams, and I know which ones are prophetic. Others in Dodge may have the same innate capacity, but they only believe in their daydreams, which are largely about material goods, riches, power, pleasure, and Texas longhorns."

That was a mouthful, and I was so glad he didn't attempt to impart that information on paper. At the same time, I felt something was lacking in me, for I hardly ever remembered any of my dreams, let alone the ones that were potentially prophetic. I went back and forth on whether to believe in Mr. Matters' dream or to dismiss it. I decided to check with some people I knew on the subject.

Will Lee Washington told me he had experienced so many dreams at night involving Monique Taylor that he had lost count. But he did remember one troublesome dream a few days after William Taylor died in which Congress repealed the Ku Klux Klan Act and the Dodge town founders subsequently passed an ordinance saying no blacks were permitted within town limits unless they became slaves again. "Damn glad that dream wasn't prophetic," Will Lee told me. Monique elected not to acknowledge my question. Will Lee explained that while she loved owning a restaurant and working every day, she no longer had time for dreams.

When I asked Robert Wright during a busy day at work if any of his dreams had ever come true, he pointed out the window toward Front Street where steers were rumbling past right through town and said: "It's happening right there before our eyes, son — Dodge City, the new queen of the cow towns." When I posed the same question to Alice Wright one night when I was looking after the children, her face lit up and she cried out, "I got exactly what I dreamed of every night when I was just a girl — a rock solid husband and five children who delight me most of the time, and when they don't, I let you borrow them." I felt like reminding her that she was only thirteen when she married Robert and that wishing and longing for something all day was not the same as night dreaming. But she enjoyed responding to my question so much I didn't want to spoil her mood. Next, I asked the same to daughter Clara Belle, who amazingly enough was already older than Alice had been on her wedding day. "The only man I ever dreamed about is you," Clara Belle said without hesitation, and she didn't even accompany that shocking statement with a giggle. I decided it was best to not pursue the subject of dreams any further.

As dubious as I was about Wyatt Matters' Boot Hill dream, I often took strolls to the tracks when a train steamed into town, and each time the anticipation caused my palms to sweat, my stomach to churn, and my heart to beat faster. I wasn't sure if it was because I was nervous about seeing Jane again or anxious about seeing Luther for the first time or some of both. Each time I didn't see the pair on the platform I would return to the general store or blue house feeling better to a degree but also somewhat the fool. When walking to and from the tracks I sometimes ran into one of Dodge's law enforcers, usually Wyatt Earp or Bat Masterson on their separate patrols. Both were striking figures — Wyatt with his handlebar mustache and blue eyes more piercing than even those of Mr. Matters, Bat with his derby hat and a cane he liked to spin. Neither man walked hurriedly but always stepped with an air of confidence that suggested they knew that anyone who confronted them would be overmatched. While they were out to arrest men, for each arrest meant a $2.50 addition to their monthly salaries, Bat always tipped his hat to me in passing and Wyatt usually paused to say a few words, even if he called me Mr. Harrington. "How is little old Wyatt doing today, Mr. Harrington?" he'd ask multiple times, referring to Wyatt Matters. And twice he said, "Now, Mr. Harrington, you be sure to tell your friend Wyatt that I haven't run into Luther Perkins yet, but I have my eyes and ears wide open."

It was July 7, 1876, with the cowboy herds pouring into Dodge and the citizens trying to digest the shocking news out of Montana Territory that Lieutenant Colonel George A. Custer and his immediate command had been wiped out on June 25 by hostile Indians at the Little Bighorn, when Luther and Jane Perkins (how it hurts to call her a Perkins!) came to town. Bat Masterson was the first to see them. Jane was the one to catch the attention of Bat, who had an eye for the ladies and at age twenty-two was three years younger than Jane. He had tipped his derby to her and was welcoming her to Dodge City and such when Luther took exception and, ignoring Bat's badge, seized the lawman's cane, jabbed it into Bat's belly, and shouted, "Keep your distance, big man, that's my wife!" Luther turned out to be a small man, somewhere in height between Mr. Mathers and me, but he was in such bad temper that Mr. Masterson's size didn't matter. But, as was expected, Luther was overmatched. Bat yanked his cane free of the newcomer's hand without difficulty and could have easily thrashed Luther with it but instead spun it in dramatic fashion and spoke calmly: "Now mister, you settle down. I have never in my life offended a lady or overreacted to a man who thinks he has been slighted. I am Bat Masterson, sir, and I have just kept you from assaulting a peace officer — me."

At that point, Jane stepped in, apologized for her husband, introduced him and herself as "the Perkins of Lawrence," and told Mr. Masterson that she was a former resident of Dodge City. Mr. Masterson then explained that he was an old buffalo hunter who had come and gone from Dodge over the years but had only just settled in as a lawman. "Things can get a bit boisterous here this summer with all the cowboys in town," he added, "but if you stay north of the tracks, you should get along just fine, ma'am. We have the saloon crowd without doubt, but there are plenty of folks in Dodge who desire a peaceful town where folks like you can raise a family, send the kids to school, attend church, and partake in community activities."

"We ain't staying long," said Luther. "And those cowboys better steer clear of my wife."

"Just don't go looking for trouble, Mr. Perkins. Cowboys are like buffalo hunters; they spend too much time away from civilization. When they finally get to town, those boys are in high spirits, and sure as a full house beats a flush, they'll get drunk. And drunkenness, sir, often leads to wild behavior."

"Cowboys don't scare me. I've handled them before in Texas. I'll do the same here."

"That so? In Dodge, Mr. Perkins, you best let the law handle any misbehaving cowboys."

"They better just leave us alone. Everybody better."

"I see you are not wearing a visible firearm, Mr. Perkins. That's good. We also have a town ordinance against concealed weapons."

"Some reason you're harassing me and my wife?"

"I don't harass anyone. I'm a lawman. What, may I ask, brings you and your wife here all the way from Lawrence?"

"That badge don't mean nothing to me. We don't have to tell you a bloody thing."

"We're here to look up a couple of men we know," said Jane.

"*You* know," said Luther. "One of them is my wife's daddy. Name of Wyatt."

"Wyatt Earp? Can't be. He's too young to have . . ."

"Never mind. Noisy lawmen don't have to know everything. Come on, Jane, let's get this over with."

"Thank you, officer," said Jane. "I know where to find them."

Bat Masterson watched them go and did nothing more right away. When he crossed paths with Wyatt Earp in the early afternoon, though, he mentioned the tough-talking Perkins and his pretty wife, who happened to be looking for her father, named Wyatt.

"You don't say," said Wyatt Earp. "Interesting."

"Sure is. But hard to imagine. I'd say you're no more than five years older than her, tops."

"There is another Wyatt in town. He's old enough to have such a daughter. I wouldn't necessarily expect her to be pretty, though."

"Nevertheless, she is that. Gorgeous reddish-brown hair. What Custer's killers wouldn't give to take a scalp like that. The young lady is well-formed, too, in an eye-catching red dress, but she's polite and respectable, nothing like her husband. My instinct says we could have trouble before long with Mr. Perkins."

"Luther Perkins, right?"

"I suppose. Don't recall mention of his first name. How do you know him? He's new to Dodge."

"Don't know him. Heard he could be trouble."

"From Marshal Deger? How would he know?"

"No, not from Deger. From the other Wyatt. Didn't know he had a daughter. I promised I'd let him know if I saw this Luther Perkins in Dodge. But it'll keep. You saw him, not me. You hungry, Bat?"

As I later learned, Luther and Jane found Wyatt Matters before Wyatt Earp got around to telling my mentor that the couple was in town. First, Jane took Luther to Mr. Matters' tent, which stood weatherworn and half-collapsed in its old location, and they found nothing inside except two crumpled pages from the 1874 *Dodge City Messenger,* several blackened cans in the fire pit, the remains of an Arkansas River largemouth bass, and three mice making themselves at home. They had a brief conversation about it, according to Jane.

"Your old man must have left town," Luther told her. "We came here for nothing."

"He told me he was never leaving Dodge alive, and he says what he means."

"Could be he's as dead as your other two fathers — the one murdered by Bloody Bill and the one who made himself your stepfather."

"He was *your* father, and you murdered him."

"No loss. I did Lawrence a favor. Hard-headed, deceitful Calvin Perkins never gave anyone an even break. He sent his own son to prison."

"You did rob his bank."

"Sweet Jesus! Get over it, Jane. You never liked the son of a bitch any more than I did. My old man was asking for it."

"No man deserves to be shot that way."

"Now, don't you start asking for it, wife."

"All I've asked for is to be allowed to see my father. It's been far too long."

"We're here, aren't we?"

"OK, then. I won't be threatened. I've stopped being afraid of you."

"We went over this ten times in Lawrence and twenty more times on the train. We can't stay here. We got to catch the next train to Pueblo. No telling when they'll find Papa Perkins' body and put two and two together."

"You catch the next train to Pueblo, Luther. I have only one blood father and I'm not leaving Dodge till I've seen him and . . ."

"You're my wife. You go where I go today and forever. You promised."

"And you promised I could see my father if I left Lawrence with you."

"All right. Stop talking at me. I hate people who talk at me. This town is growing, but it ain't that big. If he's here, we'll find him. Where would he go?"

"He obviously moved. Let's go ask someone."

"All right. All right. But we better hurry. We're on the run."

"*You* are. I thought you only wanted to show your father you had me back with you and maybe frighten him some. I had no idea you were going to tie him up, press that derringer to his temple, and pull the trigger."

"You're in this as much as me. You're my wife. You hated him, too."

"I've never fired a gun in my life."

"I could have blasted him with a shotgun or one of Calvin's beloved hunting rifles, but I know how you hate the noise of big guns. You were dozing off in the next room, and I didn't want to disturb you, so I kept my voice down when scolding Papa Perkins and then pressed that tiny, quiet double-barreled derringer to his head and fired from one barrel and then the other. He didn't even whimper."

"Such a considerate husband. But an evil son. You didn't give your father any kind of break."

"I made it quick for him. Now, let's go find your daddy."

I have no reason to doubt that's what they said to each other before they left the tent. Jane has always been one to tell the truth. After that I was an eyewitness to everything, for the person Jane went to for information about Wyatt Matters was me. She knew she could find me at the general store. I was manning the store by myself because Robert Wright had gone to see business partner Charlie Rath, who was still bringing in buffalo hides from Texas even while Texas cattle were stimulating another economic boom in Dodge. I didn't see the husband at first and I was so enraptured by seeing my true love again, in a dress no less, that I took her into my arms without thinking. Yes, I initiated the long hug, but I swear that Jane squeezed me right back. I didn't realize Luther Perkins was there, too, until he picked off the counter one of the wooden mallets that were on sale and came after me. I took only one blow to the shoulder before I wrestled the makeshift weapon away from him and dropped it to the floor. As he bent down to retrieve it, I pinned back his arms and told him to stay still if he knew what was good for him. Of course, a demented person doesn't always do what's good for him.

"Another man!" shouted Luther after finding out he couldn't squirm free. "Another lover in Dodge! It's not even one of your cowboys. It's just some hot-blooded storekeeper."

"What do you mean one of *my* cowboys," said Jane. "There is only one, and you left him shaking in his boots in Fort Worth."

"Would have killed him if you hadn't gotten in my way. I hate cowboys. I hate storekeepers, too."

"And bankers and barbers and businessmen and everyone else, maybe even yourself."

"That one was the Babe. What do you call this one — Honey Pot? Nosey? Sweet Lips?"

Even as I restrained Luther, I began thinking what a terrible shame it was that I had never once kissed Jane full on the lips. At least I had enough sense not to mention that Babe Herrera was still in town after driving the herd up with Maverick Washington's outfit.

"Let me go, Sweet Lips!" Luther shouted, squirming again. "That's my wife! That's my wife! You have no right interfering, storekeeper!"

I ignored him. It wasn't as if Luther and Jane were married the way normal people were, like the Wrights and the Zimmermans. Anyway, I wasn't ready to let go, not when this was the most satisfying, most manly thing I had done since October 1874 in the Long Branch when I smashed that whiskey bottle over the black-hatted cowboy's noggin and probably saved Wyatt Matters' life. Now, gripping Luther with all my might, I had no idea the demented man had shot his father twice in the head and was on the run from the law. With that knowledge, would I have been so bold? It's hard to say. I was just fortunate the demented man had gone at me with a wooden mallet instead of a firearm and didn't have the physical strength to even deal with a store clerk.

I began to tire from gripping him so hard. I wasn't sure how long I could hold on, but I believed I must for he started butting me with his backside. The word *demented* pounded my brain. "What will you do if I let you go?" I asked him.

"You'll see, you wife-stealing weasel!"

I didn't want to see, but then Jane spoke in a manner that was both helpful and disturbing. "Don't be a bloody fool, Luther," she yelled. "You're wasting time. This man means nothing to me. He's a friend of my father's. He can tell us where Wyatt is, if you promise to be nice."

He didn't have to promise because those words *This man means nothing to me* were doing the pounding in my head now, driving away *demented.* I suddenly was totally fatigued, my strength gone, my spirit flagging. Luther slipped away and immediately picked the wooden mallet off the floor. He was determined to try again.

"Don't!" Jane shouted at her husband as she slid between him and me, probably the same way she had protected Babe Herrera from the madman in Fort Worth. "He'll tell us." She then jabbed me in the belly. "Where the hell is Wyatt, Harry? He's left the tent. Where'd he go? Don't worry. Luther doesn't want to hurt my father. It's me who wants to see Wyatt. I want to apologize for not getting in touch with him all this time and keeping him out of my life. I did miss him down in Texas. Heck. He's the only father I have."

Not a word about me, the one who loved her so much. I resisted saying: *And didn't you miss me just a little bit?* Instead, I gave her the information she wanted: "He's in your old place. Wyatt and I are renting the blue house from the Zimmermans."

"Blue house?" said Luther. "What the hell is a blue house?"

"It's blue," said Jane. "Thank you, Harry. You're a good man." She gave me a quick kiss on the forehead and then dragged Luther off by his free arm before he could wield the mallet. He might have resisted more, but at that moment Mr. Wright and Mr. Rath came into the general store from the back.

"What's going on?" Mr. Wright said. "Who were those two running out the front door?"

I was biting my lip. I couldn't speak.

"Did that man pay for that mallet?"

"Take it out of my salary," I finally said. "I got to go."

"Where? It's the middle of the afternoon. Things figure to get busy. I need you here, Harry."

"Could be someone might need me more," I said, and I also ran out.

Luther and Jane must have raced all the way to the blue house. I followed at a brisk pace, but by the time I got inside the house and to the doorway between the kitchen and Wyatt's bedroom, Jane and Wyatt were already well into their reunion. He had a slight summer cold and had been reading in bed. I noticed the title of the book on the floor — *Little Women; Or, Meg, Jo, Beth, and Amy*. Jane was kneeling next to the book and leaning over the bed, holding his hand. Wyatt wouldn't stop talking — so many words he needed to get out now that his silent time was finished. He repeatedly told her how much he had missed her and how he knew she was coming home again, that he'd seen it in a dream. He didn't mention having seen Luther in the same dream. Jane mostly just kept apologizing for not having been a better daughter. Like her father, she ignored Luther, who stood in the corner, swaying back and forth, sulking, and wringing his hands as if he had been sent there by his stern father. Little did I know — or Wyatt know, for that matter — Calvin Perkins was dead in Lawrence and Luther was guilty of patricide.

Luther paid me no mind. He had dropped the mallet somewhere along the way to the blue house, so I didn't see any reason to pay him any mind either. I felt I could handle him if it came to fisticuffs. His presence did keep me from moving in closer to the bed to become an active part in the reunion, not that Wyatt or Jane were paying me any more attention than they were Luther.

When the conversation turned to whether Jane had come back to stay and Jane mentioned a promise to leave with Luther, maybe that very day, things started to get ugly.

"You can't go," said Wyatt. "Dodge City is your home, our home."

"She's my wife," shouted Luther. "She goes where I go. And we can't remain in Dodge."

"Nobody asked you to stay in Dodge, mister. If he is keeping you with him against your will, Jane, I can do something about that. I can . . ."

"I'm his wife," Jane said meekly. "We made a pact. If I went to Pueblo with him, I'd be allowed to stop off in Dodge so I could see you."

"You can't steal a wife from a husband even if you are her father," said Luther. "As her father, though, you can give her presents — better yet, gold and silver and greenbacks. Where do you keep your dough, old man?"

"Nothing here for you," said Wyatt.

"Damn right. Say what you have to say to each other and then it's on to Pueblo for the Perkins."

"What's in Pueblo?" I asked.

"Keep your nose out of this, storekeeper. You don't even belong here."

"You're wrong. This is my home. Isn't that right, Wyatt?"

"The blue house can be Jane's home again, too, at least until we build us a big white house further out of town on a little hill to get away from all the cowboy noise and commotion."

"Quit talking," said Luther, now pushing past me to reach the side of the bed. He tapped Jane's shoulder, but she shrugged off his hand. "Look, old man, I didn't come here to do you any harm. But keep it up, Jane's father or not, and the only hill you'll end up on is Boot Hill. Tell him goodbye, wife. We have a train to catch."

"Why rush?" I asked. "And what does Pueblo have that Dodge doesn't?"

"It's on the Kansas-Colorado border," said Wyatt. "The Atchison, Topeka & Santa Fe Railroad reached Pueblo earlier this year. It's the end of the line."

"Not for the wife and me," said Luther, who was now tugging on Jane's arm. "From there we can go on our own farther west, or north, or south, anywhere that suits our fancy. I've always had a hankering to see Old Mexico."

"What about you, Jane?" Wyatt asked. "You have your sights set on Mexico, too? You really want to go there with him? Cruelty, threats to shoot and kill, and neglect of duty are all legitimate grounds for divorce in Kansas."

"You got no right to say such things, old

man. I never threatened to shoot and kill Jane. After I got out of that hellhole prison, I traveled all the way to Texas to reclaim my wife from some worthless cowboy. I had a right to threaten to shoot and kill that son of a Mexican whore. Lucky for him, he backed down, and I brought my wife safely back to her home in Lawrence." Luther suddenly stopped tugging and talking and began swiveling his head like a barred owl.

"But you left Lawrence," I said.

"What of it!" Luther shouted at me. "We're out to make our *own* home together, right Jane?"

"Not exactly," Jane said. "He needed to get away and I . . ."

"Shut your damn mouth," said Luther. "Don't tell them nothing. You're my wife and you promised."

"To love and obey till death do you part?" said Wyatt.

"What the hell do you mean by that crack!" yelled Luther.

"In some cases, wedding vows are nothing but words, and words don't mean much without substance behind them."

"Never made any vows when Calvin Perkins forced us to get married," said Jane. "Can't break any vows if there never were any."

"You promised we wouldn't linger in Dodge. We need to keep moving, wife. A promise is a promise is a promise."

"Yes, I promised that, but that's all I promised."

"You shall obey, wife," Luther said as he roughly took hold of Jane again and pulled her toward the kitchen door. "It's my right. I'm the man in charge now. I say what goes. There's no Calvin Perkins around giving orders anymore. Damn that man and damn you, too, Wyatt Matters. No way I need stand here listening to any more garbage. I need answer to no man. Move it, Jane. No more blue house for us. No more daddies. No more Dodge."

"Stop him, Harry," called out Mr. Matters as he climbed off the bed but then stepped on *Little Women* and froze. "We can't let him take her to Pueblo. He won't give her up. He'll force her to keep going with him and they'll never stop moving. Jane won't ever return."

I didn't move right away because I was thinking too much. Earlier it had been me defending myself against Luther's attack by mallet. But now he had no mallet, and he was fleeing. I would need to go on the offensive, which was something I was unaccustomed to doing. But I wouldn't be doing this for myself. I told myself it was for Jane; everything was about Jane.

Luther was now pulling her by her auburn hair — the ogre! I needed to save her because while he had his rights as a husband, I figured a demented husband lost those rights. I went after him with my bare fists. He kept hold of Jane with one hand while he reached into a pocket with the other and pulled out a concealed weapon — a two-shot derringer. First, he pointed it at me. I staggered but kept advancing. He redirected the barrel to Jane's head and that stopped me cold.

"Don't think I won't do it," Luther said, his eyes aglow like those of an owl at night. "I'd rather kill my wife than have her run out on me again and take up with another man."

"I'm not another man," I said, even as I took another step forward. My legs seemed less cautious than the rest of me.

"Stay there, Harry," Jane said. "He means it. I know. He killed his own father with that same gun. I'll go with him. I must. Nobody else need get hurt."

"Nobody talk — nobody do nothing!" Luther screamed. "I don't want to hear one more word from any one of you."

Luther kept gliding toward the door with Jane in his control and the barrel of the derringer now mostly inside Jane's mouth. I kept quiet. So did Wyatt, which surprised me. He didn't try to talk Luther out of it. But he did do something, rather foolish I thought. He hurled a pillow at the gunman. It's hard to say what he hoped to accomplish. The pillow was a fluffy one. It seemed to me like a spontaneous act, no thinking through his action. But whether it was his intention or not, he succeeded in diverting Luther's attention. When the harmless pillow bounced off the back of Jane's head, Luther yanked his derringer out of Jane's mouth so hard that he chipped one of her front teeth. He spun toward the bed and fired at Wyatt, certainly a long range shot with such a little pistol. I remembered my mentor once telling me that derringers were only accurate up to ten feet and only effective as a last-resort defense weapon by gamblers and prostitutes. Wyatt was standing by his bed at least fifteen feet from the shooter. Nevertheless, Wyatt dropped onto the bed clutching his side and let out a groan that for some reason made me think of Monique Taylor. I wasn't sure if Luther intended to fire his second shot at Jane or me, but he never got one off. That's because the other Wyatt, Wyatt Earp, burst through the door with six-shooter raised and realized there wasn't time to issue a warning or to get close enough to Luther to crack him in the skull with the gun butt. Wyatt Earp had only come there to let Wyatt Matters know that the potentially dangerous Luther Perkins was in town. It could be argued that Mr. Earp should have come earlier, but his appearance was timely, possibly lifesaving. Mr. Earp put three slugs in Mr. Perkins, any one of which would have been fatal.

Epilogue

There you have it. Wyatt Matters' clairvoyant Boot Hill dream poem about Luther and Jane coming to town had come true, but not entirely — and that was a good thing. After Deputy Marshal Earp stopped firing his gun and Mr. Perkins hit the floor like a sack of general store potatoes, I hurried to the bed with the last four lines of his poem rushing through my head:

I KNEW NOT THEIR INTENTIONS
SHE WAS MY CHILD BUT
LUTHER'S WIFE
THERE WAS A RECURRENCE
OF GUNFIRE
MORE THAN ONE MAN
LOST HIS LIFE

"Are you all right?" I asked Wyatt, who was holding his hip with some blood seeping out between his fingers.

"It's only a scratch," he said. "My God. Where's Jane? Did she run off?"

"Only to get Dr. McCarty," said Wyatt Earp. "She'll be back in a jiffy."

It was more than a scratch, but nothing like the first time Mr. Matters had been plugged at the Long Branch saloon. Luther Perkins was the lone fatality that July day in the blue house. He would be buried on Boot Hill with no ceremony and no marker. My mentor was on his feet again in two weeks, and it only took that long because he was enjoying Jane's before-unseen talents as a nurse. He would not only recover but also go on to live another twenty-three years — yes, all the time in Dodge City and barely missing the twentieth century. He would see a lot more of Wyatt Earp, Bat Masterson, Robert Wright, and numerous other Dodge characters and find much more to complain about as the saloons flourished and shootings occasionally occurred until the mid-1880s. One of his proudest moments came in 1878 when the town's leading lights finally agreed to put up a sign that Mr. Matters had long been pushing for. The sign on Front Street boldly stated *The Carrying of Firearms Strictly Prohibited*. Once the railroads, with their hundreds of stock cars, began rolling into Texas closer to the grazing lands, Dodge

City's days as a cattle town ended. By then Monique Taylor and Will Lee Washington had become tired of the restaurant and saloon businesses and departed for New Orleans, not yet married but perhaps on the verge (at least according to Will Lee).

I continued to live with Wyatt Matters in the blue house until he died peacefully on New Year's Eve 1899 just minutes from midnight. Earlier that evening he had displayed enough gumption to make a last resolution while lying in bed: *To get to heaven as quickly as possible to discuss with God possible ways life could be made better on Earth.* His mind undiminished, he continued to lie there listening to me read to him from William Ralston Balch's mammoth 1891 encyclopedia *The Complete Compendium of Universal Knowledge: Containing All You Want to Know of Language, History, Government, Business and Social Forms, and a Thousand and One Other Useful Subjects.* Wyatt Matters' last words, though, were not particularly uplifting: "That's a helluva thing. I should have written it myself."

Despite several salary boosts grudgingly given me by Robert Wright, I had finally quit the general store in October 1887 to go to work for Frank Aikins, who had just taken over as editor and publisher of the *Dodge*

City Times. Mr. Matters readily approved of me becoming a newspaperman since Aikins believed in the value of education and declared he would have no sympathy for "scheming politicians in any party, who buy their nominations and pay money for votes." Aikins soon bowed out, but I kept working for his successors until 1892 when I became a retired gentleman (at age forty-two, about the same age Wyatt Matters was when he first came to Dodge City) and began an account of my mentor's life as I knew it. Well into the next century the manuscript remained unfinished.

For all you romantic-minded readers who were wondering, I have not forgotten Jane Hankin, and rest assured, I never will. No, sadly to say and even more sadly to write, I never did land my true love, so to speak, but she remained a part of my life — and that of Mr. Matters, too, up until his death. After nursing her father back to health following the shooting, she stayed around Dodge for several more months, repairing her relationship not only with him but also with me, Monique Taylor, Frederick and Matilda Zimmerman, and, yes, Babe Herrera. She forgave Babe for allowing Luther Perkins to take her away from him in Texas, determining that he wasn't in fact cowardly but was nobly respecting the sanctity of marriage. She still loved the Babe, and the one obstacle (at least the only one I was aware of) to their happiness had been eliminated by Wyatt Earp. To make a long story short, Jane became Mrs. Herrera that year and went on a long honeymoon in Old Mexico (her husband's native country), after which they lived in south Texas but would keep coming north to Dodge each summer, with the cattle drives at first and then on their own once the drives to Kansas ended. As I write this, the couple is still together and without regrets in the Lone Star State. Jane and I do write letters to each other regularly, and she says the good old Babe doesn't mind. I usually stick a little poem in each of my correspondences. Some habits die hard.

I won't say much more about the well-known Wyatt Earp, who stayed on in Dodge for some time and then continued to make his mark in Tombstone, Arizona Territory, and many other Western places, including Alaska, as the frontier days came to an end. Last I heard he was out in California hobnobbing with cowboy actors like William S. Hart. Interestingly enough, his shooting of Luther Perkins has somehow slipped through the pages of history. It could be that in early July 1876 the citizens of Dodge and the *Dodge City Times* were preoccupied with Colonel Custer's demise. It could be Wyatt himself never cared to mention the time he fired three .44-caliber slugs into a pathetic little crazy man who at that moment had only one bullet left in his derringer. After all, the stalwart Wyatt was even reluctant to discuss his heroics in the famous 1881 gunfight near Tombstone's O.K. Corral. Now Bat Masterson did write quite a bit about his friend Wyatt Earp and their many adventures in the Old West, but the lawman-gambler-turned-journalist never bothered to bring up Mr. Earp's non-gunfight with loco Luther. As far as most history books are concerned, between January 14, 1876 (when jealous John Tyler shot the wrong man), and April 9, 1878 (when somebody killed Bat's brother City Marshal Edward Masterson and Bat exacted immediate revenge), not one person was fatally shot in Dodge. It was as if the July 7, 1876, "Incident at the Blue House," as Wyatt Matters later referred to it, never happened.

In the twentieth century, I got tired of being a retired gentleman (plus I no longer had the financial support of the late Wyatt Matters, who in 1899 had fittingly left almost all that remained of his father's railroad fortune to his daughter, Jane) and got back into the newspaper business. I eventually wound up in New York City working for the *Morning Telegraph* with Bat Masterson, who at age 67 on October 25, 1921, would die of a massive heart attack at his desk. I was forced into retirement two months later because management found out I was seventy-one (yes, I had been lying about my age and barely looked sixty) and didn't want a second old Western character to die on the job. I soon after made a New Year's resolution to finally finish my Matters manuscript. As you can see, dear reader, I have kept that resolution. And I live on.

During Bat's last years, we mostly talked about prizefighting, horse racing, baseball, war, and politics, and only rarely about the old days in Dodge and then only to recall the legendary, if largely forgotten, Wyatt Matters, whom Bat dubbed, "the Fastest Brain in the West." I was no Wyatt Matters, by any stretch, but I had become a much more knowledgeable and confident speaker and writer in the twentieth century. Luther Perkins' name never came up in my conversations with Mr. Masterson, and I mentioned Jane Hankin's name only once. It happened the day before he died. We were relaxing in his office, shooting the breeze and drinking more than usual (him, Canadian whisky, me, red wine), when he spoke about Emma, his wife since 1893. Bat interrupted himself to ask me why, with all the worldly women out there, I was a lifelong bachelor. It took me only a second or two to come up with my answer. I told him I would have had many, many years of happy matrimony under my belt if not for this handsome, peace-loving Texas vaquero who first rode into Dodge City in the spring of 1874 merely to play ball.

ABOUT THE AUTHOR

Gregory J. Lalire majored in history at the University of New Mexico; worked for newspapers in New Mexico, Montana, New York, and Virginia; and was the editor of *Wild West* magazine 1995–2022. He is the author of the children's book *The Red Sweater* (1992) and seven novels: *Captured: From the Frontier Diary of Infant Danny Duly* (2014), *Our Frontier Pastime 1804–1815* (2019), *Man from Montana* (2021), *The Call of McCall* (2022), *Mountain Woman* (2023), *Two Kids: Willie and Billy* (2024), and *On Blueberry Hill: The 19th-century Boyd vs. Bender Feud* (2025). He won a Western Writers of America Stirrup Award in 2015 for his nonfiction article about baseball in the West and was a WWA Spur Finalist for his article "Custer's Art Stand" in the April 1994 *Wild West*. He lives in Leesburg, Virginia.

The employees of Thorndike Press hope you have enjoyed this Large Print book. All our Thorndike Large Print titles are designed for easy reading, and all our books are made to last. Other Thorndike Press Large Print books are available at your library, through selected bookstores, or directly from us.

For information about titles, please visit our website at https://www.gale.com/thorndike.